# PATH OF
# THE INCUBUS

MORR AND HIS opponent stood almost toe-to-toe,
their klaives carving glittering arcs as they swept
together, clashed and whirled away to attack again.
Morr used his greater height to rain down blows
like thunderbolts, causing his enemy to sway and
finally take a step back to escape from beneath the
storm. His foe responded by redoubling his attack
and unleashed a rapid series of eviscerating strikes
from left and right.

Morr was put on the defensive, his grip spaced
widely on his klaive as he blocked one strike
after another. Suddenly the towering incubus was
staggered by an unexpected overhead swing that he
barely managed to block with his upraised klaive.
Morr fell back a pace and his opponent rushed
forward to keep up the pressure, hammering at his
guard without respite.

*By the same author*

· **THE DARK ELDAR SERIES** ·

Book 1: PATH OF THE RENEGADE
Book 2: PATH OF THE INCUBUS
Book 3: PATH OF THE ARCHON (Coming 2014)

THE MASQUE OF VYLE
(Available exclusively from blacklibrary.com
and Games Workshop Hobby Centres)

MIDNIGHT ON THE STREET OF KNIVES
*A dark eldar short story*
(Available exclusively from blacklibrary.com)

BELLATHONIS AND THE SHADOW KING
*A dark eldar short story*
(Available exclusively from blacklibrary.com)

THE TREASURES OF BIEL-TANIGH
*A dark eldar short story*
(Available exclusively from blacklibrary.com)

*More tales of the eldar from Black Library*

· **PATH OF THE ELDAR** ·
*Gav Thorpe*

Book 1: PATH OF THE WARRIOR
Book 2: PATH OF THE SEER
Book 3: PATH OF THE OUTCAST

THE CURSE OF SHAA-DOM
*An eldar short story by Gav Thorpe*
(Available exclusively from blacklibrary.com)

FARSEER
*William King*
(Available exclusively from blacklibrary.com)

A WARHAMMER 40,000 NOVEL

# PATH OF THE INCUBUS

## ANDY CHAMBERS

BLACK LIBRARY

*For Jessica, little Eris.*

**A BLACK LIBRARY PUBLICATION**

First published in Great Britain in 2013 by
Black Library,
Games Workshop Ltd.,
Willow Road, Nottingham,
NG7 2WS, UK.

10 9 8 7 6 5 4 3 2 1

Cover illustration by Neil Roberts.

A CIP record for this book is available from the British Library.

UK ISBN: 978 1 84970 299 7
US ISBN: 978 1 84970 300 0

See Black Library on the internet at
**www.blacklibrary.com**

Find out more about Games Workshop
and the world of Warhammer 40,000 at
**www.games-workshop.com**

Printed and bound by CPI Group (UK) Ltd, Croydon, CR0 4YY

Torturers and sadists, nightmare made real, the dark eldar are evil incarnate. Cold and beautiful, slender of bone, their lithe appearance belies their deadly talent for slaughter and cruelty.

From the hidden city of Commorragh, the dark eldar launch their lightning raids into the depths of realspace, sowing terror and leaving devastation in their wake. They hunt for slaves, fodder for the hell-pits and the petty amusements of their lords who draw sustenance from the blood shed in ritual battle. For in this hellish realm, living flesh is currency and Overlord Asdrubael Vect rules above all with the greatest share.

Beneath their supreme master, the archons of the darkling city murder and cheat to keep one step ahead of She Who Thirsts. For the dark eldar harbour a terrible curse, a wasting of their flesh that can only be slowed by the infliction of pain. Life eternal is the reward for this soul harvest, and the favour of the ancient haemonculi can extend an eldar's mortal coil yet further... for a price. The alternative is damnation and endless suffering, a withering of body and mind until all that remains is dust.

But such hunger cannot ever be sated. It is a bottomless pit of hate and depravity that lurks within the dark eldar, a vessel that can never truly be filled, even with oceans of blood. And when the last drop has bled away, the soul thieves will know true terror as the daemons come to claim them...

# PROLOGUE

*Welcome fellow traveller, welcome! Whether you are a simple observer or perhaps an unwitting participant in the unfolding drama before us please be most welcome. Unfortunately I must begin by breaking with some of the ordinary dramatic conventions at this juncture. You see this is the second of a series of three parts, a triptych if you will. Hence we must perforce begin with a recap, a résumé and a reappraisal of what has already occurred, as tiresome as that seems.*

*Those of you who have followed this darkling tale thus far will already know most of these facts and so I hope you can forgive my indulgence of those only lately arrived. If you are confident in your recollections then I invite you to proceed without diversion. However, some perspective is useful both for those ignorant of prior machinations and for those many great minds that failed to grasp their immediate import at the time.*

First then, our stage: Commorragh, the eternal city. Dark, terrible, delicious Commorragh, where pain and subjugation are the meat and drink of ageless creatures of unfathomable wickedness. To fully understand Commorragh one must understand the wider universe that bore it. So, to begin with here is a secret that if properly understood might change your perception forever. All of reality, everything we see as static, safe and secure, is in fact in constant flux. The grains of sand on the beach demonstrate more solidity and longevity than the cherished absolutes of the worlds we believe in.

You see our material universe is born of Chaos and our reality is nothing more than a passing fancy of the Dark Gods; an infinitely short moment when anarchy is frozen for long enough for us, myopic and stunted as we are, to perceive substance and believe that there is such a thing as 'natural order' in the universe.

Such hilarious conceit! What amazing hubris!

Mighty Commorragh is a facet of reality born out of hubris, and a very different one to the random dross thrown up by nature. It is a pearl consciously aggregated out of the spittle of creation by ancient, mortal minds that thought themselves the equal of the gods. And what a place they made for themselves.

Beyond Commorragh and its enslaved sub-realms the material universe moves on: civilizations rise and fall, stars implode and the whole rough scrimmage over ownership of the galaxy continues apace. Within Commorragh a long, dark midnight reigns that has gone on unchallenged for millennia. Its inhabitants eternally cheat death and avoid their ultimate fate at the claws of

*She Who Thirsts*, the daemon-goddess of their own creation. Sensuous, sadistic, pleasure seeking, these are the dark eldar, last remnants of an empire that spanned the galaxy in its time. Few have fallen as far as the inhabitants of Commorragh without being destroyed utterly.

Still, pity the poor Commorrites, trapped upon a stage of their own making. They can take brief forays in the material realm to assuage their gnawing hunger, snatching what they can to carry it back to their eternal city, but they remain ever-hungry. Every day *She Who Thirsts* drinks a little more of their soul and that growing emptiness can only be filled with the suffering of others.

The players: A group of Commorrite nobles intent on reclaiming lost glories in one of the endless power plays of the eternal city. These were unified by their ancient bloodlines and a contempt for the new order imposed after their forefathers had been overthrown. Incidental characters included: the master haemonculus Bellathonis employed to effect a proscribed resurrection, Lileath a young Exodite worldsinger kidnapped to be used as pain-bride for the operation, and Sindiel, a craftworld renegade who was eventually persuaded to save her. Perhaps most significant of all at this point in events was a bodyguard and executioner by the name Morr, a member of that curious warrior cult known as the incubi.

To their scheme, then. The primary obstacle in the noble's path to glory was, as ever, the Supreme Overlord of Commorragh, the great tyrant himself, Asdrubael Vect. Alas, the nobles could match Vect with neither brute power nor subtle intrigue. Confronted with these facts the leader of the conspiracy, one Archon Yllithian, persuaded his co-conspirators into a singularly dangerous course of action.

As they were unable to overcome Vect themselves the nobles would attempt to raise one of the tyrant's more successful prior opponents, a Lord called El'Uriaq, from the dead to guide them to victory. Predictably their scheme miscarried and they instead raised something beyond their power to control – the soul of this great noble corrupted by an entity native to the ever-changing realms of Chaos. This composite entity – quite possibly an emissary of She Who Thirsts – appeared wrapped in the seeming of the leader they sought.

The consequences fell thus. Of the nobles but one survived the immediate aftermath. The bodyguard Morr, to his great distress slew his own noble master, Archon Kraillach, when he realised that Kraillach had become corrupted by the entity. The entity itself murdered the third noble, Archon Xelian, with a memetic curse when she proved intractable to its aims. Yllithian proved clever enough to be useful to the thing he had unleashed and so survived only to be near-fatally struck down during the monster's destruction.

These consequences alone are, of course, really quite inconsequential when compared to the harm that all of these dramatic events conspired to inflict on the metaphysical fabric of Commorragh itself.

Here another brief moment of explanation is in order. It is best to imagine Commorragh as a bubble maintained by equal pressure across its entire membrane. If the membrane is breached the external pressure forces what is without to come within to the great detriment of *anyone in the vicinity at the time.*

*Over the centuries Commorragh has incorporated many other little pearls into its bubble, encrusting itself with a hundred stolen realities to be enslaved and exploited. Ripples in the surface of the membrane can also dislodge these satellites realms, setting them free to drift and realign chaotically.*

*These phenomena are collectively known to the inhabitants of Commorragh as a 'Dysjunction', and most rightly feared. This tale revolves around the Dysjunction the noble's schemes accidentally brought about, its effects and its resolution.*

*So, now you know all that brought the tale to this point. Invaluable knowledge that will pay dividends later, I feel sure, although I promise there will be no quizzes. And who am I? Player or narrator or both, I don't doubt that it will become readily apparent as the drama unfolds. For the present it would be boorish to take centre stage if only for fear you might think this tale is about me. The correct questions for you to address to yourself at this time are these: What do I want? How will I get it? What stands in my way?*

# CHAPTER 1
## CONSEQUENCES

THE COLONY HAD existed forever. Cradled in darkness the feeders lurked awaiting the call to hunt, the breeders quietly gestated future generations after receiving the caustic seed of the patriarch. The younglings suckled and worried at the feeder's veins in blind hunger while they impatiently grew and grew to become something *other*.

The colony lived in eternal night, a soft umbral world made in equal parts from their environment and the woven excrescence of generation after generation of feeders and breeders living and dying. Beneath the colony flowed the river of life, a viscous and unchanging ribbon that gurgled along between the walls of the universe. Food came via the river, sometimes cold and soft as it drifted just beneath the surface, at other times warm and upright as it waded in the gentle current. The feeder's sensitive spiracles scented every morsel, living or dead, and their ultrasonic shrieks summoned their broodmates to come join the feast before it left the colonies' world.

Recently, for the first time in uncounted generations, change had come upon the colony. It was something unknown even to the patriarch with all his long-digested wisdom. The breeders trembled with fear and trepidation. The feeders fluttered angrily this way and that, seeking the source of disruption, but the source lay beyond their world and seemingly beyond the walls of the universe. Those seemingly impenetrable walls shook like a birthing breeder and strange, alien sensations swept through the densely clustered bodies of the colony. Food was becoming plentiful, particularly the cold and soft kind, but the colony was not thriving. Madness had gripped some of its members and sent them fleeing into the great unknown. The remainder clustered more tightly than ever, their fear bringing them closer together in the patriarch's sinewy embrace.

Now a new stimulus had entered the colony's consciousness. Lights bobbed and slid along the river of life. Light, that hateful invader, meant only one thing – that it was time for the feeders to broach forth in a fluttering wave and quench it with their leathery bodies and their hooked claws. Sometimes light brought food: hot blood to be drunk and raw flesh to be torn and consumed. Other lights were hard and inedible, useless to the colony and only a source of distress until the river bore them away into the great unknown. In either case the feeders would clutch and worry at the source until it was gone and the comforting darkness closed in once more. Individuals mattered not at all – the continuation of the colony was everything.

THE POWERED EDGE of the blade was inactive but its inherent weight and molecule-sharp edge still sheared through flesh and bone as though it was little more than wet tissue paper. The victim gave a last, despairing high-pitched shriek as it tumbled to its death. This small drama did not serve to silence the speaker for moment.

'Really? This is the only way out of Commorragh that you could think of on short notice? Even in the midst of an imminent Dysjunction there must be better paths to follow.'

'Your presence is not required,' the towering incubus named Morr grunted in response. The incubus viciously swatted at another gloomwing with his great double-handed blade, his *klaive* to use its correct title. Morr was very keen on being correct, Motley knew, and that was probably the only thing that was preventing the incubus from attacking him. The tunnel was wide but the ceiling was low – Morr could have laid a gauntleted hand flat against the filth-encrusted roof without stretching. Even so the incubus wielded his two-metre long blade in the constricted space with consummate skill and precision, keeping it in constant motion as he tracked his elusive attackers.

His unwanted companion, a slight figure dressed

in stylish, if archaic-appearing grey, skipped nimbly to one side as the flying gloomwing flopped into the viscous sludge flowing around Morr's ankles in two neatly bisected pieces. It joined the pieces of at least a dozen other hook-winged predator-scavengers that had already whirled out of the darkness to attack and found Morr's klaive waiting for them instead. The simple beasts seemed not to realise the dangerous nature of the prey they were trying to drag down with their numbers so they simply kept coming. What light there was showed an incessant flutter of dark wings circling determinedly just out of reach.

'Oh come come,' said the one in grey. 'We're on the verge of becoming such fast friends. It would be truly tragic to cut short our glittering association now, surely?'

Morr reversed his klaive and whirled it with both hands, grunting as he slashed out at another darting shape. Traditionally all klaives feature an impaling spike or disembowelling hook projecting forward a hand's span or so from their flat tip. Morr used his klaive's hook to snag the gloomwing and drag it within range for a lightning-quick downward stroke. The unfortunate creature tumbled to join its bisected fellows in the muck.

The incubus's companion swayed negligently to one side to avoid another diving gloomwing but never stopped talking. 'I confess I'm a little hurt by that, Morr, I mean after all we've been through together you might at least indulge me with a verbal response rather than grunting at me...'

The incubus ignored the speaker and waded forwards, slashing left and right in a continuous figure of eight. The other skipped after him keeping up a continuous chatter. 'I came all this way, after all. Found you in that dank hole you were hiding in and warned you we had to get out while we still could. The thanks I get is you stomping off into what can only be described as a sewer without a word... besides which, you still need my help. Who else can testify on your behalf when there were no other witnesses to Kraillach's death?'

Morr paused and turned to face the grey-clad figure, swinging his klaive without a glance to skewer another leather-winged assailant as it flew at his back. Morr's blank-faced helm regarded his companion with unmistakable malevolence. When viewed at close quarters it became clear that the other's clothing was not grey but a form of motley, tiny diamond panes of black and white that endlessly repeated. The too-mobile face below the domino mask was bright and smooth like that of a painted doll.

In contrast the incubus was covered in dark armour from head to foot with scant decoration saving short horns and tusks curving from its sinister, narrow-slotted helm. There was something about the incubus's resolutely taciturn nature that implied that, by extension, he found this loquacious individual irritating in the extreme. Morr's klaive twitched involuntarily as if he were only barely manageing to suppress the urge to strike down his companion through a heroic exertion of willpower. For once the armoured warrior broke his customary silence in what amounted, for him, to a lengthy declamation.

'I cannot prevent you accompanying me... Motley, and I do owe you... a debt,' Morr admitted reluctantly, 'but do not imagine I need you or want you to help me again. The hierarchs shall be the final judge of my actions and they will hear no testimony but my own.'

Motley frowned sadly. 'I'm afraid that despite your cogent disputations destiny has yet to have her wicked way with us both. Even were we parted I feel positive we would be cast back together again momentarily until the Dysjunction is resolved – you know it's no coincidence that the masque sent me to you in your hour of need.

'All is not lost, Morr, but only if we play out our roles in the drama together. There are forces that you do not, indeed cannot, know of in the greater universe that are moving speedily towards a resolution that will bode very ill indeed for Commorragh if it transpires as they would have it. If you'll just accept my help again I can guide you to a better future.'

The incubus gazed at Motley silently for a moment more before turning and stomping away through the ooze without further comment. The sudden movement scattered a handful of gathering gloomwings like leaves. The motley-clad one pursed full red lips beneath its domino-mask and then followed with a sigh. Further back along the tunnel, unnoticed by either the incubus or his unwanted companion, stealthy figures dogged their steps.

ARCHON AEZ'ASHYA STOOD upon a narrow path of silver above the kilometres-deep caldera of the volcano-like arena of the Blades of Desire. The thin, cold air of High Commorragh blew chill against her exposed flesh and the captive suns, the *Ilmaea*, circling above seemed to give little warmth. The uppermost edges of the arena were etched with gleaming white stone terraces where she could see a sparse-looking gathering of shivering spectators. Distance and the size of the arena made the numbers deceptive at first glance. In reality hundreds of kabal members had come to see the challenge in person, and many more were watching by indirect means. She could feel their presence hovering around her like a pack of silent, hungry ghosts.

The silver path ran from one edge of the rim to the other, leaping arrow-straight over the centre of the hollow cone at the heart of the fortress. Anything falling from here would have an unbroken plunge until it hit monofilament nets strung above the forges, cell blocks and practice areas at the bottom of the pit. At its mid-point the path widened into a disc no wider than Aez'ashya's outstretched arms from its centre to its periphery. Her challenger was already waiting there for her with readied weapons gleaming. Aez'ashya strode out confidently and brusquely acknowledged the cheers of her followers on the terraces. The cheers of her loyal kabalites seemed somewhat muted and in this case it wasn't only the distance that was to blame.

Aez'ashya had no illusions – she was archon of the Blades of Desire only because another had made it so. There were plenty who doubted her ability to hold onto the position, and some who hoped to gain it in her stead. To truly rule the kabal Aez'ashya knew she was going to have to prove herself over and over again. The very smallest beginning of that was disposing of her immediate challengers, three so far, four including her current opponent, Sybris.

Sybris had been member of the clique of hek-atrix bloodbrides who were present at Archon Xelian's 'accidental' death. Previously Sybris had been well favoured, well enough to aspire to replacing Aez'ashya as succubus until Xelian's sudden fall had frustrated her ambitions. That frustration had quickly flared into open antagonism when Aez'ashya was thrust into the position of archon in Xelian's stead. Aez'ashya knew Sybris well, they had sported together both on the battlefield and off it in the past. In fact Aez'ashya knew enough about Sybris's style and methods to have a small qualm of doubt about the upcoming bout.

Sybris favoured two half-moon shaped blades that she used with a hip-swinging, straight-armed, momentum-driven technique she'd learned from Quist disciples in Port Carmine. The blades were heavy enough to smash through a parrying blade and Sybris was agile enough to snap them outward to catch a would-be dodge with eye-blurring speed. But it wasn't her enemy's weapons that particularly

PATH OF THE INCUBUS

concerned Aez'ashya. It wasn't even Sybris's lustrous, wire-strung braid of hair. The braid was tricked out as a flexible weapon some two-metres long and tipped with barbs and blades. Aez'ashya knew that Sybris could seamlessly work strikes with that braid into her other attacks. One flick of her neck just *so* and Sybris could cripple or kill an opponent. An unexpected slash from the side or below... those half-moon blades whirling up for a decapitating strike and it was all over. But that wasn't what was giving Aez'ashya doubts either.

Before every other challenge someone had sent Aez'ashya advice on how to defeat her opponent: a weakness pointed out, a poison suggested, a habitual manoeuvre to avoid. This time there had been nothing, no sly messenger with words of wisdom and so Aez'ashya was truly on her own. She repeated to herself that it didn't matter, and that it didn't mean that Sybris had received a message of her own that revealed the secret of how to defeat Aez'ashya.

It didn't matter. Aez'ashya was wearing a pair of hydra gauntlets, skin-tight armoured gloves that sprouted a profusion of lethal crystalline blades from fists, forearms and elbows. She could feel the sharp tingle of the drug *serpentin* coursing through her veins, the mélange of hormonal extracts heightening awareness and sharpening her already preternaturally quick reflexes even further. She would overcome this challenge with or without outside help.

All these thoughts had raced through Aez'ashya's

mind as she walked out along the narrow silver path. Now she was within a dozen strides of the centre disk and Sybris raised her twin moon-blades in salute. The movement seemed a little awkward, shading just beneath the fluidity and poise that could be expected of a hekatrix bloodbride. Aez'ashya kept her face in a cold, haughty sneer but she laughed warmly inside. Others might be unwilling to help but she still had her own tricks to deploy, as Sybris would discover to her dismay very soon.

THE SLAVE'S FINGERS had been cut down to little more than stumps. Burn tissue on its hands and face made it look like it had been a necessary surgical procedure, but most probably it wasn't. Kharbyr still found himself vaguely admiring the deft agility the slave demonstrated in chopping and weighing powders, the thick stumps gripping the narrow blade and handling the thin twists of paper with easy familiarity. Kharbyr looked at the slave's horribly burnt face disinterestedly for a moment and yawned, wondering when his contact would arrive. He was waiting beneath an awning fashioned in the appearance of trailing orchids of silver and gold outside a drug den on the Grand Canal and his patience was rapidly running out.

Once upon a time a wide promenade of polished stone tiles a hundred strides across had separated the black, sinuous loop of the Grand Canal from the lower palaces of Metzuh tier. Over time the drug dens and flesh halls of Metzuh had sprawled out to clutter the open space with furnishings, slave cages, awnings and apparatus. Each expansion had been the subject of a bitterly fought turf war between neighbouring establishments, forming an untidy patchwork of feuds and vendettas as varied as the objects themselves. The slave's little hutch off to one side of the entrance had probably cost a thousand lives in duels and murders over the years, the silver and gold awning had been around for so long that it had probably cost a million.

The battles for ownership of the banks of the Grand Canal were a crucible that had done much to form the network of petty kabals making up the current power structure of lower Metzuh. Eventually a point of equilibrium had been reached where no one dared to claim the last twenty paces up to the canal's edge for fear of upsetting one or other of the self-proclaimed lords of lower Metzuh. The uneasy peace was normally good for business yet right now the slave was bereft of customers. The miserable creature still kept cutting, re-cutting and weighing its wares with all the eagerness of a pet performing a trick. Kharbyr, for his part, had already sampled all that the slave had on offer and decided he would rather stay sober.

He glanced up and down the empty canal bank for the hundredth time and considered whether to bother keeping his rising anger in check any longer. There was no sign of anyone watching him right now, but that meant nothing. There had been an indefinable sense of someone or something following him for days now, and Kharbyr had taken elaborate measures to shake off any stealthy bloodhounds on his way to the meeting. The fact he could sense nothing now could just mean they were being more careful. It didn't help that the wrack he was here to meet was late, again, and his choice of meeting place was a reminder of past transgressions that Kharbyr had worked hard to overlook. He had a dozen other places to be that all promised better entertainment and profit than this particular corner of Commorragh. The only thing keeping him here was that the wrack, Xagor, only ever ran errands on his master's account and that meant it was probably important to find out what he wanted.

Most of the Epicureans were out holding a noisy processional along the open space at the bank of the Grand Canal. It was partially a diversion for bored pleasure seekers and partially a display of power – an implicit warning to the adjacent districts not to mess with lower Metzuh. The city had been tense of late, taut with anticipation of… something. There was change in the air, a forest-fire scent of imminent disaster that the inhabitants of Commorragh were always quick to sense and react to. Rumours were rife about murders and skulduggery up in High Commorragh and it was said that the great tyrant was distracted by sinister machinations even his castigators could not seem to fathom. In back alleys and hidden souks soothsayers and rune casters muttered of dire portents. The desperate and the dispossessed were gathering in dark corners and plotting how to seize advantage in the coming troubles.

So it was that the Epicurean Lords had summoned their coteries for a show of strength. All over Commorragh similar scenes were being played out as restless cults, covens and kabals gathered to promote their claims to dominance in the prevailing climate uncertainty. Kharbyr could have confirmed a lot of their worst fears based on what he'd witnessed in person over the past weeks, but he chose to stay in the shadows and smirk at their posturing instead.

First came rows of oiled and naked slaves of a variety of races holding the leashes of the Epicurean's pets. Slinking sabercats snarled at imperturbable massiths, blade-legged helspiders marched beside drooling, heavily sedated bhargesi. A kaleidoscopic display of fur, feathers and scales was guided slowly along by the sweating slaves under the watchful eyes of the beastmasters. Occasionally a sudden disturbance in the ranks marked where an irritated pet had turned on their handler, but the steady flow of exotic beasts never halted.

Behind the pets came the favoured slaves. Most of them had been freakishly altered by the flesh-carving arts of the haemonculi into walking sculptures of bone and meat. A few opulently dressed turncoats moved among the staggering, skittering throng and shouted grovelling praises to their masters for their continued existence. It was hard to tell if the braying and moaning of their heavily altered compatriots signified their agreement or disapproval.

Next came the artisans: cadaverous haemonculi with their wrack servants in their barred masks, they mixed freely with master weapon smiths and forge overseers resplendent in their kilts of blades, gravity sculptors walking with wheels of knives spinning above their heads. Here and there gaudy mixologists and painted Lhamaens warred with another to produce the most overwhelming musks and pheromones. Brightly coloured clouds leapt in to the air from their flasks and vials like flights of escaping birds.

The artisans were favoured enough to wear the sigils of their sponsors, all being members of the host of minor Epicurean kabals that passed for authority in lower Metzuh tier. Here was the triple slash of the Soul Cutters, there the rearing serpent of the Venom Brood, or the sickle blade of the Shadow Reapers or a score of others. The artisans mingled despite their temporary allegiances. Their skills were in such great demand among the Epicureans that their loyalties shifted frequently, and for them today's rival might become tomorrow's ally in the anarchic lower courts. False flattery and insincerity thrummed through their ranks as they greeted one another over and over again with the most extravagant courtesies.

Kharbyr tensed. The feeling of being watched was back, as sudden and direct as if someone was standing right behind him and breathing down his neck. He anxiously scanned the slowly moving column trying to identify the source. There, a masked wrack still quite far away down the procession, just occasionally bobbing into view among other apprentices and journeymen. But that particular iron-barred masked looked too frequently towards the awning where Kharbyr stood for it to be coincidence. Was this his contact finally approaching or an imposter? Anything was credible right now. Kharbyr loosened his knife in its sheath before settling back into the shadows to wait and find out.

# CHAPTER 2
## THE QUESTION OF ESCAPE

THE GLOOMWINGS BECAME progressively less numerous while at the same time becoming larger and more corpulent. Some were big enough to engulf a person whole, but they were much slower and less aggressive than the rest. Large or small, Morr tirelessly slaughtered everything that came within reach of his klaive and drove the remnants before him in a shrieking, chittering wave.

Eventually a break among the filth-encrusted walls showed an unfamiliar gleam of metal. Closer examination showed a low side-shaft sloping upward at a gentle angle. It had once been guarded by a grillwork of bars, but time and the gloomwings had eaten away at the soft metal to leave only broken stubs like rotten teeth in an open mouth. Morr crawled inside without hesitation, using his klaive to lever himself up against the slippery walls and rapidly disappearing from sight.

The motley one sniffed and peered after the incubus with comical dismay. 'Really?' he called. 'I say again, this is really the best you could come up with?' Stubborn silence met his jibe and after a while, and with an audible sigh, he bent down and followed.

The shaft proved to be short, no more than a dozen metres long, before it emerged into the side of another, larger, sloping shaft at right angles. The filth here was so prevalent that it was pitch dark, almost like swimming in black water. Rustling, chittering noises echoed weirdly around the shaft, along with the scraping sounds of something big moving around.

'Morr, is that you I can hear?'

Guided by instinct alone the motley one skipped aside as something came rushing out of the blackness. Its impact against the wall of the shaft was shattering, a thunderclap sound in the enclosed space.

'Oh enough is enough!' The motley one muttered as he threw a small object on the ground. The inky blackness was riven by a flash of light so bright it was as though a sun had blinked into existence for a microsecond and engulfed that dark hole in its brilliant photosphere. The momentary glare revealed a monstrous, cloaked figure poised over something that thrashed and struggled in the leaping shadows. A flock of tiny gloomwings overhead shrieked and died in the flash, their nerveless bodies tumbling down like a sudden storm of black snowflakes.

Darkness swiftly descended again, but only for an instant. Red lightning flared from where the cloaked figure had stood, followed by the pure white flash of a power weapon strike. The armoured figure of Morr wielding his klaive was revealed in the actinic afterimage. He seemed poised in the act of striking at rippling curtains of dark flesh surrounding him. Another strike flashed followed by another, the flickering stop-motion progress of the incubus's assault speeding up into a continuous blur of light.

The monstrous figure was revealed as not cloaked but winged – many-winged, in fact – as was shown when it reared back to try and escape its tormentor. It gave a deep, ululating cry of despair as the klaive bit deep into its flesh again and opened its body sac to disgorge a tidal wave of offal. The thing collapsed into a writhing mass, its fleshy wings flailing at the stone with horrid strength. Morr dodged through the thrashing mass to cleave through its primary nerve stem, reducing its dying spasms to a few shuddering twitches.

Morr eventually rose from the centre of the dying mass like a gore-smeared phoenix, his klaive sizzling and steaming with caustic ichor. Motley applauded him lightly.

'Bravo, Morr, once again you prove more than equal to the challenges set before you!' Motley smiled before coughing theatrically into his sleeve. 'Though of course we mustn't overlook the small contributions made by your gallant companion.'

Morr glared at the implication. 'The creature was under control before your intrusion,' he argued hotly. 'It may have hastened matters but it did not change the outcome.'

'Well time is of the essence so you are welcome anyway, my friend, we've only a short while before Commorragh becomes isolated by the Dysjunction and we're stuck here among a lot of people that want you dead,' Motley said brightly as he nudged an outflung wing with one elegantly pointed toe. 'So… I assume *this* is why not many people come this way?'

Morr snarled something unintelligible and stomped off up the sloping tunnel. Motley edged carefully around the dying creature that had once been known as patriarch to a thousand offspring and skipped nimbly after him.

The tunnel levelled out ten metres before it, and the roof opened to admit another vertical shaft with no visible means of climbing it. The tunnel itself came to a dead end dominated by a wide ellipse of sparkling metal and silvery stone that was reminiscent of the outline of a great eye. Blank stone showed behind the structure and it seemed to hang in the air unsupported by any of the tunnel walls. There was an aura of quiescent power about it, as though a swift, silent river was flowing nearby.

'Ah ha!' exclaimed Motley. 'This looks like an old ship gate, well a smallish one anyway. That's why I love this city you know, Morr? Turn a corner and you never know what you might stumble across.'

Morr directed a withering gaze at him in return. 'Archon Kraillach secured this gate long ago to be his own secret means of entrance and egress to the city. It is not locked to a destination, nor is it monitored in any way.' Motley blanched a little at the incubus's words.

'With a Dysjunction imminent doesn't that mean…?' Motley asked.

Morr continued as if Motley had not spoken at all. 'When the Dysjunction occurs this gate may collapse altogether; it will certainly be forced open for a time and anything that finds it might come through into the city. We must be far from here before that happens.'

'We? Oh Morr, I didn't know you cared!' effused Motley. 'You see? We're becoming such good pals already!'

'I cannot prevent your unwanted attentions, I must endure the inevitable consequences of my actions,' Morr intoned. The words seemed to form a personal mantra for him and he repeated them quietly. 'I must endure the inevitable consequences of my actions.'

'Not merely endure. I'm afraid, my old friend, that you must atone for them too,' Motley said sympathetically, 'and not just the actions you're thinking about.' Morr turned his blank helm to face Motley, its crystal eyepieces seeming to flash with red flames. Motley obediently lapsed into silence for a moment before changing the subject.

'So is it safe to assume you know how to activate the gate? Is there a mechanism for sealing it behind us?'

Morr grunted and turned his attention to a panel on the lower edge of the gate. Initially Motley took a mild interest in Morr activating the gate but became increasing distracted by the tunnel behind them. He glanced back several times before wandering aimlessly a short distance away from where Morr crouched with head tilted as if listening. Motley suddenly snapped his fingers together, plucking something out of the air in a half-seen blur of movement. He examined his prize with interest.

'Oh, interesting,' Motley said. 'I think you should look at this, Morr.' He thrust something tiny towards Morr, something small enough that it was barely visible pinched between Motley's gloved thumb and forefinger. An insect, seemingly, but surely no living insect was ever spun so finely from metal and crystal as the spying device Motley held.

'The flare must have blacked out their primary sources so they had to send up back-ups at short notice, no doubt there's more of them around.' For a moment Motley's voice held none of its usual levity or hidden jests, then he brightened again and smiled capriciously. 'Someone is watching us, my friend,' Motley said and turned the device towards himself before enunciating clearly into it. 'I do hope they just watch and don't intend to do anything to interfere, that would be unfortunate,' Motley crushed the spy fly between his fingertips and blew away the dust of its wreckage.

'Let us find out what our watchers intend,' Morr said ominously, straightening and stepping back from the gate. A curtain of shimmering energy began to coalesce within the gate. At first it was made of pure silver light but as the curtain strengthened it became shot through with flashes of gold and umber. After a moment coiling threads of green and blue snaked across the surface. There was something venomous-looking about the portal, an intrinsic malevolence that made both Morr and Motley take another involuntary step back from it.

'Is it…?' Morr began, but left the thought unfinished.

'The Dysjunction. Yes,' Motley said hurriedly, his ordinarily light demeanour suddenly serious. 'It must be only moments away. We have to leave right now or at best we'll be trapped here for the duration. At worst, in about five minutes, we'll be up to our ears in daemons.'

A weight appeared to lift from Morr's shoulders. He took up his klaive and went to stand facing the centre of the gate. 'Then let them come,' he intoned. 'I am ready.'

Motley goggled incredulously at the incubus. 'Now is not the time to make the supreme sacrifice trying to hold this one portal in a city of a million portals!' he shrilled desperately. 'Go to your hierarchs if you must, but we must tackle the root cause of this Dysjunction together and quickly! We have to go!'

Morr shook himself reluctantly out of the death-fantasy. It was so much easier to seek atonement through self-destruction than by facing his crimes that it seemed unfair to be robbed of the chance. The fact it was easier would have convinced him that it was the wrong path to take even without Motley's screeching imprecations. The portal throbbed and shimmered before them both uncertainly, a threshold to the webway, itself a path to a billion other places known and unknown, hidden and obvious, open and forbidden. The place Morr must go to was well hidden, but forbidden to none. Any might seek the hidden shrine of Arhra; the true question was whether they would survive to leave it. Morr took a single step towards the open portal with Motley close at his heels before a harsh shout from behind caused them both to halt abruptly and turn.

'Stop right there! You're not permitted to leave the city!'

'LAST CHANCE, SYBRIS,' Aez'ashya said as she stepped onto the platform. 'Back down and join with me. I'll even make you one of my succubae if you still want it.'

Sybris's braided hair gave her an angular, statuesque profile above her high-necked skinsuit. She raised her chin defiantly and shot Aez'ashya a look of withering disdain.

'An honour that should already rightfully be mine,' Sybris spat. 'You offer me scraps from your table when you aren't even fit to be an archon, let alone a *ynnitach* in High Commorragh.'

*Ynnitach*, bride of death. So be it, Aez'ashya thought, as she raised her hydra gauntlets and closed her fists. The crystalline shards protruding from her wrists and elbows crackled as they grew outward into wickedly hooked blades. Sybris needed no more invitation than that to launch into her attack. She pirouetted lazily towards Aez'ashya, her half-moon blades swinging out like pendulums.

Aez'ashya ducked beneath the glittering arc of the first blade, then sidestepped away from the second to reach the centre of the disk. Sybris instantly reversed her motion with a high kick and came after Aez'ashya hard. The deadly spirals of Sybris's sweeping blades tightened inexorably to make a double strike on Aez'ashya. The blades sliced down with unstoppable power as the hekatrix threw her full body weight behind them. Aez'ashya rolled away from the attack, snapping up to her feet at the edge of the disk. She was just in time to catch Sybris's counter-swing on one of her gauntlet-blades and twist it savagely.

Sybris backflipped to avoid having her weapon wrenched out of her grasp and Aez'ashya easily avoided a backhanded blow as Sybris fought to recover. The razor edges of the hydra gauntlets whispered within millimetres of the silky surface of Sybris's skin as she twisted away, swiftly pirouetting again to build her momentum back up. Aez'ashya grinned wolfishly.

Every one of Sybris's moves was just a fraction slower than they should be, a fact that Sybris herself didn't seem to be aware of just yet. She swung in again, straight arms sweeping the blades at Aez'ashya's exposed throat and belly. This time Aez'ashya stood her ground and struck out at the slashing blades, not aiming to block them but merely redirecting them so that they sailed harmlessly past her. One of Aez'ashya's gauntlet blades seemed to glide across Sybris's midriff as she returned to a guard position, carving a crimson line through skinsuit and flesh. The tip of the blade broke off in the wound with a high-pitched crackling sound and Sybris gasped as she jerked back.

Sybris's blade-tipped braid whipped forward like a striking snake. There was no fractional delay to the move and it caught Aez'ashya by surprise. A bunched fist of scalpel-sharp, finger-long blades came swinging at her eyes, provoking an immediate and instinctive reaction. Aez'ashya grabbed the braid and pulled, forcing Sybris to backflip over her. Aez'ashya drew one of her elbow blades across Sybris's flashing thigh, carving another red trail and leaving another crystalline shard behind to work its way into the wound. Sybris swung viciously at Aez'ashya's imprisoning gauntlet, forcing her to relinquish her grasp. Aez'ashya let go and allowed Sybris to spin away from her, re-occupying her position at the centre of the disk.

It all came down to the planning, as Aez'ashya had come to appreciate after recent events, preparation meant victory. The old Aez'ashya would simply have taken up this challenge with whatever was at hand and wherever was convenient. The new Aez'ashya understood the value of picking your ground and choosing your weapons carefully. The fighting area was just a little too constricted for Sybris to build up to her full speed, the gravity in it just a shade heavier than Sybris was used to. Aez'ashya was of the firm opinion that too many wyches trained in low gravity environs, that many became seduced by the more spectacular fighting styles they permitted. Sybris was living proof of the fact.

Now it was only a matter of time. The crystalline blades of Aez'ashya's gauntlets had already regrown. Fragments that they had left in Sybris's wounds would keep them bleeding freely despite the best efforts of her skinsuit to seal the cuts. Sybris's style relied on momentum, now that constant motion was causing her to bleed out all the faster. Aez'ashya settled herself to wait for the inevitable opening.

THE MASKED WRACK separated from the Epicurean's procession and approached openly. As he did so Kharbyr surreptitiously drew his knife and held it ready beneath his cloak. The wrack held up both hands to show they were empty of weapons, although the curved, bird-like claw grafted in place of the wrack's right hand would have made a passable weapon on its own. A new addition, Kharbyr judged by the way the wrack struggled with it while removing his mask. The thick-browed and morose face that was revealed looked familiar enough – but that meant nothing in Commorragh where flesh could be twisted and reshaped for the price of a hot meal. Kharbyr smiled insincerely and spoke first.

'Greetings, "Xagor". How many daemons at the gate?'

'Six, and Kharbyr was almost taken,' the wrack responded evenly.

Kharbyr's face flushed angrily at the memory. 'Very clever, now what is it you want?' he snapped.

'Too open here. Inside?'

Xagor stepped towards the entrance to the den, perhaps a little too eagerly, but Kharbyr stopped him with an outstretched arm.

'Out here is fine. No one is going to be paying any attention to us with all this going on.'

He nodded toward the canal bank where lines of warriors were now filing past to the accompaniment of thundering drums and clashing cymbals. They were irregularly armed and armoured in a dark, curvaceous style that was barbed and bladed in a fashion that would put a scorpion to shame. Several of the warriors bore trophy poles hung with brightly coloured, almost spherical, helmets and a variety of shrunken heads like obscene gourds. The warriors kept to rigid files dictated by their kabals and woe betide any of them that should step into the path of their rivals. In contrast to the mercurial artisans a faithless warrior was worthless, a weapon that could not be trusted. It was better for warriors to die than betray their sworn masters (at least according to the masters). Kharbyr mused uneasily that there might be a lesson to be learned there somewhere.

Xagor's forehead furrowed unhappily, but the wrack stayed obediently where he was and settled for expressing himself in a hoarse, ear-grabbing whisper in order to maintain his ham-fisted attempts at intrigue.

'The master... sends greetings.'

'That's nice,' Kharbyr sneered, without bothering to drop his voice. 'Where is he?'

Xagor, if it was Xagor, hedged for a moment and Kharbyr grew even more suspicious. Even the trooping warriors seemed wary, their masked helms turning constantly as they scanned blindly for threats. Omnipresent suspicion and a simmering undercurrent of suppressed violence swept along with the warrior's section of the processional like a glowering thunderhead.

'Secret... the master has had much work to do.'

'So I can see, although I can't say I'm too impressed by the work he's done so far on you.'

Xagor's ordinarily dull eyes flashed with anger at the jibe. 'Do not mock the master!' he snarled, momentarily forgetting his ridiculous stage-whispers act. The slave over in his hutch paid absolutely no heed and Kharbyr laughed derisively in the wrack's face.

'He can't protect us!' Kharbyr hissed. 'He can't protect himself! We should just run–'

'The master said Kharbyr would want to run,' Xagor interrupted hotly. 'The master said it was a good idea. Run far! Hide well.' The wrack turned suddenly to leave. Kharbyr was astonished by the turn of events.

'Wait, what? You can't just leave!' Kharbyr stepped in close and grabbed the front of Xagor's robes, holding his naked blade to the wrack's neck. 'I'm told nothing and expected to perform like a pet on command! I'm being followed – you know that? I am, and they'll be catching up pretty soon so tell me what's going on or I'll slit your throat here and now!'

The wrack grinned back at him triumphantly. 'The master said that when Kharbyr wanted to run Xagor should leave and see what Kharbyr does next. If Kharbyr then follows and demands answers then the master asks Kharbyr to guard something while he runs. Bad times are coming very soon and Kharbyr must protect this.'

The wrack was suddenly holding an object in its normal hand, a flat, finger-thick metal pentagon with a spiralling groove in its surface.

'What is it?' Kharbyr eyed the thing suspiciously and didn't touch it. It didn't even look valuable to him, but he also knew that in Commorragh looks could be deceptive. An object that small could still hold the compressed form of something much, much bigger. Like a small starship, or a portal to another world, or a bomb large enough to ensure that no part of Kharbyr would ever be recovered.

'It is a secret…that Xagor does not know,' the wrack glanced at Kharbyr almost with embarrassment as he said this. The implication seemed to be that threatening or torturing Xagor, as much as Xagor might enjoy it, would not reveal anything more.

'Then… how does it help anything?' Kharbyr said as he lowered his blade with a sense of resignation.

'The master says it will,' Xagor said soothingly.

'There had better be a reward in this.'

'The master said to remind Kharbyr that the master's patronage is worth Kharbyr's life many times over.'

'Much good it has done me so far,' Kharbyr muttered bitterly.

'The master also said he has already done more for you than you know.'

'Apparently Bel–,' in his anger Kharbyr barely stopped himself from mentioning the master haemonculus by name. 'Apparently the master says a lot, only not to me.' Kharbyr fumed, chewing at his lip uncertainly. As he looked up he saw the end of the Epicurean's processional was coming into view. Last of all (saving for a rearguard of more warriors, even Epicureans having some sense of self-preservation) came lower Metzuh's petty archons and nobility of mixed blood. They came two and three abreast in an order of precedence that had probably been the source of much bickering and in-fighting. As it was Lord Naxipael of the Venom Brood led alongside Bezieth of the Hundred Scars, archon of the Soul Cutters. Both were lesser archons that Kharbyr recognised and had had some peripheral dealings with. Ornate palanquins and biers bore the Epicurean lords along elevated above a throng made up of their immediate cliques of bodyguards, confidants, lackeys and hangers-on.

For all his flippancy the patronage of the master haemonculus Bellathonis was worth more to Kharbyr than he cared to admit. It had already cowed enemies and opened doors for him that had never existed before. Recently Kharbyr had changed the cliques he moved in and begun to ascend no small distance up the slippery slopes of kabalite politics despite his lowly blood. If he ever hoped to ride on one of those palanquins himself he needed powerful allies like Bellathonis. The wrack was waiting with a smug grin on his face, holding the metal thing out as if he expected Kharbyr to take it, but Kharbyr still hesitated. He could never aspire to anything by endlessly serving others; somehow he had to take control of the situation himself.

The noise of the processional made it hard to think: horns blared and drums beat incessantly, the sound of skirling pipes carried back from the artisans, shrieks and screams filtered back from the pets. The warriors were silent now, their tramping steps their only accompaniment. Over all the background noise Kharbyr's ears caught a distinctive high-pitched sound that grabbed his attention immediately. He turned back to Xagor and took the metal octagon from his hand.

'I think,' Kharbyr said hurriedly, 'we had better go inside after all.'

# CHAPTER 3
## DYSJUNCTION

'WHO IS IT that dares to impede an incubus in his work?' intoned Morr slowly and dangerously. 'Show yourself and I'll judge your worth to give me commands.'

Mocking laughter came out of the darkness. 'We'll stay where we are, thanks, being not such great fools as to come within reach of your klaive nor the clown's blade.'

'Oh?' said Motley as he stepped forward as lightly as a dancer. 'Then how do you plan on doing any impeding at all, friends? We need but take two steps and we are gone from here. How do you intend to allow or disallow that?'

'You aren't the only one with grenades, fool.'

If the assailants hadn't bragged they might have been more successful in their efforts. As it was Motley spotted the first tiny bulb of metal tumbling through the air, caught it and threw it back in one fluid motion. A blast of static lightning lit the tunnel where it landed that illuminated running figures in its crawling afterglow. Haywire, Motley opined to himself, they were using Haywire grenades to try to knock out the gate. Any moment now they would think to throw more than one at a time. Motley glanced backwards to find Morr and shout a warning.

There was no sign of the towering incubus and the gate was in the process of powering down.

Motley took in the whole scene within a frozen instant of panic. Time slowed, stretched while each intimate detail imposed itself. Angry red lines were spreading across the metal and stone of the gate's structure. It was intended to be a permanent shut-down, one that would leave behind nothing but a pile of useless slag. The veil of shimmering energy was still held within the gate for the present, swirling and opalescent now, but it was thinning by the moment. Motley darted for the dying portal just as a shower of small grenades came tinkling down in his wake.

A vicious pattern of detonations raged around the gateway, electro-magnetic discharges and gouts of plasma (some of the assailants having already escalated their intentions from capturing to killing) intermingling in a catastrophic storm of energised particles. In the aftermath the gate was gone, just a fused and twisted mass was left in its place. Of the incubus and the harlequin there was no sign.

The agents poked, prodded and analysed the area

in a desultory fashion but it was clear there was nothing more that could be done. They consoled themselves that their master was currently otherwise engaged and unreachable. The unpleasant task of informing him about their lost quarry could be safely deferred for another time.

HAD THE AGENTS but known it their master was not far away at that moment. Archon Nyos Yllithian of the Kabal of the White Flames was staggering through the worming guts of the Commorragh's vast foundational strata. He was now only minutes away from the Dysjunction he'd unwittingly had such a large hand in bringing about. Judgment, seemingly, had already caught up with him. He rebounded from moist stone walls in the near darkness as he desperately sought a way out, his numbing hands stretched out before him as he fumbled along dank, slimy tunnels. Kilometres above him there were silver towers taller than mountains, manses the size of cities, fortress-like continents and island-palaces of surpassing beauty and grandeur. His own fortress lay agonisingly close by, filled with retainers and warriors and slaves to do his bidding. But Archon Yllithian was alone, trapped in the foetid entrails of the world and he was dying.

By his nature Yllithian was not a creature given to regrets. All in all he shared the almost pathologically forward-facing attitude of his race. The past was the past and nothing more could be said; such was the healthy attitude of the average Commorrite

– saving, perhaps, for the propensity to recall slights, vendettas and feuds with crystal clarity. Even so Yllithian felt the bitterest regret now. Not regret for unleashing otherworldly forces beyond his capacity to control by resurrecting the beast El'Uriaq. Not regret for the overweening hubris that had caused the deaths of his allies, nor for the mass murder in the accursed El'Uriaq's banquet hall left now so ominously silent behind him. No, Yllithian's only regret was that he had been unlucky enough to get caught up in El'Uriaq's downfall.

Yllithian had to admit to himself that it had been a pretty scheme to destroy El'Uriaq. He had only recognised the true danger of it in the last moments, and even then he'd chosen to flee instead of trying to warn El'Uriaq or prevent it. Too slow, too slow by far and now his skin was vitrifying before his rapidly clouding eyes, turning to a lustrous jade colour that would soon darken to black. The master haemonculus, Bellathonis, had contrived to release the Glass Plague upon El'Uriaq and his guests. It was a viral helix created to turn living flesh in glass, meaning a true death for a Commorrite as their body was completely destroyed in the process. No regeneration, no resurrection was possible from the Glass Plague and so any Commorrite of any value was normally immunised against it. That had been the clever part – the haemonculus had persuaded the Exodite witch, the worldsinger, to turn the plague into something that could overcome any form of defence. Being able to communicate with lower forms of life seemed such a safely mundane ability until someone used it to bypass your immune system. Yllithian knew he was as good as dead.

The archon of the White Flames still drove his stiffening limbs forward, some animal instinct for self-preservation bright in his mind. A coolly logical part of it was telling him it was hopeless, that he should lie down and preserve his remaining energy. There was a distant siren whisper of She Who Thirsts in that call for surrender, she eagerly awaited his soul and all woes, all cares would be obliterated in her all-consuming embrace. Yllithian croaked defiance through stiffened lips and tottered onward.

Bellathonis and the crone, Angevere, they were the ones to blame. They had made El'Uriaq's ill-starred return possible in the first place. Yllithian had seen himself as directing events, making the plans and gathering the resources. Now it was clear he was the one that had been directed all along... No, that wasn't right – Bellathonis had been as surprised as anyone, and in fact almost fatally injured by the newly risen El'Uriaq. The crone and the Exodite, then, some scheme of theirs to bring ruin to Commorragh, poisoning all of Yllithian's plans with their sorcery. That seemed closer to the mark, but even then it didn't seem quite right. Some greater architect had been at work, he sensed now, a being unconstrained by time or space that apparently had nothing better to do with its energies than bring about Yllithian's downfall.

The archon's dying mind continued churning

with recriminations and paranoia as it had done all his life. For perhaps the first time in his existence he was denied any means to exact vengeance or even level his accusations. He had already been caught and killed by his invisible slayer, he was just not quite dead yet.

His dimming senses alerted him to a trembling, as if the floor of the tunnel was vibrating like a taut wire. The crone had been right after all, may Lhilitu eat her stitched-shut eyes, a Dysjunction was really coming.

SYBRIS'S SINUOUS GRACE was faltering. She spun like a broken toy around the edges of the disc, worrying constantly at Aez'ashya's guard but always finding it impenetrable without throwing her whole strength against it, which now she dare not do. The silver surface was crisscrossed with crimson rivulets and smears. Not much longer now. Aez'ashya was anticipating a final, despairing assault before Sybris endurance leaked away completely. She flexed her razor-edged hydra gauntlets in anticipation of the moment.

The end came with a violent lunge from Sybris. She flung herself forward to smash at Aez'ashya with full force, her half-moon blades seeming to blur into a solid ribbon of steel. Aez'ashya gave ground before the onslaught, ducking or redirecting strikes with both fists and forearms. In truth Aez'ashya had little choice, Sybris's eyes were glassy and beads of foam flecked her mouth – sure signs that she'd used a dose of *Splintermind* to maintain her fury. Aez'ashya found herself being driven to the edge of the platform with a kilometres-deep drop yawning at her heels.

Aez'ashya delivered a sudden kick to Sybris's hip that sent the hekatrix reeling. She quickly followed through pivoting and stepping inside Sybris' superior reach. The hydra gauntlet's fist blades crunched below Sybris's sternum, parting her steely bodice and ripping open the smooth, white flesh beneath. Sybris eyes flew wide open, she staggered and coughed blood before lashing back viciously at Aez'ashya. This was the danger point, the time when an opponent knew they were already dying and would suffer anything to drag their killer down with them.

Aez'ashya caught Sybris's descending wrist and used it to swing her out toward the edge of the disc-shaped platform. A desperate slash from Sybris's other blade was contemptuously knocked aside as Aez'ashya relentlessly bore the hekatrix over the edge. Sybris screamed as her feet lost their grip and kicked helplessly over emptiness. Aez'ashya smiled and let Sybris flail desperately for a moment before reaching a quick decision, abruptly grabbing her by the throat and dragging her back from the brink.

'You know what, Sybris?' Aez'ashya panted. 'I think I'm actually grateful to you. I'd had my own doubts about whether I could prevail as archon and now you've confirmed that I can. Now the question is – can you be clever enough to accept that?'

Sybris nodded numbly. There was little else she could do with Aez'ashya's blades at her throat.

There was no doubt that Sybris would go on to cause more trouble, that she would attract other malcontents and plotters into her sphere. Aez'ashya now realised there was value in that too. Sybris was a known quantity that Aez'ashya could defeat one to one if need be. If Sybris also became a lightning rod for other schemers then so much the better, they would be that much easier to identify and deal with. Aez'ashya released Sybris's throat and grabbed her by the braid instead.

"You get to live this time, Sybris, for old time's sake and because you've helped to prove me worthy,' Aez'ashya said, 'but I'll be keeping this as a souvenir!' She sliced off Sybris's braid close to the scalp and held it aloft to show off to the distant spectators. To her annoyance Aez'ashya noticed that Sybris was no longer looking up at her. The hekatrix was gazing off into the upper air of High Commorragh, her attention focused somewhere above Aez'ashya's shoulder with a look of horror growing upon her face. A small tremor ran through the platform beneath their feet. Wary of a trick, Aez'ashya glanced quickly in the direction Sybris was looking. What she saw almost froze her heart.

High above them the circling *Ilmaea* were changing. The black suns were outlined by crawling circles of white fire, whip-thin solar flares curled outward from them like slow lightning. The sun's light glinted poisonously and washed everything with an oily, unclean look. Something was very, very wrong.

\* \* \*

THE BLACK VELVET surface of the Grand Canal bore a small armada of pleasure barges following the Epicureans' procession. The crafts' occupants called out encouragements or mockery according to their mood, played music and danced. Most gained their sport from trying to lasciviously tempt those on the bank to plunge into the Grand Canal and swim out to them. It was cruel game considering that the curious mixture of narcotics, wastes and other chemicals that made up the 'waters' of the canal promised madness or oblivion to any that touched them. All in all, Bezieth, Naxipael and the other lords of the Epicureans could reflect that things were going well.

Too well in the eyes of some of their watchers. The first herald of trouble came in the high-pitched snarl of multiple engines. A welter of wasp-like jet-bikes with wild looking riders swiftly followed the sound, swooping down onto the processional from above. The bikes screamed low over the heads of the kabalites, wheeled, looped and returned in less time than it takes to tell it. This time their hooked bladevanes swept past within a hand's breadth of the Epicureans. Crests were parted, trophies were shredded and a handful of the unlucky tallest slaves decapitated by the reavers' second pass.

The ranks of pets snarled and reared dangerously at the intrusion, the warriors flourished their weapons defiantly and the artisans carefully watched the unfolding events. As the reavers reached the rear of the procession Bezieth reared up from her palanquin with an inarticulate roar, seeming ready to swat the interlopers out of the air with her djin-blade. Violence shivered in the air. Its imminence was almost palpable, crystallised and ready to fly apart into a frenzy of action at any moment.

A few sharp words from Lord Naxipael seemed to abruptly quell Bezieth's ire. She sat down with a thump as the reaver pack raced away over the canal and scattered upward like windblown leaves.

'They're nothing but bait,' Naxipael hissed.

And so they were. A few moments later a second, and far larger, pack of reavers droned overhead with insouciant slowness as they trailed after the first. The first group had been a decoy to provoke an attack and draw fire while the real threat manoeu-vred for position above. Someone was trying to draw the Epicureans into a messy brawl along the Grand Canal – doubtless a setback intended to illustrate to the individual kabals that their loose coalition offered no real protection. A simple test passed just as simply by not rising to the bait.

However, the procession remained stationary even after the reavers departed. Every eye was drawn to the warding where it rose from the far bank of the Grand Canal. The warding extended as far as the eye could perceive, a swirling, darkly opalescent boundary that curved away in all direc-tions. Beyond it lay the untamed energies of the void held forever in check by arcane technolo-gies. Nearby a slender bridge curved across the canal to seemingly pierce the warding at the Beryl Gate, a permanent portal to the sub-realm of the Aviaries of Malixian. Hazy images of other realms occasionally swam into view within the warding, visions of fey towers or strange landscapes, but to the inhabitants of lower Metzuh the shimmering energy was a boundary as solid and unremarkable as a stone wall.

Now it was obvious that something was changing. The oily, sickly colours of the void were swirling faster, now whirling into impossible new shapes, now pulsating as if shot through with lightning. A spider's web of bright and terrible light was slowly spreading outwards over the surface of the warding from the beryl gate, chinks of a deadly effulgence leaking in from realities beyond Commorragh. A low, animalistic moan of terror swept through the procession at the sight. Some individuals broke and ran for the palaces but it was already too late for anyone to save themselves. The Dysjunction had begun.

The first shock was physical; the city shook as if it were in the grip of an angry giant. The canal churned to froth as shockwaves ran through it. Pleasure craft were upended and tipped their occupants into waters where their screams were rapidly stilled. On the bank people were thrown off their feet as chasms yawned in the polished stone that swallowed parts of the procession whole. Stone split and metal screamed as portions of the lower palaces gave way and toppled outward to crush those unlucky enough to be beneath them.

On the heels of the first physical shock a psychic shock came blasting through the warding, a wave of empyrean energy that twisted reality itself before it.

Some simply went mad as the stones rippled beneath their feet and sprouted screaming faces or clutching hands. These tore at one another like wild beasts, snarling wordlessly as they clawed and bit. Others cast themselves into the churning canal, screaming with laughter as the black, viscid ooze closed over them. Some died where they stood, bursting into incandescent flames, or being torn asunder by lightning, or ravaged by invisible claws or melted like hot wax. These were all the lucky ones. The rest, by far the bulk of those present, survived the immediate shock only to attract the attention of other, more sentient entities as they breached the warding.

These predatory beings feasted on souls and the raw suffering of mortals. In some ways they were very much like the Commorrites themselves, but where the methods of Commorrites were refined to a high art of sensuous cruelty, these beings were crude and atavistic. Their manifestations were the stuff of nightmares – pincer clawed temptresses, whirligigs of living flames, foetid cadaverous things lurching on stick-thin limbs and a hundred other daemonic terrors made real. Their appearance was accompanied by waves of sickness, fever-dream emotions and hysteria. The spectral horde coalesced, spread and tainted the air before it like ink dropped into a pail of clear water. They tore into the Epicureans with joyous abandon and weapons flashed as the Commorrites tried to defend themselves, but for each abomination that was shredded or blasted apart a dozen more crowded forward to take its place.

At the rear of the procession Bezieth of the Hundred Scars wielded her djin-blade with desperate skill. No daemon-spawn could lay a claw upon her as she hacked her way free of the struggling mass at the head of a handful of other survivors. For once the angry sentience of the djin-blade seemed to be entirely on her side with none of the unexpected twists and turns it liked to make at inopportune moments. The enraged spirit of the previous archon of the Soul Cutters, Axhyrian, was trapped within the crystalline djin-blade and made a ready source of energy for Bezieth to call upon when she needed it. Axhyrian's rage could make for a treacherous weapon, but right now Bezieth needed every advantage she could lay her hands on. Lord Naxipael followed closely in Bezieth's wake felling invaders left and right with a pair of finely crafted blast pistols. Behind him a loose wedge of retainers was forming, but their numbers were thinning by the second.

'It seems our superiors in High Commorragh have truly given us the "noble treatment" this time!' Naxipael cried over the screams.

'No time for talking, snake!' Bezieth replied furiously. 'Just... kill!'

The other members of the procession had completely disappeared under a mass of writhing, feasting daemons. A continuous stream of snapping, clawing monstrosities came against Bezieth and Naxipael as she cut her way towards the ruined palaces hoping to find a place to make a stand. It was only a hundred paces from the canal side to the lower palaces yet it seemed more like a hundred miles. The ghostly energies flowing through the breach in the warding brushed constantly across her mind. They spawned strange visions and alien emotions there: spiralling iron towers that reached up into infinity, skies of blood and rivers of entrails, meadows of fingertips and clouds of lies. Tiny static-like shocks of joy warred with darting release and morbid satisfaction for the contents of her soul.

A quartet of single-horned, cyclopean daemons with rusting swords came lurching at her out of the kaleidoscopic mental fog, their drooling maws emitting the buzzing of flies. She hacked them down with short, chopping strokes as if she were cutting wood. Their obscene bodies yielded readily to the djin-blade and split like ripe fruit wherever it fell.

A sixth sense sent her diving to one side just as a barbed and serrated mass of metal crashed down where she had stood a moment before. A glance upwards showed more fragments of pillars, colonnades, statues, minarets and arches tumbling down from high above. Flights of multi-coloured fireballs swept past overhead and plunged into the lower palaces, the dancing flames eating unnaturally into the ruins with joyous screams. Bezieth found that she had made her way to a twisted pile of slave cages and decided that was her best place to turn at bay.

It was a timely decision. Behind her the ravening

horde of entities was spreading out to seek more prey. They had finished feasting on the procession, which by now was just a mess of tattered banners and gory debris, and were looking hungrily towards the palaces and, coincidentally, Bezieth and the other survivors. She spat defiance at the daemons as they bounded forward, seeing them skittering and squabbling with one another over these fresh morsels. The rotting ones and the fiery ones seemed at odds, as apt to attack each other as come for her; a fact she immediately used to her best advantage.

Bezieth's djin-blade snarled and sheared through tentacles, claws, tongues and pseudopods with equal abandon. Retina-scarring flashes from Naxipael's pistols burst more of the running bodies and for a brief instant the area around Bezieth was cleared. The creatures seemed to be becoming weak and uncoordinated. A change was sweeping through them and they were beginning to show the first signs of fear. Now Bezieth felt as if she was cutting at smoke, each sweep of her blade seemed to dissipate half a dozen of the entities at a time.

The pulsing, crackling spider web of light around the Beryl Gate was dimming. Bezieth glanced up to see images in the warding, like great towers or tentacles or tornadoes, vast, titanic forces that were all thrusting blindly at the gate from impossible angles. She forced herself to look away before her sanity unhinged completely, focusing on what was close by and material before she lost her mind to the enormity of the forces rageing beyond her reality. The awful light was continuing to dim despite their attempts to bludgeon their way through; the glowing cracks were fading as if they were composed of cooling metal. The daemonic horde wavered in and out of existence as the eons-old failsafes of the warding struggled to seal the breach. One by one the temptresses, lurching corpses and dancing flames collapsed in on themselves or vanished like wind blown flames.

An awful not-quite silence descended over the scene. There still sounded in the distance wrenching, grinding and screams beyond number, but a momentary bubble of comparative calm seemed to have encompassed the canal bank in the absence of the screeching, whirling daemon horde. The Beryl Gate was gone, replaced by a shifting, multi-hued star that now doubtless led to many places other than the Aviaries of Malixian the Mad. Too many places. The void beyond the warding looked bloated and menacing, storm clouds ready to break. The shrunken band of survivors grouped around Bezieth and Naxipael looked at each other uncertainly. There were many unfamiliar faces among them.

'Is it over?' one said.

'Over? It has barely begun!' Naxipael hissed angrily. 'Until all the gates are sealed–' As if to underline his words Archon Naxipael was interrupted as another tremor ran through the canal bank. The multi-hued star that had once been the Beryl Gate twinkled ominously. Naxipael refused to be daunted '–until all of the gates are locked there will be more incursions, more daemons!'

'That seems like a handy blade to have at a time like this,' a voice close behind Bezieth remarked casually.

Bezieth whipped around to cut down the speaker for his impudence, the razor edge of the djin-blade singing through the air. Then it happened, the grim inevitability of it unfurling before her very eyes. The blade was stronger than ever, glutted on stolen daemonic power. It twisted treacherously in her tired grip, the razor-edge slipping sidewise to bite deeply into her thigh. Bezieth felt the sudden, cold rush of adrenaline from a really serious injury. She felt her leg begin to buckle beneath her and fought to push the djin-blade away from her throat as the ground rushed up to meet her. The pounding blood in her ears sounded like the laughter of Axhyrian.

# CHAPTER 4
## THE GLASS PRINCE

GUIDED AS MUCH by good fortune as quick reflexes, Motley emerged into the webway in an untidy heap but thankfully unharmed. There was no mistaking that it was the webway he'd landed in (which was a relief in itself): the strangeness, the sense of unreality, the feeling that the surrounding gossamer walls were just barely stretched over infinity and that if you peeked behind one you would see the whole universe laid out before you. Motley picked himself up and dusted himself down fastidiously even though there was no dust, dirt or anything else so crude and elemental to be seen. The webway tunnel surrounding him was made up of all-encompassing, hazy whiteness that seemed to slide away from the eye when viewed directly.

Only as Motley started to walk along did the view resolve itself into wide, almost circular tunnel that undulated gently before him. Behind him there was no sign at all of Kraillach's secret gate to Commorragh. Ahead of him the pure whiteness stretched away to some infinitely distant vanishing point. The purity was marred only by a stark, black shape that wavered and jumped in the middle distance, no more than finger-tall and fast vanishing from sight altogether. Motley sprinted rapidly after it.

The distance proved deceptive and Motley soon caught up to Morr, who was striding along with his klaive over one shoulder. As Motley approached Morr seemed to hunch over a little and begin striding faster.

'Fear not, Morr, your trusty companion is unhurt and ready to accompany you once more,' Motley said brightly to Morr as he jogged up level with him. The spoken words seemed curiously flat and hollow in the webway, as though their tiny noise was lost in the vastness surrounding them. Morr growled deep in his throat, and the guttural sound seemed to be more successful in making an impact.

'So, a ship tunnel, then?' Motley chattered on. 'Your archon was an uncannily canny fellow. I don't suppose he also hid a ship around here too, did he? I have no objections to strolling, but time–'

'Is of the essence. This has been already said,' Morr said heavily. 'Repetition of tropes will not serve to endear you to me. No ship exists that can travel to where we must go.'

'Hmm, that's true enough – though I can't tell you how thrilled I am that you said "we" again.'

'I have come to accept the burden of your

presence as part of my punishment.'

'That's true enough too, if a little self-castigating, but I think you have cause and effect about right.'

Morr stopped abruptly and turned to face Motley, swinging his klaive from his shoulder in an easy, practiced motion. 'You admit that you are here solely to punish me?' Morr's question was devoid of all emotion, a dead thing that hung in the air between them. Motley wrung his hands miserably as he stepped adroitly back out of immediate reach.

'No! No! Not at all. I came to help you, Morr. You were the one that asked for help dealing with your archon and his kabal, and I was the one sent to help!'

The klaive raised fractionally, a movement more subtle than the tremble of an insect's wing but Motley saw it immediately. He was supremely confident in his ability to avoid Morr's attacks should it come to that, but the incubus had proved himself quite shockingly quick and possessed of a reach with the massive, two metre-long klaive that was hard to overestimate. Motley took another step back just to be safe as he kept talking.

'Think, Morr! Without my help the corruption would have spread further, more kabals would have fallen under its sway, who knows what might have happened! Your archon was already lost, gone, you only acted because you had to... to...'

'To preserve his memory,' Morr finished quietly. 'As he was, not as he became.'

'Yes, yes and you did the right thing, no matter what the hierarchs may say to you when, and if, we reach the shrine of Arhra. Kraillach was already dead, you only killed the thing that was inhabiting his corpse...' Morr's klaive twitched at the thought and Motley decided that Kraillach's death was a bad topic to pursue altogether.

'Look...' Motley said, moistening his lips and putting on his most earnest expression. 'You have to see beyond those immediate consequences now and remember that Commorragh itself is at risk!'

The klaive slowly lowered again. Motley made a mental note to make more capital out of Morr's sense of duty. Morr's blank-faced helm turned to Motley, seeming to see him for the first time. Motley kept talking, the words bubbling out of him like a clear flowing brook.

'The city needs your help, Morr! A Dysjunction won't simply end of its own accord, oh no. That would be too simple! A Dysjunction will only be resolved by identifying the root cause and acting upon it–'

'Do not think to lecture me,' Morr interrupted. 'You might have wandered further in the webway than most, but it belongs to Commorragh. Always and forever. These things are known.'

'I don't doubt the archons will be scratching their heads and looking around for someone to blame, or that Vect is about to make one of those terribly overt demonstrations he is so fond of. None of it will change anything, don't you see? The Dysjunction will continue until the real source of the disruption is found, and *they won't be able to find it.*'

Morr simply looked at him, unmoving and

unreadable in his dark armour as he lowered his klaive to rest on the hazy, white ground. Motley shut his mouth, conscious that he had probably said too much already. The towering incubus was unwilling to let him off so easily. Long seconds drew out before Morr spoke again, when he did the single word that emerged from his speaker grille was freighted with threat.

'Why?'

YLLITHIAN HAD INITIALLY been dashed to the floor by the shock of the Dysjunction, the impact triggering howling agony as his skin splintered and drove glass shards into his living flesh. It proved to be just the first in a series of shocks that made the tunnel jump and writhe like a frightened animal. Yllithian could do nothing more than clutch ineffectually at the stonework and try to scream as the roots of the world were shaken.

An interminable period seemed to pass before the immediate violence of the Dysjunction had quieted to an infrequent trembling. Yllithian found he was lying where he had fallen and was unable to rise. His limbs were now too stiff and heavy to move. One eye was completely blind, and the other dimmed by a layer of glass spreading across it. Despite such impediments Yllithian could sense the Dysjunction was far from over. A sense of wrongness and change pervaded the air that was as distinct and dangerous as the sulphurous fumes of a volcano. Periodically shockwaves ran through the foundation strata, either more of the city wardings being breached or the unthinkable megatonne impacts of falling debris that had been shaken loose from High Commorragh.

Yllithian was surprised to discover that he could still hear sounds. At first he thought the sense of hearing the distant, thunderous shocks as they occurred was an illusion created by his vitrifying body. Perhaps, he'd thought, a sympathetic resonance of some kind was generated as even unliving matter recoiled from the distant violence being done to its fellow matter. His chuckle came out as a staccato hiss and he knew then that he could still hear. He wondered if this was to be his perverse fate, to be frozen into immobility and able only to hear the world dying around him.

Yllithian's growing self-pity was interrupted by awareness of a small, regular sound approaching him. Slow, shuffling footsteps that came closer with agonising deliberation, as if belonging to someone badly hurt or heavily burdened. Yllithian tried to twist around to see from his one, dimmed eye but he could not turn his neck. He tried to speak but only a whistle of air escaped from his rigid lips. Suddenly a dark, spider-like shape crouched before him, metal glimmering on its stick-thin limbs. Yllithian could only watch helplessly as it darted some sort of stinging barb into his prone body three or four times, each penetration felt as a dull, distant impact.

More time passed. The enigmatic figure remained squatting over Yllithian's recumbent form and more details emerged about it little by little. The face was a pallid blur, the body wasp-waisted and narrow shouldered, with finger-thick metal pins protruding from its limbs and spine. Long white hands searched over his body assuredly, stopping here and there to brush away flakes of black glass. Tingling spread gradually through Yllithian's limbs and face. Recognition dawned suddenly and he tried to speak again.

'B-B-hronss,' Yllithian managed.

'Ah very good, my archon, mobility returns,' the spindle-limbed figure replied. 'It is indeed I, loyal Bellathonis, come to your succour in your hour of need – a fact that I would ask you to recall later when we achieve happier circumstances.'

'K-K-K–' Yllithian struggled to get anything out of his frozen lips. The indignity of his situation was coming close to driving him insane but he persevered doggedly. Bellathonis watched him with ill-concealed amusement. 'K-Ku-Kurd?' Yllithian said at last.

'Ah. Not entirely, for now the plague has been placed into temporary remission by the antigens I was fortuitously carrying about my person. We must seek a more permanent solution at my laboratory, or whatever is left of it. In the meantime there will be considerable discomfort, I'm afraid, as the irreversibly transformed tissue sloughs away.'

'Y-yu-yuh-you…' the word came out as a satisfactorily low, threatening growl. Yllithian revelled in his tiny triumph. Bellathonis seemed to be less impressed.

'Oh come now, Yllithian, don't be disagreeable.

If you really blamed all this on me you'd scarcely be warning me about it now, would you? Most certainly not at the moment when I hold your life literally in my hands. You and I both know you're cleverer than that. Please accord me the same courtesy.'

Yllithian's next attempts at framing words became incomprehensible as the Glass Plague loosened its grip enough to enable him to scream. One thought kept his sanity intact through the molten crucible of pain. No matter how clever, how courteous Bellathonis thought himself, he would receive this agony a thousand times over when Yllithian finally took his revenge.

AEZ'ASHYA SPRINTED ALONG the narrow silver path with Sybris' braid still fluttering, forgotten, in one of her fists. The path bucked and jinked treacherously beneath her flying feet as tremors ran through the fortress walls. Shrill, unearthly cries could be heard coming from above, and an awful tearing sound that seemed to stretch endlessly like the turning of a great wheel. She did not look up.

The poisonous light of the *Ilmaea* was brightening unbearably, turning the silver path to a molten strip of white light. Aez'ashya narrowed her eyes and powered forward, bounding metres at a time as she left the zone of heightened gravity behind. She was still not moving fast enough to reach safety before the first real impact hit. The very air flared into luminosity with a thunderclap suddenness that heralded a shockwave of devastating intensity.

Aez'ashya was pitched screaming into the abyss as the path shattered beneath her, falling amid a storm of bright shards.

In sheer desperation she kept moving, running, leaping, swarming through the air from one tumbling shard to the next. It was a show of preternatural agility that would have put her trainers to shame but it was still not enough. The termination of her fall into the monofilament nets was only seconds away.

Something shot upward past Aez'ashya, a winged, flying figure followed by another and another. A pack of scourges were beating upwards on their powerful wings, flying desperately to escape the debris tumbling down from above. Aez'ashya hurled herself outward without hesitation, kicking off from the falling ruin of the path to arc down onto the last scourge in the pack with arms outstretched and the hook-like blades of her hydra gauntlets fully extended.

The scourge caught a glimpse of her form plummeting towards him at the last moment and tried to twist aside to no avail. Aez'ashya caught the scourge in her bladed embrace and pulled him to her like a long-lost lover. Wings beat furiously, buffeting Aez'ashya as the scourge fluttered helplessly in her grip. The scourge was dying, streamers of arterial blood flying from its body as it struggled, but its instinctive efforts to stay aloft were enough to slow Aez'ashya's fall. She rode the winged warrior unmercifully, using her weight to pull the falling, fluttering pair of them towards the fortress's inner wall. Instinct kept the scourge's wings beating right up to the moment that Aez'ashya released him to crash into the wall as she leapt free.

She landed on a sloping expanse of fluted metal and dug her hydra gauntlets into its surface as the scourge flopped and rolled past before disappearing from sight over the edge. Shortly afterwards several of the crystalline blades on the hydra gauntlets snapped clean away and sent her slithering several metres down the slope after him. Aez'ashya punched down desperately and managed to bring the movement to a scraping, screeching halt, but her hold still felt horribly precarious. She paused for a moment to gather her senses. Her heart was still pounding and limbs shaking from the adrenaline coursing through her system. There was no sense of fear, she was pleased to find, only tremulous excitement.

She glanced about her, trying to make sense of where she had landed. Above her the sky was a circle of white fire pressing down above the glowering walls of the fortress. Falling debris roared as it plunged past her en route to the bottom. Rumbles and shocks ran through the metal beneath her hands and feet. The air seemed full of tumbling detritus and the tiny, flying figures of scourges, hellions, reavers and others trying to escape the mayhem. A score of metres up the sloping surface she was on became a vertical wall with a row of narrow windows looking out. Aez'ashya tried to crawl towards them but only succeeded in almost losing her grip and fractionally sliding backwards. With their frangible crystal blades the hydra gauntlets were ill-suited to this kind of work, and Aez'ashya fervently wished she had her ordinary knives to use instead.

She noticed with amusement that Sybris's braid was still fluttering around her fist, caught on the crystal hooks there. A thought struck her as she looked at the braid and she cautiously disengaged one gauntlet from the slope in order to grasp the dangling tip. The blade was still attached, a hand-long, serrated fang of monomolecular-edged steel. Aez'ashya grinned and plunged the blade into the metal beneath her, the molecule-fine tip shearing through it just as readily as if it were soft flesh. With a firm handhold to work with she began to work her way slowly upwards to safety.

BEZIETH COULD TELL immediately that she was close to death. She could feel the warmth and life readily draining out of her through the self-inflicted gash in her thigh and leaving a terrible, paralyzing weakness in their wake. Somewhere in the distance she could sense malignant forces gathering. They seemed to be watching her slow demise with hungry eyes as they waited impatiently for her soul to slip from her body. The djin-blade still lay nearby on the cracked stones, vibrating gently. No one seemed willing to pick it up after what they had seen it do to Bezieth.

Archon Naxipael hovered anxiously at the edge of her dimming vision, unwilling to stoop to helping her himself but also unwilling to entirely abandon one of his doubtless few surviving allies. The snake-archon's narrow eyes suddenly locked onto a member of the small band of survivors surrounding them.

'You there!' Naxipael snapped. 'Yes you wearing the wrack mask. I hope for your own sake that you're the real thing. Tend to her wound immediately, I want her able to fight! The rest of you – we'll be moving out in five minutes. Search the fallen for anything useful.'

Part of Bezieth's mind was nodding with approval even while another was planning how to survive what came next. Naxipael was taking charge, giving the survivors something to do so that they wouldn't start to think about what was happening, but Bezieth understood that there was a new kabal forming here and now, with Archon Naxipael at its head. Naxipael was going to look for other survivors to assimilate them into his ever-strengthening group. They would likely be glad to join him, for the most part, to enhance their continuing chances of survival. Anyone intractable enough to refuse would become another victim of the catastrophe. Depending on how the fates fell Archon Naxipael might come out of the whole disaster immensely stronger than he was before. He might even push his way up into High Commorragh in the chaos.

A darkly robed figure was obediently shuffling across to squat down next to Bezieth. She fixed her gaze on the wrack's grilled mask as he bent to start examining her injury. Naxipael saw her as an asset still but that wouldn't last. Soon he would start wondering why he should risk keeping her around…

'What's your name?' she demanded imperiously. She didn't feel imperious. She felt as if she were trapped at the bottom of a well with the wrack's mask hovering above her, blotting out the sky.

'Xagor. This one's name is Xagor, Archon Bezieth,' the wrack said meekly. Well, that was something at least. An uncomfortable heat was rising in her wounded thigh as the wrack worked, but she doggedly showed no sign of discomfort. She found that it helped to have something to focus on, a tiny measure of control to exert.

'Who is your master?' she asked more reasonably.

'Master… Bellathonis,' the wrack replied a little hesitantly, an odd detail that Bezieth filed away for later.

'Who else do you know here?'

'No one, Xagor only came to witness the procession,' the wrack murmured, intent on whatever he was doing to the wound now. Bezieth looked at him shrewdly.

'Why would you do that? Bellathonis hasn't served anyone in the lower courts for years, he thinks he's too good for us no-oww!' Fire unexpectedly lanced through the wound and set Bezieth's teeth on edge. For an instant it felt as if it was being opened up anew.

'All finished,' the wrack said hurriedly as he stood up and backed away.

Bezieth cursed him ferociously and levered herself up onto her feet. The wound subsided to a dull throb but her whole leg felt stiff and wooden. She tested her weight on it a few times with an angry grimace before bending down to scoop up the untouched djin-blade. The febrile energy Axhyrian's spirit had demonstrated before seemed gone for now, the sword nothing more than inanimate object. Naxipael glanced over and nodded approvingly. Yes, she thought as she turned the blade warily in her hand, still an asset.

She looked around the canal bank, now a wasteland of fallen masonry and shattered slabs tilting drunkenly at all angles. A handful of heavily armed survivors were in view picking over the remnants of the procession. Naxipael was in the process of haranguing them to find a functional palanquin, but everything of that ilk looked to be mangled or half-melted into useless scrap. In the distance the multi-hued star still shimmered over the canal like the eye of a baleful god. It was time to get to work.

'Forget all that, we have to get moving,' she said as she walked over to him, striving not to limp. She jabbed an accusing finger towards the broken gate. 'We can't stay near that thing a moment longer.' Naxipael's face showed a momentary irritation that was quickly smoothed over.

'Are you sure you're fit enough to walk?' Naxipael asked solicitously. 'I had thought to find some means to carry you.' An unlikely story, Bezieth thought, more likely Naxipael was seeking a quick means to enhance his prestige.

'I can walk, and I can fight too. We must go. Now.' Bezieth realised it wasn't just bravado that was making her push Naxipael to leave. She really did have a sense of mounting dread, she could see it in the nervous faces around her too. Something about the light itself was disquieting. It was as if it cast an invisible, profane heat against both mind and soul. It was a sensation that made Bezieth want to run away and hide somewhere deep and dark.

Naxipael had the common sense to detect the prevailing mood and soon led his small group into the ruins, clambering across splintered stonework and twisted metal. The fascia of the palaces was a hollow-eyed mockery of its former grandeur, yet most of the damage was superficial. Decorative colonnades and balconies had fallen by the thousand but the underlying structures were built of more solid stuff. Darkened corridors and tilted steps led inside. A scattered detritus of cups, vials and crystals crunched beneath their feet as they advanced. Periodic bursts of screams and howls echoed from deeper within, accompanied by weird, plaintive strains of music that drifted in and out of perception. The survivors clutched their weapons and advanced warily.

Towards the back of the loose column Kharbyr walked cautiously alongside Xagor. The haemonculus's pentagonal talisman of metal was hidden away inside his bodysuit, as cold and lifeless as it had been when he first took it from the wrack. When the Dysjunction struck Kharbyr had hoped the thing was meant to protect him somehow and had clutched at it desperately but to no visible benefit. Instead he'd had to fight for his life alongside Xagor, and only their shared experiences in Shaa-Dom enabled them to survive the tidal wave of extra-dimensional filth that came washing through the warding. Then Bezieth and Naxipael had showed up cutting their way through the mess. Sticking with them had been an easy, and wise, decision at the time. Less so once Bezieth turned on him and tried to cut him down on the spot with that insane sword of hers.

'We should strike out on our own, go and look for Bellathonis,' Kharbyr whispered to Xagor.

'The master will find us when we are needed,' Xagor replied with an irritating degree of confidence.

'And in the meantime we tramp around in the guts of lower Metzuh helping Naxipael and Bezieth build an army?'

'Xagor wishes to know the alternatives.'

'Strike out on our own and hide out somewhere.'

'There is safety in numbers.'

Insane laughter came rattling down the broken corridor from somewhere ahead of them. Firelight, or something very like it, was painting dancing shadows on the ceiling and walls. As they got closer to its source it became clear that the corridor opened out into a larger hall. Figures could sometimes be briefly glimpsed cavorting inside.

'I'm not so sure about that,' Kharbyr said grimly.

# CHAPTER 5

## A TALE OF ORIGINS

ON THE HUNDREDTH day after the calamity on the maiden world of Lileathanir the survivors of the bright lakes clan finally came within sight of the Lil'esh Eldan Ay'Morai – the 'Holy Mountain of dawn's light first gleaming'. The survivor's journey across the riven face of the maiden world of Lileathanir had been a hard one. What little food had been saved from the initial raid had been lost in the calamity that followed it and so privation had tormented them every step of the way. The clan's ablest leaders and warriors had fallen in the great sky battle against the dark kin. Those brave warriors had given their lives to drive away the slaver-takers even as catastrophe struck the land, and by so doing they had left their people leaderless in the dreadful aftermath. So it was that the pilgrimage north to seek the World Shrine began as a straggling crowd of mostly the young and the old, the infirm and the cowardly.

They had looked to Sardon Tir Laniel for guidance at the beginning. She was tall and unbowed by her many winters, her hair still the colour of ripe corn. Her service as a protector and a worldsinger a half-century before had been much admired among her clan so it was natural that they sought her leadership at a moment of crisis. The only thing Sardon could think to do was to journey to the World Shrine and seek help. At first she had intended to travel alone but the other survivors would hear none of it; the ghost paths were too dangerous to enter, they said, and the land was in turmoil. The great pterosaurs refused to fly and the pack beasts quickly sickened in the ash-choked air. A journey to the World Shrine on foot would take months. The frightened survivors raised all these objections and more, but no one argued against making the journey only about who should go. In the end the whole clan, all that was left of it, simply picked up their meagre possessions and joined her in walking north.

The great forests of Lileathanir had burned like torches in its oxygen-rich air. Far off on the horizon to the south and east the sullen glow of distant fires continued to light the sky. The fires remained visible throughout the survivors' march, but the regions they passed through were already dead and cooling. In many places the cloud-scraping trunks of mighty trees still stood upright like cities of blackened towers, at other spots violent earth shocks had uprooted hundreds of the forest giants and created impenetrable mazes of charred timber. Thick drifts of grey ash lay across everything that muffled all sound and kicked up choking clouds with each step. Periodically they had to divert around shuddering clefts in the earth or sluggish flows of lava from the host of young volcanoes rising across the land.

On the eleventh day they had found other survivors. They were members of the fen clans that had hidden themselves in underground holdfasts until the trembling of the earth drove them to the surface. They found the world transformed. As the days drew into weeks they found other survivors or were found by them. Singly or in small groups they drifted in day after day, shocked, confused, and increasingly malnourished. The lake clan took all of them in and cared for them as best they could, although they had precious little to share. Other than the steady trickle of fellow survivors, they saw virtually nothing else alive in all of the regions they travelled through – every creature still able to move had long since fled or given up its bones to join the blackened pyres scattered across the forest floor.

At the time of the calamity the skies had closed over with thick, ominous clouds and the temperature had begun to drop. The sun became visible only at dawn and dusk, red and bulbous as it peered out briefly beneath a solid roof of heavy cloud. The trapped heat from the forest fires and volcanoes had compensated at first with an unhealthy, bonfire-scented breeze but this subsided as the fires marched away south and east. Three weeks after the march had begun the morning dew settled as frost and brought a blessed respite from the omnipresent ash. From the fortieth day onward they began to encounter snow. These were real crystals of frozen water that were totally unlike the flakes of settling ash that had become such a part of their daily misery. A few nights later the first deaths began to occur as the bone-wracking chill and malnutrition took their toll. Their path north became marked by lonely little cairns of stones thrown up over the bodies of those that succumbed each night.

Some had left the march, dropped out to find their own ways and hack out a new existence from the world that had so suddenly turned against them. More joined to take their place, and still more, until the tiny rivulet of lake clan members became an intermingled stream with other clans and then a flood of the surviving peoples of Lileathanir. Most of the travellers seemed to be motivated by the urge to cling together and to reassure themselves that they were still part of a greater whole. All craved some understanding of what had occurred to their world. Some sought a means to avenge themselves upon the guilty. At some point it had taken on the aspect of a pilgrimage with the normally fractious clans of Lileathanir bonding together in the face of their common adversity. That was when Sardon had started to become afraid.

Sardon certainly believed the journey had taken on a higher meaning for the people, yet as the weeks passed she had become increasingly frightened by

PATH OF THE INCUBUS

what she might find at the holy mountain. She could still feel her connection to the world spirit lurking the edge of her consciousness. The presence that had been with her from childhood was still there but not as she remembered it. The collective essence of the world spirit had encompassed many aspects: playful, nurturing, protective, wise, but its beneficent presence was a constant source of joy and reassurance to all. Now that had changed. A twisting serpent of atavistic rage boiled at the back of her mind: furious, negative, destructive, terrifying. All of them could feel the change yet none of them dared speak of it. They all looked to Sardon with pleading eyes as if somehow, miraculously, she could mend the unmendable and set the world to rights.

The burden on her soul had grown heavier with each step that she took towards her destination. When the holy mountain came in to sight many of the pilgrims danced and sang at the prospect of an end to their journey. Sardon did not rejoice with them, it felt to her too much like her journey was only just beginning.

Lil'esh Eldan Ay'Morai was a truly titanic peak. Its flattened top was normally wreathed in a permanent cloud layer that laced its flanks with rainbow-girt waterfalls and sparkling rivulets. Now it seemed as black and frozen as the dead forests below, with leprous-looking snow banks dotted across its jagged rock face like growths of mould. A series of black-mouthed openings had been torn into the mountain by the violence of the earth.

Vapours issued from them as if a whole nest of dragons was laired below. The World Shrine had existed within the roots of the mountain safely protected by hundreds of metres of solid rock. It had been only reachable through the most secret of the ghost paths with no physical connection to the outside world. Sardon had dared to hope that the World Shrine would still be unreachable but looking at the broken mountain she knew with a grim sense of inevitability that there would be a path down to the World Shrine through one of those fissures.

Sardon eventually took her leave of her companions and set out on the last leg alone. They tearfully bid her farewell but none of them tried to follow her. They understood that one must go alone to confront the dragon spirit, they would wait at the foot of the holy mountain until she returned or the cold and hunger took them. Sardon clambered inexpertly away under a crushing sense of responsibility towards her people. She slowly edged her way towards the lowest opening she had seen from below, crawling across rocks, pulling herself up ridges and jumping across crevasses. The mountain trembled beneath her feet and hands constantly, often dislodging gravel and stones that rattled and chattered dangerously past her head.

Many times the opening was lost from her view but the plumes of vapour rising from it guided her inexorably towards it. As she got closer she began to appreciate just how big the opening really was. Seen from miles away it had looked like a thin black crack, up close it yawned across a vast swathe of the mountainside, higher than a Carnosaur and wide enough for a whole clan to march inside shoulder to shoulder. Sardon slithered across the last few fallen stones to reach the ledge jutting out before the entrance and peered uncertainly inside.

Hot, sulphurous breath washed across her face, a stiff, constant breeze coming up from below. Distant grinding, hissing sounds welled up from the depths in a fearsome medley. Sardon nerved herself as best she could and began her descent.

SIMPLY, AND WITH what he felt to be creditable brevity Motley explained the cause of the Dysjunction wracking Commorragh and Morr's own role in creating it. The incubus had received the news in silence and then continued on his way as if Motley did not exist. In truth it was a better reaction than Motley had hoped for.

Morr's silence had stretched out for what seemed to be aeons while they marched through the webway. Motley chattered, observed and even sang at times to fill the emptiness but he could draw nothing from the towering incubus he followed. Motley took Morr's lack of overt hostility as a positive sign and simply smiled through it. The incubus had, after all, asked him for a direct answer and it wasn't Motley's concern if he didn't like what he heard. The webway flowed smoothly past as they took smaller and smaller filaments, the incubus seemingly sure of his path at every turn. The curving etheric walls became increasingly tenuous as they advanced into regions where the cohesion of the webway had become broken and discontinuous. There Morr stopped, turned to Motley and finally spoke again.

'I have considered your premise,' Morr said slowly, 'and I find it... feasible... that you may be correct.'

Motley smiled with genuine warmth. 'Then things may still be rectified! Come with me and, while I can't guarantee all will be forgiven and forgotten, you can most certainly save Commorragh.'

'I cannot,' said Morr.

Motley's smile vanished as quickly as the sun going behind a cloud. He sighed heavily. 'You still feel you must go to the shrine of Arhra and atone for killing your archon. This, of course, before you'll even consider going about the clearly less pressing business of saving your city from imminent destruction. Predictable enough, I suppose.'

Morr nodded solemnly.

'And you still feel the need to present yourself for judgment before these hierarchs of yours at the shrine even though you know that they will probably kill you for what you've done.'

Morr nodded solemnly again. Motley rolled his eyes. 'I don't suppose,' he said somewhat desperately, 'that you've con–'

'I ask that you accompany me to the shrine,' Morr said.

Motley shut his mouth in surprise, but only for a moment. 'Well, I'm flattered, Morr, not as a sacrifice, I hope, or perhaps a scapegoat?'

Motley's impudence had no visible effect on the armoured incubus. 'I see now that should the hierarchs see fit not to end my existence that I may need you,' Morr continued imperturbably, 'and it would be expeditious for you to be close at hand.'

'And what if the hierarchs should see fit to try to end *my* existence on, oh I don't know, some obscure point of principle?'

'As to the chance of that I cannot say.'

'Hmmph, well regardless of that possibility I will be delighted to accompany you to the dance, Morr,' Motley said brightly. 'It makes me very happy that we're becoming such good friends, companions, and, if I may say it, scions of a better future battling in the face of adversity.'

'Do not mistake an alliance of convenience for friendship, little clown.'

'All right, all right don't worry I won't,' Motley replied a little peevishly. 'I sought only to elevate our unique association as it rightly deserves, knowing that I could trust you to once more lower our collective expectations almost immediately.'

'Very well. Then follow and do not stray from the path I tread.'

'You don't have to tell me that, of all people,' Motley sniffed, and followed closely on the incubus's heels.

Before them the webway opened out into a hazy tangle of criss-crossing filaments, some wavering in an ethereal wind, some ragged and showing glimpses of multi-hued colour spilling through. The overall impression was that of a vast cave filled with phosphorescent webs swaying in the spectral breeze. Morr led the way toward a rippling fringe of colour that was alternately shot through with ochre, amber and jade. A broken portal, now a multi-dimensional weak spot that still connected to many other paths and realities, but in an uncertain and capricious fashion.

'Does this lead to the shrine?' Motley asked as his curiosity got the better of him. 'We need to be sure of where we're going before we pass through or we might end up, you know, absolutely anywhere.' At closer range fine threads of green and blue could also be seen coiling hypnotically in the veil, evidence that the Dysjunction in distant Commorragh had subtle effects reaching even here.

'No, I must retrace my steps to return to the shrine. We must go back to the beginning.'

Morr swiftly waded into the veil of colours like some titan striding into an ocean. Motley huddled in closely behind the incubus as the swirling energies rose to engulf them. Cross currents tugged fiercely at them as disassociating realities stripped them down into fundamental blocks and whirled the pieces back together again. Floods of alien concepts and strange stimuli washed across them both only to flash away in the instant that they were perceived. Through the horrid rending, tearing, soul-ripping experience Morr's continuity of purpose drove forward with Motley cowering in his slipstream. Morr's self-belief was overwhelming, it bent and twisted the vagrant realities to his will. There was a moment of weightlessness as the portal grudgingly surrendered and ejected them… elsewhere.

They stood upon an expanse of white sand that had the crystalline brilliance of fresh snow. It was night time but the darkness was lit by continuous flashes from horizon to horizon. A staccato drumbeat of explosions melded together into a continuous thunder that rolled back and forth in the sky. In the middle-distance ominous, hulking shapes the size of mountains leapt and shifted in the uncertain light.

'What is this place?' Motley asked in quiet awe.

'Somewhere that no longer exists, a land of ghosts,' Morr rumbled enigmatically as he set off across the white sands. Winds had sculpted the sand into a series of perfect ripples across their path. Morr tramped up the ridges and slithered down their opposite sides without breaking stride. The flickering hell-light of explosions and the rolling thunder never lessened.

'Can I at least ask who is, or rather was, fighting then?' Motley asked after they reached the third such ridge (he ran easily up and down each of them, leaving no imprint). 'Call me an incurable historian if you will.'

'A people that should have known better are fighting against themselves,' Morr intoned. 'Their petty dispute has been entirely resolved now.'

Motley caught no small sense of satisfaction in Morr's words. He surveyed the flicker-lit horizon. 'Why is it that I imagine that there has not been a happy outcome for them?' he wondered aloud.

Morr said nothing in reply. He was busy scanning the leaping shadows in the middle distance. The incubus jabbed out an armoured finger, pointing into the darkness. 'There I am,' Morr said. 'Follow, but do not approach too closely and do not speak.'

Motley obediently followed the dark silhouette of the incubus into the shadows. Morr's helm and shoulders were hard edged with the reflected glare from the distant barrage but otherwise he was only a blacker shape amid blackness. As they left the wave-like ridges of sand behind them the mass of hunched, mountainous shapes ahead resolved themselves as titanic growths of brain-like coral. A row of calcified ribs protruded from the sand nearby, the self-made tombstones of some megalithic beast. Two shapes were moving in the shadows between the ribs. Morr slowed his pace, dawdling to ensure that both got well ahead before moving after them.

To describe Motley's sight as cat-like or hawk-like would do disservice to all of the noble beasts involved. Suffice to say that his vision was of a fine acuity and ranged into wavelengths not normally enjoyed by either mammalian or avian life. He watched the shapes ahead of them carefully, resolving them into: first and closest to the path Morr so carefully tread upon – a young, lanky-looking eldar splashed with blood. The youth was haggard and near-naked, clad only in rags and holding one arm awkwardly as if it were injured. The youth's other hand clutched a curved cudgel with its ball-like head caked with gore.

The youth crept after a second figure that could barely be glimpsed with clarity; a night-black armoured warrior whose many-bladed helm would have over-reached even Morr's lofty height. The figure seemed out of place and unearthly even in this strange setting. Motley gained the impression of burning eyes as it gazed back once before continuing to move unhurriedly in the direction of the coral bluffs. The youth seemed drawn after the armoured figure, fearful yet determined as he crept along in its footsteps.

Motley glanced from the gangling youth over to Morr and back again, suddenly understanding. 'There I am,' Morr had said. His earlier self still lived here where the infinite possibilities of Chaos spilled into the broken coherence of the webway. The frozen instants of Morr's first steps towards his initiation as an incubus still existed as a shard of memory, a moment to be replayed so that the same path could be found again – a path to the hidden shrine of Arhra.

Motley wondered if what they saw leading the younger Morr was an avatar of Arhra made manifest. Legends about the father of the incubi were manifold. Most of them were false or contradictory but all agreed on one key point – that Arhra himself was destroyed long ago, and that the foundation of the incubi was his one abiding legacy. More likely they simply saw what the boy saw, or believed that he saw, reflected in this recreation of that explosion-wracked night.

The coral began to rise in frowning cliffs above

them as they drew closer. At the foot of the folded, curving masses of pale stone lay the vast wreck of a vessel. Blunt ribs of rusting iron poked through a patchy hide of rotting armour plates along its broken-backed kilometre of length. Great turret housings on the upper surface of the wreck pointed the frozen fingers of their cannon seemingly at random into the sky. As the dark figure and the youth vanished around the cloven bows of the great wreck Morr increased his pace again to close the distance.

Motley became aware of more and more detritus lying in the sands at the bottom the coral canyons; metal components mangled and rusted beyond recognition, the half-buried wreckage of many smaller machines ranging in size and design from skeletal-winged flyers to smaller cousins of the great vessel they were approaching. And bones. Bones and teeth were everywhere, sometimes in such density that they covered the sand completely. Thousands, perhaps millions, of bones stretching as far as the eye could see.

They rounded the bows of the great wreck and ahead Motley could see the sands bulked up higher, forming a saddle between two cliffs. Beyond the saddle the inferno of bombardment could clearly be seen lighting the sky. Long, grotesque shadows leapt out behind the armoured figure and the youth as they climbed upward seemingly heedless of the danger. Morr strode forwards, attention locked on the distant figures as they vanished from view over the top of the saddle.

The steep slope shook with the fury of the barrage on the other side. Morr forged upward through continual small avalanches of loosened sand. A rank smell of burning hung in the air from the bombardment. It was punctuated by blasts of hot wind being blown into their faces by the crisscrossing pressure waves of the closest impacts.

Morr and Motley reached the ridge-like saddle together and stopped. Before them spread a vision of hell. A pockmarked plain alive with gouts of flame and whirring traceries of light. No living thing could be seen below but the leaping fires gave an illusion of life given triumphant, elemental form as they cavorted over the tortured sands. A single flame of jade held bright and steady on the horizon, a spear point of green light that had been dug into the earth.

Morr's helm turned back and forth frantically looking for his earlier self, but there was no visible sign of the would-be neophyte or his mysterious patron.

'No! This is wrong!' Morr roared in disbelief above the cacophony of detonations.

'What? Where should we be?' shouted Motley.

Morr pointed to the unwavering green flame that hung on the horizon. 'The gate,' the incubus said grimly.

# CHAPTER 6
## NEW ARRIVALS

DESPITE ITS SUBTERRANEAN location the World Shrine of Lileathanir had been a pleasing and naturalistic place. Sardon remembered that the living rock had formed sweeping buttresses and towering pillars that gave the caves an open-air feeling, as if the viewer had wandered into a narrow valley beneath a starlit sky. Glittering waterfalls had rushed from cracks in the stone to fill plunge pools so crystal clear that they could seem like empty clefts at first glance. The stars in the upper reaches of the shrine had been made with a forgotten craft and shed light wholesome enough for living things to grow there far from the sun and sky. The whole shrine was alive with greenery from simple ferns and mosses to miniature Eloh trees and gloryvine. Mineral veins and crystal outcrops that twinkled among the pools and grottoes had lent the place an aura of fey otherworldliness as though shy magical beings gambolled just out of sight.

The altered shrine had few, if any, of its original characteristics intact. Sardon had to squeeze along a narrowing crack to even reach it, not the broad and welcoming path she had imagined. Instead the jagged edges of the volcanic rock lacerated her hands and knees unmercifully. Eventually she was forced to wriggle on her belly like a snake before finally dropping out of a metre-wide fissure and into the shrine in an undignified heap. Hissing and bubbling surrounded her, the sounds magnified by the enclosed space. Not two metres from her outstretched hand a pool of boiling mud spat dollops of caustic slime, and there were palls of smoke and vapour wreathing a dozen similar spots. The floor had been tilted and torn open. Great fissures lit by inner fires gusted hot air into the chamber like a hellish furnace. In places the roof had collapsed into a jumbled mass of slabs where a handful of the fallen stars still glowed from their recesses like evil eyes.

The World Shrine represented the symbolic and metaphysical confluence of a planet-wide system of psychic conduits. The disruption of its material fabric was symptomatic of a far greater underlying harm. The psychic aura of the place was a sickening miasma of impotent rage, a swirling hate so strong that it had turned inward and poisoned its source. Sardon wept to feel it so closely, the world spirit a rageing monster pounding at the walls of her sanity and threatening to suck her into its whirlpool of fury and loss.

Every living thing on Lileathanir was connected to the world spirit, and at their passing they joined its essence and strengthened it. It felt as if all of the mass deaths of the cataclysm had fed only the most dangerous aspect of the world spirit: the dragon. The dragon was the destroyer, the force that swept the slate clean to allow new growth. He was the forest fire and the great storm, his fury raised mountains and drank seas. Sardon honoured the dragon, and admitted the necessity of such forces having to exist but she had no love for it. Now the dragon was unleashed and consuming all of Lile-athanir in its fury.

After what seemed a long time weeping in the semi-darkness Sardon finally levered herself to her feet, coughing in the acrid fumes. She wavered about what to do next. Seeing the shrine had confirmed her worst fears, but did nothing to resolve them. She could return to the refugees outside and see their hopeful faces drop as she told them that there was nothing to be done. She could remain sitting inside and weep until she choked on the fumes or she could try to investigate further, however futile that might be. Demonstrating the inherent resilience of her people she opted to investigate.

Here and there polished sections of stone were carved with complex runes that pulsed with their own phosphorescent witch-light. None of these had been touched by the convulsions, their connections to other mystic sites on the planet remained intact. Sardon could not dare herself to reach out and use the runes to connect with the world spirit fully. She tried to sing a soothing chant as she had been taught in her days as a worldsinger, her song seemed nothing but a hollow and lifeless mockery screeched by a crone. Afterwards she felt a distinct feeling of resentment gathering about her and the walls shook disapprovingly. She determined to try and sing no more.

As she stumbled across sloping stones she came across a skeleton wedged between two slabs. The body belonged to one of the shrine wardens judging by his aggressive-looking male attire. The warden had been crushed, but that had happened later. Falling stones or boiling mud had not killed him. Straight-edged knife cuts covered his bones from virtually head to toe, none of them deep enough to be immediately fatal. Such flagrant cruelty could only mean one thing – the dark kin must have penetrated the World Shrine itself. Sardon's mind whirled at the concept and the rush of sick relief that she felt come close on its heels. *Someone else did this, not us.*

It had always been too great a coincidence to imagine that the slave-takers raid was unrelated to the cataclysm that followed it. But in her worst imaginings Sardon had never truly entertained the idea that the children of Khaine might have actually penetrated the World Shrine. Everything made sense now. The rage of the dragon had not been unleashed by the clans as she'd feared, but by the vile depredations of the dark kin in the very heart of the world. Sardon could conceive of no reason why they should come and violate the World

Shrine, but she could conceive of no reason why they did any of the nightmarish things that were attributed to them. Evil, pure and simple, seemed their only motivation.

Sardon spat in an attempt to get the noxious taint of death out of her mouth but it lingered stubbornly as she tried to think. The lower caves of the shrine had held gates to the spirit paths… and a secret that had been forgotten by many. She began to work her way downward as far as she could get, trying to mesh together in her mind's eye the layout of the shrine as it was now in comparison to how it had been fifty years before. She eventually found a sloping ramp that was only half-choked with debris and followed it. At the bottom it opened into a domed chamber that was riven with cracks and slicked with drying mud but otherwise miraculously intact.

Seven arches were carved into the chamber's stonework, doorways that opened onto only blank walls behind. The runes carved around their edges seemed dim and lifeless but Sardon could sense their latent energies flowing just out of reach. She moved to the central arch of the seven, one that was just a shade larger than the others. The twining runes on the central arch were more intricate too, older looking than their siblings to either side. Sardon struggled to recall her teacher's lesson from five decades before.

*'In time of most dire need the attention of the far-wanderers can be summoned to this place. They are haughty and judgemental but their powers are great and*

*it is said they will help if they perceive the need.'*

The words were there, but the instructions were not. A sequence of runes touched in the proper order would send out the call, but Sardon could not remember what the sequence was. She turned away and attempted to centre herself, closing her eyes and clearing her thoughts with a moment of meditation. Her eyes flew open after only a second, the relentless beat of the dragon's fury too strong in her mind to concentrate. Her memory kept returning the teacher's warning, an unnecessarily dour admonishment as she had thought it at the time.

*'Lileathanir has not called out to the far-wanderers for succour in a hundred centuries – give thanks that it is so and never think to call upon them lightly. The wings of war beat ever at their backs.'*

Sardon was suddenly startled to realise she could see her own shadow. It was stretching across the muddy floor and back to the ramp as light grew stronger behind her. She hesitantly turned to look at the source, one hand raised to shield her eyes against the glare. The central arch was filled with silver light, its framework of runes blazing with internal fire. A figure was silhouetted against the arch, unnaturally tall and misshapen-looking. Antlers spread from the figure's bulbous head and it gripped a blade almost as tall as itself that crackled with etheric energies. Sardon's knees wobbled treacherously beneath her as she stifled a cry. The newcomer swept its blazing, amber-eyed gaze over her and advanced with one empty hand raised. More figures were emerging from the arch behind it, skinny, straight-limbed and even taller than the first.

*'Peace,'* the word sounded in Sardon's mind like the tolling of a bell. She felt her fears begin ebbing away at the mental touch, but she angrily shook it off. The dragon was too strong here to be assuaged by such a simple trick. It boiled with outrage in a corner her mind, converting her momentary fear into fury.

'Speak your words openly, invader,' Sardon bristled, 'and declare yourself before I call for the Shrine Wardens to eject you.'

The figure halted and lowered its arm before sketching a bow that seemed devoid of mockery.

'Forgive me,' the figure said in a rich, mellifluous voice of pleasing timbre. 'I sought only to reassure, not to offend.'

The light dimmed as the arch reverted back to an unremarkable stone carving. Six figures now stood in the domed chamber with Sardon. She could see that the first to emerge and the one that had spoken was swathed in tawny robes from neck to ankles, its head enclosed by an amber-lensed helm affixed with thick bone-coloured antlers. The robes were covered with austere looking battle-runes of fortune and protection with an ornate chest guard of woven wraithbone. The long, straight sword in the figure's hands bore still more runes, these of destruction and of the witch path. This could only be one of the fabled warlocks of the far-wanderers, a battle-seer of the craftworld clans and something that had been unseen on Lileathanir in hundreds of years.

The other five newcomers remained silent, their attitudes ones of alert watchfulness. Each of them wore sapphire-tinted armour of subtly varying design, but all were well-proportioned and heroic-looking like animate statues. Their full-faced helms were adorned with tall crests marked in alternating bands of blue, white and yellow. They carried long-necked ancient weapons Sardon knew only as *Tueleani* – star throwers that were reputedly able to slice through a pack of charging Carnosaurs or the bole of a forest giant with equal alacrity.

The warlock reached into a satchel at his side and drew forth a miniature carving of a rune. He released it in the air between them and it hung there, slowly spinning. The rune of weaving.

'My name is Caraeis. I tread the Path of the Seer. I have come at your call,' the warlock intoned. 'This path was so ordained.'

Caraeis reached into his satchel again and drew forth another rune. He placed it in conjunction with the rune of weaving and it span around it in an erratic orbit. This was the jagged, scimitar-like rune of the dark kin. The world spirit came next, and then the profane shape of the soul-drinker. Finally there was Dysjunction. The twisting, spinning runes formed a pattern in the air that was painful to Sardon's eyes. She held up her hands and looked away.

'Enough tricks,' she said. 'You know of our pain, you know of our world spirit's pain. I believe you. Can you help us?'

'The pain of Lileathanir is felt far and wide,' the

warlock said. 'It must be healed before it can cause yet greater harm.'

'How can all this be healed?' Sardon murmured in disbelief. 'The very core of the world is violated, the spirits hunger only for bloodshed and revenge.'

'Precisely,' said Caraeis. He released another rune above the whirling confluence and it steadied the dissonant patterns immediately. The rune of vengeance. 'I have tested a thousand other variants,' the warlock said, 'each with the same result. This is the only path forward.'

'Vengeance?' Sardon cried bitterly. 'How can we avenge ourselves against what we cannot reach? With so few of us left, how can we even think of fighting back?'

'I ask only that you permit us to be your instrument in this. Allow my companions and I to bring the perpetrator of this heinous crime to justice.'

Sardon blinked in disbelief. 'You-you could do that?' she stammered, daring to hope for an instant. 'Find them and punish them?'

The warlock's antlered helm nodded solemnly. 'It is within my power to trace the destinies of the dark kin that came here and violated the shrine. The pattern is shifting and diffuse, but there are junctures yet to come where decisive action can be taken. Do you give your permission for this to occur?'

Punishment, vengeance. Ugly words to Sardon, but what she had seen in the World Shrine had shaken the very core of her beliefs. If the warlock was right and they were the things to begin the healing process who was she to deny the dragon its due? A part of her wished she could consult her people and hear their wishes, another part knew precisely what they would be. The hard life of the Exodite clans gave them an uncompromising view of justice – an eye of an eye, blood for blood. It would be hard to restrain their basest instincts after all they had suffered.

Sardon wasn't even sure she could find her way back down the mountain in her weakened state. Would the warlock be prepared to sit by while the trail grew colder and she wrangled with the clans? Probably not. He stood patiently watching her, the pattern of runes rotating between them silently as he waited for her response.

'Very well. Bring them to me, I ask this of you, Caraeis.'

'You wish to render judgement yourself?'

'I want to look them in the eye before I give them to the dragon,' Sardon said with finality.

THE FLICKERING LIGHT and close horizon made it hard to judge how far away the gate truly lay across the ravaged plain. Perhaps as little as a few thousand metres, perhaps as much as twice that.

'Will they actively try to hit us or is it in the hands of lady luck?' Motley demanded.

Morr looked across at his slight companion with a sharp movement that denoted surprise. 'I do not know,' he admitted, 'but the weapons are crude and highly inaccurate, they rely on blast and impact.'

'And real? Here and now real, I mean!' Motley yelled.

'Very real.'

'All right, then I'll try to draw their fire while you make for the gate,' Motley shouted over the shell impacts. 'Don't. Leave. Without. Me.' With that final admonishment Motley ran swiftly down the slope and out onto the plain. As the slender grey figure ran its silhouette flew into a storm of brightly coloured shards that whirled and darted capriciously. A new multi-coloured, kaleidoscopic explosion leapt up among its sullen cousins of orange and red, and it danced among them.

The traceries of fire were the first things to react to the upstart presence. They whipped around to chase after the dancing motes of light as they raced away across the plain. Moments later the explosions came crowding in, their roar and tumult overlapping as they sought to crush the newcomer.

Morr struck out towards the gate across sands that were still warm from the pounding of the bombardment. Tiny, twisted fragments of smoking metal lay everywhere – *shrapnel* to give it the properly archaic term. Occasionally there were fragments of what used to be living things too, chunks of meat and bone barely recognisable as having once been part of a greater whole. Blackened pits showed where larger shells had landed in contrast to the almost comically small scorch marks from smaller bombs. Not all of the incoming rounds were chasing after the madly running harlequin. The heaviest of them continued to rain down on the plain seemingly at random, each one shaking the ground with its impact and throwing up a huge plume of dust. Morr bent low and pushed on toward his goal, the drifting clouds of dust soon swallowing him completely.

The ground shivered beneath Motley's flying feet. The air was filled with the whoops, whistles and shrieks of flying metal. He listened intently for the distinctive slobbering noise each shell made as it flew through the air incoming, and the dopplering whine of the shrapnel outgoing from each impact. He twisted back and forth to spoil the aim of his unseen attackers, dancing through the inferno with seemingly reckless abandon. His Domino field dispersed his image and made it impossible to pinpoint him exactly. Unfortunately most of the primitive weaponry being used did not need to pinpoint him exactly – in fact it only needed to get lucky once. The slow-seeming swarms of tracer fire would have been the most dangerous without the field, however, and even with its help he had to skid aside or leap over its questing fingers a dozen times.

Even Motley's preternatural agility had its limits. He was forced into doubling back as the fire became too intense to go on. Unfortunately that placed him in just as much danger of running back beneath a stray salvo behind him. A chain of explosions erupted within a dozen metres and threw Motley off his feet. Shrapnel whirred around him like a swarm of angry bees busily stinging at his chest and upper arms. He tumbled instinctively with the blow, bouncing to his feet and coming up running. Within a few paces he staggered, still dazed from the impact and almost fell.

'No time for a sit-down right now, old boy,' he told himself drunkenly, tittering as he mastered his wobbling legs, got them beneath him and ran on. A cold ache was spreading across his chest, never a good sign. Motley decided that he'd had enough of playing at being a target, the audience seemed unappreciative and surely Morr was approaching the gate by now. He deactivated the Domino field and became an invisible flicker of grey among the flames as he sprinted off on a straight course for the gate.

Morr emerged from drifting curtains of dust onto a beaten circle of dirt surrounding the gate. It loomed over him from a hundred metres away, an angular-looking sheet of jade six stories high that shone with its own inner light. With the barrage shifted away in pursuit of Motley's distraction the area seemed almost peaceful for a moment. Morr's headed snapped up at the sound of rifle fire crackling close by. He wasn't the only one taking advantage of the distraction.

The barrage raged impotently behind Motley, blindly smashing down on where he had been rather than where he was or (better yet) where he would be. However some of the tracer-gunners kept coming uncomfortably close as they sent their bursts of fire after his flitting grey shape. Motley increased his pace, each bounding stride taking him five or more metres at a time. Ahead and to the side he could see a flickering of tiny sparks on the ground. Two groups were firing rifles at each other as they tried to creep closer to the gate. Beyond them he could see the tiny figure of Morr standing beside the gate itself.

Motley grappled with the moral implications of the situation for an instant before reactivating his Domino field. His running form splintered again into an explosion of light, a stained-glass image that flew apart virtually above the riflemen's heads. Bullets zinged past him as they fired wildly at the swirling motes but he sprinted through their positions without a scratch. Whips of tracer-fire pursued him as the unseen gunners re-acquired him. Seconds later the first slobbering sound of an incoming round could be heard.

Up ahead Motley saw Morr turn and quite deliberately enter the gate without him. Motley cursed in a rich and scorching stream as he flung himself after the treacherous incubus. A sheer face of glowing jade reared up before him even as the first multi-throated howl of the barrage was renewed behind him.

# CHAPTER 7

## AN INTERLUDE IN THE DEPTHS

THE HAEMONCULI ARE the final arbiters of life and death in the eternal city, gaunt gatekeepers to the great beyond. With their blessings no wound is fatal and any fatality short of complete destruction can be undone. They are essential to the ageless rulers of Commorragh. Only with the help of the haemonculi can they continue to cheat death and spin out their long, wicked existences. Such power could surely allow the haemonculi to rule Commorragh if they desired it, and if any of its inhabitants would countenance it, but their true passion lies only in the pursuit of their arts. Or at least so they would have it believed.

In the lightless pits beneath low Commorragh lie the lairs of the haemonculi covens. It is there that this dark brotherhood of flesh sculptors and pain artists practice their arts in the most diabolical ways imaginable. A thick miasma of anguish pervades the narrow cells and crooked passages that make up their demesnes. Here altered throats gabble in endless torment as base flesh is sculpted and re-sculpted over and over, twisted and cracked into endless new forms of suffering. In this benighted realm the haemonculi covens each plot their own aggrandisement and the downfall their rivals, hatching centuries-long schemes of genetic black-mail and manipulation to secure their access to the most powerful and influential kabals.

The Coven of the Black Descent lies within a twisting labyrinth of utter blackness filled with traps for the uninitiated. It is said that the depths of their labyrinth extend beyond Commorragh and into the webway itself, touching on split filaments and crushed strands long since abandoned by those whole and sane. Members of the Black Descent are taught the routes they must use to navigate the labyrinth between separate 'interstices' step-by-step according to a strict order of precedence. At the lowest ranks wrack apprentices know only the route necessary to reach the first interstices. As a coven member descends through the ranks more routes are revealed, the correct paths towards the second, third and fourth interstices where the true labyrinth begins. A Perfect Master must learn dozens of individual routes, an intimate secretary has memorised hundreds, while a patriarch noctis knows thousands.

A single misstep along these memorised routes would bring a messy death or, at the very least, violent dismemberment upon the transgressor. Just one step need be miscommunicated to send the victim off-course into a maze of monofilament nets, singularity traps, blood wasp collectives and corrosive mists from which there will be no return. The number of times this technique has been used by members of the coven to dispose of undesirable rivals would fill volumes, so much so that it has acquired the status of a tradition.

At the sixty-fourth interstice of the labyrinth a gathering of coven members was taking place. Four masked secret masters stood in attendance on a fifth, one in the viridian and black of an intimate secretary. By accident or design the sixty-fourth interstice was a pentagonal chamber with archways entering through each of its five walls. Each member of the gathering had stepped from a separate arch into the space only moments before as if summoned by a single call. Even the emotionally-neutered haemonculi could sense the miasma of rage built up within the chamber. It pressed on the subconscious like an inaudible, endless scream of inchoate fury.

A glass-fronted sarcophagus stood upright in the exact centre of the chamber, its contents invisible due to a blood-red mist swirling within. Several chains of dark metal enwrapped the sarcophagus and connected to rings set into the floor. It appeared an extreme measure of security in view of the already sturdy construction of the sarcophagus, a heavy, unlovely thing of ochre-coloured stone only rudely given humanoid shape. Nonetheless the assembled coven members appeared to view the chained artefact with exaggerated caution.

'Check the restraints again,' said the intimate secretary to the secret master to his right.

'Secretary?' the sable-masked haemonculus responded nervously.

'If I have to repeat myself I'll shear those deaf ears from your head. Do it. Now.'

The secret master stepped forward reluctantly and began to examine the chains, twisting them expertly to test their flexibility and strength. The masked haemonculus tested all five ringbolts first but eventually he could not avoid moving closer to the sarcophagus to check the chains wrapped around it. The red mist inside swirled rapidly in response, its tendrils seeming to jab towards the secret master only to dash themselves against the impermeable barrier between them.

'There is some exceptional wear apparent, secretary,' the secret master pronounced after a brief examination. 'I find it hard to ex–'

Two skeletal red claws slammed against the glass with sudden violence, making the secret master recoil with a curse. The claws scraped down the glass for a second and then withdrew to be replaced by a face in the mist. It was hideous, grinning mockery of a face. Red flesh stretched into a facsimile of cheeks and lips, open wet pits instead of eyes. The coven members gathered to look upon the ghastly apparition with wonder.

'How-how can this be?' stammered one of the secret masters.

'Impossible!' exclaimed another.

'Silence!' hissed the intimate secretary. 'You chatter like slaves!' The secret masters quieted at once and obediently turned their masked faces toward him.

'This function now exceeds your degree in the descent. Leave now and speak to no one of this. I have summoned the Master Elect of Nine. He will determine the correct course of action. Remember, tell no one! Your lives depend on it!'

The secret masters were eager to leave that accursed place and fled through their respective archways without further comment. The intimate secretary smoothed his robes and stared back steadily at the impossible face grinning at him from behind the glass.

'I confess I don't know how you've managed to recover so quickly either, but it will do you no good,' he told the face primly. 'When the master elect arrives we will simply determine a new way of restraining you here.'

Fastidiousness and a general distrust of underlings had done much to gain the intimate secretary his current rank. It wasn't long before he began testing the chains for himself while he awaited the arrival of the Master Elect of Nine. The secretary's taut, viridian-stained lips twitched and writhed as he whispered to himself and his captive.

'The instructions were precise on that point, very precise. There can be no escape, no resurrection except under specific conditions. You will not be leaving us just yet.'

The chains were slack and the secretary found himself wondering uneasily how they had got into such a state without visibly loosening at all. Re-tensioning the chains would require releasing one chain from its floor-set ring to draw more links through. He glanced back at the sarcophagus but the face had vanished and once again nothing but roiling mist could be seen inside. He reached out hesitantly to unhitch the chain from its ring.

'Don't touch that,' said a voice behind him.

The intimate secretary whirled to find himself face to face with the hatchet-faced Master Elect of Nine. The master elect's eyes had been replaced with plates of black crystal that winked ominously at the secretary.

'Assuming you wish to live, of course,' grated the master elect. His voice was a special torture, a grinding sound of sharpening blades, shrieking wheels and saws cutting through bone. To hear it was to have ears and senses mercilessly flensed by its hideous timbre. The intimate secretary recoiled as if he had been burned.

'Forgive me, master elect!' babbled the secretary. 'I sought only to undertake necessary preventative maintenance while I was awaiting your arrival.'

'Not a threat, secretary, merely an observation,' the master elect grated pedantically. 'In point of precision, you were trying to let her out. You simply didn't realise it.'

The master elect stepped closer to the sarcophagus and gazed at its contents before moving out to circle the chamber and examine each of the tethering chains in turn. He tested nothing, touched nothing, the haemonculus keeping his hands tucked within the sleeves of his slate-grey robe at all times. He walked with a curiously precise, stiff-legged gait as though his limbs were constructed of wheels and steel rods. The sickening psychic miasma within the chamber seemed to be thickening into a palpable aura that beat upon the mind in waves. The intimate secretary found that he was sweating despite the chill air. A faint tremor ran through the floor when the master elect finally turned back to the intimate secretary at last.

'There is danger here, but not from the source you perceive. This is ultimately Bellathonis's doing. The bitter fruits of his labour, the Dysjunction is fuelling this one's efforts to revive. Her desire is strong and draws strength to it.'

The master elect paused as another tremor ran through chamber, longer and more distinct than the first.

'Bring acid to refill the sarcophagus and enough wracks to keep her distracted while we do it.'

'Very good, master elect,' the intimate secretary grovelled before daring a question. 'It-it is certain then? Bellathonis initiated the Dysjunction?'

'Certain.' The word fell from the master elect's lips like the blade of a guillotine. The intimate secretary paled visibly at the prospect before his face contorted with fear as another ramification dawned upon him.

'If the Supreme Overlord learns of Bellathonis's involvement...' he whispered.

'Dissolution of the coven. Exile or true death to its membership for their crime of *association* with the culprit.' The master elect's tones cut the word *association* into screaming fragments steeped in an acid bath of revulsion. 'There is precedent for this on the basis of prior events.'

'But Bellathonis is a renegade!' the intimate secretary screeched. 'He fled from our ranks! We gave him no succour!'

'Irrelevant. Supreme Overlord Asdrubael Vect will mete out punishments regardless of the culpability of the recipients. The guilt of past association will be more than sufficient pretext to make the Coven of the Black Descent a target.' The master elect was dispassionate, almost mechanical in his dissection of the likely future of the coven. Fear and vindictive rage warred for possession of the intimate secretary's face. Rage quickly won.

'This cannot be borne!' the intimate secretary spat. 'Bellathonis is the one responsible, he should be the one to pay! We must silence him before he is taken by Vect!'

'Such words have been spoken before,' grated the master elect. 'The one who spoke them was sent against the renegade and failed in his task. It is believed that Bellathonis has destroyed him.'

'Then another must be sent! And another! Until...' the intimate secretary suddenly understood the path he was being led down and baulked, stammering. 'I mean... with respect, master elect, I meant no–'

'Your enthusiasm and loyalty is warmly noted,'

the master elect smiled with no discernable trace of warmth. 'You may begin your preparations immediately.'

# CHAPTER 8
### INHERITANCE

A BLINDING FLASH, a wrench of disassociation and for a moment Motley found himself falling into a green pool. No, the pool was behind him, and he was falling away from it. Up and Down fought a brief civil war over their respective claims for territory while Motley tumbled helplessly between their frontlines. Armistice only occurred when the green pool was declared the sovereign territory of Down and Motley obediently began falling towards it. The numbing pain in his chest and arm throbbed in anticipation of a return to its point of origin. His fall back into the pool was abruptly halted by an armoured arm that reached out to seize Motley's limp body and drag him aside.

Motley blinked up gratefully at Morr towering over him. Over to one side of them lay a flat pool that spilled jade light into what appeared to be a cave. Motley puffed and blew for a second before bounding onto his feet with exuberant energy. He then struck a warlike pose with a slight wince.

'Brothers in arms!' he declared with bravado. 'Equal to any and all challenges precisely as previously advertised!'

Motley abruptly slid back down onto his haunches with a bump and looked back up at the incubus. 'Don't you think?' he said a little plaintively after a moment. Bright beads of red showed on his clothing where the shrapnel had pierced it. The holes themselves had already been knitted over by its clever fibres even as they set to work on the torn flesh beneath.

'That was as brave an act as any that I have seen,' the incubus said thoughtfully. 'I was… surprised by your survival.'

'I thought you'd left me behind again.'

'There was no time to explain that the emergence would be vertical. Once I was sure that you would follow I entered the gate to ensure I would be in a position to prevent you falling back.'

'That world was your home once upon a time, wasn't it, Morr?'

The silence stretched for long moments before the incubus answered.

'That was my home long ago,' Morr said slowly. 'Ushant, a maiden world. It is my eternal shame that I was born there of Exodite blood.' Morr paused again and gazed down at Motley, his blank-faced helm studying the harlequin for indications of judgment or contempt. Motley smiled back uncertainly and feebly waved a hand for the incubus to continue. Morr snorted.

'Perhaps you had imagined all maiden worlds to be virginal paradises like Lileathanir? Not so, Ushant. My elders told me that the world was once covered by mighty oceans, but in my time they had become little more than deserts. The Exodite clans were hardy and endured, some even thrived. They remained numerous if not prosperous throughout the slow draining of the seas. Fourteen centuries before my birth the clans gathered to fight off an invasion entering Ushant through the gate that we just used.' Morr nodded across to the greenly glowing pool and lapsed into silence.

'Were they victorious?' Motley prompted. 'The peace they won would seem to have been sadly temporary if they did.'

'The clans were victorious but they became cursed in the process. In the conflict they learned new ways of making war from their enemies. Crude, indiscriminate, effective ways. Once the immediate threat was overcome the clans turned their war machines on each other.'

'What?' Motley was incredulous. 'Why would they do that?'

'Honour, pride and stupidity in equal measure. The dispute began over which clan should control the gate and guard against future incursions. The strongest clans – the Far Light and the Many Islands – each opposed the other gaining the prestige of controlling the gate. The two sides' blood-kin and allies aligned with them in pressing their claims.

Many had become so invested in making war during the conflict with the invaders, so my elders said, that they were loathe to give it up when peace was won.'

'Tragic,' Motley frowned unhappily. 'I'm ashamed no one came to intercede and make peace between the clans.'

Morr laughed, a mordant cough of humour soaked in bile and bitterness. 'Oh, they came. Many times. Finely dressed ascetics came from those drifting cradles we call craftworlds to tell us how to improve our lot. They hid behind their masks and shed crocodile tears at our misfortunes while discomforting themselves not one iota to help. In my own time they came once again and sat in judgment of us like celestial beings that had reluctantly descended into the common muck. They had finally tired of the dispute and announced their intention to give their support to the survivors of the Far Light clan.'

Motley pursed his lips but did not speak as he wondered which craftworld it was that had so thoroughly bungled their guardianship of Ushant. Each craftworld accepted nominal responsibility for a number of the maiden worlds scattered across the great wheel. Some viewed the maiden worlds as the hope for the future of the eldar race, the seeds from which the eldar might once more grow to prominence on the galactic stage. Other craftworlds viewed the maiden worlds as no more than a burden, mere primitive backwaters, the resource-sucking wreckage left behind by a failed survival plan.

'Instead of quelling the conflict the decision lent it renewed vigour. The Many Islands clan attacked the Far Light and their craftworld patrons that very night... they appeared to be surprised by this turn of events. They defended themselves poorly.' Morr's helm tilted up at the memory, its bloodstone tusks catching the light and creating the illusion that they were slicked with fresh gore.

'Is that when you saw the figure that you followed?'

'Arhra,' Morr spoke the name with conviction. 'Make no mistake – it was Arhra himself that came to me then. He told me without words that I was worthy to test my strength at his shrine. He challenged me to do so.'

'The legends say that Arhra was destroyed.'

'Nothing ever truly dies.'

'Perhaps the legends meant that he was changed beyond recognition.'

'Tread carefully, little clown. You know nothing about what you speak of.'

'My profuse apologies. I am cursed with a propensity for asking impertinent questions at inopportune moments. Forgive me.'

Morr grunted and walked away. Motley saw that the incubus was making for an exit from the cave, a ragged gash in the stone that showed a pale hint of daylight beyond. Motley wearily pushed himself to his feet and began to follow. The gash opened out into a narrow cleft in bare rock that soon became a treacherous ledge. One wall disappeared to reveal an almost sheer drop into a valley on that side, the other wall extending up in a cliff face softened in places by moisture-dripping clumps of grass and lichens. Above that was a golden haze of indeterminate source, sunlight with no sun. Below them the ledge descended towards a layer of coiling mist that covered the land like a blanket. There was a suggestion of the skeletal silhouettes of trees poking up through the mist, but they shifted and wavered uncertainly in a sea of whiteness.

'Would it be impertinent to ask where we are and where we're going?' Motley said hopefully as he skipped nimbly down uneven steps after Morr.

'We come to journey's end,' the incubus said eventually. 'The shrine of Arhra lies in the valley below.'

Motley began brushing fastidiously at the dried blood on his tunic, even though it was fast becoming invisible against the cloth anyway. 'Well that was a good deal easier to reach than expected,' Motley exclaimed a little unconvincingly. 'Always a positive sign, I say, smooth sailing ahead!'

'The swamp is not without challenges,' Morr cautioned pedantically. His tone could not disguise that even his melancholy spirit seemed to have risen fractionally.

BEZIETH EDGED CAREFULLY forward, aware of the dull ache in her leg and the way everyone else was clustering behind her as if she were some sovereign shield of protection. There was music playing ahead of her, a wild, disquieting tune that skirled and whined in a way that set her teeth on edge. There had been doors at the end of the corridor, ornate sheets of precious metal pierced and worked into the form of twin phoenixes. These had been twisted and thrown aside with unthinkable force. Shadows from within flickered and danced across the opening, the music twisted and contorting around their shambolic rhythms. Bezieth of the Hundred Scars feared nothing living or dead, but even she hesitated to look inside.

She could feel the pressure of a dozen eyes on her back willing her to step forward, while the amorphous, unknown horror ahead of her held her back. The pressures were equal for a moment, but pride drove her relentlessly forwards to look around the door jamb and reveal the scene. The floor was made up of runnelled porcelain tiles leading to hexagonal, silver-topped drains. These, the clustered stab-lights overhead, and the hanging chains showed the place had been a slaughter faire where passing denizens could enjoy exhibitions of the public torture and humiliation of slaves and eager masochists.

Now the chains hung empty and the only light came from acrid bonfires that had been rudely piled around the hall out of debris. Figures cavorted madly around the flames in time to the piping music. Most of them appeared to be slaves, looking even more twisted and ugly than usual, but there was also a smattering of pure-blooded Commor-rites leaping and capering with uncommon vigour.

At the centre of it all lay the source of the mad-ness – a great mound of pink and blue flesh with only vague approximations of limbs and a head.

It writhed and wriggled obscenely like a questing maggot while rows of flaring, hollow spines opened up and down its length emitting the hideous, piping music. The revellers danced around it, dashed offerings of wine and food over it, suckled on it and screamed out their devotion. Periodically the skirling pipes became insistent, almost whining. At this the dancers would seize one of their own number and hurl them onto the fleshy mass. The piping became ecstatic as the mound closed over the sacrificial victim like a blunt-fingered hand. In the last moments the victims would suddenly snap out of their ecstatic revelry and scream piteously in the grip of the thing. The insane piping interwove mockingly with their dying howls.

Bezieth had seen enough, the piping was starting to get to her too. She pulled her head back behind the ruined door jamb. Naxipael looked at her questioningly. She shrugged slightly and nodded back the way they had come. Naxipael shook his head in irritation and raised his blast pistols, his motion silently echoed by the other survivors. They were feeling frightened, angry and powerless – they all wanted to fight something. Bezieth rolled her eyes and gingerly hefted her djin-blade too. It emitted a chafing whine as if irritated by the hideous fluting sound ahead. Bezieth held it out before her and virtually let it lead the charge into the room.

She attacked silently, cutting down two of the dancers before they even registered her presence. darklight beams suddenly slashed across two more of them, vaporising the leaping bodies in nebula-dark explosions of matter. Naxipael tried to hit the piping beast but revellers hurled themselves in his path to make a living shield of themselves. He laughed cynically as he blasted his way through them one by one.

Bezieth carved her way forward too, outpacing Naxipael as she waded through the minions striking left and right almost disinterestedly as she concentrated her energies on limping towards the beast. Too slowly. The piping was changing, becoming a shrilling saw upon the ears as it called its children to war. The remaining dancers turned on Naxipael and Bezieth with hostility written over their mad faces. Pallid fires glowed in every eye, and phosphorescent drool fell from every lip. The marks of corruption could already be seen: flesh melting into tendrils or fur or feathers or scales, limbs that were strangely twisted and a distinct surfeit of orifices was in evidence.

Hypervelocity splinters and disintegrator bolts ravened across the chamber as the rest of the Metzuh survivors opened fire, mercilessly cutting down the revellers where they stood. Some of those hit vanished like hydrogen-filled balloons sent alight, the skin peeling back as its contents ignited in a multi-coloured flash. Most of those struck accepted the wounds as stolidly as if they were made of clay rather than living flesh. The pink, fleshy craters that opened on their bodies dripped the same phosphorescent slime as drooled in ropy tendrils from their lips.

The piping beast's minions raced forward, their

outstretched hands flashing with etheric flames. Fire leapt up around Bezieth and Naxipael, deceptively vaporous pink and blue gossamer blazes that seared armour and charred flesh at the slightest touch. Both archons were forced onto the defensive, concentrating only on trying to fend off the capering horrors that leapt around them. Shrill screams sounded from behind as some of the survivors trying to push into the hall were consumed by the scorching blasts. Bezieth saw one warrior burning like a torch, still firing his splinter rifle as he was overwhelmed. The fires leapt higher still, creating the illusion that the entire hall had become a pavilion of woven flames.

Bezieth sheared through a leering face, ducked a gobbet of multi-coloured fire and cut off the arm that spit it at her. Axhyrian's captured spirit energised her through the channel of the djin-blade, obedient and deadly in her hands for the present. Her enemies fought with no method, they leapt back and forth randomly, tumbling over each other in their haste to grasp and burn. She doggedly fought her way closer to Naxipael, who was reaping a great ruin of his foes but had been badly burned over his chest and back.

The other survivors were formed in a tight knot just behind them and were likewise badly beset on all sides so she could expect no help from them. The numbers of their attackers did not seem to be lessening at all, if anything there seemed more of them now than when Bezieth had entered the hall. The shrill piping was becoming triumphant, a mad cackling sound that drove against the soul.

A hoarse cry made her twist around to look back at the other survivors again and she gaped at what she saw. The wrack that had tended her, Xagor, was being hoisted onto their shoulders while the rest were fighting almost back-to-back to protect the execution of this peculiar manoeuvre. The wrack was in the process of awkwardly trying to level a long, thick-barrelled rifle.

Bezieth understood what they were trying to do. The survivors were lifting up the wrack up to get a clear shot over the heads of the capering minions at their daemonic master beyond. The wrack's heavy rifle wobbled around alarmingly in the melee and the flame-handed dancers leapt madly everywhere, obscuring his target. The long-barrelled rifle finally spat once to no visible effect. To attempt such a thing only showed the survivors' desperation. They had taken a fool's chance, a futile last throw of the dice before the end came and it had failed.

The horrific fluting suddenly oscillated wildly, wailing up and down scales with agonising swiftness. The dancers whirled away clutching flame-wreathed hands to their heads, staggering even as Bezieth, Naxipael and the other survivors fought back a wave of sickness. The fires guttered out and the beast was revealed to be rearing and bucking, seemingly twisting in pain as its flesh rippled obscenely. With a final heave the fleshy mound split from end to end, unleashing a wave of bile, maggots, foulness and corroded bones across the floor. The mad piping ceased abruptly. The dancers wavered and collapsed into sacs of deflating skin. Naxipael and the impromptu pyramid of survivors fell too, depositing the wrack unceremoniously on the floor. Bezieth stood speechless for a moment, waiting to see if some new horror was about to burst forth. The hall remained silent and dark.

Bezieth noticed the wrack was quick to scurry after his dropped rifle, cradling it to himself protectively as if it were a cherished pet. To her surprise one of the other survivors offered his hand to help pull the wrack to his feet. Now several more clapped the wrack on the back and congratulated him as if he were one of their own pulling off a tricky shot, rather than the surgically-altered meat puppet of a mad torturer-scientist. Bezieth shook her head. Part of the curse of the Dysjunction was to create strange bedfellows out of necessity, ripping apart the societal fabric of the city as well as its physical one.

There were only seven survivors left now, not including herself and Naxipael. The odds against his ascension to High Commorragh had lengthened considerably and he was not happy about it. She looked toward Naxipael and called the wrack to attend him, her voice a whip-crack of discipline. The wrack jumped to obey, almost dropping his beloved rifle again in the process.

'Possessed!' Naxipael raved. 'Traitors all, every damn one of them! Giving their own flesh away! Bah!'

The wrack hurried up and carefully laid his

weapon on the floor before seeing to Naxipael's injuries.

'We were too late,' Bezieth shrugged. 'Whatever got in there first was nasty enough to hold on when the warding closed. Every major daemon within a league probably squeezed itself into the first warm body it could find to avoid being drawn back. We can expect to see more possessed.'

'I bow to your superior expertise in the field, Bezieth,' Naxipael said through gritted teeth.

'That's right, I didn't get a hundred scars in Necropolis street fights.'

As with Bezieth the wrack's methods were not kind but they were quickly effective. Raw wounds that were showing through Naxipael's partially melted armour quickly scabbed over. Naxipael's face took on a mask-like grimace of pain and he cursed volubly.

'With respect,' the wrack said deferentially, 'this one would ask why no possessed were at the canal.'

Bezieth regarded the wrack coolly for a moment before coming to a decision. 'Because the big ones, which is to say the smarter ones, don't stop for a feast as soon as they get inside the warding,' she said, her eyes momentarily unfocused and distant with the memory. 'They go deep and bury themselves somewhere where they can find sustenance, somewhere they can grow like a cancer.' The wrack nodded while bowing and scraping so low that it was virtually banging its head on the tiles. Naxipael was muttering again as the scabs flaked off him to reveal patches of pink, new skin.

'Xagor, isn't it? Tell me about the weapon, Xagor,' Bezieth said, looking at the rifle more closely. It was an ugly thing, owing more to the aesthetics of a butcher's tool or a collection of tubes than the elegantly sculpted lines of a Commorrite weapon.

'This device is called the hex-rifle, honoured one,' the wrack said with some pride. 'Acothyst's weapon, Xagor found it in the processional among the entourage of Master Re'ryrinx. Most unfortunate.'

'Never mind that. What does it fire?'

'Cylinder impregnated with accelerated viral compound, normally Glass Plague. Xagor does not know what compound this device uses, perhaps mutagenic, perhaps not. Xagor has fired only one shot with it and suggests finding more test subjects for more accurate analysis.'

'Well whatever it is it works, keep it by you in case we need it again,' Bezieth said before pushing down her distaste and clapping the wrack on its leather-clad shoulder. 'And nice shot, by the way.'

Naxipael seemed more aware of his surroundings again, his cursing tailed off into a string of short expletives as he stood up somewhat shakily. He gave Bezieth a peculiar look and then shrugged painfully.

'All right, Bezieth, I'll listen to your suggestion of what to do next,' Naxipael said with equanimity.

'Then make for Sorrow Fell,' Bezieth said, 'and do it quickly.'

'Reason?'

'Things have been stable for a little while but that won't last, it'll get worse. Sorrow Fell surrounds

Corespur and it's the only tier that will be organised enough to survive the worst, Vect will keep it that way.'

'You're assuming our glorious and beloved Supreme Overlord has survived,' Naxipael sneered. 'Some revenant might be eating his entrails at this very moment.'

'More likely some High Commorragh pureblood is trying to stick a knife in his back, but I don't find either possibility very likely. Vect still lives, you know he does. When the universe ends Vect will still be alive in the nothingness that comes after, floating in an unbreachable bubble of his own deviousness and sense of self-satisfaction.'

Naxipael scowled but didn't deny it. Asdrubael Vect had ruled Commorragh with an iron fist for six millennia. The Supreme Overlord had maintained his rule through disasters, rebellions, civil wars, alien invasions and Dysjunctions before. If anything Vect seemed to thrive on the experience, emerging stronger and with notably fewer opponents after each one. Naxipael had to grant that Bezieth's plan had merit, contrawise to ordinary times it would actually be wise to seek protection from Vect's presence rather than stay away from it.

Between them Bezieth and Naxipael managed to get the survivors moving again, haranguing them for their laziness and threatening the tardy with lurid punishments. There were three warriors left, each from three different lesser kabals so they watched each other suspiciously at all times. There were a pair of Ethondrian Seekers in maroon cloaks and hoods, their half-seen faces constantly questing back and forth like weasels. They stayed close together and guarded one another's backs religiously. Finally there was the wrack and a ragged-looking sell-sword that she vaguely recognised.

They were sullen and unwilling to move, but all of them understood the peril they were in and obeyed after some grumbling. Not much of a force to take into Sorrow Fell, Bezieth thought, but any of them that could make it through the ruins of Low Commorragh should be able to find ready employment among the high archons at a time like this. Ready employment and relative safety until the Dysjunction was over.

At least so she hoped.

THE IMAGES ON the wall flickered, and the soft, amber light in the room fluctuated unpredictably. Distant, disturbing sounds flickered at the edge of hearing (or perhaps the edge of consciousness) but they seemed reassuringly far away for the present. It was still possible for the occupants of the chamber to set concerns of the Dysjunction aside for a moment and concentrate on their vital work.

One of the images was briefly outlined and expanded to fill the wall, the face of a somewhat slack jawed, flat-faced, raven-haired specimen of Commorrite nobility. One of the room's occupants spoke up as twisting skeins of data unfurled around the image.

'This is Kvaisor Yllithian, eleventh sibling on the Mol'zinyear branch, my archon.'

'Too ugly,' the room's only other occupant snapped. 'Next.'

A different image promptly replaced the first, this one closely resembled Nyos Yllithian save for a certain dissipated look and what looked to be a permanently distracted expression.

'Razicik Yllithian, seventy-third sibling on the Vatinyr branch, my archon.'

'Seventy-third? Are you insane?'

'There is a strong matrilineal quantum on the Vatinyr side of the family, my archon.'

'You *are* insane. Next.'

Face after face, name after name. All of them sharp featured, haughty, gazing at the viewer with naked contempt. There were certainly variations: pallid skins and dark ones, flamboyantly flowing manes or close cropped skull-caps, but every face bore a familial resemblance to Nyos Yllithian that was unmistakable. The master haemonculus Bellathonis stood nearby, scrolling through the ancient records of the noble house of Yllithian as they attempted to find a suitable candidate.

Despite all of the haemonculus's allegedly best efforts Yllithian was still dying. The Glass Plague was mutating aggressively, marching across his skin like a conquering army. His hands could no longer grip, his legs could not walk and he could only speak thanks to a succession of temporary skin grafts and devices. The plague had bound itself inside Yllithian's own body in a way that made it impossible to completely eradicate. Perhaps as little as days remained to him but he'd thought it would be enough time to find the right individual to use as his successor. A message he had just received denied him even that, now he had only hours.

'What about that one?'

'Zarils Yllithian, second sibling on the Oanisis branch, my archon. According to this you strangled him with your own hands and then cast his body into the void.'

'Ah yes. I knew there was a reason he looked so promising.'

'If I may make a suggestion, my archon?'

'You may,' Yllithian sighed. 'Apparently I shan't be going anywhere anytime soon. Nothing too pressing on my mind.'

'Well quite. It strikes me that with the limited time we have available it may be best to set aside aesthetic concerns and concentrate on finding a... robust enough character to survive the trans-migration of power. Physical appearance is, after all, mutable,' Bellathonis smiled his disturbingly shark-like smile at this and cocked his head to show off his own sharply altered profile with its long, pointed chin and hooked nose. 'No addi-tional charge, of course.'

'The face and the blood is everything, Bella-thonis,' Yllithian told him pedantically. 'I would be a fool to trust my household's future to the vagar-ies of your knives however talented you may claim them to be. This must be perfection itself.'

Asdrubael Vect, the Supreme Overlord had called a convocation of the surviving archons. Any kabal that failed to send its leader to the

Corespur forthwith would be judged rebellious and destroyed on sight. Vect must be desperate if he was taking such steps, or so Nyos fervently hoped. Unfortunately attending the convocation in his current state would be worse than suicide and so for the sake of the noble house of Yllithian he must find a successor.

'Well if the face must take precedence then the blood must suffer,' Bellathonis continued smoothly. 'That, too can always be rectified, of course.'

'You make your points with the subtlety of a pit slave, Bellathonis, do you know that? I just find it hard to believe that among my vast, extended and frankly bloated bloodline not one of them is suitable to take my place.'

'If I may say so, at the risk of exhibiting the subtlety of a pit slave once again,' you may have been entirely too successful in securing your own position to leave any viable contenders for your replacement. More bluntly still – you already killed them all. Furthermore these are only the blood-kin in the fortress itself. So many are missing in the Dysjunction that the pool is distinctly shallow at present.'

'Tell me again why you aren't growing me a new body right now.'

'Aside from the fantastically high chance it would be subject to possession at a time of Dysjunction, my archon? The other reason is that it could not possibly be ready in time. A third reason, if you desire it, is that it would have to be vat-grown and

you have already made your feelings on that subject perfectly clear.'

Yllithian snarled something incomprehensible.

'I'm sorry, my archon, could you repeat that?'

'I said send for young Razicik then, currently
seventy-third in line to absolutely nothing. His fortunes are about to change drastically.'

# CHAPTER 9
## THE HUNTERS

MORR AND MOTLEY descended through the banks of mist until it became a low overcast above their heads. In the valley before them the shrine of Arhra rose tier upon tier to where its conical spires vanished into the golden haze. Pillars and archways of obsidian clustered upon its faces in dizzying profusion, all enwrapped by trailing nets of parasitic vines and extravagantly flowering greenery. A heavy, humid atmosphere hung about the place creating thin tendrils of mist that flowed from the darkened entrances and down its cracked steps. Plinths dividing the steps at irregular intervals bore eroded statues; some of the carvings still recognisable as warriors and beasts while others formed bizarre and otherworldly shapes born of madness and decay.

The land surrounding the shrine gleamed with low-lying waters. The rearing shapes of mangroves bearded with hanging streamers of moss and lichen jutted out of the murk. Insects buzzed industriously and a few winged shapes wheeled high above. Beyond these few signs of life no other creatures were to be seen near the shrine. A pregnant sense of watchfulness pervaded it as if hidden eyes gazed upon the newcomers from its deeply shadowed recesses.

'Here I was reborn,' intoned Morr with reverence. 'The child that escaped the prison of its birth learned the true path to destiny and honour in this place.'

Motley glanced at the incubus with frank surprise but did not speak. Morr's words were clearly not intended for him and to respond to them might only drive the incubus back into his shell. It was remarkable enough that this living weapon had found a voice of its own if only for a moment. Morr hefted his blade and strode away, picking his way over mossy stones towards a causeway that led across the swamp. The path was treacherous in the extreme but Morr never so much as glanced downward. His gaze was locked on the distant spires of the shrine. Motley skipped after the incubus with his heart full of foreboding.

'Morr... Does it strike you as unusual that this place does not appear to have been affected by the Dysjunction in any way?'

Morr seemed puzzled by the question. 'Why should it be? There is no direct connection to Commorragh.'

'True, but the effects of the Dysjunction are being

propagated elsewhere throughout the webway, I would expect to see... to feel some evidence of its impact even here.'

'Many are the shrines to Arhra, but it said that he gave up his mortality in this place, and that this shrine was forged from his flesh and bones. His spirit is certainly strong here, perhaps it is strong enough to protect the shrine.'

'Perhaps that's it... I, well I'm sure that you're correct.'

Morr halted and swivelled to regard Motley balefully. 'You sound as though you fear some lurking corruption. There is nothing to fear in this place for those who come to it untainted by weakness.'

'Weakness in this case including concepts such as empathy, charity or mercy I would imagine,' Motley replied somewhat tartly. Morr only grunted in response before turning back to continue his journey.

As he did so he stopped short. A figure now stood on the causeway ahead of them, waiting. It was clad in green-black armour and rested a double-handed klaive on the ground before it. After a moment Morr addressed the apparition cautiously.

'Greetings, brother, I seek passage to the shrine. Have you come forth to greet us?'

The figure remained silent and made no movement, it may as well have been carven of green-black stone for all the signs of life it betrayed.

'If you will not speak then stand aside and let us pass, or there will be a passage of arms between us that you may regret.'

By way of reply the figure swung its weapon to a guard position. Morr automatically reflected the movement by raising his own klaive in both hands and taking a step forward.

'Are you sure you are entirely welcome in your old haunts, Morr?' Motley asked impertinently from behind him. 'This fellow seems to think you are not.' A short, curved blade and a long, elegant pistol had appeared in the harlequin's hands as if by magic.

'Stay out of this, little clown,' Morr warned as he continued to advance on the silent sentinel.

A battle between two incubi is a formidable sight to behold. Both wear armour capable of warding off any but the strongest blows, yet they wield weapons capable of tearing through that self-same armour like paper. Against skilled but lesser armoured opponents an incubus must fight warily – constantly on the move, feinting and shifting to keep their comparatively slow, heavy klaive balanced and ready to unleash a killing strike. Against a horde of unskilled foes an incubus can concentrate on maintaining a steady rhythm, overpowering and overawing their enemies before they use their weight of numbers to advantage. In either case the incubus can rely also on fists, knees and feet to deal crippling damage, moves that against a fellow incubus would leave them as a pile of severed limbs in moments.

Between two incubi the contest becomes one more of speed, strength and endurance. They trade blows and counters faster than the eye can follow, each swing perfectly directed at a vulnerable spot, most often the wrists, head or neck. Each parry must be delivered with just enough power to deflect a descending klaive but not so much that the defender overextends and drops their guard to the inevitable counter swing. Maintaining the momentum of the moving blades while interweaving strikes and parries is key, the first fighter to slow or falter is apt to lose their head.

Morr and his opponent stood almost toe-to-toe, their klaives carving glittering arcs as they swept together, clashed and whirled away to attack again. Morr used his greater height to rain down blows like thunderbolts, causing his enemy to sway and finally take a step back to escape from beneath the storm. His foe responded by redoubling his attack and unleashed a rapid series of eviscerating strikes from left and right.

Morr was put on the defensive, his grip spaced widely on his klaive as he blocked one strike after another. Suddenly the towering incubus was staggered by an unexpected overhead swing that he barely managed to block with his upraised klaive. Morr fell back a pace and his opponent rushed forward to keep up the pressure, hammering at his guard without respite.

Morr's klaive flicked out to snare his advancing foe's weapon with its hooked tip as he tried to buy time to recover. Instantly both warriors spun their klaives to gain the necessary leverage to drag their opponent's weapon out of their hands. Neither of them succeeded but Morr's opponent momentarily lost control of his klaive as it was flung outward from his body. Morr's recovery was quicker and he instantly slammed a blow into his enemy with his full weight behind it. His opponent blocked the strike just in time, but could not fully deflect it. The two warriors were left locked blade to crackling blade for instant before, with a mighty heave of his shoulders, Morr hurled his enemy back with brute strength alone.

The other incubus was thrown off his feet but reacted with cat-like quickness by rolling into a crouch. Morr's klaive sang as it flashed down, being only partially deflected by a weak, cross-armed parry before its hooked tip gouged into his opponent's thigh. Morr tugged the blade free in a shower of armour fragments and gore, leaving red ruin in its wake. His foe lurched up to make a desperate riposte that Morr caught easily on his klaive. He stripped the blade from his opponent's grasp with a practiced twist, leaving the other incubus completely defenceless.

Morr swung again without hesitation, a horizontal cut at the neck with every ounce of his weight and every iota of his strength behind it. The other incubus had been raising his arms, perhaps in an effort to catch the swinging blade, or to ward off the blow or perhaps even to plead for mercy. It mattered not one jot. The monomolecular edge of the klaive flared with power as it crashed through both armoured wrists and neck without slowing. A handless, headless puppet sprayed crimson as it toppled to the causeway with its strings cut. The helmed head clattered down several yards away and rolled, splashing tiny carmine spirals in its wake.

Morr grunted with satisfaction and went to retrieve the helmet and severed hands. Motley blanched as Morr produced a spool of wire from his belt and threaded the grisly trophies together prior to hanging them from the skeletal rack that rose behind his shoulders for just such a purpose.

'Is that really necessary?' Motley protested. 'Is it not enough to take a life in honest combat that you must play the ghoul afterwards?'

Morr stood and looked at Motley through glittering crystal lenses, his face unreadable behind his blank-faced helm. Motley regretted his outburst immediately. He had allowed himself to forget that Morr was a denizen of the dark city where grisly trophies are always at the height of fashion. Hearing the story of Morr's maiden world origins had softened Motley's already somewhat empathetic view of the incubus's plight even further. He told himself to recall this moment if he found himself making the same slip again. To Motley's surprise when Morr spoke it was without any trace of rancour.

'If one brother opposes my approach to the shrine then there is a high chance there will be others that feel the same way,' the incubus intoned. 'The sight of their predecessor's remains may give them pause.'

'Surely the hierarchs won't tolerate any such interference?' Motley asked. 'You've come here to seek their judgment, how can they accept such disregard for their authority as waylaying plaintiffs before they can even reach the judge?'

'The right of one Incubus to challenge another is sacrosanct. It is a law beyond the authority of any hierarch to overturn. Thus it has always been.'

'So you're saying you may face a succession of challengers then?' Motley snorted. 'The path to the shrine will be littered with their corpses at this rate.'

'It is more likely the remainder would attack as a group, and from positions of ambush,' Morr said imperturbably, 'there is no ordinance that the challenges must occur singly or openly.'

'But why would they be so set against you seeking judgment?'

Morr was silent for a long moment before answering. 'They believe, rightly, that my guilt is manifest and incontrovertible,' Morr said, 'I killed my liege lord and there is no denying the fact. For them that is the end of the matter. They believe that there is no possible mitigation for the actions I have taken and that I will dishonour the hierarchs by even bringing the case before them.'

'So they want to stop you reaching the shrine before anyone's feathers get ruffled or any awkward questions get asked?' Motley asked incredulously. Morr nodded solemnly in response.

'If they come at us again there will be no discrimination,' the incubus said, 'they will try to kill you as well as me. Turn back if you wish, you are not beholden to me to continue.'

Motley grinned wolfishly at the notion. 'More

fool them, I'm not just a pretty face, a fantastic wit and an inordinately good dancer, you know.' He skipped energetically through the first few steps of a complex pavane to illustrate his conjecture. 'So do I have your permission to get involved next time?' Motley asked brightly. 'Defend my honour and, coincidentally, my life and all that?'

Morr nodded again and turned to continue down the causeway without another word.

'Of course there is one other possibility, Morr,' Motley called after him. 'They might think you're the one that's been corrupted – you know, got the story backwards. Happens all the time.'

Morr made no response. Motley hurried to catch up with the towering incubus before he vanished into the coiling mist.

THE INTIMATE SECRETARY was furious. It was not an uncommon state of mind for him, although ordinarily it derived from less certain causes and felt empowering rather than emasculating as it did now. This was a truly impotent fury and it tasted bitter on the secretary's serrated tongue. The Master Elect of Nine had given him with the task of dealing with Bellathonis, before Asdrubael Vect learned of the role the renegade had played in triggering the Dysjunction. No doubt by doing so the master elect had fulfilled his own instructions from a deeper degree of the Black Descent – a patriarch noctis or perhaps even a Grand Reeve – to 'do something' about the renegade master before the coven suffered Vect's wrath. It left the intimate secretary with little choice to obey and get it done right after Syiin's prior failure to do so. Unfortunately the intimate secretary found himself quite unable to devise any suitably cunning schemes at present because he was fully engaged in staying alive.

The intimate secretary was concentrating on creeping through the spiralling labyrinth of the Black Descent. He was moving through the seven hundred and ninety-one motions necessary to travel from the sarcophagus chamber at the sixty-fourth interstice across to the twenty-ninth interstice where his own workshop-laboratories lay. Ordinarily this would have given him no cause for concern. The steps necessary to navigate the labyrinth were etched into his memory in symbols of indelible fire – but that was before the Dysjunction. The Dysjunction had riven the labyrinth just as badly as the city above. Traps had been triggered, hostile organisms had been released and whole sections were rumoured to have collapsed into the oubliettes below. The wracks that had returned from investigating had reported traps completely choked with fiends, ur-ghuls and a thousand other wretches that had broken loose from their cells.

Even so it was necessary to go through all the necessary motions to reach the interstice. Many of the labyrinth's traps reset automatically, and some would work as efficiently as ever no matter what happened as they were inimical to life by their very nature. The intimate secretary fumed and ground his filed teeth together at the delay as he ducked beneath an invisible monofilament web that might, or might not, still be in place to slice through an unwary explorer at waist height. There were better, faster routes with few or no traps that could take him to his destination, but his degree of advancement in the coven was insufficient for him to know them. He moved six more paces and sidestepped to avoid a pressure plate connected to a trap alleged to be so heinous that he had never been informed of its function. He could not tell if the stupid thing had been triggered or not.

He had to improvise the next ten motions, hidden spigots overhead had cracked and deposited their loads of organic acid onto the plain basalt floor below. The black rock still bubbled and spat where the acid had touched it and was forming searing puddles that stank evilly. The intimate secretary climbed along the wall with spider-like agility to avoid the whole mess, stepping back onto the floor to perform the six hundred and eighteenth through to six hundred and thirty-first motions required to avoid a sequence of moving gravitic anomalies along the next stretch of corridor. Another sidestep to avoid a timed flame funnel and he was at the entrance to the twenty-ninth interstice. He cautiously stepped inside and surveyed the chamber.

To his relief he found two hulking grotesques were stationed guarding the entrance, blocking the entry as effectively as a pair of thick, fleshy doors. Their puny heads covered by their black iron helms seemed like afterthoughts amid thick ridges of bulging muscle and sharp bony growths. The hunched giants drooled as they recognised him, their thick, ropy spittle dangling down from their grilled masks like jellied worms. The intimate secretary cursed the brutes and drove them back with blows from his short rod of office in order to get past.

Beyond the grotesques low walls divided a long, gloomy hall up into stalls occupied by various wracks working at benches and the handful of haemonculi that were directing their efforts. The benches groaned beneath a collection of multi-coloured glassware, bubbling retorts, jars, assorted metallic plates and components, surgical blades, organs pinned to boards, crackling wires and runic grimoires. Hisses, pops and bangs accompanied their work and combined to produce a drifting miasma of choking vapour and noxious fumes.

The intimate secretary ignored all of the activity for a time as he pondered. Syiin had attempted to use subterfuge to eliminate Bellathonis. Clearly the time for subtlety was past. The wracks and haemonculi in their stalls were all busily preparing weapons. All the deadliest creations of the haemonculi were present: virulent toxins, viral swarms, liquifier guns and needle-fingered flesh gauntlets, agoniser-flails and hex-rifles, traps for the soul and devices to destroy the mind were all here.

The secretary gnawed his lips as he sought the answer. Weapons were all well and good with someone to carry them. Perhaps a sudden rush of grotesques and wracks armed for slaughter? But how would they find their quarry and who would lead them? If a member of the coven was sent they might inadvertently draw the tyrant's eye to precisely what they sought to hide and that would not do at all.

As he thought his eye was drawn to a particular stall where no activity appeared to be occurring. This area was occupied not by benches and wracks but by a pair of curved two-metre high, three-metre long objects currently hidden beneath dirty grey cloths. The moment he saw it his fury rekindled, here was the answer – discarded and forgotten! He stalked across to the stall with all of the dignity he could muster.

'Ah intimate secretary, you have returned!' a secret master said ingratiatingly as he came forward from an adjacent stall. This master was masked in steel and adamantium, his smooth, oval head craning out on a thin neck above robes of layered metal mesh. A cluster of tiny lenses over one of the master's eye-holes rotated spastically until it settled on a satisfactory configuration.

'Why are these engines not functional? Are they damaged?' the secretary snapped impatiently, jerking his head sharply at the cloth-covered shapes.

'Not as far as I am aware, secretary,' the master replied warily. 'I have not tested them since… the event began, there should be no reason to believe them otherwise, that is–'

'Then ready them for action immediately!' the secretary almost shrieked.

Somewhat nonplussed the secret master tilted his smooth head enquiringly. 'To what purpose, secretary?' he asked carefully. 'By which I mean what configuration should be used?'

The intimate secretary half-raised his rod of office to strike the secret master but mastered himself. It was not truly an unreasonable question – how best to ensure Bellathonis's death? The secretary thought quickly.

'They must be self-directing,' the secretary said. 'Able to hunt down their quarry independently. Their target will be an individual, when they find the target they must destroy every atom of it.'

'I understand, secretary,' the secret master nodded, ruminating. 'A psychic trace will be sufficient to find the individual if an imprint can be supplied.'

'It can,' the secretary sniffed.

'And the capabilities of the target?' the secret master asked patiently, as if ticking off articles on a mental checklist. 'Would they be a runner or a fighter by nature?'

The intimate secretary paused and considered. From what he knew Bellathonis could be either, but if he tried to run from the engines while the city was in the grip of a Dysjunction he was unlikely to survive the experience.

'A fighter, with a high chance of being in a defended location,' the secretary declared confidently.

'Very good, secretary,' the secret master said with satisfaction. 'I'll begin the preparations to receive the imprint immediately.'

The secret master turned and nimbly flicked the cloths away from the front of one the hidden shapes to reveal a curved, gleaming prow of metal. A nest of knives and needles could be glimpsed tucked up underneath it, a set of jointed metal limbs folded as neatly as insect legs.

The intimate secretary stared thoughtfully at the engines that would encompass Bellathonis' inescapable doom. His taut, viridian lips pulled back into a disquieting smile as he found himself warming to his scheme. It would work, it had to work.

'Dispatch them the moment they are ready,' the intimate secretary instructed. 'The imprint will be supplied momentarily.' The secret master nodded silently, already busy with his work. The intimate secretary moved on to find sufficient acid and enough wracks to quell the occupant of the sarcophagus at the sixty-fourth interstice.

# CHAPTER 10
## ANOTHER SORT OF INHERITANCE

YOUNG RAZICIK YLLITHIAN was hunting in the lower halls of the White Flames Fortress when the archon's summons came. Some Venomyst infiltrators had been found sneaking their way up from the catacombs shortly after the Dysjunction so Razicik and his clique had taken it upon themselves to hunt down more of the vermin. It had been a frustrating business with scant diversion to it. The infiltrators set traps and ambushes, ran away like slaves and were generally annoying about the whole affair. It wasn't too surprising really, the Venomyst were just a remnant and more used to running than fighting. The late, great Zovas Yllithian had forced the last vestiges of Archon Uziiak's Venomyst kabal out of the fortress centuries ago. The Venomyst had been forced to scrape an existence among the somaphages and starvelings in an adjacent spire as their fortunes sank ever lower. It was debatable, really, whether the Venomyst were attempting to invade the fortress or just trying to escape from whatever hell-pit their own spire had become.

So the arrival of the message gave Razicik an opportunity to bow out from the frustrating hunt with good grace by casually mentioning that the archon was calling for him in person and so he must go at once. He suspected a trick at first, some cheap attempt by his siblings to jump him when he was alone, but the message carried the personal sigil of Nyos Yllithian, archon of the White Flames. There was no doubt as to its authenticity. Razicik left his companions to their poor sport and began springing up the first of the innumerable stairs he would have to climb in order to reach the top of the fortress with youthful exuberance. Now was not a time to trust one's fate to malfunctioning grav risers and definitely not to portals so the whole climb would perforce have to be made on foot.

Razicik thought briefly about trying to secure transport to fly around the outside of the fortress instead. The sloping, armoured eaves of the fortress's precipitous rooftops overhung a three-kilometre drop on two sides to where its foundations abutted onto Ashkeri Talon and the docking ring. The closest two spires on the remaining sides were controlled by kabals nominally allied to the White Flames. Archon Uziiak's poisonous offspring and a number of other petty archons dwelled in a skeletal spire of dark metal close by, but they posed no threat out in the open. The profusion of decorative barbs, columns, rosettes and statues that encrusted the exterior of the White Flames' palace concealed Dark lances and disintegrator cannon by the score.

The immediate vicinity should be safe and it would be quicker and much easier on the knees. Of course under the circumstances those very same disintegrator batteries might well pick off anything they detected flying close to the fortress quite regardless of its allegiance. The anarchy of the Dysjunction had wrought a sense of febrile excitement in the air, a feeling that anything could happen and probably would. It prompted a distinct inclination to shoot first and ask questions not at all. Such an unfortunate 'accident' would be too convenient for some of Razicik's siblings to resist arranging it, and so the stairs it must be.

Razicik was amused to note how quickly the stairs altered as he climbed up through the fortress. At its lowest levels the stairways were narrow and twisting with the steps worn to almost U-shaped declivities in cheap, porous rock or corroding metal. Climbing upward they straightened out and became noticeably wider and more richly appointed. Here the steps were unblemished and made of gleaming metal or polished stone.

Razicik couldn't remember the last time he had met the archon, old Nyos Yllithian, face to face. Most of his blood siblings felt it was generally safest to steer clear of the old schemer and avoid drawing excessive attention to oneself. Old Nyos could be positively restrained in comparison to some of his peers, but he was still a cold-blooded killer with no compunction about strangling a potential rival at birth. It dawned on Razicik that Nyos might want to do away with him, but summoning him to do the deed seemed unnecessarily convoluted unless some personal affront was involved. Razicik wracked his memory for anything he might have done to arouse the archon's ire. He could think of nothing and failing to appear would mean a death sentence anyway so he continued to climb, albeit less exuberantly than before.

Higher still and the stairways became sweeping curves of alabaster and onyx that were festooned with decorative balustrades and finials of frozen flame. On these levels Razicik encountered two of the archon's incubi standing waiting for him. They directed him to an antechamber with an entry arch that was sculpted in the shape of great overlapping wings of platinum, gold and silver.

The incubi did not accompany Razicik inside and as he passed the entrance the sculpted wings animated and folded into place across it, leaving him in semi-darkness. The walls were exquisitely decorated with frescoes of White Flames victories and hangings made from the skins and banners of fallen foes. As Razicik's eyes adjusted to the dim light he beheld a small circular table in the centre of the room. A simple throne at the far side of the chamber was its only other furnishing. Razicik realised with a start that a cowled figure appeared to be slumped in the throne. As he stepped forward to investigate the figure shifted slightly and spoke.

'Ah Razicik, you're here at lasst,' the voice was

that of the archon but twisted somehow, sibilant sounding. Ghostly fingers of fear brushed Razicik's spine for the first time. What was going on?

'I am here, my archon, at your command,' Razicik replied uncomfortably. 'How may I serve you?'

'I have dedicated my life to this kabal, Razicik, I've laboured endlessly to ressstore the noble housess. Every action I take iss born out of the love I bear for my housse and for the presservation of all our futuress, but now my time iss done. Do you understand? Thiss body of mine can sstand it no longer…'

Razicik was both shocked and delighted. There had been rumours that the archon had been injured and was incapable, but to have face-to-face admission of the fact meant two things – the archon was taking him into his confidence, and that old Nyos was weak and vulnerable. Razicik eagerly stepped closer.

'No! Say it isn't so!' Razicik protested convincingly. 'Oh my beloved archon, what cruel fate has befallen you?'

'Sspare me your condolencess!' the archon spat. Like every other member of my bloodline you are unworthy of the name Yllithian! Sslack, ssybaritic, sself-indulgence ingratess – every one of you! None of you are worthy to lead this housse!"

'I regret not conforming to your ideals better, archon,' Razicik replied icily as Nyos's rant subsided into a medley of hissing and hacking coughs. Razicik still carried his sword and pistol from hunting in the catacombs and the incubi had not thought to disarm him. He wondered how quickly he could cross the chamber and plunge the blade into the archon's heart. Pretty quickly, he decided. He sidled a little to one side to get an angle around the table in the centre of the room. As he did so he noticed that there was a gleaming object on the table. It was a crown of dark metal with two points elongated so that they would protrude like horns on the wearer's brow.

'Yess, the crown,' the archon said quietly. 'You can kill me momentarily, but you musst hear of thiss firsst–'

'Oh I don't think so!' Razicik cried, ripping out his sword and lunging forward. To his surprise the archon didn't move, staying seated even as the point of the blade crunched home. The first thrust felt like it didn't penetrate flesh at all, some kind of armour perhaps? Razicik didn't waste time pondering it, he thrust again and again into the unyielding body. The thrill of murder-lust gripped him and he started hacking madly at the figure on the throne until it toppled over with a despairing hiss.

He stopped hacking and started laughing, panting and laughing again as his hands shook with the burst of adrenaline. He'd expected the incubi to come charging in at any second, but they hadn't. Now he, Razicik, was archon and those incubi were his to command along with every other soul in the White Flames fortress. Where to begin? Gifts for his friends and retribution on his enemies would be a good start. He caught sight of the crown still lying on the table. Actually, that was a good place to start.

Razicik picked up the crown and felt its weight for a moment as he marvelled at its workmanship. Doubtless Nyos had intended to pass along a symbol of ancient rulership that would show the kabal that its new leader had his blessing. Razicik laughed again at the old archon's hubris, fancy thinking that kind of thing even mattered any more. Still, as a trophy it had intrinsic value, and wearing it would always remind Razicik of this glorious moment. He slowly placed the crown on his head, feeling himself growing into the role of archon even as he did so. He would be a fearsome archon, fearsome and mighty and… memorable.

Unbearable pain lanced through Razicik's temples, a searing hot whiteness that burned out all thought, all volition except for the need to scream. He frantically tore at the crown but it stayed firmly in place as if it had been welded onto his head. There was a wrenching sensation, deep rooted as though something at the very core of his being was twisted free. If Razicik could have still seen he would have witnessed twisting tendrils of light extending from his eyes and mouth to the fallen corpse of his archon at the foot of the throne. If he could have still discerned sounds he would have heard his own screaming rise to an indescribable intensity before falling suddenly and ominously silent.

The tendrils of light faded away, leaving the chamber in semi-darkness once more. Razicik swayed for long seconds, staggered abruptly but did not fall. He gazed about him uncomprehendingly for a moment and then cursed richly.

'Thank you so much for doing absolutely nothing while the little bastard was stabbing me,' he called out angrily.

The master haemonculus Bellathonis appeared from behind a hanging holding an over-sized syringe full of red fluid in one long-fingered hand and a curious looking helix-barrelled pistol in the other. Bellathonis showed no chagrin at the other's outburst as he hooked the unused pistol back onto his waist harness, if anything faint amusement was playing around the Haemoculus's withered lips.

'I told you from the outset that the best chance for the device to function correctly was for the subject to don it voluntarily,' the haemonculus said mildly. 'I felt it probable he would still do so in his moment of triumph despite his rather egregious diversion off-script.'

'Probable? Have you ever been stabbed, Bellathonis?'

'Many times, my archon,' Bellathonis murmured as he advanced and plunged the needle of the syringe deep into Razicik – now Nyos's – neck and slowly depressed the plunger.

'Well it's not something I enjoy, even with the vitrified flesh,' Nyos Yllithian snarled.

Inwardly Nyos was thrilled to feel his lips and cheeks moving freely again, he grinned, frowned, yawned and snarled again in quick succession. It felt good despite the ongoing ache of the injection. Bellathonis finally withdrew the syringe and looked at Nyos's new face appraisingly.

'I would not have believed it when Razicik first entered the room,' the master haemonculus opined, 'but he really does look like you now. Something about the eyes.'

'A sense of determination and the vaguest whiff of intellect, haemonculus, nothing more.'

Nyos bent down and scooped up Razicik's sword from where it had fallen from his grasp. Having a weapon in his hand felt good too. He thrust it savagely into the fallen body that was now the repository of Razicik's worthless soul. An agonised hiss emerged from it that was all too familiar to Nyos's ears. He bent down to look into the ruined face of his old body.

'Still with us Razicik? Good – I know you can hear me,' Nyos murmured as he slowly twisted the blade. 'Don't worry, you'll master being able to talk again in what little time you have left – or at the very least I guarantee you'll master being able to scream.'

A wretched, hissing burble was all Razicik could manage at present. Lots of room for improvement there, Nyos thought to himself. He left the sword protruding from the body and turned back to the haemonculus with something like appreciation on his face. 'Come with me,' he said simply before turning to press down on one arm of the throne. A section of the wall slid up to reveal another, larger chamber behind it.

'And what of the young pretender here?' Bella-thonis said, nudging the glassy mass with his foot.

'Leave him for now – you can freeze him or

something? Extend his life somehow?'

'Of course, I'll save him for you until you have the time for a proper audience,' the master haemonculus said. He drew forth another vial, of greenish fluid this time, and fitted it into the syringe. Kneeling down, Bellathonis punched the needle into the vitrifying body in several spots.

'Excellent. Now come – I must prepare myself.'

The room revealed beyond was much wider than the first, which was evidently little more than a vestibule to this one. It was so wide that the ceiling seemed low and its corners were lost in shadow. The only illumination came from one wall which was curved and made of glass-like bricks each a metre across laid many courses deep. The view it gave onto the outside appeared astoundingly clear, the light that was filtering in brightened and dimmed anarchically in time with lightning flickering outside. A mismatch of cabinets, divans, tables and other furnishings were revealed scattered rather forlornly around the space in a way that only served to emphasise its shadowy emptiness. What Bellathonis at first took to be ornamental pillars near the wall of glass proved to be a row of gnarled black trees with drooping fronds sitting in metallic urns.

Yllithian began stripping off his garments as he crossed to one of the cabinets. He stood naked as a newborn as he reached inside and drew out fresh clothing of unornamented black. Bellathonis stepped closer to the glass wall to look outside, just like they always did. Yllithian smiled to himself, it was all too easy.

'What do you intend to do with yourself now?' Yllithian asked casually as he dressed himself and watched the potted trees silently extending their fronds towards the haemonculus. 'And be careful of the Black Eloh trees, by the way,' he added maliciously at the last possible moment. 'They bite.'

Bellathonis turned and batted away a questing tendril fondly. 'Oh I'm well aware of the proclivities of the species, my archon. I am greatly impressed by the breadth of your accomplishments – I hadn't taken you for a fellow enthusiast of carnivorous horticulture.'

Yllithian shrugged and waved away the compliment with unconvincing humility as he reflected that he had been right, the master haemonculus was never going to be caught out so easily. 'Only a passion of my great-grandfather Zovas Yllithian,' Nyos told Bellathonis. 'I merely honour his memory by keeping them alive. To be honest they remind me of him a little – grasping and eternally hungry.'

Now that he was closer to the glass wall Bellathonis could truly see outside the spire that formed the White Flames' fortress. The view was astonishing. Ashkeri Talon stretched out far below him, its sharp angles and innumerable jutting spines vanishing off into the distance. The point where it joined the artificial horizon formed by the city's immense docking ring was virtually lost in the gloom yet it still showed as a pale line to the unaided eye. Three kilometres below him the juncture between talon and spire was covered with the leprous districts of Low Commorragh growing over each other like competing patches of fungus. Despite the sweeping curve of the glass wall no other High Commorragh spires were visible from this angle, which was probably the only reason such a structural weak spot had been permitted to exist.

Ordinarily the vista below would be bustling: ships moving to and fro on the docking spines, shipments of slaves being brought into the city and raiding forces heading outward in endless caravan. Now the only things moving were fires burning out of control. In the multi-hued void a thousand more rosettes of flame burned brightly – the hulls of shattered ships being consumed by their own fusion fires as they drifted helplessly. The insipid light cast by the *Ilmaea* over the scene was shifting constantly as if they were obstructed by clouds where no clouds could possibly be. Some part of Bellathonis hesitated to look up to see what was making the fluctuations and he obeyed the instinct, fixing his gaze outward instead.

The shifting veil of the void beyond the wardings was normally diaphanous, sometimes opalescent but most commonly dark with only a hint of shifting, nacreous colour. Now it was vivid and poisonous looking, a storm-wracked sky filled with angry, competing thunderheads of blue and deep green interspersed with spears of flickering, multi-dimensional lightning. The ominous thunderheads seemed to be rolling ever closer, piling up above the height of the spire, above all of High

Commorragh and above the entire city like a frozen tidal wave... Bellathonis realised that Yllithian had stopped part way through pulling on a pair of iron-grey sabatons and was waiting for his answer.

'Forgive my distraction, my archon, the scenes outside are rather... dramatic. With your permission I had hoped to remain in the comfortable, and safe, environs of your fortress for a while.'

'Oh did you now?' Yllithian smiled. 'That hadn't really crossed my mind. I suppose you could always take over Syiin's old quarters temporarily. If I gave my permission, of course.'

'Of course.'

Yllithian lifted a black, glossy cuirass from a stand and fitted around his torso. The armour sighed lightly as it gently enfolded him and moulded itself perfectly to the contours of his body. 'There's been no sign of Syiin for quite some time,' Yllithian remarked idly. 'A curious business, that.'

Bellathonis failed to rise to the bait. Both of them knew full well that Yllithian's previous haemonculus, Syiin, had been murdered by none other than Bellathonis himself. However High Commorrite etiquette, after countless centuries of scheming and backstabbing, had come to eschew outright commentary on such things as a sign of being excessively gauche or obtuse.

'It would seem unlikely that he will turn up again at this point,' Bellathonis mused, still gazing distractedly outside. One of Bellathonis's favourite personal modifications had been to implant a pair of stolen eyes into his bony shoulder blades. By concentrating on a corner of his mind he could enjoy a fully panoramic view of his surroundings and so keep an eye on Yllithian even while he looked out at the destruction. The scenes below were no doubt being replicated a thousand times over around Commorragh. An almost palpable sense of suffering was in the air and Bellathonis found it was most intoxicating.

He stroked another questing Eloh frond under its ventral vein to make it curl up involuntarily as he considered his options. Yllithian was fishing for more information about the clash between himself and Syiin, a line of inquiry that seemed unlikely to be in Bellathonis's own best interests. On the other hand Yllithian could grant security for the immediate future on a whim, or, if it came down to it, he could simply summon a fortress full of retainers to exercise his will. Bellathonis decided it was probably wise to give the archon something.

'It is perhaps possible,' Bellathonis said, 'that Syiin's jealousy over my association with your noble self drove him into a fit of madness, causing him to undertake acts eventually harmful to himself.'

Yllithian was attaching the second of two barbed pauldrons to his shoulders. He pulled on a pair of gauntlets attached to hooked vambraces that covered his arms from wrist to elbow. 'It's true that Syiin seldom seemed to have the best interests of his archon at heart,' Yllithian said. 'I have wondered if his coven had some hand in his disappearance. He was a member of the Black Descent wasn't he? Just like you?'

And there it was. Not a difficult thing to find out, but it proved that Yllithian had been doing his homework. Bellathonis began to worry that he had underestimated Yllithian's resourcefulness. He turned to look at the archon directly. Yllithian was now resplendent in full war armour and vermillion cloak, with a tall helm held in the crook of one arm, a sword at his side and the horned crown on his head. Bellathonis had to admit that he looked every inch an archon. Yllithian's steady gaze held no hint of softness, indecision or mercy as he awaited Bellathonis's answer.

'I parted ways with the Black Descent quite some time ago, my archon,' Bellathonis said carefully. 'It was the subject of some acrimony at the time – a trifling business really. I suppose it's possible that the Black Descent eliminated Syiin in retribution for his association with me. I understand that he did draw your attention to my abilities in the first place.'

Yllithian watched the haemonculus's face carefully as he spoke, trying to judge his veracity through the mask-like distortions of countless surgeries. Not an outright lie, Yllithian thought, but a half-truth at best. Bellathonis certainly seemed to think the Black Descent had some hand in the matter, which was an interesting fact that Yllithian mentally filed away for later examination. Right now more pressing matters demanded his attention, even more pressing than vengeance on the haemonculus that had crippled his former body. The thrice-cursed Supreme Overlord Asdrubael

Vect could not be kept waiting.

'Very well, you have my permission to occupy Syiin's quarters until further notice,' Yllithian said, waving away the haemonculus's grateful bow. 'I must go to Corespur and attend to the Supreme Overlord's wishes. Ensure that you are still here when I return, we will have more to discuss.'

Yllithian ignored Bellathonis's acquiescing bow and stalked out of the conservatory with his cloak billowing impressively. The haemonculus hurried to exit close at his heels – perhaps fearing to be trapped inside the hidden chamber. A sudden thought struck Yllithian as he reached the vestibule.

'What became of the crone's head, Bellathonis? I carried the damned thing to El'Uriaq's banquet as you suggested but I left it there. Do you know where it is?'

'I do not, my archon,' Bellathonis replied just a shade too quickly. 'I could initiate a search for it if you wish, although I fear it will have been destroyed in the Dysjunction.'

Lie. Lie. Lie. Yllithian felt radiantly good, as if his machinatory powers were returning to him in blazing flashes of insight. There was no doubt in his mind that Bellathonis still held the crone, Angevere, within his power. By extension that meant she was still in Yllithian's power too.

# CHAPTER II
## THE MANY BLADES OF ARHRA

MOTLEY WAS THE first to sense something wrong. In truth a sick feeling of disquiet had crept into his belly after the first duel and stayed there. The bloody-handed code of honour of the incubi had seemed somehow laudable within the confines Commorragh, but out in the webway it seemed a very different thing. It was like seeing some predatory undersea creature that can be admired for its deadly beauty in its own environment. When that same creature is removed and examined under the harsh light and differing pressure of the world above it is revealed as something foul and monstrous, an aberration.

The harlequin found himself wondering if the sub-realm of the shrine was really a sub-realm at all, or the dreams of Arhra made solid. What Motley truly knew of Arhra could be comfortably inscribed on a napkin while leaving enough room for a sonnet or two, but he mentally reviewed the little he did know. Arhra, so the legends recounted, was one of the legendary Phoenix Lords that had appeared in the immediate aftermath of the Fall. As the scattered, pitiful remnants of the eldar race struggled to survive in a hostile universe the Phoenix Lords had come to teach them the ways of war.

Different branches of the eldar told different tales of the origins of the Phoenix Lords. Some believed them to be the last fragments of the gods, driven like Khaela Mensha Khaine into taking mortal form to escape the depredations of Slaanesh, the entity that the eldar call She Who Thirsts. Others maintain the Phoenix Lords were the ancestor spirits of the mightiest eldar warriors to ever live, called forth to save their people once more. Yet others believe they were something new, beings sprung from those that lived through the Fall and became something greater. Gods, demi-gods or ghosts, the Aspect Warriors they trained never spoke of their mysteries.

Arhra was known as the Father of Scorpions, and his disagreements with the other Phoenix Lords were said to be deep and vitriolic. The Phoenix Lords preached discipline and caution, a slow rebuilding around the preserved kernel of the eldar of the craftworlds. They foresaw that the heightened passions of war could destroy what was left of the eldar in the centuries that followed. Motley knew that Aspect Warriors learned to adopt a persona, a 'war aspect' that could insulate their souls from the carnage and prevent them developing a taste for it. As with so many other things, the craftworld eldar saw the allure of bloodletting and senseless violence as a gateway for Chaos to enter their hearts and complete their ruination. What Arhra believed was a secret known only to his followers, the incubi.

'Morr, would you tell me more about Arhra?' Motley ventured finally. 'As we're going to his shrine I feel I should know more about him. I've heard what the craftworlds have to say, but I suspect their version may be a little biased.'

Morr snorted. 'I'm sure they portray him only as a fallen paragon, another one of their lessons about the dangers of Chaos. Very well, I will tell you of Arhra as it is told to postulants at the shrine. You may judge the truth for yourself.'

The causeway was slick with slime, its tilted slabs occasionally disappearing entirely into pools of flatulent mud. The lower-lying mists were thicker here. They hung across the path in moist tendrils, and made the trees appear to be flat, two-dimensional images like scenery on a stage. Morr's voice was the only disturbance in the silent marsh as he paced along telling the story of Arhra.

'After the great cataclysm of the Fall the eldar peoples were left scattered and leaderless. Debauchery and hedonism had eroded any form of discipline they had and left little knowledge of how to defend themselves. The eldar survivors were preyed upon by the slave races and driven from one place to another as they wavered on the verge of extinction.

Finally a group of heroes arose who could stand against the enemies of the people. These were the Phoenix Lords the craftworlders speak of, some called them heroes that because they believed them to be reborn of the essence of their dead gods. Asurmen was the first but others quickly followed, including Arhra himself.

'The heroes fought on behalf of the people, and they taught others to fight to protect themselves. Each hero gained a following of devotees committed to their particular style of combat: Asurmen's warriors were fleet of foot and deadly in their aim, Baharroth's hawks took wing and fought from above, Maugan Ra's killers reaped souls from afar, while Arhra's followers learned to fight with the true gift of fury.

'Arhra taught his followers how to direct their fury with discipline, how to harness the power of their rage and strike out with it. Soon none could stand before them. The other heroes quarrelled with Arhra's methods. They wished the people to learn to lay down and take up the role of warrior at need as if donning a mantle, they wished to abandon the peoples of Commorragh and fight only for the craftworlds. Arhra saw that the long fight against Chaos would require true devotion from all of the peoples, not weak compromise for the benefit of a few. He refused to accept the heroes' ideals and went his own way.

'Followers flocked to Arhra's shrines and he tested them for their worth. The weak and corrupt he slew, he taught discipline and martial skill only to those possessed of sufficient fury to stand against him. Where Chaos threatened Arhra always stood against it. It is told that in his final battle Arhra stood alone and without respite through days and nights when the other heroes failed to come to his aid. At last Arhra was pierced through the heart by the dark light of Chaos. What returned to the shrine showed Arhra's face yet burned with an unholy fire that drove Arhra's students into terror and madness.

'When all seemed lost the students heard their master's voice from amid the flames. It bid them to marshal their fury and stand against him, that now was the ultimate test of their discipline. Such was their devotion that they obeyed despite their terror. They slew Arhra's corrupted mortal form and partook of his untouched spirit, taking it into themselves so that the way of Arhra should endure for ever more.'

Morr fell into silence and Motley wondered where the truth lay between the legends told in the craftworlds and those of the shrine of Arhra. Both seemed to agree he had fought against Chaos and fallen to it, but the stories diverged in regards to the outcome thereafter.

It was almost a perfect ambush. The trees had begun to cluster more closely around the causeway as they got closer to the shrine, and they became bigger, and more gnarled with great exposed root systems that arched completely over the path itself in some places. The assailants had chosen a spot that was not so obvious as a passage beneath roots

ANDY CHAMBERS

or through a particularly dense section. When Morr
and Motley came to the natural amphitheatre created by four especially large trees they had already
passed through a dozen similar sites already, and
many better ones for assailants to lurk in waiting so
they thought nothing of it. The spot was unremarkable rather than the perfect spot for an ambush,
and because of that it came that much closer to
succeeding.

Motley stepped lightly along the causeway behind
Morr with weapons out, projecting more confidence than he felt. He was straining every sense,
probing the dark, misty hollows and tree boles
around them. The great black mass of the shrine of
Arhra had vanished behind the trees but he could
still feel its presence, weighty and ominous, ahead
of them. Suddenly as Motley looked forward on
the causeway he caught sight of a darker shape in
the mist. A flicker of movement and it was gone,
but that was more than sufficient for Motley to cast
caution to the winds and shout a warning.

'Look out, Morr!' Motley screamed. As the words
left his lips a rustling and cracking of branches
sounded all around. Four incubi sprang into view,
surrounding them, two dropping from the over-
arching canopy like ugly spiders just as two burst
out from behind concealing barriers of roots with
flashing sweeps of their klaives. The black and
green warriors were upon them in an instant,
their double-handed klaives raised to hack and
slay. Three closed in on Morr while the remaining
one came for Motley with an easy slowness that

176

betrayed his contempt for his allotted task.

As quick as thought the bloodstone tusks affixed to Morr's helm flashed with baleful energy. Spears of ruddy light transfixed one of the advancing incubi and sent them reeling back in the grip of a palsied shiver. Morr lunged forward to strike his incapacitated attacker, but his other two opponents quickly rushed forward and drove him onto the defensive. Klaives streaked through the air back and forth, block and counter, too fast for the eye to follow as Morr tried to hold his ground in the clash.

The fourth incubus hefted his klaive to cut down Motley with a single stroke from neck to crotch. The long-barrelled pistol in Motley's hand spat twice, striking sparks from the incubus's warsuit but not materially impeding his progress. The klaive swept downward in an unstoppable killing blow and Motley seemed to explode into blinding shards of light. The incubus's strike fell on empty air as Motley whirled away from beneath it, entirely hidden for a second by the activation of his Domino field. The incubus twisted his downward cut into a disembowelling swing, the two-metre blade sweeping after the frenetically dancing blur of colours.

Motley leapt upwards and flipped himself backwards over the klaive as it rushed by beneath him. He got an inverted glance at Morr as he did so. Morr was lunging for one of his attackers again, but he had to turn and defend himself as the other immediately came at his back. The two incubi were circling to keep the towering incubus flanked while the third recovered from Morr's opening blast of neural energy. The incubi would overwhelm Morr in seconds once all three came against him at once. Their three klaives to his one would beat down his guard, tear through his armour and spray his life-blood across the causeway.

Motley planted one foot on the flat of the blurring klaive and used it to boost off for a kick into his assailant's face. His soft shoe did no damage at all to the incubus's rigid war helm, but the buffet was enough to disorient the warrior for a split second while Motley leapt completely over him. The harlequin landed behind the incubus's back and spun to tap him lightly on the shoulder. The incubus roared in frustration and twisted to bring his klaive whistling around. As the incubus turned his arm was raised shoulder-high to drag the klaive in its glittering arc. Motley punched into the incubus's armpit with deadly precision, striking for the chink where the armour plates separated for an instant.

The incubus staggered at the seemingly weak blow and the klaive fell from his hands. The warrior reeled for a second more before collapsing back with blood leaking from every joint and seal in his armour. He was a victim of the harlequin's kiss – a simple, deadly weapon unobtrusively strapped to Motley's forearm. The tubular device contained a hundred metres of monomolecular wire tightly wound like a spring. By punching forward the monomolecular filaments were sent looping outward and then instantly withdrawn. If the tip of the wire pierced a target's flesh the unfurling wires would turn their innards into the consistency of soup in a split second.

Motley wasted no time in mourning his opponent's messy demise. He snapped his attention back to where Morr was fighting for his life against the other three attackers. Morr had succeeded in driving one of his foes into the marsh at the edge of the causeway. He was keeping the other at bay with vicious swipes of his klaive in between hammering blows down on the one he had trapped, but his third opponent had recovered and was re-entering the fray. As Morr turned to hurl one last, desperate blow against his foe in the marsh the others seized their chance and leapt forward with klaives swinging for Morr's back. Motley was already moving, his pistol levelling for a shot into the swirling melee that could not possibly change the outcome.

Too late Morr's attackers realised they had been duped. The towering incubus altered his klaive's direction at the last moment and he swung with it, spinning aside with the momentum to bring the deadly blade looping around into the two behind him. The blow was wild and poorly-aimed, either one of the incubi would have dodged or parried it alone. But the two close together, one with reflexes still slowed by neural bombardment, interfered with one another's defences fatally. The hooked tip of Morr's klaive crunched home and wrenched free in a bloody spray. One of the incubi fell back with a partially severed arm flopping grotesquely.

Motley bounded across the intervening space, the pistol in his hands pumping shots into the injured incubus almost as an afterthought. He hoped that

Morr would understand what he was attempting to do and not accidentally eviscerate him with a wild swing. The towering incubus appeared completely focused on his duel and the glittering arcs of swinging klaives bisected the air without cease. Motley angled off the causeway and into the marsh, his light steps leaving no imprint in the quagmire as he ran.

The incubus that Morr had driven back was struggling his way out of the morass when he saw Motley closing in on him as a scintillating blur of colour. His klaive came up defensively and Motley slid in beneath it, creating a small tidal wave of muck as the harlequin skidded inside the incubus's guard. Motley struck faster than a snake, punching his harlequin's kiss up where the incubus's helm met his cuirass – precisely at the point where the weaker neck seal could not resist the deadly, unfurling wire. The incubus's head left his body in a spectacular gout of crimson, the gore-slicked, hair-fine medusa's nest of coiling wire visible for a fraction of a second before it retracted inside the harlequin's kiss.

Motley turned to see Morr hacking at the two remaining incubi with a lethal onslaught of blows. The injured one was struggling to wield his klaive one-handed as Morr relentlessly drove him into his compatriot in an effort to entangle them both. Recognising the danger the surviving incubus ruthlessly cut down his companion without a second's thought. Motley tensed to leap to Morr's aid but then stopped himself. Morr would never accept his help in a one-on-one fight without resentment. Instead Motley forced himself to stand quietly to watch the dazzling storm of blades, allowing himself to enjoy its lethal precision for a moment.

Back and forth the blades swung, tireless as metronomes. Morr's greater size and reach was slowly wearing his opponent down, but Morr, too, was tiring. The frenetic energy Morr had used in defending himself against multiple opponents was taking its toll. His klaive was moving a fraction slower, his parries were a modicum less sure. His opponent sensed the change and settled into a punishing rhythm intended to leach away the last of Morr's endurance. Whenever Morr tried to give ground to buy himself respite his opponent followed up relentlessly. Morr circled to avoid being driven off the causeway and countered with a murderous assault of his own, flinging back his smaller foe with a flurry of blows that used the last dregs of his strength.

Only at the last moment did Motley realise what Morr was trying to do. Intent on Morr, the other incubus had his back to Motley and Morr's assault was pushing him virtually into the harlequin's arms. Morr's blank-faced helm glowered straight at Motley for a moment and then he understood. Motley exploded into action, leaping forward to punch his harlequin's kiss down into the nape of the incubus's neck. The last assailant jerked once spasmodically and collapsed like a puppet with its string cut. An eerie silence descended over the bloodstained scene.

'Sorry,' Motley panted. 'Didn't realise you'd want me interfering in your little duel at the end there.'

'Fair fights are for fools and romances,' Morr grated, his voice still taut with bloodlust.

'But you said before... Well, never mind I suppose,' Motley said. 'I'm just glad there were only four of them.'

'There was a fifth,' Morr stated flatly. 'I do not know why they did not engage us, it would have tipped the odds in their favour.'

Motley recalled the flicker of movement he had seen before the trap was sprung. Morr was right, none of their four assailants had come from the same direction. Someone was still ahead of them on the causeway, between them and the shrine.

'It would seem the odds were already in their favour, my old friend, but no match for us,' Motley preened. 'I'm happy I could be of assistance.'

Morr grunted and hefted his klaive on to his shoulder. He started to walk away along the causeway and then paused for a moment in uncharacteristic indecision. The blank-faced helm half-turned towards Motley.

'I was grateful for your help,' Morr said slowly. 'I have underestimated you in the past. I will not do so again.'

Morr quickly turned and strode onward before Motley could respond. The harlequin trailed after the towering incubus wondering if he had been complimented or threatened, or both. He decided not to ask Morr exactly what he had seen along the causeway, it was unlikely the incubus's visual acuity was better than Motley's own. Aside from that Motley was unsure just how Morr would react if he knew that Motley had caught, just for an instant, the distinct impression of burning eyes set into a many-bladed helm before the mysterious figure vanished into the mist.

IN THE LIGHTLESS pits beneath Commorragh a curious procession was cautiously worming its way through the labyrinth of the Black Descent. A secret master masked in metal led two creatures made of metal. They glided easily through the air at the master's heels like obedient hounds, small for their kind but still as sleek and deadly as hornets. Behind them a group of wracks struggled along bowed down by the weight of cables, tripods and fluid-filled alembics. The secret master leading them, a haemonculus known as Mexzchior, loved the engines like a father – and they were indeed his children, after a fashion.

From his earliest days Mexzchior had developed a supreme fascination with metal in all its aspects, its purity and malleability. He had dedicated himself to finding ways of imbuing metal with life, transforming life into metal and, most of all, teaching metal how to scream.

The two engines that accompanied him, entities Mexzchior designated as *Vhi* and *Cho*, were living beings with spirit, direction and purpose – of that he had no doubt. They represented the pinnacle of his art, part organic and part mechanical. Pain engines of their ilk had been built in many forms by many different haemonculi over the millennia, everything from the unlovely chainghouls of the Prophets of Flesh to the intricate masterworks of the legendary master haemonculus, Vlokarian. Despite this Mexzchior liked to believe that his creations were truly unique.

It was true that there were many larger engines, the segmented carapaces of Vhi and Cho were narrower and shorter than most. They slipped silently through the air a scant half-metre above the ground with their scorpion-like tails curving up to just above head-height. Some had mocked his creations as being puny but Mexzchior had quickly silenced them when he demonstrated the speed and agility gained through their design. Very few of the critics had survived the demonstration.

Mexzchior had configured Vhi closely after the classic Talos pain engine style. Its scorpion tail mounted a heat lance for a barb while its underbelly was a swinging mass of chain-flails, razor-edged pincers and surgical saws. Vhi could burn through bulkheads, burst in doors, crush, maim and disembowel with a fierce glee that was a pleasure to behold. Cho was more esoteric in her outfitting, closer to the Cronos parasite engine in function. Cho attacked its victim's vitality in an altogether different fashion than Vhi. Its weapon were fluted, crystalline devices of sinister import, its armoured shell was covered in bristling antenna and twitching resonator-vanes.

Mexzchior would have been hard put to choose one of his children over the other, but if the great tyrant were to descend from Corespur and demand that one of his engines be destroyed he would have to keep Cho. She had developed a distinctive personality in Mexzchior's mind, subtle and almost playful in comparison to the brash, direct Vhi. Cho was a time-thief rather than a destroyer, a macabre hunter that could drain the very life-essence from its victims leaving them as nothing more than wizened husks.

Mexzchior felt both thrilled and nervous. Thrilled because the intimate secretary had entrusted him with a vital task, selecting him above all the other secret masters. The secretary had ordered him to send his engines into the Dysjunction-wracked city to find a very specific target. A pouch at Mexzchior's waist carried the vital imprint materials that would lead his engines straight to their target. The wracks carried a large supply of the vital fluids and nutrients the engines would need while they undertook their task. When they reached the periphery of the labyrinth they would be refilled and then released. That independence was what made Mexzchior nervous. The intimate secretary's instruction had been very precise, indeed exacting, on the subject once released the engines would operate without assistance as they hunted down their prey.

The intimate secretary had implied that the engines should simply be released into the labyrinth the moment that they were ready. Mexzchior could not bring himself to do that and so he had stretched the secretary's orders somewhat to guide

his children out of the labyrinth before sending them on their way. One last drink and then
they would fly the nest to strike and return. They
would return, he told himself, some engines went
rogue but not his children. They would return to
him with evidence of their success and Mexzchior
would be finally be exalted by the Black Descent for
his true genius.

Mexzchior had briefly wondered who the target
might be before thrusting such thoughts from
his mind. Someone important and well guarded,
clearly, or both engines would not have been
demanded. Ultimately it did not matter whether it
was a personal enemy of the intimate secretary or
a foe of the entire coven, Vhi and Cho would end
their existence this very night.

AMONG THE TRACKLESS paths of the webway warlock
Caraeis paused at a confluence and pondered for
a time. The skein of probabilities was tightening
inexorably but he was confounded by this particular juncture. Each path led forward but only one
of them would bring him to the optimum location in time and space. He reached down into his
satchel and brought forth a rune, releasing it from
his fingers without looking at it first – a forgivable
transgression of Form, so he told himself, under
such circumstances of heightened emergency.

The rune of weaving hung before him again, just
as he had known it would. It dipped and swayed
towards one of the filaments of the confluence, its
psycho-sensitive material reacting to the faint trace

left behind by the dark kin. The rune of weaving had come to his hand so many times now that he felt a special kinship with it, almost as if it guided him personally. The rune drew him ever onward and showed him paths of destiny he had not dared to even dream of. The skeins of fate were tightening to a point where he would be at the confluence of events, the key piece in a great change that would touch the lives of billions.

Caraeis recaptured the rune and returned it to his satchel as Aiosa, the leader of his bodyguards, approached. Beneath his masked helm Caraeis grimaced unhappily. The Aspect Warriors were coolly professional in their demeanour yet Caraeis could not escape the impression that they had been assigned to watch him as much as to watch over him. If their exarch was making a point to speak to him directly it was unlikely to be good news.

'You overstepped your mark with the promises you made on Lileathanir,' Aiosa said without pre-amble. 'Your dishonesty could impugn the honour of the Just Vengeance shrine.'

'There was no dishonesty,' Caraeis replied while carefully keeping his voice even and reasonable. 'I merely made no definition of how swiftly we would return. Naturally I omitted to mention that our first duty would be to return to the council and seek their judgment in the matter.'

'You deliberately misled the Exodites' repre-sentative.'

'I gave her hope. There is every reason to believe that the farseers will accept my proposal for action.

I am confident that it will prove to be the correct course.'

'And if they do not? The Exodites' hope will be in vain and they will perish awaiting succour that cannot come.'

'Such a decision falls to hands and minds other than my own. The council is beyond our questions and fears.'

'Yet you still attempt to manipulate their decision.'

'Of course, just as they, in turn, manipulate our decisions. Everything is manipulation.'

'It sits poorly with me to see you manipulate the people of Lileathanir.'

'They have chosen to hide themselves from the universe. There are limits to how far we can protect them when the universe finds them.'

'That is a harsh judgement.'

'The universe is a harsh place, as we well know and would do well to remember. I must note that you made no effort to intercede at the time, has your disquiet over my words only developed recently?'

The exarch looked at Caraeis silently for a moment, the tall crest and helm she wore lending her an aura of imperious disdain. Not for the first time was Caraeis reminded that in some regards there was but a wing beat between the Aspect Warriors of the craftworld shrines and the incubi of the dark city. Some even whispered that there was common ancestry between the two. Certainly a warrior code bound them both, the assumption of a strength greater than themselves to make them able to endure the terrible things they must do. One of Caraeis's colleagues had opined that the difference between Aspect Warriors and incubi was only one of degree, and that where exarchs entered the equation the line blurred almost completely.

'You should know that I intend to report your actions to the council of seers,' Aiosa pronounced flatly.

Caraeis mastered his voice carefully before responding. 'It is your right to do so. I am confident that they will support my decisions. In the meantime may I rely on your continued protection and support?'

'We will continue to discharge our duties with honour until such time as justice is done or we are recalled.' The response was passionless and robotic, a rote recitation of dogma. Caraeis accepted it as being as much as he could hope to get.

'Then... we must continue on our way. The one we seek is close, the action of capture will be challenging in the extreme.'

'We are equal to the task. Proceed.'

Caraeis turned and led the way into the confluence. The narrow-minded pride of Aspect Warriors was none of his concern. Soon, he thought, very soon his auguries would be completely vindicated.

# CHAPTER 12

## THE DREAMS OF DRAGONS

IN THE ACRID, trembling World Shrine of Lileathanir Sardon, the unwilling messiah of her Exodite people, slept a sleep of pure exhaustion and dreamed of the dragon.

She had spent her energies attempting to cleanse the shrine and set it to some sort of order even though it seemed like a hopeless task. In the end she had settled for concentrating on disposing of the remains she had found. One-by-one she had dragged seven sets of skeletal remains to the edge of a fiery crevasse before carefully rolling them in.

Unlike more 'civilised' societies, Exodites have no horror of death, they live side by side with the raw thews of nature where death is a daily occurrence. The fleshy vessel in which the spirit had resided was of little consequence to an Exodite like Sardon once the spirit had fled. No, handling the dead did not trouble her, but the sight of their terrible injuries did. A handful had seen quick, clean deaths, sheared into pieces as neatly as if giant shears had shut on them. Most were more like the first she had found. They had been crippled and then carved like joints of meat. It sickened her to imagine the pain that had been so gratuitously inflicted upon them.

Most troubling to Sardon was that she had found no female remains. The body of the shrine's worldsinger was missing. Sardon had imagined that it could have been buried in one of the collapsed areas of the shrine, or even that the worldsinger had cast herself into a pit to end her own life rather than fall prey to the children of Khaine. Deep down she knew that neither was the truth. There was a keen sense of loss in the dragon's rage that she had struggled to understand at first, now she believed she understood. The young worldsinger who was present at the shrine when the cataclysm began had been taken. She had been kidnapped and dragged off into bondage by a pack of the most evil, sadistic violators imaginable.

Once the thought had entered her mind it would not leave. Physically and emotionally exhausted Sardon had curled up on a flat slab of fallen stone, shoulders quivering as she allowed herself to weep for wardens and their lost worldsinger. Sleep came as a mercy, her brain finally blotting out the horror beneath a wave of sweet oblivion. But the restful darkness did not endure for her. Freed of their conscious bonds her dreams flew free and became intertwined with those of a greater being. She found herself dreaming the dreams of the world spirit itself.

At first she saw herself lying in a cave, her pale form looking soft and vulnerable amid the black, jagged rocks. The cave was like and yet unlike the World Shrine. This World Shrine was a vast, shadowy space that was old beyond reckoning, older than the stars themselves. Its wall crumbled and fell back to reveal caverns and tunnels beyond that were beyond numbering. The openings stretched impossibly into the distance. Some held glimpses of other places and other times, bright tableaux that formed for an instant and then were gone. Others moved through stately cycles of ruin and regrowth before Sardon's dreaming vision.

Sardon became aware of the invisible conduits of power running through the place, the pulsating life force of the planet whirling past on its eternal loop through the foci spread across its surface. Barrows and cairns and obelisks knit the psychic flow into a lattice, a self-propagating diamond compounded of the spirits of every being that had ever lived and died on Lileathanir. Their essence girdled the world, insulating it from the hostile universe beyond with a psychic shield so dense that no corruption could breach it. The world spirit of Lileathanir had become a mighty thing, the land had become it and it had become the land.

Hubris. Sardon could sense the bitter reek of it everywhere. The world spirit had become mighty, a nascent godling in its own self-contained universe. In its pride it had overlooked the threat from beyond, trusting that its strength in the meta-physical realm would apply in the material realm also. Instead it had been hurt in a way it could barely understand and now it raged with puerile petulance . In a distant corner of the caverns flames licked hungrily as the dragon grumbled and hissed in its slumber. Sardon's dream-self quailed. She did not want to get caught in the dreams of the dragon. Its rage would consume her, burn her to ash like the broken lands beyond the holy mountain. Sardon tried to master her fears, to direct herself and travel through the dream as she had been taught long ago.

Her disquiet made the place she was in even more frightening, solidifying the caverns into drip-ping walls black with moisture. Stalagmites and stalactites crowded everywhere like petrified piles of dung and hanging slabs of meat. Beyond and around them roamed the hiss and whisper of dead spirits, their dry voices rustling horribly on the edge of perception. The billions of dead souls trapped in the Lileathanir matrix flowed around her like smoke, individually no stronger than any single mortal but collectively… Collectively they became the world spirit and a gestalt psychic power capable of so much more.

Sardon found herself before a crack in the weep-ing rock wall, wide and low like the one in the mountainside she'd had to crawl through to reach the real World Shrine. She pushed inside, crawling into the narrowing split towards a chink of light on the far side. The roof and floor pressed so closely together that she had to force herself between them, edging forward with shoulders flat and head turned to one side to get closer to the light. Claustrophobia gibbered at the edge of her dream-consciousness, threatening to send her into a blind panic thrashing against the implacable rock. She stopped, and breathed deep (mentally, at least) to quell the emotion. Finally she wriggled herself close enough to bring her eye to where she could peer through the chink.

Beyond it lay the World Shrine as it had been before the cataclysm, full of light and life. Sardon's point of view was constrained, seeming to come from high up at one moment, then through the eyes of a different Shrine Warden in the next. Every point of view told the same story with more or less grisly detail. Sardon soon became sickened by the violence and tried to crawl away. She found that she could not back out of the crack. The rock seemed to have closed up even more closely and held her as if petrified. She was constrained to watch the violation of the shrine enacted over and over again.

A small group in black appearing suddenly, shifting and barely seen... sharp blades glittering as the Shrine Wardens were butchered like children... The worldsinger captured just as she attempted to take her own life... her limp form carried off through a portal into the webway... and the world spirit, for all its metaphysical strength, helpless to intervene.

It had tried, its attempts wrecked first the shrine

and then the world as it lashed blindly at the attackers. It was all for naught. The perpetrators slipped away into the webway like thieves in the night and beyond the reach of the world spirit of Lileathanir almost before it had perceived them. An entity that had dreamed for aeons was stung into wakeful wrath, and the vengeful fury of the dragon found full expression in that waking. The stones around Sardon's body still shook with the memory of it.

A sinister, imposing figure in all-enclosing armour had directed the dark kin, its red-eyed helm tusked and horned like a beast. It bore a terrible double-handed blade that was the ruin of all who came before it. This one was the last to leave, turning before the portal to sweep its gaze around the shuddering shrine. The burning eyes seemed to look straight at Sardon and the figure spoke with a voice like the tolling of a great bell.

'Only the naïve try to forgive and forget!' the voice roared. 'Arhra remembers.' As the words were spoken the rock holding Sardon began to move, grinding slowly shut like huge, black jaws. She felt a horrible sensation of compression, suffocation and finally... blackness.

Sardon awoke in the hot, foetid darkness of the World Shrine gasping for breath.

'SORROW FELL?' KHARBYR muttered to Xagor. 'Just how the hell are we going to get all the way up there on foot?'

'This one does not know,' the wrack responded

mournfully. 'These were the archon's words, not Xagor's.'

In the baroque, anarchic geography of Commorragh, lowly Metzuh tier was about as far as you could get from Sorrow Fell without disappearing into the pits beneath. Even before the Dysjunction no direct connection had existed between the two districts. The rare physical interactions between their denizens meant chancing a flight through the hostile upper airs or using a well-guarded portal.

'The long stairs might still be standing, I suppose,' Kharbyr said uncertainly. 'If we can find our way up to Hy'kran somehow.'

'This one does not know,' Xagor repeated. The wrack's passivity was starting to irritate Kharbyr immensely. Given even the most basic leadership the wrack seemed content to go along unquestioningly with whatever he was ordered to do.

Led by Naxipael and Bezieth, the small band of survivors seemed to be pushing towards the core. They had left the slaughter faire and taken to the covered streets and wider passageways of Metzuh, occasionally crossing open plazas that were eerily devoid of people and mounting stairways more or less choked with debris. As they moved further from the Grand Canal there was less evidence of intrusion. The bodies they found increasingly showed signs that they had died at the hands of mortal foes rather than twisted entities from beyond the veil.

Always inward, always upward. Kharbyr began to suspect that the archons didn't really know where they were going and were just making a confident show of following their noses. Kharbyr took another pinch of *Agarin* to clear his head, savouring the clean bite of it and the shiver it sent down his spine. The one bright side of recent events was that Kharbyr's pouches were now bulging with looted stimulants and narcotics. If he lived through this he would be rich, or at the very least well supplied. The flat metal pentagon Xagor had given to him still rode inside one of his inner pockets. It had remained dead and lifeless but it gave him a vague sense of protection that he was happy to accept under the circumstances. Touching it made him think of a new angle to take in prodding Xagor into action.

'Xagor, we just need to find a good place to hide until this blows over,' Kharbyr said in what he hoped were his most reasonable and persuasive tones. 'We both have a duty to protect what the master gave me – it simply isn't safe to be wandering around with it like this.'

That made Xagor hesitate for a moment. Kharbyr knew the wrack was dedicated to his master with a kind of pet-like devotion that he found hard to fathom. The very suggestion that Xagor might be in danger of failing Master Bellathonis in some way was enough to give the wrack pause for thought.

'This one is not so sure,' Xagor admitted eventually, 'that Sorrow Fell will be safer for anyone except archons.'

'You see! Now you get it!' Kharbyr hissed. 'If we show up at Sorrow Fell we'll just get thrown back into whatever mess happens next, and the one after that, and the one after that until we're dead!'

Kharbyr shut up quickly when he saw Bezieth look sharply back in his direction. He prayed she hadn't overheard his words – Bezieth was looking dangerously frustrated and in need of something to take it out on by way of diversion. The survivors walked on in complete silence for a time accompanied only by the creaks, crashes and distant screams of the disaster-wracked city.

Eventually Xagor dared to whisper, 'We two are not strong enough to survive alone,'

'I have a plan,' Kharbyr said smugly. 'You just need to stick close and follow my lead when I make my move.'

Xagor looked at him uncertainly for a moment and then shrugged fatalistically. 'Xagor will remain with the master's gift. If need be this one must be on hand to retrieve it.'

'Eh? What do you mean "retrieve it"?'

'If Kharbyr dies, Xagor must retrieve the gift. The master indicated the gift would survive extremely high temperatures, entropic energies and significant crushing forces unharmed.'

'Oh. Thanks for the vote of confidence.'

They had come to another shattered street, this one open above to a view of luridly tainted skies. Needle-fine streaks of fire and false lightning flared on high. Their passage traced battles taking place kilometres up in the air at a distance too great to discern the antagonists by anything other than their weapon discharges. Whoever was doing the fighting it seemed very lively up there, reflected Kharbyr. His plans for just stealing a jetbike or sky-board from somewhere and making off suddenly seemed less appealing. The plan had been vague on the where to go part anyway, but the hostile skies definitely weren't the place to be right now.

The street ahead widened into an open space, a courtyard the width of a parade ground where broken fountains leaked sluggishly across the flag-stones in several places. Three sides of the court held an assortment of tumbled buildings and blocked street entrances. The far side of the court was delineated by an iron-grey wall that rose for half a dozen metres up to a jagged, crenellated top. A good way beyond the fang-like merlons at the top of the wall another sloping face could be seen off in the distance, this one of deeply grooved silver that ran upwards until it vanished from sight. The grey wall had a suspiciously uniform-looking gap running along its base rather than a foundation, and no gate or bridge in evidence. On seeing this Kharbyr suddenly realised at once where they were.

'Latiya's steps,' he muttered to himself. 'It seems our archons knew what they were about after all.'

Latiya's steps were an interconnected series of moving platforms that gave access to the higher tiers of Commorragh around Ashkeri Talon. The stories said that long ago Archon Latiya had been so deathly afraid of flying that she had caused the steps to be built to give herself easier access to the upper tiers. It was a farfetched tale but stranger things had happened in Commorragh in the past, and much worse legacies had been left behind by less mundane phobias. The steps were simply considered quaint and old fashioned in modern times, typically well guarded but seldom used for anything practical. Kharbyr had heard the steps operated by some kind of fluid metal under pressure moving the platforms. He'd never considered that they might still be working.

The survivors moved warily into the open space, spreading out instinctively to present a less tempting target for any lurking snipers. When they were part way across the court Kharbyr spotted a flicker of movement between the crenellations and shouted a warning. All nine survivors vanished behind pieces of shattered stonework in the twinkling of any eye. No matter how skilful a fighter was they all knew that a lance blast or disintegrator bolt could end their life in an instant.

Kharbyr was crouched behind a bitten-off half moon of fountain bowl. Xagor lay a few metres away behind a chunk of fallen rock barely big enough to hide him. The wrack poked out his ridiculous rifle to scan the battlements and Kharbyr watched with interest to see whether Xagor would get shot. Being armed with only a pistol he felt justified in hanging back out of sight for now. Not for the first time he regretted not picking up something heavier back at the processional, but it had looked like a lot of extra weight to be dragging around at the time. Xagor was not shot or even shot at. After a few seconds Kharbyr called softly to the wrack.

'What can you see?'

'Some few heads bobbing,' Xagor said before adding unnecessarily. 'No shoot yet.'

Kharbyr peeped over the rim of the bowl and caught sight of four helmeted heads and gun barrels between the battlements. Nothing bigger than a rifle was in evidence and they were all angled to point at no one in particular – either a good sign or part of a very elaborate trap. Kharbyr ducked back down and checked the streets behind him. A band of warriors (or truth be told even a band of small children) bursting out on them now would put the survivors into a deadly trap. Nothing could be seen or heard in that direction either, but a spot between Kharbyr's shoulder blades that he'd learned to respect in the past still felt itchy. Something was surely amiss. Naxipael stood up in full view and called out in a commanding voice.

'I am Lord Naxipael of the Venom Brood. Who is it that speaks for you? Come down and join us, our strength must be combined.'

There was a pause before a shout came back – not from one of the exposed warriors, Kharbyr noted wryly, but from someone keeping out of sight. He wondered how many more of them were hidden behind the wall.

'Venom Brood is lower courts dreck, you shouldn't even be out of Metzuh,' came the sneering response.

That was interesting and said a lot about the respondent. Not from Metzuh or affiliated with the lower courts, that was for sure. The tier rivalry sounded like something Hy'kranite, they always had special contempt for Metzuh being directly beneath them, just as Azkhorxi had nothing but contempt for Hy'kran and so on all the way up to Sorrow Fell and Corespur. Just as importantly, the hidden speaker didn't feel strong enough to face a petty archon or command him to leave, a fact that was not lost on Naxipael. He laughed cynically.

'You can't come down, can you? You're stuck up there because the controls are locked. Guess who has the key?'

A faint horizontal line had appeared on the silver slope beyond the battlements, descending at a deceptively unhurried pace, thickening and darkening swiftly as it came. Naxipael saw it and jabbed a finger towards the approaching apparition.

'You'd best join me while you still can, you've got company coming,' Naxiapel shouted merrily. 'Or perhaps they'll turn out to be more amenable to using common sense in a crisis.'

Curses and the rattle of armoured figures running sounded behind the wall as the helmeted heads vanished. The descending line had resolved into another battlemented wall, this one gunmetal in colour and lined with warriors. The sharp crack of splinter fire intermingled with the throatier bark of disintegrators indicated that there was going to be no negotiation with the newcomers. The answering fire from their superior location was immediate and intense.

'All right!' the voice shouted with a new edge of desperation to it. 'Help us and we'll join you!'

Naxipael sang out five oddly twisting words and,

after a slight quiver, the whole iron-grey wall began to descend. First the gap at its base narrowed and vanished, while the battlements kept sliding downwards until they became little more than a row of sharp teeth across the courtyard that could be stepped between. Beyond the row Kharbyr could see a dozen bronze and green warriors crouching behind scanty barricades they had thrown up from fallen rubble. The gunmetal wall was still a dozen metres up, the underside of it clearly showing where its risers connected to the grooved slope.

'Everybody on!' ordered Naxipael. The survivors scrambled to obey – except Kharbyr and Xagor. They hesitated for a moment, each looking at the other. This would be the ideal time to split from Naxipael and Bezieth's clique before they got into another pointless fight at bad odds. On the other hand Xagor was right, just two of them left alone on daemon-haunted Metzuh tier might not stand much of a chance.

'You two! Come on or I'll kill you myself!' Naxipael shouted, already waiting at the first row of battlements with his blastpistols leveled meaningfully. The momentary thoughts of escape vanished and Kharbyr ran over to the archon with Xagor close behind. The moment they passed between the crenellations Naxipael called out four words and the iron-grey platform began to ascend. High velocity splinters were tearing chips from the scant cover available on the platform, a dark lance beam flashed and shriveled a warrior along with the stone he hid behind in its awful glare of anti-light.

The distance to the top of the gunmetal wall was shrinking rapidly as their platform rose to meet it. Kharbyr guessed that it had already halved, just a few more seconds and they would come level. Grenades flew back and forth seeding bright blossoms of plasma fire on both sides of the wall. With three metres to go Kharbyr ran forward, dodging and leaping for all he was worth as envenomed splinters and rageing energy bolts hissed around his ears. Two metres to go and he could see their enemies clearly now, Azkhorxi warriors in black and purple, their helms crested with a half moon of silver. Kharbyr rolled aside from a burst of splinters and darted for a point on the wall where a grenade had just detonated on the far side. One metre to go and Kharbyr leapt up, springing nimbly between the sharp teeth and hoping fervently that he wasn't the only one doing so.

# CHAPTER 13

## ASCENSION

THE SCULPTED FACE of the shrine of Arhra rose before
Morr and Motley like a cliff. Tier upon crusted tier
of frowning archways were shadowed by thickly
clustered columns. Steeply sloping flights of steps
interwove among crumbling plinths weighed down
with a wide variety of grotesque statuary. The
shrine was built of darkly lustrous obsidian that
seemed to suck up the light falling upon it. A riot
of foliage was festooned around the lower reaches
of the shrine, a green wave frozen at the point of
breaking across a black mountain. The fleshy looking creepers and bright blooming lianas softened
the brooding edifice somewhat, but their verdant
fecundity contrasted so sharply with the lightless
stone that it lent the whole an alien, intrusive air
that sickened the stomach.

Motley expected some kind of final challenge as Morr approached, but the towering incubus mounted the first steps without incident. The shrine was silent as a tomb, even the natural sounds of the surrounding swamps seemed muted in its presence. The sense of brooding watchfulness he had sensed from far off was overwhelming this close, as though every shadowed archway hid a silent sentinel. As Motley placed his first foot on the steps he felt an empathic chill run up his spine. Passion and murder-lust were etched into the very stones of this place, an echo of millennia of blood-shed and violence being honed to an artform with the kind of depth and clarity that only the eldar race could achieve.

Morr climbed steadily, seemingly confident of where he was going as he passed the first tier of archways and kept moving upwards. Motley forced himself to follow, passing plinths with their crouching beasts and towering warriors. There was a strong preference for low slung, multi-legged monstrosities that Motley assumed were scorpions from different worlds and realities. Some exhib-ited disturbingly humanoid characteristics: hands instead of claws, saucer-eyed faces. Unlike just about every other shrine Motley had ever seen all of the statues faced inward towards the structure itself, rather than out to the world.

Three tiers up and Morr vanished inside one of the archways without so much as a backward glance. As the incubus disappeared from sight a bell tolled once from deep within the shrine, the dolorous tone of it seeming to hang in the still air. Motley hurried up but then paused on the threshold despite himself, poised for a moment between the world of light outside and the darkness within. A cold breath seemed to blow into his face, a thing welling up from deep in the underworld and before him lay only shadows. Motley finally screwed up his courage and stepped inside the archway. No peal of the great bell greeted him, which was a fact he found to be disquieting and reassuring in more or less equal measure.

Within a few steps from the archway the path twisted and darkness became complete, Motley could barely see his own hand when he fluttered it in front of his eyes. The urge to kindle a light was strong, almost overwhelming, and yet it felt as if it would be somehow… profane and unwelcome to do so. An oppressive presence hung in the darkness and some deeply primal part of Motley had no wish to see it revealed. He decided this was a wise piece of counsel and perforce had to feel his way forward as the path twisted and twisted again between pillars. Sometimes the stone beneath his feet was level, sometimes it sloped roughly downward, but never up. The only sounds were of clattering, verminous things that scuttled or slithered amid the shadows, giving way ahead of Motley and trailing faithfully behind.

The sensory deprivation made it feel like hours were passing when it could only be minutes. An unmistakeable sensation began to seize Motley that he was descending into an open grave, a charnel house with no escape. The taint of death was so pervasive it felt as if it were burying him alive. After what seemed an interminable period Motley perceived a faint vertical line of light ahead of him. A feeble spray of photons was manageing to edge past an obsidian pillar and give relief to the inky blackness.

Motley eagerly took a step towards the light before a slight breeze against his face stopped him short of taking another. He looked down. A pit gaped at his feet, a headlong fall into darkness for any that rushed forward at this particular point, complete with superfluous-looking spikes glinting a long way down at the bottom.

'Rather mean,' Motley complained as he sprang across without difficulty and, coming to the pillar he had seen, found himself looking out into a long hall.

The floor was sunken, with steps leading down to it on all four sides. Many of its slabs appeared to have fallen into a chamber below, creating an irregular pattern of smooth-sided pits throughout the hall. Motley was willing to bet they all had spikes at the bottom too. There were many other archways leading into the hall, open mouths of darkness lurking behind a forest of black stone pillars. More massive columns supported a roof that was lost in shadow. The only light came from a scattering of tallow candles on the steps, simple things that would have been in keeping with stone knives and bearskins. In their fitful illumination two things were apparent: First that Morr was there, standing facing away from Motley and towards the far end of the hall. Second, that the far end of the hall was dominated by the enormous figure of what could only be Arhra.

The legend stood easily a hundred metres tall in his many-bladed helm and ancient armour, a great klaive held at the ready to destroy. The statue's gigantic ruby eyes gleamed down from high above, the tiny, moving flames of the candles lending them a frightful semblance of life. Motley paused, unwilling to precipitate any violence by his sudden appearance. He was about to clear his throat to politely to announce his presence when Morr spoke.

'You may enter here, little clown,' the incubus said. 'This is the hall of testing. By tradition it is open to any worthy supplicant. You have already proved yourself worthy to tread these stones.'

Motley stepped into the hall and approached warily. Something was amiss, the incubus's words were edged with bitterness. This was apparently not the homecoming Morr had sought.

'Where are the hierarchs?' Motley ventured.

'Where indeed?' rumbled Morr. 'A worthy supplicant would be received by them in this place, a wandering incubus of the brotherhood would be welcomed here by the hierarchs no matter what shrine he hailed from. For me: Nothing. They hide from me.'

'So… what now?'

'I will go to the inner sanctum and confront them,' Morr said with icy deliberation. 'I'll tear down this shrine stone by stone if I must. Their cowardice insults the Dark Father and proves them unworthy to carry forward his creed.' Morr took a step forward and then stiffened. Within the flicker of a candle flame a figure had appeared in the hall, or perhaps been revealed where it hid in plain sight all along.

A tall warrior in segmented and bladed amour of an ancient pattern now stood between Morr and the statue. The newcomer was armed with the metre-long hooked-tipped double swords that the incubus call demi-klaives, held now loosely at his sides.

'Stay back!' Morr warned Motley. 'Raise no weapon if you value your life!'

Although the incubus barring Morr's path stood perfectly motionless there was a poised readiness to his attitude that spoke of explosive action less than a heartbeat away.

'What's happening here?' Motley whispered. 'Who's that?'

'He has no name for he never speaks. We call him *Drazhar* – the living sword,' Morr said with something like reverence. 'He is the deadliest of our brotherhood, the undefeated, the true master of blades.'

'Not a hierarch then?' Motley asked a little hopefully.

'No. Drazhar has slain hierarchs but he does not claim their place. Some say he is Arhra reborn and yet he slays those who attempt to venerate him. Drazhar exists only to kill.'

Motley made a silent 'O' of dismay. Morr addressed the silent warrior directly.

'Drazhar! You bar my path but you do not attack. Have the hierarchs sent you to keep me from their door?'

A miniscule tilt of the horned helm of the incubus affirmed that he had been sent for precisely that purpose.

'Morr! Don't take the bait!' Motley hissed urgently. 'They want you to destroy yourself. It'd make a tidy solution to a problem they don't want!'

Morr hesitated; the harlequin was right. The hierarchs were against him, and so by extension his whole brotherhood of bloody-handed killers. His life was truly over.

If anything the hot coal of rage he had nourished in his heart for his entire existence burned even brighter at the thought. It was a monstrous injustice for the hierarchs to turn their faces from him when had held absolutely true to the central tenets of Arhra's teachings.

The reek of political expediency clung to the hierarch's actions, or rather the want of any action at all: to punish Morr for destroying his Chaos-corrupted archon would be to fly in the face of everything that Arhra had taught to the incubi – even at the cost of his own mortal existence. To exonerate Morr would send a tacit message to every archon in Commorragh that the day could come when their own incubi bodyguards could turn against them, citing the edicts of a long-dead Phoenix Lord as justification.

The entire relationship of the incubi to the myriad other entities in Commorragh's power structure
would be irrevocably altered in either case, the
brotherhood would be weakened, fractured by the
schisms already becoming apparent. Better if the
problem simply didn't exist at all, then the hierarch's judgment could never be questioned.

'I see it now,' Morr said to Motley. 'To save the
brotherhood I must be destroyed. Not for the sake
of honour or vengeance, but for convenience.'

'Oh Morr,' Motley replied sadly. 'You'll always
find such noble concepts as honour become increasingly rare as you ascend through the ranks. The
pursuit of power virtually requires the abandonment of resolution for pragmatism, cooperation for
coercion and principle for convenience. Sadly it's
the way of these things.'

Morr tore his gaze away from the figure of
Drazhar, still patiently waiting, to regard the slight
figure in motley beside him.

'Now will you please come with me to Lileathanir?' Motley asked somewhat petulantly. 'You did
agree to do it if you survived coming to the shrine
and look – here were we are, surviving.'

After a moment Morr turned back to face the
master of blades. 'Survival alone is not enough,'
Morr said slowly. 'I learned this on Ushant before
I ever saw the wider universe. Life without purpose
has no intrinsic value.'

'You have a purpose! You can save Commorragh
from the Dysjunction!'

'No.' Morr intoned as his blank-faced helm

swiveled back to Motley. The bloodstone tusks of Morr's helm suddenly flared with ruby energy that burst upon the unsuspecting harlequin in a tsunami of red-edged pain. Caught completely unawares by the treacherous strike Motley fell to the flagstones twisting in agony. Every nerve was jangling as if fire raced along it. Paralysed, Motley could only look on with anguished horror as the towering incubus bent over him.

'My path is clear to me now. Farewell, Motley.'

KHARBYR SHOT THE first black and purple figure he saw then ran forward to plunge his blade into another that was leaning over the battlements to shoot. He caught sight of Bezieth hacking her way into a group of three, the gore flying from her djinblade as it sheared through armour and flesh. He just had time to think that they had the numbers over the Azkhorxi before one of them almost skewered him with rifle-blade. He twisted aside from the thrusting point and shot the owner in the face. Murder-lust gripped Kharbyr as he jammed the curved half-metre of razor sharp metal that was his own blade up under the warrior's chin and into their brain. He pulled the blade free in a shower of crimson before plunging it beneath the warrior's chest plate again and again.

Something slammed into Kharbyr's shoulder, instantly knocking the breath out of him. Pain lanced through his nervous system like white fire, ripping a horrific scream from his lungs. Kharbyr wheeled around to see another warrior in black and purple calmly shooting into the melee from a short distance away. Kharbyr's pistol hand shook as if he were palsied, but he raised it and shot back wildly in desperation. The warrior collapsed as if poleaxed – cut down by either Kharbyr's uncertain rounds or someone else's blind shot in the whickering cross-fire. Suddenly it seemed there were no more black and purple warriors left standing. Naxipael's ragtag clique had triumphed again. Kharbyr's knees buck-led beneath him as poison raced through his veins.

Xagor was at his side almost before he could draw breath for another scream. The wrack still laid his stupid rifle down with the most infuriating care before looking at Kharbyr's wound. Xagor's bird-like metal claw clamped onto Kharbyr's shoulder authoritatively and elicited a blistering series of imprecations from him.

'Kharbyr squirms like a child,' Xagor admon-ished. 'Only splinter-kissed, no major tissue loss.'

'Poison you idiot!' Khabryr shrieked. 'I'm poisoned!'

Xagor had produced an ugly-looking metal syringe in his gloved hand. The wrack made a dis-parageing noise as he dug its thick needle around in the wound.

'Bloodsong and sournyl – neurotoxins like faerun, but cheap and nasty,' the wrack said with elaborate disdain. 'Easily fixed.'

The fire in Kharbyr's veins was abruptly washed away as if by a dash of ice water. In the aftermath of it his limbs started trembling and his shoulder began to ache abominably. The wrack sprayed some sort of sealant over the wound to prevent it bleeding.

'Xagor thinks Kharbyr needs to wear armour in future,' Xagor suggested. Kharbyr treated him to a withering look in return.

'Armour won't save you from anything that'll kill outright,' Kharbyr replied through gritted teeth. 'Being quick on your feet will!' It was something of a personal philosophy for him, but it was rapidly assuming the dimensions of a full and comprehensive explanation for his dislike of being weighed down. Xagor made the disparageing noise again.

'Kharbyr trusts his skills too much, skill cannot protect against luck. Fate is stronger.'

The wrack picked up his rifle and hurried off to tend more of the injured. Kharbyr sat up cautiously and looked about him. The meeting of the two sections of the steps had formed another broad courtyard with a row of gun metal teeth across it. To either side broad archways led away into parkland. Judging by the scatter of bodies the Hy'kranii had taken the worst of the casualties in the Azkhorxi attack. The survivors from Metzuh had lost just one of their number, some nameless warrior lay nearby torn in two by a disintegrator blast. The archons Bezieth and Naxipael had a prisoner, or rather an enemy who hadn't died of his injuries yet. Kharbyr edged a little closer to better overhear their questioning.

'Who holds the other steps?' Bezieth shouted, one foot on the prisoner's chest.

'Take a ride up and find out!' the prisoner

managed to spit before his voice rose in a yell of agony. 'I don't know! Archon Jhyree sent us to seize the lower steps from the Hy'kranii.'

'Oh? And why should she do that?' Naxipael asked almost gently. 'Was she under orders from Corespur?'

'Ask him why!' the prisoner shrieked, gesturing towards Kharbyr. Both archons glanced at him with disturbing intensity as he struggled to make sense of the accusation. He realised that the prisoner was indicating not him but a Hy'kranii warrior in ornate armour standing nearby. Judging by his green and bronze battle gear this was a dracon or at least a trueborn kabalite. He was probably the one in charge of the guards on the first step that had joined themselves to Naxipael. The Venom Brood archon arched his brows inquiringly. The dracon, if such he was, shuffled his feet a little uncomfortably at all the attention he was suddenly getting.

'Well?' Naxipael prompted. 'And why is it we should we ask you, Sotha?'

Dracon Sotha shrugged expansively. 'Archon Osxia held the view that Metzuh was already lost and had plans afoot to quarantine the whole tier.'

'Hmm, quarantine sounds like a nice euphemism doesn't it?' Naxipael mused to Bezieth. 'We can safely assume Osxia means "lock it down until everyone inside is dead" by that.'

'Osxia is slippery and has no love for Metzuh,' replied Bezieth, 'but I'll wager there's more to it than our new friend here is letting on.'

The half-forgotten prisoner beneath Bezieth's

heel was laughing, a horrible choking sound as he drowned in his own fluids. 'You should tell them the rest!' the prisoner coughed. 'It's a fine jest and well-deserved.'

'What did you do, Sotha?' Naxipael's tone was icy.

'I did nothing!' the dracon spluttered. 'Osxia sent the word to Vect, I had no part of it.'

'What word?'

'That Metzuh was completely lost and… needed to be purged.'

The prisoner laughed again, blood bubbling from his mouth in a pink froth. 'We intercepted your messenger!' he babbled in a rush of words. 'We sent it upward with an addition of our own and now Vect thinks Hy'kran is lost too. You're all as good as dead!' The prisoner coughed, convulsed and then loudly expired with wild laughter etched on his blood-flecked lips.

Bezieth and Naxipael exchanged an inscrutable glance before stepping away from the corpse of the prisoner to discuss the revelation with more privacy. Kharbyr could guess what they were thinking. If the Supreme Overlord received word that entire tiers of low Commorragh were lost he would activate certain ancient failsafes. These served to lock areas off from the rest of the city with impenetrable fields of energy. Vect had used them before when incursions from beyond the veil grew to the point where they threatened the city.

Assuming the outer wardings held the entities would be trapped, growing progressively weaker as they destroyed all the living creatures capable of sustaining them. When the time was ripe the overlord's forces would re-enter the sealed area and make it a point to hunt down anyone still alive on the not unreasonable assumption that they must have been possessed to survive. Talon Cyriix had met a similar fate back in the day when one of its archons decided that allying with daemons was a good way to overthrow the Supreme Overlord.

That was if the outer wardings held. If they didn't then the sealed areas would become living hells like accursed Shaa-dom – lost forever to the anarchic energies of the void. Would Asdrubael Vect even get the message? If he did, would he believe it? Kharbyr had no clue, but the great tyrant had a well-deserved reputation for ruthlessness that would certainly encompass sealing off whole tiers of the city if he believed they constituted a threat. He caught sight of Xagor returning from tending the other injured, the wrack glared with professional disdain at the corpse of the prisoner as he passed it.

'Amateur talents,' Xagor sniffed quietly as he looked at the archons still deep in conference.

'They got what they needed,' Kharbyr said. 'Apparently word has gone up to the tyrant to seal off both Metzuh and Hy'kran.' Xagor shivered visibly at the thought.

'Lies come easily from dying lips,' Xagor said. 'The master teaches us to return to the same question over and again without death interceding.'

'I'm sure he does, but right now even the

possibility that it's true is enough to kill us all, so in this case I'd take the risk of believing a dead informant.'

'This one thinks it is not his choice to make.'

'You need to think about what the master wants more,' Kharbyr sneered. 'Us caught in the middle of inter-kabal wars or us hiding out somewhere safe.'

'Let this one know when you find that place,' Xagor nodded eagerly. 'Xagor cannot cure whole kabals of clients, too many hurts in each fight.'

Kharbyr gazed up the grooved slope to where the next step lay out of sight. If he remembered correctly the next step was copper-coloured, the one after that was bronze, then silver and then gold for Dhaelthrasz just one tier beneath Sorrow Fell itself. Unconsciously he rubbed at the flat metal pentagon in its hidden pocket again and a thought struck him.

'We're going the wrong way,' Kharbyr muttered to himself. 'We need to be going down, not up.'

'This one does not understand: death above, death below, death wherever we might go,' Xagor half-sang in his flat, monotonous voice.

'Look – the upper tiers are full of kabalites on high alert, the whole place is in anarchy right now and getting mixed up in their fighting is going to be nasty. The lower tiers might get completely sealed off. What's a place that's always in anarchy, even without a Dysjunction?'

'Sec Magera,' Xagor replied promptly.

'That's right, Sec Magera – Null City. We go there and join whoever's strongest.'

'Xenos and outcasts,' Xagor spat with surprising distaste.

'Which is why they'll be concentrating on just surviving, not treachery and revenge like the kabalites are doing. Besides I have friends there that can help us if they're still alive.'

Xagor nodded slowly at Kharbyr's words. 'How to escape without consequence?'

Kharbyr looked over to where Naxiapel was arguing with the Hy'kran dracon, Sotha. Bezieth stood nearby looking thunderously angry. The other survivors from Metzuh and the remaining Hykranii warriors had picked up on what was going on and were clustering around the archons in two discrete groups. The nearest arch into the parkland adjoining Letiya's steps on this tier was less than hundred metres away.

'Now is as good a time as any,' Kharbyr said, tilting his head towards the arch. 'Move that way like you're checking the bodies or something then just walk out quick and quiet. I'll follow you in a moment.'

Xagor immediately sidled off with exaggerated nonchalance, poking and prodding at the fallen Azkhorxi as he went. Kharbyr turned back to where Naxipael and Bezieth were now arguing with Sotha. The followers of both sides were eyeing their opposite numbers resentfully and violence was in the air. Kharbyr started pondering how he could turn that into a big enough distraction to secure his own getaway.

# CHAPTER 14
## THE LIVING SWORD

MORR TURNED HIS back on the collapsed harlequin and took a step towards the colossal statue of Arhra looming at the end of the hall. Drazhar responded instantly, racing forward and bounding over the intervening pits faster than a running Gyfrlion. An instant later he landed before Morr, physically barring his path with demi-klaives held ready to strike. The two incubi stood in frozen tableau like twin colosii with tension crackling in the air. Neither moved, staring rigidly at one another as they locked in a silent battle of wills. Moments seemed to draw into minutes and still neither twitched so much as a muscle.

The tableau shattered into sudden violence without warning. The swiftness and ferocity of the first exchange was too quick to follow with the naked eye, with no hint of who had been the first to strike.

Only glittering after-images were left by the ballet of leaping blades: Morr's klaive licking downward, one of Drazhar's demi-klaives deflecting the blow even as he whirled to unleash a devastating riposte with the other. Drazhar's twin blades hewing, mantis-like, Morr leaping aside to avoid being driven back into a pit.

Motley finally began to regain some control of his treacherous limbs after Morr's paralysing nerve-jolt. He still felt sick to his stomach as he pulled his legs beneath him and shakily stood. The duelling incubi paid him no heed. They were caught in their own universe where there was only Morr and Drazhar, like twin neutron stars whirling around a common axis. Any attempt to interfere in their contest now would be instantly fatal. All hope was lost, Motley was forced to admit, and all he could do was watch the tragedy unfold while marvelling at the deadly skill of the combatants.

Both were masters, of that there could be no doubt. The difference in armaments made the contest one of speed against strength. Even mighty Drazhar, the living sword, could not block Morr's heavier klaive as it swept through its lethal arcs. Neither could Morr match the darting speed of Drazhar's demi-klaives. The battle was constantly shifting, always moving, always dodging among the irregular patchwork of open pits and solid slabs without so much as a downward glance. The footwork and agility alone was breathtaking, the scream of their blades tearing through the air was terrifying.

The fight raged back and forth through the hall, around and across the pits, up to the feet of Arhra and back again. Grotesque shadows cast by the duellists capered and leapt around the walls as if an army of daemons fought through the hall, all eerily silent except for the scuff of armoured sabatons against stone and the soughing clash of blades.

The two incubi broke apart after a particularly furious passage of arms, frozen once again in tableau. Drazhar crouched with demi-klaives held at the ready, one arced overhead like a scorpion's sting, the other pointed unwaveringly at his opponent's heart. Morr's armour was mauled and he dripped crimson from a score of small wounds. The towering incubus swayed alarmingly for a moment and Drazhar rushed forward to deliver the coup-de-grace against his weakened opponent... and almost lost his own head in the attempt. Morr's klaive hissed forward faster than a striking snake. With an unbelievable twist Drazhar caught the hurtling klaive on both of his blades and was physically driven back, heels scraping, across the stones.

But that was the last of Morr's strength, a last gasp. His recovery was slow and sloppy as Drazhar – relentless as ever – came bounding straight back onto the attack. The demi-klaives rained down like a hammer on an anvil, sparks flying as Morr's klaive swept aside each attack in turn, but each defense was a little slower now, a little weaker as Morr's lifeblood drained from him, and with it his prodigious strength.

Motley saw the death blow coming in the most

vivid detail, unfurling with agonising slowness. Morr's klaive hooked out too far to return by Drazhar's first strike, the second strike coming as an uppercut. The hooked tip of the demi-klaive gleaming as it curved up in a perfect parabola and caught Morr beneath the chin. A flash and Morr hurled back as if he had been launched. Morr landed at the edge of a pit with a crash, his shattered helm spinning away into the darkness, his klaive skittering across the flagstones as it fell from nerveless fingers. Drazhar leapt on his fallen enemy, his merciless blades raised for a decapitating strike. Motley covered his face with his hands and turned away, unable to watch what would come next.

*To live as a true eldar is to live on a knife edge, to live as an archon is to live at the very point of the knife.* Yllithian repeated the catechism to himself as he mounted the steps to the landing field at the top of the White Flames' fortress. So the insufferable tyrant Vect had summoned him like a slave – Yllithian would go and brazen it out like the pureblooded Commorrite that he was with a smile on his face and murder in his heart. Survival was important now, survival so that he could set about wreaking the most consummate revenge.

Yllithian had ordered the seneschal to assemble all the warriors and auxiliaries that could be spared from the immediate defense of the fortress. Without counting his personal barque it came to just five Raiders full of warriors with an untidy mix of scourges, hellions and reavers to escort them. It was a substantial enough force for a time like this, but certainly not enough to rescue him from Corespur if Vect knew more than Yllithian hoped he did. Then again, the Supreme Overlord was always careful to ensure that no single force in Commorragh could hope to assail Corespur under the best of circumstances. The White Flames' fortress, mighty and storied as it was, was nothing more than a child's model in comparison to the enormity of the Supreme Overlord's demesne. The forces on hand would have to suffice.

Looking over the warriors Yllithian noticed a certain air of reluctance about them – downcast eyes, backward glances, a nervousness that was readily spreading to the undisciplined hellions and reavers. He thought it appropriate to address his retinue and remind them of their obligations so he raised his voice so that it would carry to all of those assembled.

'Hear me! Our city is in peril and our Supreme Overlord calls for our aid in setting all to rights – as well he should, knowing the power of the White Flames! We go now to Corespur to hear his counsel and accept his just commandments. Now is not a time for fear, now is a time for strength and rigor of the highest order, any who stand before us are abominations to be destroyed, any who fall along the way are lost. Now I bid you by my lawful command as your archon and master in all things, obey me now or I shall end your existence before you take your next breath. Look up! Look up and gaze upon what we must overcome ere we reach our destination this day!'

As one they looked up into the hellish, vaulted skies over High Commorragh and beheld a scene from nightmares. The *Ilmaea* were weeping black tears. The stolen sun's ragged coronae flared with multi-hued energies from beyond the veil and dripped foulness. The suns gazed down from the heavens like monstrous burning eyes in whose awful light there could be seen twisting clouds of their pinioned offspring. What could be glimpsed of the warding beyond the now twice-stolen suns was a vivid riot of colour: thick brush strokes of blue and purple clashing against swirls of jade and emerald, lugubrious clouds of grey and brown swelling out of nowhere only to be dispersed by flickering storms of blue-white static.

Another storm was about to break upon them. Etheric energies crackled through the air, ghostly fire danced on pinnacles and livid thunderbolts made the whole fortress quiver with their impact. Harsh cries and screams were carried on the rushing winds, alien tongues crying out in languages that were forgotten before the eldar race ever took to the stars. Yllithian gazed upward without fear and noted with pride that his kabalites obeyed promptly and without question. A few individuals had fallen to the ground convulsing horribly at the sight, it was true, but they were weaklings best disposed of now before they failed him later.

Satisfied, Yllithian stepped aboard his personal barque, a singular grav-craft of quite stunning beauty. Its fiercely jutting prow was inlaid with ruby and alabaster depicting the icon of the White Flames. The graceful lines of the barque's narrow hull swept majestically backward from the prow before flaring to accommodate pods containing gravitic engines at the rear. Yllithian mounted the open platform at the centre of the barque and settled himself into a richly appointed throne. His incubi bodyguards moved to take their positions at long-throated splinter cannon and disintegrators ranged on mountings along the barque's bulwarks. At a nod to his steersman Yllithian's craft smoothly ascended from the landing field. A swirl of Raiders, scourges, jetbikes and skyboards rose below his craft and swiftly oriented themselves around the barque. Yllithian gestured again and the barque shot forward like an arrow released from a bow.

The jagged landscape of High Commorragh lay before them, its dark towers, bladed spires and sharp-spined steeples pushing upwards in mad profusion. Fires were burning in many places, the winds pushing dirty streamers of smoke outward like tattered banners. Partially collapsed towers and ruined manses jutted out of the haze like broken teeth. Here and there the flash of weapons fire lit the darker recesses between mountainous spires. Vicious battles were being fought, no doubt, neighbours exorcising their pent-up frustrations and ambitions against neighbours, kin set against kin. Some of Yllithian's own allies were fighting down there, but in comparison to the awesome energies roiling overhead their squabbles seemed petty and inconsequential. Yllithian and his retinue swept implacably onwards across Sorrow Fell.

Yllithian indicated for his steersman to climb higher to avoid weapons fire striking at them from below. It was a calculated risk to accept the greater odds of lightning strikes and flying daemons coming against them but Yllithian knew all too well the awful accuracy and potency of the armaments in use by the warring kabals. He would take his chances with daemon claws rather than suffer his meagre force being gutted by a burst of well-directed lance fire from ambush. As they rose thunderbolts smote the air with retina-burning strokes of raw energy all about them. The crash and roar of the storm shook every cell in the body, jarred the skeleton and made the ears quail at the unleashed violence. There was blinding flash and a pair of hellions simply vanished, their racing skyboards instantly smashed into flaming fragments falling away from the formation.

Yllithian's retinue raced on through the tumult, throttles open to the maximum and engines screaming. A reaver was transfixed by another spear of lightning, its power plant detonating instantly in a silent blossom of orange fire. A sleek-hulled Raider was struck and dropped away trailing smoke and flames. Tiny, flailing bodies spilled from its deck as its steersman fought for control. The Raider disappeared amidst the jutting spines and towers beneath with no sign of recovery.

Yllithian's retinue began bobbing and weaving instinctively – as if they could somehow spoil the aim of the random discharges. Yllithian rebuked his steersman for his stupidity while inwardly reflecting that he had personally experienced artillery barrages that were less terrifying in their intensity. The untutored mind always refuses to believe that it cannot somehow avert the random strokes of fate. Yllithian had taught himself better than that. His barque had inbuilt force fields that would shrug off the lightning if he had the misfortune to be struck. His only concern, and it was a slight one, was that a sufficient fraction of his force would survive the ordeal to be of use to him in what was to come.

BELLATHONIS MADE HIS way down through the White Flames' fortress quite openly. He leaned on Yllithian's patronage shamelessly to get him past the obstructive incubi, paranoid warriors and overly-inquisitive trueborn that he encountered along the way. The mere mention of the archon seemed enough quell any desire to impede him, so it was really all quite gratifying. The lower reaches of the fortress were in a shambles. Fewer and fewer White Flames kabalites were to be seen, and those that were flitted cautiously through the shadows. The smell of burning was everywhere and Bellathonis came across occasional bodies scattered through the twisting corridors and deep cellars. Psychic phenomena began to manifest as he went lower still: walls that wept crimson tears, hazes of frost and oily mists that muttered and sang in alien tongues.

Bellathonis sighed and finally resigned himself to draw his own weapon. It was something he ordinarily felt was almost demeaning to do, a sign of poor planning. He consoled himself that the circumstances were far from ordinary. Yllithian had bid him take up residence in Syiin's old quarters in the pits but Bellathonis found himself rapidly souring on the notion. Who knew what half-finished experiments and maddened, uncaged grotesques roamed free in Syiin's little kingdom? Before Bellathonis could venture into the pits he would need reinforcements of similar ilk.

Coming to a decision he turned aside down a little-used stair at the next junction. The narrow stair twisted tortuously towards one of the fortress cisterns, a lapping subterranean lake of ooze and foulness. Within that chamber, Bellathonis knew, lay a certain alcove containing a hidden door that would take him beyond the confines of the fortress. It was a risk, but certainly no greater than counting on the obedience of Syiin's surviving wracks to the murderer of their master.

Bellathonis paused at the archway into the cistern, listening intently for any sound that might betray occupants. He heard nothing but the slap of wavelets against stone and stepped cautiously within. Piers of mottled rock reached out over a vast black expanse that was barely visible in the dim light. Countless identical, featureless alcoves etched the walls to either hand. Bellathonis counted his way along to the alcove he and Yllithian had used to enter the fortress after he had discovered the White Flames archon dying of the Glass Plague in the tunnels below.

The Haemoculus slid one long-fingered hand along the apex of the alcove until he found a series of tiny projections almost impossible to distinguish from the surrounding stonework. As he was about to press them he caught a flicker of movement in his all-round peripheral vision. He focused on it without turning by giving full attention to the eyes implanted into his shoulder blades. He saw two tattooed eldar no more than a dozen metres away creeping silently towards him. They were naked save for fanged helms and scaled loin cloths, their limbs and chests covered by spiralling rows of tooth-like dags. Their bare feet made not a whisper of sound as they advanced and both clutched poison-streaked daggers that promised a quick death with a single scratch. These must be the Venomysts that the guards in the upper part of the fortress had warned him against.

Bellathonis lowered his arm and turned slowly to face them, clearing his throat as he did so. The two Venomysts froze like statues as if their immobility would somehow render them invisible.

'I really have no argument with you,' Bellathonis said reasonably. 'By all means run along and go find yourselves some White Flames to kill.'

One of the Venomysts glanced minutely to the other one for guidance. Bellathonis raised his pistol and shot that one first, his spiral-barreled stinger pistol emitting only a slight hiss as it punched a toxin-filled glass needle into the Venomyst's chest. In the twinkling of an eye the Venomyst's tattooed flesh swelled outward like a balloon, expanding around the wound site to become a sphere that encompassed the unfortunate eldar's entire body. There was a creak of straining skin and then a snap as the flesh-balloon popped messily to shower his compatriot with gore.

'That one was a compound called Bloatwrack, boring but effective and… so very quick! You might want to run now,' Bellathonis suggested as he levelled his pistol at the second Venomyst. To the haemonculus's surprise the Venomyst did nothing of the sort, instead hurling his dagger with deadly accuracy. The stinger pistol fired almost accidentally, Bellathonis's reflexive shot zipping off into the darkness a hand-span from the Venomyst's masked face. The haemonculus tried to dodge the spinning blade but he was no wych gladiator that could pluck knives from the air. The dagger took him in the shoulder, provoking a curse of mixed pain and surprise.

The surviving Venomyst took off running, his bare feet slapping on the stones as he disappeared into the gloom before the haemonculus could fire another shot. Bellathonis gritted his teeth and concentrated on pulling the dagger from his shoulder. He had to admire how quickly the lips of the fresh wound were blackening. The Venomysts may have lost their sartorial sensibilities but they lived up to their name when it came to poisons. He tasted the blade tentatively with his black, pointed tongue and grimaced a little. It was a necrotising soporific, something intended to make you lie down and quietly rot to death. A composite toxin, one with overlapping effects and probably some unpleasant surprises that were only activated by trying to use the appropriate anti-venoms.

Bellathonis's gaze swam alarmingly and he dropped the dagger to brace himself against the corner of the alcove in order to avoid falling. The blade striking the stone echoed weirdly in his ears, a stretched and dream-like ringing. The haemonculus tried to summon the will to reach up and trigger the latch to the hidden door, but it suddenly seemed horribly far away.

FREE TO CHASE and hunt at last, the terror engines Vhi and Cho found their way up from the pits into a region known as Splinterbone. Their exit brought them out into the flow of an acid-green subterranean river that wound its way around and through the outermost districts from the Corespur. The engine's implanted memory engrams told them that this would serve as ideal cover for an approach and the quickest route to their prey's immediate vicinity. The river's twisting course was shrouded in darkness and hung with toxic clouds as it slipped beneath arches and through ducts between a series of chambers and atriums that had long since been abandoned by all but the desperate and the wretched.

The two wasp-like engines sped along just above the river's toxic surface, the imprint of their gravitic impellers leaving perfect V-shaped wakes behind them. The psychic scent of the prey was weak at this point, but it exerted a definite tug on the engines' narrow consciousness. Right now the faint spoor could belong any one of the millions of lifeforms detected in the direction the engines were taking. As they drew closer the trace would intensify to the point where they would discern their target as an individual, track its movements and discover its lair. All this was pre-determined, a set of absolutes imprinted into their higher cortex functions that was as inescapable as death itself.

But they still had autonomy, that most precious of gifts to automata. Cho wove back and forth happily on the spurious justification of testing attitude controls. Vhi aggressively probed the surrounding sub-strata for information nodes and test-fired its weaponry with joyous abandon at anything that moved. They remained unimpeded in their progress, flashing past a few shattered grav-craft that were drifting lazily in the flow but finding all to be devoid of detectable life signs. Vhi detected ongoing seismic damage to the surrounding structure and advised abandonment of the projected route, citing a high probability of blockage. Cho resisted the proposal, citing the enhanced speed achieved by following the river course as far as possible. Vhi agreed and the pair swept onward together towards Ashkeri Talon.

Vhi and Cho were soon cruising slowly through the ruins of Lower Metzuh, crossing and re-crossing the psychic spoor they were seeking. The source was close, or had been close to this area in the recent past yet there was confusion in the readings. Cho was the more sensitive of the two and could detect recent indicators that were an acceptable match for their target. Vhi had found older traces that matched the parameters exactly, but that were quickly lost as they entered the vicinity of an uncontrolled webway juncture. They argued silently about their findings, Vhi being quickly overthrown in his proposal to enter the juncture due to the poor probability of re-acquiring the trace on the other side.

Cho fluttered vanes and sensor rods in agitation. Logic dictated pursuing the most recent traces of the target but Vhi stubbornly refused to accept the validity of Cho's findings. Vhi proposed backtracking the trails he had detected for further investigation while Cho advocated pursuit of the existing traces before they became diffuse. No precedence had been placed on accuracy over expedience, only blanket elimination protocols applied and so the two engines found themselves to be deadlocked.

After a few moments of drifting silently in cogitation Cho proposed the solution of exercising the autonomy they had been granted to the fullest. They would split up: Vhi would follow his trace, Cho would follow hers. In the event of both trails leading back to a single lair they would combine their efforts to eliminate the target. In the event that one of the targets was found to be a false positive it would be eliminated and the engine responsible would rejoin the other as quickly as possible. Cho advocated this as the absolutely optimal solution to the problem.

Vhi pondered the proposal for a considerable time. Core combat algorithms warned of the undesirability of force dispersal, yet a line of reasoning that might be termed 'experience' or 'confidence' in a living organism encouraged Vhi to accept Cho's proposal.

The two engines went their separate ways, Cho nosing deeper into the wreckage beside the Grand Canal while Vhi followed the psychic trace he had detected aloft. The trail had been confused and muddied by the events in the city but Vhi was drawn upward as if by invisible threads. Vhi experienced a rush of conflicting data that a mortal creature would have described as 'excitement'. The hunt had become a contest between the two engines each following their own course to success or failure. Their beloved creator would be proud.

# CHAPTER 15

## THE QUALITY OF MERCY

SECONDS PASSED AND Motley heard nothing. No final curse from the fallen incubus as his doom descended upon him, no meat slicing sound of Drazhar removing Morr's head for a trophy. The harlequin peeked between his fingers cautiously. The scene before him was virtually unchanged, Morr lay on the flagstones, with his helm-less head and one shoulder dangling over a pit, his great klaive out of reach. Drazhar was now poised above him like a great, armoured mantis with his demi-klaives crossed at Morr's throat. A simple twitch of the wrists and Morr would be decapitated in an instant, yet the twin blades were held back, unmoving.

After a long moment Drazhar slowly withdrew his demi-klaives and straightened. He took a step back, still regarding Morr, nodded curtly and turned away. Within a few steps the master of blades was lost in shadows, vanishing into the darkness as if he had never existed. Motley darted to where Morr lay, hope blossoming in his heart as he saw the towering incubus was still moving. Unmasked, Morr's pale face turned to Motley with anguish written in every line.

'Even honourable death is denied!' Morr snarled. 'Defeated by the master of blades who leaves none alive, yet he leaves me to suffer in my shame!'

It was an old face, lined and scarred by countless conflicts. Lank, pallid hair framed a strong visage with a sharp jaw line jutting pugnaciously below fierce dark eyes. The passions that had always lurked behind his blank-faced helm now blazed forth like a living thing.

'No!' Motley snapped. 'Drazhar shows more wisdom than you do. He sees that you still have a greater role to play even if you will not accept it! You said that Drazhar defies the hierarchs, slays his venerators and does as he wishes, witness him doing just that by sparing your life – he found you worthy, Morr! Worthy to live and play your part!'

Morr fell back with a groan, fingers clawing at the floor in his anguish. To live, reflected Motley impertinently, after being so resigned to death must be a great inconvenience and perhaps the thing requiring greater bravery. From deep in the shrine a bell tolled once, twice, thrice, the deep, rich tones rolling one over the other. The vibrations seem to emanate from the very stones beneath their feet. Motley cocked his head to one side, wondering what the tolling meant, swiftly concluding that it was probably nothing good under the current circumstances.

One of the fat tallow candles on the steps guttered and expired, the shadows crowding closer about them. Many of the candles were out now, Motley realised, only a handful of them still illuminating the hall.

'Morr, I feel your pain but I really think it's time for us to leave now.'

Morr levered himself painfully into a sitting position, elbows on knees and face in his hands. 'Why?' he said. 'Why leave this place now? I should remain until I starve to death. It would be a fitting end.'

Another candle expired. The shadows deepened further. The great statue of Arhra was now only a menacing shape in the darkness. Motley sensed the vaguest hint of movement at one of the many archways that entered the hall, and then another. Red eyes glittered back at him from the blackness beyond the arch.

'A pointless ending, an unworthy one!' Motley cried as he tried to look in every direction at once. 'Also quite possibly not an option – look! Drazhar might feel himself strong enough to defy your hierarchs, but they still want you dead and they send others take his place!'

There were pairs of red eyes within the shadowed archways all around Morr and Motley. The cruel, pitiless gaze of the incubi surrounded them. Morr rose unsteadily, snarling at Motley when he attempted to help. Even without his tall helm the incubus towered head and shoulders above the slight harlequin, a grim spectre in his riven and bloodstained armour. He gazed around the hall with contempt blazing from his eyes.

'So, now you come to offer me at the idol of Khaine?' Morr muttered to himself, swaying as he bent to retrieve his fallen klaive. 'You would burn me like a failed supplicant?'. The incubus seemed to draw strength from his grip on the weapon, straightening with new defiance etched on his face. Another candle guttered and went out. There were only three candles left now, three wan pools of light in a sea of darkness.

'No, Morr!' implored Motley. 'We have to leave! Is this how you want to be remembered? Struck down in your own shrine to no purpose when you could have saved billions?'

Morr hesitated for a moment and glanced at Motley uncertainly. The agony of indecision was writ large in his face. Another candle went out, leaving long shadows between them as Motley pressed his advantage unmercifully.

'Because I'll make sure of it,' Motley whispered venomously. 'For all the centuries to come I'll make sure that everyone will remember Morr only as the incubus that failed. He failed his lord, failed his shrine, failed his people!'

Morr roared and swung at Motley, the klaive hissing through the air between them. Motley negligently stepped back out of reach, theatrically stifling a yawn as he did so.

'In the state you're in you can't even fight, look at

you! You can barely lift that oversised butcher-blade you're so fond of,' Motley said sardonically. 'Have you survived a battle with Drazhar only to fall to lesser blades this day? Is that honour? Is that the perfection you've spent your whole life pursuing?'

Morr's klaive paused. Motley's stinging darts had drained the rage from his face, leaving only hollow-eyed emptiness and pain in its wake. The towering incubus lowered his blade and looked around the darkened hall as if truly seeing it for the first time. Implacable red eyes glittered at him from the shadows, jackals closing in around a wounded lion.

'No,' Morr grated. 'This is not the perfection I sought.'

'Then come with me now and we'll make a worthy legend of you yet!' Motley said passionately. 'And future generations will marvel at the path of the incubus and the strength of Morr who stayed the truest to Arhra's teachings – the most perfect killer of all.'

Another candle flickered and died, leaving only one feeble puddle of light to hold back the encroaching darkness. Morr turned slowly to face the monstrous statue of Arhra, almost invisible now in the gloom save for the malevolent gleam of its ruby eyes. The bloodied incubus raised his klaive in solemn salute to the apparition.

'I understand your lesson, master!' Morr cried aloud, his harsh tones chasing echoes from the walls. 'I shall carry your word to where uncorrupted ears will hear it. Your ways will not be forgotten by the faithful. This is I swear to you!'

Morr lowered his klaive with something of his old precision. The red-eyed shadows of the incubi were closer now, ranged all about Morr and Motley in the dying light of the last candle. If the incubi heard Morr's words, approved or disapproved of them, they gave no sign. The razor-edges of their klaives glinted with sinister intent.

'Do you have a plan, little clown?' Morr said quietly.

'It's your shrine so I was rather hoping you had one,' Motley replied softly.

'Then we will die together,' Morr said with grim finality. 'The hierarchs will not permit you to live after what you have seen and heard.'

Motley could almost swear that Morr sounded happy at the prospect.

ARCHON YLLITHIAN HAD made it his business to understand what kind of monstrous entity he, Kraillach and Xelian had allowed into Commorragh. In the months after raising the thing they initially believed to be Vect's deadliest old enemy, El'Uriaq, Yllithian had applied himself dilligently to finding out just how deep a pit he had dug himself into. The study of the void had always been something of a passion for him and he had thrown himself into the pursuit with a renewed fervour that even his jaded peers found almost unspeakably perverse. For Commorrites the forces of Chaos were something best viewed from the corner of the eye, something to be denied and ignored as much as possible. Much as a race of clifftop dwellers might try not to address too much thought to the mechanics of plunging to their own death, Commorrites tended to confine their thinking rather to ways to avoid such a fate than the details of it.

Not so for Yllithian, and his knowledge had kept him alive as El'Uriaq destroyed Xelian and Kraillach. Yllithian had gazed into the Sea of Souls and come to understand the limitless power that lay there, and something more of its monstrous perils. He had also come to understand more about its denizens – at least as far as the manifestations of madness and terror that the daemons represented could be understood by a coherent mind. Thus he knew that the daemons would be coming for them soon, unable to resist the bright sparks of the eldar souls flickering past so close below.

The Dysjunction was an awe-inspiring example of the power intrinsic to the warp, a terrifying demonstration of the forces surrounding Commorragh. Yllithian had sought out such power all his life and now he saw how it had always surrounded him: vast, untameable and unattainable. Even so, it had been Yllithian's schemes that had unleashed the current cataclysm upon Commorragh. He had forced Asdrubael Vect to summon his archons and engage his wicked intellect solely in defence of the city for a while. Yllithian smiled to think of the opportunities that would open up in the immediate future. New territories could be claimed, rivals eliminated and vendettas slaked under the guise of executing the Supreme Overlord's orders. With all that Yllithian knew there was a chance that he could do something to stop the Dysjunction, but the more he thought on it the more he could see no reason to do so.

Between the crash of thunder the shrill cries on the wind became louder, more excited. Yllithian's incubi bodyguard swivelled their weapons back and forth as they scanned for the source, the long muzzles of their cannon hunting the skies relentlessly. There! A twisting funnel descending towards them, a mass of dark-winged specks dropping from clouds the colour of bruised meat. Streams of hyper velocity splinters and darklight beams from Yllithian's retinue converged on the approaching mass and blocked it as thoroughly as if an invisible wall had been thrown up in its path.

In the daemonic hierarchies, Yllithian knew, these manifestations were little more than vermin, lesser entities that were slipping through the connection between the Ilmaean sub-realms and Commorragh itself. The great, open portals that ordinarily allowed the wan heat and illumination of the stolen suns to filter down on the city had become porous under the strain of the Dysjunction. The etheric energies leaking in around the Ilmaea sustained these lesser daemons in great flocks. Yllithian was gambling that they could not stray far from the stolen sun's immediate vicinity for long without becoming critically weakened.

Yet more dark shapes were descending on all sides, wings beating frantically as they closed in on the flying White Flames Raiders and their escorts. Most of the assailants were twisted, naked humanoids that were winged and clawed in varied fashion. A great many appeared as vast, bloated flies, darting eel-like worms or other less easily identifiable creatures. Yllithian's kabalites kept up a withering fire as the hordes approached, bursting daemons like overripe fruit wherever their shots struck true. The Raiders pulled tightly together to intensify their firepower, while the scourges, hellions and reavers snarled around the periphery in a defensive wheel. The daemons ploughed into the barrage of fire relentlessly, utterly careless of their casualties in their attempts to reach the succulent souls they could perceive.

Now the hellions and reavers were fighting hand to hand against the first wave of attackers, their hellglaives and bladevanes against fangs and claws as the daemons tried to drag the escorts from their mounts. Yllithian saw a hellion plucked from his skyboard and borne aloft to be torn apart in seconds, he saw winged scourges plummeting in a death grip with what seemed their own dark reflections, reavers being buried beneath leathery wings. He stood from his throne and drew his sword. His gamble wasn't working, the daemons were too strong, the skies were still black with them.

Shrieking, bat-faced entities dived on the Raiders and tried to seize their occupants. Yllithian slashed at reaching claws and fanged faces as they flashed past. Several of his incubi were forced to abandon their cannon and take up their klaives to defend themselves as daemons clawed their way across the bulwarks and onto the fighting platform. Yllithian led a charge to clear the deck and the twisted entities' croaks of triumph soon turned into shrieks of alarm. Yllithian paused in the slaughter long enough to snap an order to his steersman.

'Activate the shock prow!'

The curving, armoured prow of Yllithian's craft instantly crackled with power, fat sparks dripping from it as it projected a directional wave of electromagnetic force ahead of the racing barque, an atom-splitting ram-blade of force. Daemons caught in the path of the ram decohered instantly, exploding in bright webs of lightning as it plowed forward relentlessly through the infernal flock. Shrieking daemons wheeled aside only to be caught in the Raider's crossfire and torn to pieces. Yllithian permitted himself a self-indulgent grin of triumph, the shock prow was a recent addition made at his own instigation after recent events. He was gratified to see it working so well.

Suddenly they were breaking through the clouds of flying daemons as the defeated remnants fluttered upward. Sorrow Fell was spread out again before them, its light and spires seeming earthly and welcoming after the horrors of the skies. Corespur reared up in the distance as a dark, jagged mountain lit only by the flashes of thunderbolts.

A hazy ring of green light surrounded the base of the promontory that formed Corespur. In its poisonous illumination thirteen titanic statues could be seen standing sentinel over Sorrow Fell. The hated visage of Asdrubael Vect glowered down from every statue, each holding a different ritualised pose or accoutrements that represented one of the thirteen foundations of vengeance. Vect had placed these monuments to his ego to stand watch over Sorrow Fell long ago. They were a permanent reminder of the ascendance of his own power over all the aristocratic families of High Commorragh. It was a calculated affront amid a landscape with more than its share of huge statues of commemorating the deeds of noble-blooded Commorrites both living and dead.

Vect's monstrosities stood on pedestals that placed them higher than the tallest spires. Their dimensions dwarfed even the thousand metre high representations of Commorragh's heroic forebears so that they were quite literally placed in Vect's shadow. It was said that nothing that occurred within the statues' gaze escaped the attention of Vect himself. Yllithian knew from personal experience that they screamed constantly – a hideous stentorian howl that had rendered the part of Sorrow Fell closest to Corespur virtually uninhabitable. Each statue projected a standing sound wave of misery and terror that intensified the closer one came to Corespur.

Search beams quested the skies around the statues endlessly, ethereal columns of greenish light that swept back and forth like ghostly fingers. As Yllithian and his retinue approached they were caught and held by one such beam and the deck of the barque flooded instantly with its veridian glow. Yllithian instructed his steersman to slow to a crawl as they were assessed. A voice spoke out of empty air beside Yllithian.

'Identify,' the voice chimed.

'Archon Yllithian of the White Flames,' he replied boldly, reflecting that now the authenticity of Bellathonis's blood-work would truly be put to the test. Vect would care not one jot if the leadership of the White Flames had changed hands, but it would indicate a potential vulnerability that Yllithian was loath to reveal to the Supreme Overlord. Moments ticked by beneath the unwinking beam, Yllithian could feel his nape hairs rising as invisible waves probed deeper into the very fabric of the craft and its occupants: measuring, comparing, categorising.

'Confirmed. Proceed,' the voice said.

Yllithian nodded to the steersman and they smoothly accelerated toward Corespur with his reduced retinue trailing behind. They were rising now, the prow tipping up to catch the sloping promontory beneath the anti-gravity ribbing on the barque's underside. Rising tiers of blade-topped towers, saw-edged battlements and angular gables slid past beneath their hull. Endless ranks of dark, empty windows gazed out across Sorrow Fell like lidless eyes. Shoals of dark-hulled Raiders and Ravagers followed their movements from a discreet distance. These were Vect's Black Heart kabalites alert for any sign of treachery, numerous and seemingly untouched by the city's agonies as they patrolled their master's stronghold. Fortress, armoury, lair, command centre, prison by equal parts – this was Corespur, the very center of

Asdrubael Vect's power. Truly Yllithian was entering the belly of the beast.

KHARBYR SPRINTED THROUGH emerald fronds and trailing ivy. Splinter rounds hissed past him, chopping viciously through the greenery like invisible shears. He veered into a hedgerow and burst through it in a storm of snow-white petals. He could hear running steps behind him, and voices cursing at him. These only served to lend wings to his flying feet as he ran for his life. This was certainly not the outcome he had been hoping for, but it was the kind of outcome he had been half-expecting.

Like all plans, it had seemed a good one at the time – logical. He'd strolled up to listen to the argument between Bezieth, Naxiapel and Sotha. Sure enough the Dracon Sotha wanted to get back to his archon and report the Azkhorxi treachery. Naxipael would hear nothing of it and imperiously commanded, with an increasingly heavy garnish of threats, that the dracon and his warriors accompany him to Sorrow Fell. Bezieth seemed just about ready to kill both sides equally.

Nerves were on edge and weapons were being fingered as the two groups of survivors from Metzuh and Hy'kran watched their leaders squabble. It was a simple matter for Kharbyr to shout out a warning, whip out his pistol and put a few shots into the Hy'kranii. The scene exploded into violence as both sides let rip at point blank range. Kharbyr didn't wait around to see the results, he simply turned and ran.

Kharbyr angled down a pathway between grassy embankments starred with flowers of crimson and gold. The declivity took him out of the immediate line of fire of his pursuers so he concentrated on pouring on more straight-line speed in order to outdistance them. This was when you got to be glad you weren't wearing armour, he reflected, when you were running from people who were wearing it. He didn't know Hy'kran tier as well as he would have liked but he knew that the parklands stretched for kilometres. All he had to do was lose himself among the foliage and his pursuers would never find him.

He wondered briefly what had happened to Xagor. When Kharbyr had turned to run Xagor was already nowhere to be seen. It was an impressive trick for the bumbling wrack to pull off although Kharbyr didn't have much of a chance to analyse it at the time. He had got within a dozen steps of the arch into the parkland by the time both sides had stopped shooting at each other and all started shooting at him instead – or at least that was what it had felt like. Pure luck had kept him alive through that first burst of fire, splinters and energy bolts knocking chunks out of the parkland arch even as he ran beneath it.

He darted off the path, hurdled a fallen log and dived headlong into a copse of flowering Loga-niaceae. He slithered beneath drooping boughs heavy with orange flowers to find a small hollow beneath the shrubs where he was hidden from the path yet could still peep out between the leaves to watch for pursuit. He lay still and tried to moderate his breathing, convinced that the pounding of his heart was audible across the entire park. Minutes passed and then he saw Naxipael stalking furiously along the path with the two Ethondrian Seekers in their maroon cloaks and hoods trailing behind him. The Seekers constantly bent to sniff at the ground like hounds, questing back and forth as they followed Kharbyr's trail.

Kharbyr experienced a sinking sensation in the pit of his stomach. He'd forgotten about the Seekers. Ethondrian Seekers could track a scourge through the turbulent upper airs, there was no reason they couldn't track him straight to his hiding place. The Seekers were approaching the point where he had left the path and in a few seconds they would direct Naxipael straight to him. The Venom Brood archon did not look to be in a forgiving mood. Kharbyr tensed his legs to get ready to run again. Just then Bezieth emerged onto the path behind Naxipael and called out to him.

'The traitor must have doubled back or we'd have him by now,' she said. 'We have to get moving, Naxipael, we don't have time to waste on this.'

Bezieth vanished again. Naxipael snarled something incoherent and turned back to follow her. The Seekers whined discontentedly as they were dragged away from their quarry. Within a few moments the path was empty again and Kharbyr allowed himself to breathe once more. He started to think frantically about how he could disguise his trail if the Seekers came back. It struck him then that Naxipael and Bezieth had probably already caught Xagor and didn't care so much about finding him anyway. The wrack could fix wounds and keep them patched up. Kharbyr was just a nameless loose cannon to them, a traitor. Just leave him to die on his own.

Kharbyr got up, determined to put more distance between him and the Seekers just in case. Perhaps if he could find some water he could obscure his trail for a while. He froze as he realised there was someone else coming down the path. Xagor came into view, creeping along with his rifle slung over his back and looking fearful. The wrack glanced around, left the path and headed straight towards his hiding place. Kharbyr grimaced and stepped into view brushing dirt from his clothes.

'I thought I'd lost you,' he said casually. Xagor seemed genuinely startled, as if he hadn't really expected to see Kharbyr step out from behind a bush.

'Well we made our escape, what's wrong now?' Kharbyr asked peevishly.

'Perhaps it's the fact that your friend is just acting as a decoy,' Bezieth said from behind him.

# CHAPTER 16
## CAPTURE

THE RING OF red-eyed incubi had closed completely around Morr and Motley in the shrine of Arhra. Unwounded, Morr might have been able to hold off so many for some time, and even prevail against more than a few of them before they took his life. Yet Morr's wounds still dripped crimson, and he held his great klaive upright only by an effort of will. Motley had proved himself more than equal to individual incubi but against so many, in the darkness of their own holy place, they would quickly drag him down too.

'Speeded by wings of desperation a plan does occur to me,' Motley said quickly, 'but I shall require a moment I doubt these eager young gentlemen will grant us.'

'Then I suggest using the same ruse that you used

against the gloomwings,' Morr said somewhat reluctantly.

'Ah! Good plan! Yes! Now!'

Motley hurled a photonic flare that split the stygian vault with a blazing white thunderbolt. Even through closed eyes purple spots danced in his vision, for the armoured incubi the effect was multiplied a thousandfold. With their senses unexpectedly blasted by their cornered prey the iron ring of incubi staggered and broke for a moment. Mustering a supreme effort, Morr leapt among them with his deadly klaive lashing right and left with all thei fury of a wounded tiger. In the confusion klaives swung so wildly that some of the incubi wounded one another.

Meanwhile Motley cast a small silver spindle into the air that hung in place and spun around its axis emitting a trilling whine. The harlequin sang desperately, pitching his tones within the shrill warbling of the spindle. A swirling purple teardrop wavered into focus beneath it and expanded rapidly like a slit pupil opening. Morr charged through the open gate without bidding with a dozen vengeful klaives at his back. Motley gave a jaunty wave and slipped through just before retribution arrived, the gate closing instantly behind him with an audible snap.

Morr awaited the harlequin on the other side, leaning heavily on his klaive with a look of horror on his pallid face as he gazed about him. They stood among picturesque ruins, elegant pillars and porticos of undoubtedly eldar design that were overgrown with moss and briars. Fragments of statues lay underfoot, and the cracked flagstones sprouted with dry, coarse grass. The genteel-looking decay was illusory, and came to an abrupt halt at a cliff edge a hundred metres away in each direction. Beyond that torn islands of rock, some the size of continents, whirled and somersaulted through a pulsating, multi-coloured sky.

'Is this...?' Morr seemed unable bring himself to ask the question.

'Lileathanir?' Motley said. 'Thankfully no, not yet anyway. Relax, we should be safe here for the moment.'

Morr sagged, seating himself on a fallen stone with his klaive across his knees. The incubus truly looked old now, worn out. Motley decided it might be best to give him a moment to collect himself before journeying onward. Morr gazed down at the shattered face of a statue curiously, its single eye gazed blankly back at him.

'What is this place if it is not the maiden world?' the incubus asked.

'This was Ashnerryl'ti, just an outpost of the old empire before the Fall. A garden world, really, a retreat of sorts or so I'm led to believe, but a populous enough one to call down its own doom when She Who Thirsts awoke. It was caught on the peripheries of the great upheaval – touched by the trailing edge of Her cloak, as it were, and pulled beyond the veil. It was enough to shatter Ashnerryl'ti into a thousand pieces and irrevocably alter every single one of its inhabitants – in point of fact we're standing on what remains of some of them right now. They were all quite literally petrified by the sight of Her awful majesty, or so the story goes.'

Morr gazed at the tumbling sky for a moment and then at the ruins some more. He stood suddenly.

'Why did you bring me here?' the incubus asked with a strange edge to his voice.

'I didn't choose it,' Motley replied defensively. 'It was the easiest place to reach in a hurry where I knew we would be safe. Few know how to find this place, and even fewer choose to come here.'

'Then who are they?' Morr said, pointing.

Five figures in sapphire armour of a design vaguely reminiscent of the incubi were emerging from hiding behind the ruins around them. Motley recognised them instantly as craftworld Aspect Warriors of the Dire Avengers shrine. These warriors seemed slighter than incubi, well-proportioned and heroic-looking, like animated statues. Their full-faced helms were adorned with tall crests marked in alternating bands of blue, white and yellow. They carried long-necked shuriken catapults that they kept levelled at Morr and Motley at all times.

A sixth figure emerged from the ruins, this one swathed in rune-covered robes and with its head enclosed by a bulbous, insect-like helm that was affixed with antlers of wraithbone. The warlock, for such it was, bore a witchblade that was as tall as himself. It seemed a curiously delicate-looking, academic weapon in comparison to Morr's brutal klaive.

'A curious sight,' the robed figure said equably, 'to find entertainer and murderer travelling as boon companions together.'

Morr laughed mordantly. '"Murderer"? Come closer, little seer, and I'll add another to my tally. In your case it would be my pleasure.'

Motley stepped quickly to interpose himself between the warlock and the injured incubus. 'What brings you here, fellow travellers?' the harlequin asked brightly. 'This is a secluded, not to say delicate, spot. I hope everyone can be relied upon to behave themselves. Why don't we introduce ourselves, my angry friend here is Morr, you can call me Motley – now what should I should call you?'

'My name is Caraeis, I tread the path of the Seer,' the warlock said reasonably. 'We have come for your companion, he is to be taken before the council of seers and punished for his crimes.'

'Aren't you getting a little ahead of yourself there, Caraeis?' Motley asked acidly. 'Surely there'd be all that trial and judgement stuff first, an opportunity to answer the accusation thrown in there somewhere, evidence, impartiality and suchlike and so forth before we arrive at any talk of punishment?'

'This is none of your affair unless you would fight against us on his behalf,' the warlock said with a trace of irritation in his voice. 'If that is the case I'll have to regretfully order the Avengers to cut you down where you stand.' Motley noticed that his words provoked the slightest of head twitches from the Dire Avenger exarch leading the squad of Aspect Warriors. She evidently disapproved of the warlock's actions in some way.

'I would rather see the best possible outcome for everyone involved,' Motley replied carefully. 'At this very moment we are on our way to Lileathanir to attempt to rectify matters, you'd be welcome to accompany us.'

'So you do admit the culpability of your companion after all,' Caraeis said with some relish. 'Under the circumstances I think you had best accompany us to the council too, so that you can fully explain yourself and your role in the affair on Lileathanir.'

'Explain myself? I am no more beholden to your council of seers than my dear friend Morr is,' Motley responded with some heat. 'By what right do you claim to order us around like captives? Are we your captives, do you think?'

The slight harlequin stepped closer to the warlock, seeing how the robed battle-seer flinched ever so slightly as he did so. This one was full of fear and ambition, a nasty combination. Two of the Dire Avengers pointedly swivelled their shuriken catapults to cover Motley while the other three remained locked unwaveringly onto Morr. Motley stepped back again with open hands and a wide grin to show he meant no harm.

'The incubus is my prisoner,' the warlock said smugly. 'If you wish to remain with him you must also become my prisoner.'

'Motley,' Morr said quietly, 'this is not your battle, none of it has been your battle from the moment we met. Now it is time to leave me to my fate.'

Motley turned to look up at the unmasked face of

the incubus now standing close behind him with his klaive in his hands. Morr's lank, pale hair had fallen forward to hide his features but the fierce, mad gleam of his eyes still glittered between the strands. Motley could see a taste for self-destruction burning there, the exultation of slaughter to come even if it was his own.

The Dire Avengers could cut Morr down before he took a single step, the warlock could boil the incubus's brain inside his thick skull just by looking at him – but Morr still wanted to fight them. The incubus must be seeing this as his reprieve, a chance to go out fighting against a properly hated foe instead of the brotherhood of his shrine.

'I cannot do that, Morr, as much as you'd like me to. Not while there's still the faintest shred of hope left,' Motley said heavily, 'and I am truly sorry for this. I only hope you can forgive me for it later.'

Motley snapped his leg up and out so fast that even the Aspect Warriors didn't have time to react. A perfectly executed nerve-kick to Morr's temple dropped the towering incubus like a felled tree – a slight sway and then a gathering rush before he crashed to the ground.

Motley turned back to the warlock with a heavy sigh. 'There, now you can't "accidentally" kill my friend while apprehending him. I think I will come along with you, just to make sure everything stays nice and friendly.'

The warlock inclined his bulbous helm sardonically, seemingly well pleased by the outcome. The Dire Avengers came forward warily, three covering the fallen warrior as one of their number brought out a set of heavy manacles. The Dire Avenger exarch was watching Motley with her beautifully crafted star thrower held at ease in what was probably intended to be interpreted as a conciliatory gesture.

'You have not spoken of the craftworld you hail from,' Motley remarked. 'Where do we have the honour of travelling to?'

'Biel-Tan,' the exarch said before the warlock could intercede and stop her. The warlock glared at the exarch and Motley sensed some silent exchange was taking place between the two.

'Ah, that explains a lot,' Motley interrupted. 'As I recall Biel-Tan claims jurisdiction over a great many maiden worlds.'

'They are the future of our race,' the warlock said sharply.

'Not to mention excellent recruiting grounds for Biel-Tan's efforts to reforge the old empire,' Motley remarked impertinently. 'Lots of eager young Exodites ready to fight and die for a great cause with the right grooming. You should be careful, Caraeis – your bias is showing.'

The amber lenses of the warlock's bulbous helm regarded the harlequin silently for a moment before the seer turned and stalked away. Motley looked back to the exarch and her squad. Her warriors had shackled Morr's arms behind his back and strapped him to a collapsible bier that floated a half-metre above the ground. The Dire Avengers had evidently come prepared to take a living prisoner and transport him back, which Motley took to be an encourageing sign in some regards. To Motley's relief the Aspect Warriors also retrieved Morr's klaive and strapped it onto the bier alongside the thoroughly restrained incubus.

'We would have taken him alive,' the exarch told Motley. 'There was no need for you interfere.'

'Oh, I don't doubt that a group of finely honed Aspect Warriors like yourselves would have executed the plan perfectly,' Motley replied with a frown. 'It's your warlock friend over there that I'm concerned about.'

The warlock had moved off among the ruins to an intact arch of pale lavender stone. He stood facing it for a considerable time, muttering and making passes through the air with his hands. Eventually a sheen of silver drifted into being inside the arch, wavered and then strengthened into a rippling veil. Motley noted with dismay that blue and green threads coiled within the veil – even here the Dysjunction could be felt. Its effects were flooding the entire webway. The four Aspect Warriors took up positions at each corner of the bier carrying Morr. With the exarch leading they began guiding the bier to the gate. The warlock held up a hand to stop them as they approached.

'There is a disturbance in the webway,' the warlock said. 'A direct link is impossible. I must make a rune casting to divine our best path forward.'

'Well yes, that would be entirely the issue wouldn't it?' Motley snorted derisively. 'The disturbance will only get worse the longer that we stay away from Lileathanir.'

The warlock ignored him, concentrating fully on bringing forth tiny wraithbone runes from his satchel with quick, practised movements. He placed each into a growing, spinning array suspended in the air before him.

The correct interpretation of rune casting is a nuanced art form that takes quite literally a lifetime to master, as evinced by the craftworld eldar in their Path of the Seer. Eldar runes embody symbolic concepts deeply rooted in ancient mythology and philosophical schools of thought that were already old when the eldar race was young. Runecasting came down fundamentally to interpreting the alignment of the psycho-active wraithbone runes when they were set 'adrift in the ether' to reproduce in microcosm an idea of the emergent patterns in the macrocosm.

It took no special expertise to see that the warlock's reading was erratic, the broken orrery of runes twisting around one another chaotically. The warlock flinched as two of the runes actually touched, the resultant discharge of psychic energy blasting them apart with a crackle of static. Both runes dropped to the ground charred and smoking.

'Not that way, I'm thinking,' Motley suggested helpfully. The warlock only emitted a low growl in response before focusing his concentration back onto the rune casting. The wheeling runes slowed a little, re-aligned and several of them reversed direction. The warlock kept reaching into his satchel and pulling out more runes as if trying to balance the casting. Motley tried to make sense of the runes being shown to him.

There was the rune for Anarchy/Disorder/Entropy most prominent orbiting at the outermost reach of the casting, encompassing everything within it. To Motley's mind that could only represent the Dysjunction in this case, its erratic influence affecting all the other elements. His eye was drawn to the rune of weaving as it looped back and forth within the orbit of the Dysjunction, seeming to shepherd the other runes before it. It fluttered unnaturally between the jagged, scimitar-like rune of the dark kin and the serpent-like rune of the world spirit as they swung through perilously close gyrations. It sped around the dire portent of the soul-drinker rotating around the bottom of casting, and encompassed salvation orbiting the top. Numerous lesser runes wove back and forth between the major ones: the sun, the moon, the scorpion, the devoured and more. At times the rune of weaving darted between them all.

'You know I could always lead you to Biel-Tan if you like,' Motley said hurriedly. 'No one knows their paths through the webway better than me, well nothing mortal anyway.'

'That won't be necessary,' the warlock announced sharply. 'I see the way forward clearly enough.'

Motley pursed his lips uncertainly, darting a quick look at the exarch. She stood as still and imperturbable as a statue, her tall crested helm turned to the gate. Aspect Warriors, Motley lamented to himself, were always so hard to read. Caraeis was retrieving his runes now, capturing them one by one and returning them to his satchel. The moment he had the last rune secured the warlock unsheathed his witchblade and stepped through the gate. The exarch followed, then the bier carrying Morr and its four attendant Aspect Warriors.

Motley hurried to follow as it really wouldn't do to lose them now. As he passed the spot where Caraeis had performed his rune casting he saw the two blackened, twisted runes that had struck one another were still lying ground untouched and abandoned by the warlock. They were damaged but still recognisable before they crumbled to dust when Motley tried to touch them. They were the rune of the Seer and the rune of the Laughing God or, to put it more commonly, the runes used to represent the warlock and the harlequin.

'Oh dear,' Motley muttered to himself as he stepped quickly through gate at the heels of the Aspect Warriors. If he could read those runes then Caraeis had most certainly seen them too. That didn't bode well at all.

'TURN AROUND VERY slowly,' Bezieth said.

Kharbyr did as he was told, turning slowly to find Bezieth's djin-blade levelled at his throat. Somehow she had got right behind him, crept up through the loganiaceae shrubs without a sound while he was watching Xagor coming down the path. The tip of her blade was vibrating with a high, keening whine, as if it wanted to lunge forward of its own voli-tion. Kharbyr's mouth was suddenly very dry. He was dead, he'd seen Bezieth of the Hundred Scars fight and she could carve a gutter-rat like him into pieces one-on-one without even breaking a sweat. Xagor whimpered pathetically behind him, making Kharbyr reflect grimly that he could expect no help from the wrack either.

'You had better have a more detailed plan in mind than "run away into the park",' Bezieth said eventually and lowered her blade. Kharbyr experienced a giddy rush of relief.

'You're not taking us back to Naxipael?' he blurted in disbelief.

'Or killing you,' the archon reminded him pointedly, 'even though you've already shown yourself to be faithless and untrustworthy. You're lucky you have a useful friend to speak up on your behalf.'

Kharbyr glanced back at Xagor, who was nodding emphatically. 'Don't look at him!' Bezieth snapped. 'Look at me! That's better. Now, tell me all about your genius plan to get out of this.'

'By going down, not up. Down to Null City,' Kharbyr said reluctantly. 'The xenos and mercs down in Null City will be pulling together at a time like this, not pulling apart at the seams like they are in High Commorragh. I know people that'll help,' he ended weakly. It didn't sound like such a good plan anymore, not with Bezieth's eyes boring into his as she searched for any hint of evasion. He felt particularly weak and stupid beneath that pitiless gaze.

'And just how were you planning to get there?' Bezieth asked impatiently.

'I was going to find some transport and use the… travel tubes,' Kharbyr replied, even as the words left his mouth he knew that he had probably just signed his own death warrant. Anything capable of moving under its own power would be long gone from Hy'kran and probably everywhere else within a hundred leagues by now. The tubes would be blocked by debris and who-knows-what crawling out of the pits to join the fun. It was a weak plan, doomed to failure before it even began. Bezieth held his gaze for a long, painful moment before she spoke again.

'Not bad, but your chances of finding transport just lying around rest somewhere between slim and none. We'll have to steal it or do without.'

Kharbyr grinned stupidly. 'You want to go with my plan? What about Naxipael?'

'Naxipael will most likely get shot the moment he tries to set foot in Sorrow Fell. They won't be taking in any waifs and strays up there,' Bezieth said carelessly. 'If I ever see him again I'll claim we got separated in the park and I couldn't find my back to him. Believe me he won't push the point – especially if no one is stupid enough to try and contradict me.'

Kharbyr glanced at Xagor again despite himself. The wrack merely shrugged helplessly. He was right, it didn't matter what reasons Bezieth had for splitting with Naxipael – it wasn't like they had a choice whether she came along or not. Besides, her sword arm and that nasty blade of hers would be a real boon if they ran into trouble again. Bezieth seemed to be amused by watching him working it all out.

'Listen. It's Kharbyr, isn't it?' she said reasonably.

'Listen, Kharbyr, and I'll tell you the same thing I told your friend. In every crisis there's opportunity, you just have to make sure you survive the crisis for long enough to take advantage of it. I intend to survive this crisis and personally I rate Naxipael's chances of surviving as being significantly worse than my own. That assessment extends to the people with him. Don't you agree?'

'This one agrees, mistress!' Xagor squawked obediently.

'As does this one,' Kharbyr assented.

'Good, because by extension the people that stay with me have a better chance of survival too. Now let's get going, you first Kharbyr – and try not to get distracted.'

ARCHON YLLITHIAN EXUDED confidence as he unhurriedly mounted a set of low, wide steps that swept up to the doors to the grand auditorium in Corespur. He took note of the host of greater archons assembled there also awaiting audience with the Supreme Overlord. They were strung out along the steps in cliques and clumps, the leaders of the most powerful kabals in Commorragh standing around waiting at the overlord's door for their instructions like expectant slaves. Many he recognised, some he acknowledged with a nod, others he greeted warmly or pointedly ignored.

Fear lurked behind every face. It was masked by bravado or pugnacity or humour or boredom, but fear hid behind the hard, black eyes of every archon present. The assembled host were the ones who stood to lose the most in the Dysjunction. They had unleashed unspeakable terrors on the slave-races across the galaxy, revelled in inflicting exquisite pain and suffering for centuries beyond numbering yet now they were the ones in fear. Anarchy had broken upon their own strongholds and they found it had an entirely different timbre when it was rageing so close to home. Yllithian recognised the fact that there were no archons present from the satellite realms, presumably because the portals were still too unstable to find them. More pointedly every archon present was either from Sorrow Fell or one of the upper tiers, a fact which did not bode at all well for the status of Low Commorragh.

Yllithian came to an individual that he recognised, but not one that he acknowledged as a great archon. His surprise caused him to pause for a moment. The lithe succubus Aez'ashya stood before him, looking magnificent in skin-tight flex-metal and bladed shoulder guards that spread fans of knives at her back. Yllithian recalled that this erstwhile archon that had been propelled into leadership of the Blades of Desire after the fall of his ally, Xelian.

Yllithian had distinctly mixed feelings about Aez'ashya. She was trueborn but of inferior stock without a trace of noble blood. She had unwittingly become El'Uriaq's catspaw when he had decided to rid himself of Xelian and now she was left a puppet without a puppet master. He wondered how she was manageing to maintain her control over the notoriously fickle Blades of Desire. Yllithian smiled and addressed her warmly.

'Why if it isn't Aez'ashya, what an unexpected surprise to find you here,' Yllithian said with mocking gallantry. 'I am delighted to find you weathering these difficult times so well – a true test of leadership even for experienced hands like mine.'

'The pleasure is mutual, Yllithian,' Aez'ashya purred. 'It seems so little time since I was undertaking missions on behalf of Archon Xelian, and by extension her close allies like Archon Kraillach and your good self, of course. Missions of the most delicate nature, or so it seemed at the time. Now I send my own minions to do my work for me.'

Yllithian smiled with his lips but not with his eyes. She was warning him in subtle terms not to push too far. What Aez'ashya had witnessed in the accursed halls of Shaa-dom was enough to damn Yllithian five times over if she brought it before the Supreme Overlord. It felt oddly refreshing to be on the receiving end of blackmail for once. Of course such a revelation would bring doom on Aez'ashya too – entry to Shaa-dom was forbidden on pain of death, so it was a case of mutually assured destruction.

'Quite so, it must all seem so very new to you now. This will be your first meeting with Asdrubael Vect in person, will it not?' he chuckled. 'Given the circumstances he will be in rare form today, you're in for a treat.'

'Speaking of rare form I had heard rumour that you had fallen prey to a wasting disease, but I confess you look better than ever. Even a little younger perhaps.'

'Too kind, too kind,' Yllithian replied smoothly. 'It's truly a wonder what the haemonculi can achieve when all seems lost. I still await the return of my dear friend Xelian with an almost breathless anticipation.'

'Oh? I had hoped to ask you if there had been word on Xelian's whereabouts. I'm told that her most dedicated hekatrix stole away her corpse before it could be tended to. No sign has been discovered of it since, personally I fear that the noble Xelian may be lost forever.'

'I have indeed heard such tales being told.' Yllithian smiled again, sympathetically this time. 'But I have complete faith in Xelian's unconquerable spirit. That she will be found, in some form, is not a subject of doubt in my mind.'

'Perhaps you're right. All natural laws are turned on their head at present, so why not in this matter also I–'

A hideous crash of cymbals and screech of horns abruptly rent the air, rendering any further verbal sparring impossible rather to Yllithian's regret. At the top of the steps two vast, engraved doors were grinding inward to reveal a dark space beyond that was broken occasionally by an ominous, flickering light. One by one the great archons turned and walked inside in answer to the summons. The Supreme Overlord was ready to receive them now.

# INTERLUDE

*We become such slaves to continuity, insisting that we receive our portions of beginning, middle and end dished up to us in our trencher in order to feel that our repast has substantive significance. A story most particularly is expected to slide from gate to gate with the orderly precision of public transport. All aboard…on your left you'll see… on your right you'll see… and so on until the end of the line, please ensure you take all belongings with you when exiting the vehicle.*

*Of all the mortal constructs this one is perhaps the most pernicious. Our efforts to impose structure mean that things have to have a beginning, a middle and an end, that they must unroll with visible cause and effect, not to mention a sprinkling of moral lessons and insightful observation along the way. Our existence is spent crafting our own stories into a suitable lifetime, categorising every experience to fit them into self-imposed*

273

*contexts, trying to write ourselves towards an ending that we don't really want to reach.*

*Reality is not like this. Reality is spontaneous and unknowable, chaotic, abrupt, wonderful, terrible and most of all unpredictable. The sad truth is Things Just Happen. Plans go awry, unforeseen elements prove pivotal and unrelated events combine in the most unexpected ways.*

*That is to say unexpected to some at any rate. There are powers in the universe that see all possibilities and endlessly try to shift the balance towards their own ends: a nudge here, a push there and all will be as they desire it. Little do they know that powers above them also nudge and push them in turn.*

*It's said that when mortals try to plan that the gods laugh. Thus we come to where we are now. Morr and Motley both frustrated in their efforts by an unexpected third party, the world spirit still bent upon revenge against Commorragh, the inhabitants of the dark city struggling and failing to survive (and, in some cases, prosper) in a catastrophe unleashed by powers beyond their reckoning. Events still continue to spiral out of control, creating more debris as they fall into anarchy. Is there still hope for a gratifying resolution and perhaps a moral lesson or two? It's difficult to say at this juncture. Time is most certainly running out.*

# CHAPTER 17

## TRANSITION

MOTLEY EMERGED INTO an all-too-familiar landscape. Bleached dunes of dust lay all about them lit by a single, lonely-looking sun that was little more than a chilly red disk hanging high overhead. The air was bitterly cold and infected with an unpleasant acidic tang that invaded through the nostrils and sat on the back of the tongue. It was familiar as a generality rather than as a specific, hundreds of worlds bearing gates to the webway were virtually identical to this one – blasted wastelands devoid of all life. Motley looked back to see that they had emerged from a five metre tall wraithbone arch protruding incongruously from the face of a dust dune. The warlock, Caraeis, was leading the squad of Dire Avengers and the bier carrying Morr away across the dunes on an arrow straight course presumably towards another gate.

The warlock was playing it safe, taking the long way around by moving from planet to planet to keep their journey outside the webway as much as possible. Motley felt his lip curl involuntarily a little. Time was of the essence yet Caraeis was acting as if he could take all the time in the world. An unwelcome thought that had already been lurking at the edge of Motley's mind settled into a fully-developed suspicion. He fished a small object from his sleeve, a thin oblong of crystal embossed with stylised masks that laughed and cried. He surreptitiously breathed on it once, polished it and then flipped it back through the gateway where it vanished like a puff of smoke.

The harlequin turned and ran lightly after the Aspect Warriors until he caught up with them. Morr was conscious now, glaring silently at Motley as he passed. Motley liked to think there was more despair in the look than hatred, and he gave Morr an encourageing grin and wink anyway. He was most certainly going to need the towering incubus's support soon. Caraeis was already vanishing down the opposite slope of a dust dune, sending tiny avalanches downward with each footfall. Motley called out to him.

'Caraeis? I'm still not really sure about your direction here. Are you intending to take us all the way around the great wheel just to get back to Biel-Tan?'

'You well know the webway is too unstable to risk traversing long sections of it at present,' the warlock replied testily. 'Your disregard for your own safety and that of others does you no credit.'

'The safety of "others" is actually at the foremost in my mind,' Motley said brightly, 'probably more so than yours. The difference lies in who those "others" are. From your outlook you would regard two thirds of our race as not being worth taking any risks for.'

Caraeis stopped to face him evidently needled by Motley's implication. 'Pure hyperbole,' the warlock said. 'You would accuse me of caring nothing for the Exodites – that is untrue.'

'Oh, so just one third are disposable then? Who set you up as judge, Caraeis?' Motley asked in outrage. 'Of course the webway is a little unstable – that's because Commorragh is in the process of being broken apart! Meanwhile you delay and pre-varicate to do your best to ensure that the process is completed!'

The warlock did not even trouble to deny the accusation. 'It's true I would not risk a single life to see the dark city continue,' he said. 'The foul perver-sion of Commorragh has gone on too long already, I would rejoice to see it ended in my lifetime.'

'And so you would sacrifice Lileathanir too?' Mot-ley mocked. 'Because that's what Commorragh will take with it at the very least. More likely is that the entire webway finally unravels, and our race is left stranded, scattered through the stars as we finally fade away into nothing.

'You want to know something interesting, Caraeis? Commorrites refer to themselves as "true eldar". The way they see things they have continuity with the pre-Fall days that neither the craftworlds or the Exodites can lay claim to. If you really want to reforge the empire you should ask the dark kin, they're the ones that really remember it.'

Motley was acutely aware of the Dire Avengers, and especially their exarch, standing stock still behind him. The sort of accusations the harlequin was cheerfully throwing at Caraeis verged on blasphemy in polite craftworld society. They were deadly insults for one on the path of the warrior and a matter to be settled by open conflict if honour was to be maintained. The harlequin was gambling that the Aspect Warriors would not leap to the warlock's defence because they already suspected his motives in some fashion. The internal conflict that was evident between Caraeis and the Dire Avengers was only going to be intensified the more they saw him failing to live up to their standards.

'Does he speak the truth, Caraeis?' the exarch said. 'Is there a risk to the webway as a whole?'

'No,' the warlock snapped irritably. 'Again hyperbole and exaggeration, the current... ah... flexing will rectify itself with time.'

'You mean you hope it will!' exclaimed Motley. 'You can't know that's true!'

'Wiser minds than mine have studied the problem,' Caraeis said more evenly, 'and I agree with their conclusions.'

'What a shame these august authorities aren't on hand to support your claims,' Motley remarked acidly. 'I, on the other hand, speak from considerable personal experience. I can take you straight to

Lileathanir right now if you'll just let–'

'Your life of… vagrancy and your foolish doom-saying do not make you an authority on anything!' Caraeis thundered in response, he caught himself and checked his anger before continuing shakily. 'Our actions have been planned and foreseen, directed by the highest minds towards a path most conducive to the continued existence of our craftworld. You act only to provoke me and waste the time you claim is so precious in pointless argument. I will hear no more of this.'

With that Caraeis turned and stalked away down the dune. After a moment of hesitation the Dire Avengers followed him with their prisoner still in their midst. Motley followed and attempted to provoke the warlock further with a few more choice observations but got no response. Caraeis was right that Motley was trying to delay him. It was, however, a far from pointless exercise. Another tall wraithbone arch was coming into view atop the next dune. Motley hoped he had bought enough time for his message to get through.

KHARBYR SOON ABANDONED the idea of stealing transportation; the place seemed a city of ghosts. As they moved coreward the parkland quickly gave way to tightly packed slave quarters that had encroached into the manicured lawns and hidden arbours. The narrow, crooked streets were barely shoulder wide in places to give protection against marauding gangs of hellions and reavers. Scourges were usually to be found in the uppermost and outermost parts of the city, but packs of wild riders of skyboards and jetbikes were a peril just about anywhere. They saw it as a personal challenge to take their machines through the tightest streets, down inaccessible pipes and along the faces of the spires themselves when they took a mind to. Wires and chains were strung between the overhanging eaves of the slave quarters so that even riders wild enough to try their luck in the twisting streets would soon catch a swift death instead.

It hadn't saved the inhabitants. Dead slaves lay everywhere, sprawled in doorways, piled in the streets in an untidy mixture of races and sexes. They had all been cut down by splinter fire from above, probably a Raider full of warriors moving above the rooftops. Plentiful pockmarks and puncture holes in the flimsily constructed buildings showed that the slaves that had tried to remain inside hadn't fared any better than the ones that tried to run.

'Why kill them all like this?' he asked Bezieth.

'You're a pretty little idiot aren't you, Kharbyr?' she told him. 'The answer's as plain as the nose on your face. Think. Why execute the slaves?'

'Well the old joke is because they're revolting,' Kharbyr said in confusion, 'but these don't have any weapons so they didn't plan it very well.'

'Seriously? Look above your head, boy!' Bezieth snarled in exasperation. Kharbyr looked up without thinking, up through the narrow gap between the buildings to where vivid, ugly colours were being visibly plastered across the sky from moment to moment. The sight wrenched at the soul, as if he were seeing the bones of creation were being laid bare in all their base simplicity. What was worse was the feeling that he was also seeing familiar reality being rewritten into new and alien forms before his very eyes. He looked away stifling a curse.

'All it takes is one of these idiots to think he's seen god or salvation or his great, hirsute, uncle Uggi up there and we could have a whole new problem on our hands. Belief, desire, worship – the daemons would be feeding on it like a swarm of locusts,' Bezieth explained heavily. 'Not the smartest move leaving a heap of potential meat-puppets like this, but I imagine whoever did it came through here in a hurry.'

Bezieth noticed that Xagor was looking back curiously in the direction they had come from, even though the black, narrow street seemed empty save for the dead. 'What is it, Xagor?' she snapped. The wrack jumped reflexively in response.

'Sounds, quiet sounds!' Xagor babbled. 'Gone now, but whisper-quiet!'

Bezieth frowned and looked back along the street too. Still nothing moved and nothing could be heard above the distant roar of infernal winds. She looked to Kharbyr who returned her gaze with a shrug before circling his temple with one finger to indicate his judgement on Xagor's sanity.

'Well there's nothing there now, keep moving and stay alert,' Bezieth said with more certainty than she felt.

* * *

A FEW HUNDRED metres away, hidden by a trellis of climbing rose in an artfully-placed gazebo Cho studied the input of her twitching sensor vanes and needle-fine probes with some confusion. The trace to the target had been present, a strong trail existed and was developing moment by moment, and yet the target itself was not present. No comparable scenarios existed within Cho's frame of reference and it was making the data extremely difficult to analyse.

On one logic path she had now followed the trace to its termination point and not found the target she was looking for. Therefore she must turn around and rejoin Vhi to investigate his trace, and so in effect cede defeat. Another logic path took into account the additional factor that the trace was still developing, the psychic spoor appearing in the ether like oil spontaneously appearing in water. Pursuit of this ongoing development might yet lead to the target, and the contest with Vhi would remain in contention.

Taking both logic strands and twisting them together produced two potential conclusions. In the first the target was present but using an unknown technique to mask its exact whereabouts. The technique did not eliminate the spoor entirely but rendered the target, in effect, invisible to Cho. In the second a form of decoy was being used to lay false trails. Both conclusions had precedent, although neither equated exactly to the phenomena being demonstrated in this precise example. Cho fluttered her sensor spines in something akin to frustration.

Attacking a decoy would undoubtedly compromise her chances of success by forewarning the real target. Such a scenario even held the potential of incurring the level of structural damage that could critically impair Cho's functionality. This outcome held a strong negative reinforcement, elimination of the target superceded all self-preservation considerations but that only applied once the target was positively acquired. In other words Cho was quite ready to get hurt and possibly die, but not against the wrong target. This was the kind of logic that Vhi seemed to interpret as a form of cowardice.

The other engine was undoubtedly taking the most direct and bloody route possible in his pursuit of the target. That was simply the way they had been made: Vhi for speed and strength, Cho for agility and cleverness. Part of Cho was being constantly distracted by not having her companion engine close at hand, missing its brainless certainty and the enhancement of their collective capabilities when they were together.

Correct psychic parameters or not Cho could still detect four living minds moving together through the park and generating the correct psychic trace as they went. Logic dictated that they had strong probability of connection to the target even if they were only being used as decoys. Cho concluded that patient stalking/hunting protocols might reveal more information. If necessary a direct attack strategy could be used to force a decision later, but only once Cho could determine whether that was liable to drive the target into the open or deeper under cover.

The sleek machine-form of Cho rose up on whisper-quiet impellers and slid forward on the trail of the lifeforms with all the focused intensity of a stalking panther.

THE LIGHT LEAKING into the auditorium through its high windows was awful to look upon. Livid, angry colours swirled within it; bruised purples, sullen reds, diseased yellows, poisonous blues and nauseous greens fought to overwhelm the eye and baffle the mind. Its brightness jumped and leapt capriciously from moment to moment. Periodically an all-enshrouding gloom would fill the great hall in defiance of its many lamps. In the next moment retina-burning flashes sent grotesque shadows darting across its trembling flagstones from the forest of chains hanging down from above. Each chain bore a body that had been hung up like freshly killed meat, although many of them still quivered or twisted in silent agony.

Yllithian took his place amid the assembled archons ranging themselves in a half-moon before the steps to Vect's throne. The dais itself was raised, appearing as a cylinder of metal extending up to the ceiling like a thick-bodied pillar. Moments passed in uncomfortable silence with only the crackle of distant thunder for accompaniment as the archons waited. The tramp of armoured feet came to their ears as Black Heart kabalite warriors filed into the auditorium and took up positions around the dais and along the walls. A number of Vect's courtiers and playthings swept in to arrange themselves decoratively on the dais steps before, as a final touch, a troupe of trained slaves were lined up to sing an interlude passage of the *Rhanas Dreay* – the coming of the Overlord.

As the slaves' voices reached a crescendo of pain the dais slid downwards as smoothly as a piston until it became level with the steps. A hemispherical shield of entropic energy atop the dais swirled and dissipated to reveal a throne. The throne was a dark, ugly thing of sharp angles and gleaming blades. It was an artefact that looked savage and unworthy of the elegance of true eldar culture – meaning that it was a statement of intent for those wise enough to read it. It squatted on the dais with an undisguised malevolence that well suited its occupant. The Supreme Overlord of Commorragh gazed down from his bladed throne and favoured each of the assembled greater archons with a lingering look.

Vect's milk-white skin was as smooth and unlined as a child's yet his void-black eyes glowed with millennias-old hatred and unimaginably devious intelligence. The proud archons met the Supreme Overlord's gaze without flinching (as they knew they must or die), but not one of them did not tremble a little inside. Vect's sharp-featured face was normally redolent of the uncounted centuries of unbridled wickedness he had inflicted on others for his own pleasure. The Supreme Overlord normally projected amusement, or self-satisfaction or insufferable confidence by turns. Now his mouth was drawn into a bitter scowl.

'My poor, beautiful city,' said Asdrubael Vect at last, his rich voice sonorous with melancholy. 'Why is it that everyone conspires to destroy it?'

The cracked black expanse of the auditorium shivered again and flakes of the artfully decorated ceiling fluttered down like baroque snow. The archons stood silent and waited, none of them fool enough to try and answer. The Supreme Overlord of Commorragh stepped down from his throne and began to walk slowly around the vast hall.

All about him, above him and behind him bodies swung on chains suspended from the ceiling. Most were still alive, but they hung silently in their agonies. Their screams had been paralyzed along with their vocal cords at Vect's command when he tired of their repetitious and entirely pointless pleas for mercy.

The great tyrant paused before one of his 'guests' that was hanging head down and covered in gore. This had once been Archon Gharax of the Kabal of the Crimson Blossom. Like the others he had been the ambitious leader of a minor kabal possessing only a few handfuls of warriors until a few hours ago. Now he was reduced to an example, part of a display created by Vect to impress upon the greater archons the true gravity of the situation. Vect ran a long-nailed finger through the dangling strips of flesh his haemonculi had expertly flensed from the unfortunate archon's frame.

Vect's words were not truly directed at the ruin of

flesh and bone hanging before him. Archon Gharax suffered on in induced silence. His eyes radiated pain and burning hatred for his Supreme Overlord. By all accounts Gharax had been completely loyal to Vect, or at least as completely loyal as any Commorrite archon could claim to be, but Vect did not care. Gharax's puny handful of warriors had pledged their loyalty directly to him now. A time of Dysjunction was not one to allow the minnows to swim freely.

'I've pondered this often down the ages, you know,' Vect told Archon Gharax. 'In fact I believe I can say that it is a topic that has occupied my attention beyond all others – and there are always so many, many other matters that demand my constant attention.'

Yllithian and the greater archons watched impassively as Vect paced onward through the grisly display. It was rare to see the great tyrant in the flesh, and rarer still to do so in the presence of so many other archons – hanging from chains or otherwise. Yllithian calculated that over a hundred archons were present in the chamber in one state or another. United they could easily kill Vect and finally free Commorragh from his wicked rulership and millennias-long oppression.

Yllithian had to repress a snort of derision at the thought. Out of all the fearless warriors present in that great chamber no one was about to risk making the first move. As ever, the archons watched one another and looked only for an opportunity to strike down their rivals instead of the insidious puppet master that controlled all their destinies.

It was enough to make one weep, or to laugh hysterically – another urge that Yllithian was forced to quell. Something told him that if he began laughing he wouldn't be able to stop. Laughter without end until even the madness of the Laughing God seemed logical and sane. No one moved and no one spoke. Yllithian and the greater archons remained as silent as Vect's hanging victims while they patiently awaited the Supreme Overlord's command. A time of Dysjunction was no time to show weakness.

Finally Vect stalked back to his throne and sat before he spoke again. 'Naturally I have summoned you all here to discuss the current Dysjunction. Such occurrences are not without precedent just as such occurrences do not occur without cause. Rest assured that those responsible for this attempt to destroy us all will be found and will be punished for their crimes. Upon this you can rely.'

The auditorium shook violently. From beyond its walls a thunderous cracking sound assailed the ears and the soul in equal measure. Vect paused and looked outward into the rageing storm, a feat that few would dare to emulate. Yllithian thought he saw fear in the tyrant's eyes. This ageless god of the eternal city could see the end of his rule written in the roiling energies outside. Yllithian suppressed an urge to flee, to hurl himself to the ground and cover his ears or, worse still, admit all and beg forgiveness.

He was the one responsible. His actions had

brought about the Dysjunction – that he was sure of. His scheming with Xelian and Kraillach had unleashed the forces now battering remorselessly at Commorragh. Such bitter irony that a scheme to unseat Asdrubael Vect had now brought Yllithian to within striking distance of the tyrant himself. It was all irrelevant now. Xelian and Kraillach were already dead and gone, consumed by those same terrible forces leaving only Yllithian to bear the responsibility that Vect had so darkly alluded to.

If Vect were ever to divine Yllithian's culpability in the cataclysm currently enfolding Commorragh it would be the end of him. The fate of the lesser archons would be a truly blessed release in comparison to the horrors that Vect would inflict upon Yllithian for his crimes. The fear in the pit of Yllithian's stomach was a familiar one. He had plotted for long enough against Vect to weigh all the consequences. Even so, standing before the tyrant himself, with all his plans ruined and allies destroyed it was all Yllithian could do not to soil himself. Despite his fears Yllithian had to comport himself with the same aloofness as the other greater archons, each pretending they were careless about the current situation and its implications. To do any less would provoke the Supreme Overlord's suspicions.

Asdrubael Vect drew in a sharp breath and continued.

'For the present the city must be protected, a responsibility that I charge each and every one of you with from this moment forth.'

Vect stood again, his restlessness betraying an anxiety Yllithian would never have believed possible in the saturnine Supreme Overlord. As the tyrant strode through the hanging bodies again he seemed to draw new energy, his voice echoing unnaturally through the great space.

'All incursions from beyond the veil must be eliminated! Open portals will be sealed! The possessed destroyed! Many of you will believe that this is an ideal time to settle old scores and eliminate your rivals – quite rightly so – however I warn you that if your games further imperil the city you will answer to me directly... and I also warn you that I am far from being in a forgiving mood.'

As if to underline Vect's words another thunderous boom rattled the auditorium. The tyrant's frown deepened into an angry grimace.

'Enough talk. Go. Get out of my sight. Your districts of responsibility will be assigned to you,' he spat. 'Go and do what you must to save our home.'

The archons filed out in silence. Each was consumed with their own thoughts, no doubt planning how to feed each other to the rageing entities loose in the city while remaining... well, innocent would be the wrong term... more like blameless. Yllithian eyed the others with interest as they broke into cliques en route to their own transports. Surreptitious glances and minute gestures indicated predator and prey to the practiced eye. In a time of Dysjunction all bets were off. All previous alliances were in ruins, old rivalries temporarily set aside and new accommodations made while the political landscape of Commorragh shifted as suddenly and as violently the city itself as the storms engulfed it. The thought rallied Yllithian immeasurably. His own plans might be in ruins but so were the plans of every other potential rival.

The ebon corridors around the auditorium were filling up with more functionaries, representatives and yet more Black Heart kabalites from all over the city. Yllithian reflected that Vect probably had many more groups to harangue and threaten into obedience over the next few hours. Mandrake nightfiends lurked in the shadows between silver sconces guttering with ghostly wytchfire, incubi klaivex pushed past arguing helliarchs and syrens beneath arches of black opal, groups of haemonculi clustered together like colonies of bats displaying the seals of their different covens – The Hex, the Prophets of Flesh, The Dark Creed, The Black Descent.

Yllithian paused and looked at the Black Descent representative more closely. His white, glistening face was altered into a wide, permanent smile amid hanging jowls that twisted into a beard-like mass of purple tendrils at his chin. Black, ribbed robes concealed the haemonculus's surprisingly corpulent body. A pointed demi-hood rose from the nape of his neck to frame his ugly visage. The creature caught Yllithian's glance and turned to him seeming to smile, if it were possible, all the wider.

'You're here to represent the Black Descent to the Supreme Overlord,' Yllithian declared.

'I have that honour, archon,' the haemonculus

agreed slightly cautiously. The haemonculus took note of the White Flames icon on Yllithian's armour and his eyes narrowed shrewdly. His permanent smile seemed a little strained for a moment.

'Then we also have some mutual matters to discuss,' Yllithian told him frankly.

'You are... quite correct, Archon Yllithian,' the haemonculus nodded. 'We do have a great deal to discuss. Sadly I regret that this is neither the time nor the place to do so.'

'Quite. Let it be known that I am amenable to a resolution that would satisfy all parties,' Yllithian said nonchalantly as he turned and began to walk away, calling over his shoulder, 'and do send me word of your intentions at your first convenience.'

Zykleiades, Patriarch Noctis of the Black Descent, watched silently as the White Flames archon moved away through the throng. The patriarch's mind was still racing through all the implications of the seemingly chance encounter with Yllithian. Zykleiades was old even as haemonculus count their years, which is to say infrequently. He had grown to be old by being extremely cautious about the unexpected and examining new information from all angles before committing himself.

According to the reports he'd received from his underlings the renegade Bellathonis had already been dealt with, and yet here was the archon clearly implying that their mutual 'problem' was an ongoing one. That fact alone would be the source of some very great distress to those underlings later, and new plans would be needed to rectify the situation if it proved to be true.

Yllithian's averred amiability for a resolution was a coded way of saying that he would be disposed to help the Black Descent to kill Bellathonis. That of itself was potentially helpful and yet extremely disturbing at the same time. It implied that Yllithian knew more than was entirely healthy, which in turn meant another death that would have to be arranged to completely cover the trail leading back to the Black Descent – the death of Yllithian himself. The archon of the White Flames was high profile and consummately well protected against such an undertaking so it would certainly be no easy matter to remove him.

Zykleiades shook his head in dismay at the timing of such a critical distraction. It could even be the case that Yllithian was setting up an elaborate ruse to implicate the Black Descent so that any action by them against him would serve to confirm the coven's culpability in the Dysjunction. It could equally be the case that Yllithian was simply trying to throw the patriarch off his game in the hopes that he would blunder in front of Vect.

Cymbals crashed and horns blew to summon the waiting throng inside the auditorium. The patriarch tried to focus on clearing his mind of any trace of guilt or fear that could give him away when he stood before the Supreme Overlord. There were times when he simply couldn't understand how the archons did it.

# CHAPTER 18
## CAUDOELITH AND OTHER CEMETERIES

THE WORLD BEYOND the next gate was dark as night and as tumultuous as a storm. Black tongues of vapour howled past driven by a relentless, battering wind. No sun or stars gleamed from above so Caraeis raised his witchblade and called forth a wan, bluish light from it to help them find their way. The landscape was made up of glittering, blackened rubble interspersed with twisted branches of silver thrust upward like fire-blasted trees. The previous world had been bitterly cold, this one was as hot and choking as a fever dream. The ground underfoot exuded an unhealthy heat as though fires were still burning deep inside the rubble. The gate they emerged from was blackened too, its silver-chased wraithbone overlaid with a patina of blasted carbon.

Motley genuinely recognised this place; he had

travelled here before a long, long time ago. This was Caudoelith, sometimes jokingly called Vaul's workshop – one of several worlds that had claim to that title before the Fall. Caudoelith was already a battleground before She Who Thirsts awoke with competing eldar factions fighting to secure the part-built craftworld the inhabitants were constructing for their escape from the imminent cataclysm. In one of the bitter morality plays that war is so apt to generate the unfinished craftworld was destroyed in the fighting, its blazing remnants tumbling down to spread ruin on the planet below. Few eldar had survived to be consumed by the very doom they had fought to escape.

The warlock and the Aspect Warriors advanced warily across the blasted landscape. No eldar on Caudoelith had survived the birth scream of She Who Thirsts, but in the subsequent centuries all manner of alien scavengers had tried to gain a foot-hold here. Wars had been fought not only by the eldar against scavengers but scavenger against scavenger and even, tragically, eldar against eldar for possession of the planet. Motley himself had come to fight an infestation of orks, but he'd heard stories that at some point the world had played host to every race in the galaxy with opposable digits.

Legends of Vaul, the smith-god, were known even beyond the eldar race and the idea that some great treasure was still hidden on Caudoelith seemed to be unshakable. Not a generation could go by without some dusty scholar or avaricious pirate arriving to stake their claim. The fact that the eldar fought to protect the planet only confirmed the myths. The truth was that there was a treasure on Caudoelith, just not of a kind that other races would value. Caudoelith of old had tens, if not hundreds of thousands of individual portals into the webway. Everything from huge ship gates capable of accepting the most grandious of aether-sailing vessels to interconnected individual portals that allowed instantaneous travel to any corner of the galaxy within a few steps.

The fighting and the Fall had put an end to all that. Only a handful of the original gates had survived but that still made Caudoelith a vital nexus in the material universe, a connection point between innumerable strands of the webway that were normally inaccessible from one another. Small wonder that Caraeis had brought them here. Despite Motley's earlier mockery there were few places inaccessible from the gates of Caudoelith. It was even possible that the warlock could bring them directly to Biel-Tan from this cemetery-world.

They trudged onward into the teeth of the rushing, black winds. The glittering terrain varied little: tumbled slabs of jade, marble and moonstone, wrecked machineries of gold and platinum, silverfiligreed rubble all clutched in a mutual embrace and all slowly eroding into powder. A dozen more millennia and Caudoelith might resemble the world they had just left, a dune sea made of the decayed remains of a forgotten civilisation.

Motley caught the faintest flicker of movement out of the corner of his eye, something not of the billowing blackness but solid and man-like. He remained silent and waited to see if the movement was repeated. He was rewarded by a another fleeting glimpse of motion beside a tumbled slab. Still the harlequin held his tongue and only moved to get a little closer to Morr. The Dire Avengers seemed oblivious, the warlock had his attention fixed on guiding them to the next gate. He was frequently consulting a single rune held in his cupped hands, seeming to be now a little confused by its indications.

Weapons fire burst upon them without warning, trails of spurting dirt stitching through the party from multiple sources. The Dire Avengers reacted flawlessly, darting into cover and returning fire in a single fluid movement. Caraeis looked at the rune in his hands again in apparent surprise before finally obeying the exarch's decidedly forceful injunction to take cover. Motley dived over to Morr's bier and dragged it down to the ground where the incubus would have a modicum of protection from the hissing crossfire.

Their attackers had a decisive edge in firepower, any move from the Dire Avengers provoked a hornet swarm of rounds zipping and splattering into the stones about them. Every few moments there would be silence for a second and then fire would come snapping in from a different angle. Motley was stuck lying at full stretch next to Morr and became acutely aware that the majority of his own cover was provided by the body of the incubus beside him.

'You should cut me free, little clown,' Morr

rumbled. 'I would prefer to die on my feet.'

'Oh I will in just a moment, when it's safer,' Motley whispered back comfortingly. Morr laughed humourlessly as another burst of rounds sang past only millimetres away.

The exarch and Caraeis looked to have been concocting a counter attack. All five Aspect Warriors suddenly sprang to their feet and made a concerted rush into the ruins, their shuriken catapults spitting coordinated bursts as they ran. Caraeis followed with his witchblade crawling with chained lightning, one hand upthrust to shed a bright, cold light over the Aspect Warriors' advance. The moment they vanished into the darkness Motley set to work cutting the straps restraining Morr to the bier, his curved blade quick and deft as it sliced through them one after another. Morr's klaive fell free as the incubus surged up into a sitting position, arms still bound by manacles behind his back.

'Release me!' Morr said, his voice thick with emotion. Motley pressed his harlequin's kiss to the manacles, its looping monofilament wires instantly rending their locks to dust. As the chains fell away Morr swept up his klaive with reverence, a terrible, feral smile splitting his face as he did so. A barrage of stunning flashes erupted in the direction the Aspect Warriors had taken, sending shadows leaping across the scene. Morr poised the great two-metre arc of the klaive and looked towards Motley meditatively.

'Come on, we don't have much time,' Motley cried as he started running in the opposite direction taken by the Aspect Warriors. 'You can always kill me later!'

Morr glanced uncertainly towards the weapons fire and explosions for a heartbeat. The firefight seemed to be drifting further away, tailing off to occasional whickering cracks in the distance. Reaching a decision, the incubus turned and loped away along the path taken by the fleet-footed harlequin.

BELLATHONIS'S TORTURE-LABORATORIES were buried within a honeycomb of hidden chambers and secret ways touching on the White Flames' territory in High Commorragh. The main area had originally comprised a wide, high chamber with rows of cells along one dripping wall and a cracked floor. Now it was more than half-ruined. The floor had split open and tumbled the cells into a slope of broken rubble. Chunks of stone and piles of gritty dust were scattered everywhere.

A handful of Bellathonis's faithful wrack servants were digging through fallen debris looking for equipment that had survived the tremors unleashed by the Dysjunction. Several work-tables had been turned upright and bore neat rows of gleaming tools. A glass fronted sarcophagus hung from the ceiling on chains, although its twin lay smashed on the floor below it. At the centre of the reduced room an examination table bore a metre-high cylinder of burnished metal with a handle at the top. The metal casing was hinged at the front to reveal it guarded a cylinder of crystal filled with colourless fluid. The object floating in the liquid was almost hidden by long, dark hair that coiled slowly around it, but it was undeniably a severed head.

A shape moved at the entryway to the lab, staggering abruptly into the light. A nearby wrack whirled in alarm and dropped the tray of instruments he was holding with a crash.

'Master! What happened?' the wrack cried in dismay.

'Oh, it's nothing,' Bellathonis gasped as he waved the minion away. 'Don't fuss.'

'Bu-but master, your–'

A synthesised voice cut through the wrack's jabbering. The voice sighed like the wind through winter-stripped branches.

*'You appear to have lost an arm since the last time I saw you, Bellathonis, how very careless of you.'*

Bellathonis wagged the stump of one shoulder ruefully. 'As I said, it's nothing that can't be fixed in a trice,' he grinned disturbingly, 'and better than the immediate alternative, believe me.'

*'I have heard tales of animals that will gnaw off their own limbs to escape a trap,'* the voice whispered. *'The fates are closing in around you, renegade master, your death is inevitable.'*

Bellathonis walked over to the cylindrical container and peered directly at its occupant. A pale, waxy feminine face with stitched-shut eyes and mouth seemed to peer blindly back at him between the coiling locks. 'Always ready to lighten the mood, Angevere,' the haemonculus said with deceptive sweetness. 'That's what I like best about you.'

The voice sighed from a narrow grille in the base

of the cylinder and while the lips did not, could not move, the face twitched with the semblance of life.

*'I warned you to destroy Yllithian when you had the chance, now he plots against you. He wishes to become your destroyer, not your ally.'*

'That would seem uncommonly foolish of him when I hold his life in my hands.'

*'No longer. You have granted him new life and even now he uses it to betray you.'*

Bellathonis's black eyes glowed dangerously at the crone's words. Angevere hated Yllithian with a passion and not without reason. The White Flames archon was the one that had found and decapitated her after she had survived for centuries alone in the daemon-haunted ruins of accursed Shaa-dom. Finding that the crone still somehow clung to life Yllithian had then traded her severed head to Bellathonis as a curio to excite his interest in the wider, more dangerous schemes the White Flames archon was brewing. Yet Angevere also had the gift of warp-sight and not everything she said could be dismissed as self-serving doom saying.

'Well we can see about that,' Bellathonis announced. 'If it is true then Yllithian has underestimated me quite badly.'

Bellathonis awkwardly dug through several pouches one-handed before eventually retrieving a thumb-sized crimson jewel with many facets. He tapped it on the table three times and laid it flat on the surface, all the while reciting the name 'Nyos Yllithian' over it as if it were an incantation. A small, red-tinted image sprang into being above the jewel, a hazy viewpoint in the first person perspective. Bellathonis watched and listened as Yllithian (for it was his viewpoint) harangued his warriors and set out for Corespur.

'*You can read Yllithian's thoughts? How so?*'

'Unfortunately I can't read his mind, but I can see what he sees, hear what he hears and hence also hear what he says. It's in the blood, you might say… That is an awfully large number of daemons up there.'

'*Dysjunction opens the cracks in our reality into doorways, there are many outside eager enough to press inside for the feast.*'

'Hmm I understand that perfectly well, but what's to be done about it?'

'*It is out of your hands, or rather hand I should say.*'

'That is a very unsatisfactory answer, Angevere, perhaps you should reconsider it,' Bellathonis said archly. 'My resources may be limited at present but they could certainly accommodate one of your equally limited stature.'

The stitched-shut face flinched at the prospect of excruciation by Bellathonis. From prior experience she knew he was right, the haemonculus was reckoned a master in his art with good cause. The speaker grille rasped almost plaintively.

'*Two wandering souls lost in the webway approach their final destination. Dark and light, it will be their sacrifice that determines the outcome of the Dysjunction. They are beyond your reach now, or the reach of anyone in Commorragh, even Asdrubael Vect himself.*'

'Hmm, better I suppose but I still don't like it,'

Bellathonis muttered, bending his attention to the image again. 'So, it seems that our Yllithian has been placed on assignment for the immediate future. He's going to be busy for a while.'

*'It will not matter. Your doom has already been unleashed.'*

'Yes, yes, doom, gloom and so forth. You really are tiresomely repetitive at times. Oh wait who's this? Zykleiades, you old monster – ah, I see you've made patriarch noctis now. Standards must have slipped even further since I parted ways with the Black Descent.'

*'You see? Yllithian offers you up to this Zykleiades without even troubling to ask for a price. The archon wishes you dead.'*

'If only it were so simple,' Bellathonis sighed meditatively. 'Zykleiades will want me dead and disappeared, but I suspect if Yllithian is truly out for vengeance he would much rather I were alive and suffering for a suitably protracted period of time. He does tend to be very thorough. That's a terrible shame, I'd thought Yllithian more progressive in character.'

*'All hands are turned against you now, you cannot escape your fate.'*

'Oh I don't know about that, Angevere, after all just look at you. You should have died centuries ago in the fall of Shaa-dom and yet here you are. Contingencies can be a wonderful thing.'

*'The price was more terrible than you can imagine.'*

'Only because you made the mistake of paying it yourself,' the haemonculus sneered. 'Speaking of which I really should get myself fixed up. You there! Come over here where I can see you better – ah yes, that's a very fine pair of arms I see you've got there...'

THE SLAVE QUARTERS came to an end where the parkland's boundary had originally been. The architecture of the buildings changed abruptly from a maze of flimsy boards with mud underfoot into slab-sided monoliths of obsidian, steel and granite that were spaced out along wide boulevards of springy turf that had been richly fertilised with crushed bone. The blocky structures varied in size but those closest were only a few storeys high, rising higher the further they went from the park. All were richly decorated with carvings and columns around cavernous doorways and empty windows. Some featured living displays of moving light that portrayed their occupants, most showed impassive, sculpted renditions of their long-dead faces to the world. These were *Ynnealxias* – mausoleums for glorious ancestors, or more accurately monuments to them as none contained a trace of mortal remains.

The ironic contrast of slave slums being crammed alongside the array of splendid, empty edifices he now moved through never even crossed his mind. In a society devoid of gods the *Ynnealxias* were the closest things to temples to be found in Commorragh, empty houses for the dead that celebrated their achievements in life. Kharbyr advanced along the edge of a deserted boulevard feeling uncomfortably exposed. He tried to keep his eyes downward and not stare up into the maddening skies, even as a tiny, mad part of himself told him to do it. He could feel pressure bearing down on him from way up there, a sickening sensation of alien heat that made his skin crawl. The urge to look at it again was almost overwhelming, even now he could still swear that he saw flashes of unearthly colour wherever he looked.

The eldar gods had all been destroyed, so the story went, consumed by She Who Thirsts in the Fall: Asuryan, Khaela Mensha Khaine, Vaul, Kurnous, Lileath, all of them. Commorrite families of any breeding and history now venerated themselves, or rather their illustrious predecessors, instead of their contemptible failed gods. In High Commorragh the noble families erected kilometre-high statues to themselves and dedicated entire wings of their manses to the accumulation of the lore of their bloodline. Here on Hy'kran in the lower tiers the trueborn could not indulge themselves so fully in their necropoli and must perforce make do with humbler temples to their own vanity.

In the middle distance the knees of Azkhorxi tier rose above the rooftops, a jagged fence made of polished towers of obsidian and amethyst. Somewhere close to the foot of those towers, Bezieth had assured them, there would be access to the foundation layer and its vein-like substrata of tubes and capillaries. Kharbyr hoped she was right; he had an almost animalistic sense of being stalked through the mausoleums. The dark, open doorways seemed poised to suck him inside at any moment and trap him within their sterile luxury for all eternity.

Of course every trueborn lived with the avowed intent that no such house of the dead would ever be built for them. Through the intercession of the haemonculi any trueborn could return from death provided the smallest part of their mortal remains could be saved. Yet death still came for some: by all-consuming fire, by destroying energies, by deadly toxin, by enigmatic disappearance or plain perfidy over the centuries the number of monuments inexorably multiplied. The houses were decorated with trophies accumulated across centuries of reaving: the crystal encased skulls of notable enemies, the prows of captured ships, suits of barbaric armour, exotic weapons, statues and artworks stolen from a hundred thousand different worlds. Vainglorious inscriptions declared their achievements:

*'Quiver before the might that was Vylr'ak Ak Menshas who was called the Shrike Lord by his victims. So strong his blade that he would plunge it through three bodies at once, so swift his raider that in a thousand hunts not one slave ever evaded his grasp.'*

*'See here arrayed the riches of Oxchradh Lyr Hagorach Kaesos, the Soul Thief. Young or old all submitted beneath his savage caresses in the end. On the world of Sharn a hundred settlements fell to him in a single night and he declared himself not yet sated.'*

*'Witness the death house of Kassais, who needs no other name. Beneath a dozen suns his reavers did bloody work to his instruction, leaving slaves with one eye and*

*one hand only to record his passing.*

The only ghosts here were memories, yet Kharbyr could feel his nape-hairs rising as though a hungry gaze followed his progress. Amid all the background turmoil and horror of the city something was singling him out for its attention, something dreadful. He stopped and glanced back uncertainly at Bezieth and Xagor following a few paces behind him. His fears suddenly seemed too stupid and groundless to voice when he met the archon's impatient gaze.

'What is it?' Bezieth hissed.

'I… nothing, I just felt like I… like we were being watched,' Kharbyr stammered.

'I feel it too,' the archon declared. 'There's something following us, has been since the park if not earlier.'

'Do we try and catch it?' Kharbyr said softly with a sense of relief. He'd begun to fear he was going mad. Bezieth shook her head.

'No. Keep going, if it doesn't want to tangle with us there's no reason to tangle with it unless we have to. We'll try and lose it in the shafts.'

Kharbyr nodded and crept stealthily onward. The boundary towers of Azkhorxi were much closer now, dominating even the tallest of the nearby *Ynnealxias*, a fact that was no doubt the source of great ire to the Hy'kran trueborn. The ground ahead sloped downward towards a row of angular buttresses protruding from the closely set towers. Between the buttresses could be seen the raised lips of three silver rings set into the ground, each wide enough to swallow a Raider whole. These would be vertical mouths of travel tubes that emerged into Hy'kran from beneath the core.

Kharbyr increased his pace a little, eager for a chance to quit the open skies for somewhere more comfortably enclosed. As he got closer a flicker of movement among the buttresses caught his attention. He silently dropped into a crouch and strained to pierce the shadows for several minutes, long enough for Bezieth to come crawling forward to look too. She cursed viciously.

'Ur-ghuls,' she spat.

The lip of the travel tubes was swarming with the whip-thin, troglodytic horrors. They were crawling up from below like an infestation of lice looking for a new host. Their blind heads quested back and forth as their rows of scent-pits tasted the air.

Kharbyr nodded. 'They seem to be heading this way, it looks like that big pile of carrion back in the slave town has a claimant after all. There's something weird about them, though, I think they've been warp-touched.'

Bezieth grunted and looked again. It was hard to tell at such a distance but there was something unusual about the creatures. It took her a few seconds to realise what it was. Some of the ur-ghuls were missing limbs, and all of them seemed torn up in some gruesome fashion or other.

'Don't they usually eat each other if they're given half a chance?' Kharbyr asked.

'Cannibals, yes,' Xagor chirped. 'Somaphages.'

'So why aren't the ones with missing limbs in the

bellies of the other ones,' Bezieth said grimly.

'More to the point how can we get through them? Will your blade carve through them like it did on the Grand Canal?'

'No, and ur-ghuls are strong and fast enough that I'd normally hesitate to fight more than three at once without a squad of warriors at my back. There's got to be more than thirty down there and more coming. I don't think we can get through them, I think we have to get out of their way and hope they don't scent us.'

Xagor wrung his hand and claw miserably. 'Highly efficient olfactory organs,' the wrack whispered fearfully. 'Most effective hunters.'

'Then we get into a doorway where they can only come a few at a time and… wait what's that? Looks like we're in luck, not everyone's left yet.'

A sleek, angular shape had come drifting silently out of the shadows above the swarming ur-ghuls, a shape with a jutting, armoured prow that thrust out below bellying aether-sails of orange and green. It was a Raider with its narrow deck tightly packed with kabalite warriors. The ur-ghuls milled in confusion, their scent-pits flaring at the nearness of prey but as yet unable to locate its source.

'What are they doing?' Kharbyr said.

'Having some fun cleaning up,' Bezieth replied.

A shower of tiny objects dropped from the Raider into the seething mass, metal seeds that blossomed into fiery gouts of plasma wherever they landed. Whip-thin bodies flashed to fire in the sudden glare, then withered into ash in a heartbeat.

Merciless fingers of splinter fire lashed down at the survivors, cratering flesh and splintering eyeless skulls.

The ur-ghul pack went wild, running and leaping in all directions with horrid agility. By some sixth sense several leaped directly up at the Raider, their hooked claws outstretched, but the Raider's steersman had judged his height nicely and it bobbed just out of reach. The one-sided battle continued with the kabalites gunning down the ur-ghuls at their leisure. The pack was dispersing now, most trying to find places to hide even as some continued to hurl themselves pointlessly at their flying tormentor. The Raider turned to pursue a handful of ur-ghuls that were fleeing directly towards where Kharbyr, Bezieth and Xagor were hiding.

'Something's definitely sending good fortune our way,' Bezieth murmured quietly. 'Let's not disappoint it. Xagor, do you think you can hit their steersman with that rifle of yours?'

Xagor shook his head frantically, hunching his shoulders helplessly as the Raider chased the berserk pack of ur-ghuls closer.

'Let me rephrase that,' Bezieth said coldly. 'Xagor, you will hit the steersman with your first shot or I will gut you like a fish.'

# CHAPTER 19
## THE POWER OF MISDIRECTION

MOTLEY DID NOT stop running and stretched his lead ahead of Morr as they raced away through the rushing darkness. They dodged between broken walls of Lapis Lazuli and down blackened alabaster streets, wove between piles of scintillating rubble and across fields of shattered crystal, the harlequin's gazelle-like agility always keeping him ahead of Morr's pantherish, loping strides. After a time Motley perceived that Morr seemed to be content to follow, and had no trace of insane murder-lust in his eye. He dropped back to run alongside him, glancing up at the incubus's exposed face.

'Are you tired? We can rest a little if you like but we have to keep moving. Caraeis will be able to track us like a hound so we have to keep moving faster than they can catch up with us.'

'I am well rested,' Morr rumbled. 'Those prancing

fools gave me ample opportunity to regain my strength, it chafes my heart to leave them alive.'

'They would shoot you full of holes first and you know it. So... you're not mad at me for knocking you out like that? I confess I thought there would be more running and shouting involved before we made our peace.'

Morr laughed, a peal of manic sound that was lost in the battering winds. 'Little clown, you have moved among us in the eternal city yet you are still blind to our ways. That trick is so old that it has its own name. It is called a *Roc'chsa* when two slaves turn on one another in order to gain favour with their new master. I approved of your quick thinking.'

'Oh. I never thought of it like that,' Motley said, slightly perturbed. 'I suppose that should make me feel better about it, but somehow it doesn't.'

'Why do you not simply make a gate now as you did in the shrine?'

'The warlock, Caraeis, would sense it instantly, and he could block its formation for long enough for the Dire Avengers to reach us.'

'So where do we run to?'

'A permanent gate, I think, is somewhere close by. If we can reach that and enter the webway I can get us to Lileathanir.'

'Surely the warlock will hold that shut against us also.'

'It will be much harder for him to do with a permanent gate. You'll have to allow me some leeway here, I'm sort of inventing this as I go.'

'Then tell me who attacked the craftworlders and by what happy coincidence they came to help our escape.'

That… is my little secret to keep for now, just know that we have friends as well as enemies in this particular production.'

'GONE!' CARAEIS SNARLED. He kicked at the broken shackles angrily and fought with a desire to tear off his masked helm so that he could fill his lungs and scream into the howling winds in frustration. Aiosa, the Dire Avengers exarch stood to one side watching him rage, her own impassive mask coolly inscrutable beneath its tall crest.

'Calm yourself,' she said to him with mind-speech. 'Your passion has no place here, remember your path!'

The warlock tried to check his emotions and fought to breathe more calmly. Caraeis's personal investment in this mission had become like a living thing dwelling inside his chest, gnawing to break free. He ran through the thousand and one man-tras he had been taught about the hideous dangers that were inherent to uncontrolled passions for a psyker.

The runes, the mask, the Path of the Seer itself, all were ways of insulating him against the perils of the warp and lending him enough protection to safely wield the limitless power it represented. If his underlying will lacked focus and discipline it meant that nothing could protect him. If his connection with the warp became too personal, if he bared his soul even once to the daemons then he was lost and his time on the Path of the Seer would be over. He quieted the beast within his breast only with great difficulty.

'Why was no guard left behind?' he asked eventually, his tone remarkably steady in his own ears.

'I instructed you to remain on guard,' Aiosa replied. 'Why did you not do so?'

'I… that is not what I heard,' Caraeis said in confusion. 'I heard you instruct me to follow.'

Aiosa gazed at him silently, waiting for an explanation with not a shred of doubt in her demeanour that Caraeis had made an error. Caraeis searched his memory carefully, Aiosa's mind-speech had seemed a little garbled at the time but he had put it down to the confusion of the firefight. He had definitely had the strong impression of the word 'follow' being in it, although now he came to analyse it, he was unsure precisely who had said it. A cornerstone of Caraeis self-assurance crumbled perceptibly – was it possible he had been duped? As he wrestled with the implications a Dire Avenger approached and dropped several objects into the dust at Aiosa's feet with evident disgust.

'Exarch, we found these at the battle site. dark kin were here.'

A barbed, wicked-looking pistol and a tall, dark helm surmounted by a crescent moon lay in the drifting dust. Both showed signs of recent damage, shurikens had torn into the helm and the pistol had a broken barrel.

'Nothing else?' Aiosa asked. 'No blood, no bodies?'

'Nothing, exarch, no tracks either – although the ground was unsuitable for them.'

'Very well, return to overwatch positions.'

Aiosa turned back to Caraeis. 'Well?' she asked as if no interruption had occurred.

'Someone told me to follow, but I don't think it was you. I was tricked.'

'I see,' the exarch said clinically. 'Tell me your opinion of these artefacts.' Caraeis had a momentary impression that he was being addressed by an automaton, that if he peered inside Aiosa's armoured suit he would find it empty. He shook his head and tried to focus on the helm and pistol, he held a gloved hand over them, cautiously feeling for their psychometry. He shivered unexpectedly and pulled his hand back.

'There is no doubt that they are of Commorrite manufacture. The pistol has been fired recently, before it was broken. The impressions were… too chaotic to read anything beyond that. What do you think?'

'That someone is trying to mislead us again by laying a false trail back to the dark city. We were left these clues to find.'

'That seems very convoluted,' Caraeis said dubiously.

'We were not attacked by dark kin, our supposed foes went out of their way to avoid harming us.'

'Then who?'

'The answer is obvious. The harlequin called in more members of his masque and they led us in a merry dance while he escaped with our quarry.'

'What?' Caraeis spluttered, animal outrage scratching inside his chest again. 'That's monstrous! Why would they favour the dark kin so flagrantly? They're supposed to be jealous of their beloved neutrality!'

'You told the harlequin that he was also your prisoner. I believe they could convincingly argue that you committed the first affront and they acted only to rectify it.'

Caraeis fell silent. Aiosa was correct, in his hubris he had given the harlequin grounds to argue he'd been compelled to accompany them against his will. Caraeis had been so sure that his path would lead straight to the council chamber on Biel-Tan that he hadn't stopped to consider that someone would work so actively to divert him. He felt shock that events, so neatly mapped out in previous rune castings, were spiralling out of control.

'If an entire masque is against us our mission will fail unless we declare war,' Aiosa said flatly. 'And that I will *not* do.'

'There's no evidence of that being the case,' Caraeis retorted with something of his old assurance. 'We-we must reassess the situation based on what we know, not just what we suppose. The prisoner has escaped us temporarily, but I do not sense that he has left this world as yet. He has accomplices but he hasn't gone far. The incubus can be recaptured with the forces we have on hand. The harlequin knows he cannot intercede directly without entering the conflict and now we know that too.'

Aiosa's mask stared back inscrutably at him as if suggesting that she had known that particular fact all along.

THE RAIDER SLEWED alarmingly as its steersman exploded messily across its stern. The fleeing ur-ghuls, somehow sensing the sudden change, immediately turned and leapt up at the wallowing grav-craft like grotesque frogs. In a flash a trio of the needle-toothed horrors were scrambling over the gunwales and clutching at the kabalite warriors aboard. Stabbing combat blades and point blank range splinter shots hurled off the creatures in short order, but not before their combined weight had tilted the Raider so that it sank even lower to the ground. More ur-ghuls leapt aboard and the Raider's blood-slicked deck quickly became a struggling mass of hook-clawed fiends and bronze-armoured warriors fighting for survival.

Bezieth led Kharbyr and Xagor in a silent rush towards the stricken craft. An ur-ghul hissed and turned on her with rows of scent pits flaring. Bezieth's djin-blade crunched through the creature's dome-like skull without her even breaking stride. Aboard the Raider a warrior made a desperate leap to grasp its curving tiller bar and bring the craft under control. He was instantly tackled by the frenzied grey-green shape of an ur-ghul and the struggling pair tumbled overboard to fall to the ground with a bone-snapping crunch.

Kharbyr made an agile leap that put even the ur-ghuls to shame, swinging himself up onto one of the Raider's blade-like outriggers. Xagor was plying his hex-rifle indiscriminately, kabalites and ur-ghuls were swelling and popping obscenely left and right. Kharbyr ran along the outrigger and jumped across to the narrow deck near the stern. A Hy'kran kabalite, wheeling to face him in surprise, met Kharbyr's curved blade as it crunched point-first into his throat. Kharbyr wrenched his knife free and hacked off a clutching, hook-clawed hand even as he turned and sprang for the tiller bar with the speed of desperation.

Bezieth thrust her keening djin-blade through another disgusting, whip-thin body with such ferocity that it virtually sheared the ur-ghul in twain. Another leapt at her and she cut it out of the air in twitching fragments. Axhyrian's spirit was obedient in her hands, the djin-blade light as a wand as she cut and thrust. She glanced up to see Kharbyr braced at the tiller bar with it clamped beneath one arm as if he were steering the Raider through a storm. Kharbyr heaved the curving control bar hard over to tilt the wallowing grav-craft almost onto its side. Kabalite warriors and ur-ghuls, unprepared for the sudden shift, came tumbling off the deck in shrieking clumps. Bezieth grinned appreciatively and ran forward to catch at a tilted railing, hurling herself aboard the Raider as Kharbyr brought the craft upright again.

Almost as her feet hit the deck another needle-fanged horror came clambering over the railing opposite. Bezieth's sword flashed across the inter-vening space like lightning and sent the creature flying backwards in an explosion of black ichor. She turned to Kharbyr and shouted.

'What are you waiting for? Go! Now!'

'But... Xagor!'

Bezieth glanced below to where the wrack was struggling with an ur-ghul that had its claws wrapped around his rifle. Needle fangs champed for his throat as the horrible strength of the creature relentlessly bore him down. An instant of calculation flickered through Bezieth's mind, save the wrack or abandon him to his fate? If it had been Kharbyr down there the conclusion would have been instant – even though the skinny assassin had just raised his worth a notch or two in her estimation – but the wrack was actually useful. She leapt down from the Raider with a long suffering sigh, her djin-blade licking out to decapitate the ur-ghul pinning down Xagor. More ur-ghuls circled, but with easier prey at hand in the form of hapless fallen kabalites than an armed and aware opponent they warily kept their distance.

Kharbyr dipped the Raider as she pulled the wrack to his feet so that she could virtually throw Xagor straight onboard. She caught a look of calculation on Kharbyr's face as he manoeuvred the craft and swarmed swiftly aboard herself before he could form any bright ideas of his own about leaving her behind. The Raider's angular nose came up and they rose quickly upwards out of reach of the struggling ur-ghuls and warriors beneath.

'That was... nicely done,' Bezieth admitted.

'Thanks,' Kharbyr grinned, elated with his success.

He felt like he was actually starting to like Bezieth on some levels. Despite the scars and rough manner she was turning out to be the most reasonable, down-to-earth archon he'd ever encountered. It was a very odd feeling for him and it didn't last long.

'Don't get too close to those towers,' Bezieth snapped. 'The Azkhorxi will burn us down just for fun if you give them the chance.'

'Where to then?' Kharbyr asked sulkily.

'Into the tubes, the plan hasn't changed.'

'What about the ur-ghuls?'

'Just don't stop to pick up any more passengers,' Bezieth told him acidly.

VHI WAS BECOMING dangerously frustrated. Impatience, his memory engrams told him, was often the cause of mission failure but that piece of wisdom did not seem to help right now. The psychic trail was fresh and distinct. There was no doubt that the target had passed this way recently not just once but several times. The narrow sub-strata tunnels Vhi was now investigating were rank with the spoor of the target and it was absolutely clear that its lair must be nearby.

However, try as he might, Vhi could locate neither the target nor the lair and was now finding himself crossing the same spots over and over again. When Vhi had first hit upon the fresh trail he had experienced a desire for communication capability so that he could illustrate his manifestly superior hunting skills to Cho by sharing the knowledge. Now he experienced a similar desire for communication capability so that he could consult Cho on the findings. It was most puzzling and Cho was too far out of range to ask. The enhanced sensing capabilities of the Cho engine were something his protocols now told him were sorely missed.

Vhi stalked back and forth on whisper-quiet impellers through the tangle web of sub-surface tunnels, drifting through the darkness in silence as he analysed his sensor returns. Available information bore no indication of the tunnels' existence and so he had to painstakingly map them as he went, laboriously cross-referencing that information with the confusion of multiple target trails he could also sense. It didn't help that the layout of the tunnels seemed to be random and followed no discernible pattern on either the horizontal or vertical plane.

Vhi gradually came to realise that the randomness of the tunnels was because structural damage had occurred in them recently. Some had collapsed entirely, others were partially blocked, voids and crevices had opened up to make connections between sections that hadn't existed previously. The psychic spoor led straight up to walls of fallen debris in several places, yet as the three dimensional map Vhi was building grew he could see that the trails continued beyond the blockages. Clearly these trails were older and had been made before the structural damage occurred. With a rush of excitement Vhi flagged all such interrupted trails as older data and eliminated them from his calculations.

Sure enough the remaining psychic traces formed

a distinct nexus, a knot of activity that could only denote the location of the target's lair. Vhi rotated his hull smoothly in place to point directly towards the area in question. His segmented tail curved forward over his carapace and the heat lance mounted on it glowed with ruby energy. A fiery line connected the lance with the tunnel wall for the briefest instant before the dense matter of the wall began to soften and drop away in viscid blobs. Vhi modified the output of the heat lance and began pushing slowly forward into the resulting hole. Vhi was done with creeping around through tunnels, he had decided, cutting a direct course for the target's lair would achieve maximum surprise and in the meantime it was a gratifyingly destructive path to take.

YLLITHIAN STOOD ON the deck of his barque pondering the complex vagaries of so simple a matter as sending a message in Commorragh. Secure communications were always problematic in the eternal city. Even after millennia of dedicated efforts by paranoid archons to find ways to prevent it any signal could be intercepted or blocked or broken by a clever enough foe. Even supposedly unbreakable line of sight energy pulses could be interfered with, redirected or eavesdropped on.

Assuming you could get over those difficulties the simple fact of accepting any kind of communication also accepted the possibility that it had been tainted in some fashion. An innocent-seeming message might, for example, be corrupted to introduce a command into your armour systems to cut your own head off, as occurred most notably to the unfortunate Resy'nari Kraillach on receiving what was ostensibly a report of his victory over Ly'lendel the scrivener. How can you communicate when you don't trust one another or anyone else? It was a pretty problem however you sliced it.

Yllithian was diverting himself while waiting patiently to receive notification of his assigned district from Vect – however that might be achieved. Around him were arrayed his somewhat reduced band of warriors. Their reaver and hellion auxiliaries were huddled in tight around the surviving Raiders, all silently holding station together like a shoal of sleek, predatory fish. The dark, jagged slope of Corespur swept away below them to where the titanic, screaming statues of Vect stared out over the distant spires of Sorrow Fell.

Dozens of dark shoals like Yllithian's waited in the shadows of Corespur: aethersails of crimson, purple, poisonous green, acidic yellow were on every side, serpent prows with jewelled eyes thrust alongside of gilded harpies and jagged rams, chain-snares and trophies swung beneath blade vanes and serrated keels as the host silently drifted in unaccustomed quiescence. Countless different icons marked out the host of different kabals that had been summoned by the Supreme Overlord. The opportunities for them all to gain some advantage in the chaos were virtually limitless and they began right now. In the hours to come a single missed order might send an archon or a whole kabal crashing into ruin in a heartbeat.

Another reality-shaking storm was breaking across the city. World-shattering bolts of multi-coloured lightning lashed down from the warding into the spires below with terrifying violence. The strikes were so frequent that at times it seemed as if there was a forest of flickering pillars spread across the city that barely supported the sagging, rageing vault of heaven. Fires licked everywhere and fully half of Sorrow Fell seemed to be burning, its sullen red glow warring with the vivid aurora above.

Periodically groups of sleek craft would slide out of the host and descend into the maelstrom as they received their orders. Yllithian continued to divert himself by imagining the difficulties inherent in communicating with such a disparate horde. This was no raid into realspace where a plan could be pre-made, roles assigned and each part then trusted to work within the greater whole. Vect seemed to be biding his time, waiting to see where the worst eruptions were occurring while he fed kabals into the blaze one by one, but perhaps it was just the physical difficulty of actually telling them all what to do.

The problem rested squarely with the inherent deviousness of the Commorrites themselves. In realspace everyone focused on working together as smoothly possible, the city-games were suspended for a time in the interests of efficiency. In Commorragh itself even something as simple as a rival receiving a message offered boundless opportunities for mischief. Because of that signals had to be routinely encrypted, decrypted, re-encrypted, quarantined and subject to the equivalent of red-hot pokers and pincers before they could be safely brought anywhere near the attention of a living recipient. Even then there were no guarantees that some slippery foe hadn't found some new and exciting way of getting something past your defences. It all took up an inordinate amount of time and added uncertainty to a situation that was already dangerously fluid.

A beat of dark wings above caught Yllithian's attention as the lone scourge he had been half-expecting, half-dreading descended onto the deck of the barque. The altered messenger was prominently wearing the mark of the Kabal of the Black Heart to show he was one of Vect's own (although that in itself meant little, flying false colours was a trick older than Commorragh itself). The scourge furled its gorgeous, feathered wings ostentatiously and knelt in front Yllithian offering up a narrow wafer of crystal for Yllithian's inspection.

Messages delivered by hand avoided many problems while introducing a few new ones, but at least you could identify the origin more readily and, if the situation warranted it, literally shoot the messenger. As it was Yllithian took the crystal from the scourge's clawed fingertips without a second glance, shooing the feathered warrior away with his other hand. The scourge bounded to its feet and leapt away into space, the unfurling snap of its wings doing little to conceal its cynical, cawing laugh as it departed.

Yllithian examined the flat crystal plaque and turned it over in his hands: a biphase lattice genecoded to a single sender and recipient – unbreakable, unforgeable and unalterable – theoretically at least. It bore the mark of Vect and it no doubt contained his orders, sealed in such a way that they could quite literally be seen by Yllithian's eyes only. He was hesitant about unsealing them – it felt very much like donning a leash. No doubt many other archons had felt the same way but the truth was that the leash was already around their necks and what they were feeling was Vect jerking it to bring them to heel.

He slid one finger along the top of the wafer and a row of unambiguous, angular ideograms swam into view within the crystal. Yllithian read it, and then read it again before crumpling the thing in his fist. It crushed into fine, glittering dust, slipping away instantly between Yllithian's fingers in a twinkling cascade. He meditated for a moment on the missive's contents, thinking that unseen eyes would be watching and waiting for his reaction. He hesitated for only a heartbeat, what choice was there but to obey? For now at least... At his gesture the shoal of White Flames grav-craft slid away from the slope of Corespur and set course into the maelstrom.

In another section of the waiting host Aez'ashya stood on the small, open deck of her Venom skychariot reading her own crystal-encased message. A wry smile played across her lips as she did so. At her call the Blades of Desire began rousing their skycraft, the high whine of booster engines rising around her moment by moment. She swept her arm forward and the Venom shot away following the course Yllithian had taken, a snarling swarm of reavers and hellions at her back.

# CHAPTER 20
## ESCAPE ATTEMPTS

'THEY'RE COMING,' MOTLEY called suddenly, still running. 'I'd hoped they would take longer to decide on what to do but apparently we've been fated to be disappointed in that regard.'

Morr, loping beside him tirelessly, glanced at the harlequin without questioning how he knew what actions the craftworlders were taking. They had been running for minutes through the glittering ruins and the place they had escaped from was well out of sight in the darkness by now.

'Will your allies be able to intercede again?'

Motley shook his head regretfully. 'They've already done more than I should ask, and besides I think Caraeis will be wise to their tricks now.'

'How far is it to the nearest gate?'

'Too far unless we can think up a way to throw them off our trail,' Motley grimaced. 'Those Dire

Avengers run quicker than hunting hounds.'

'Alone you are considerably faster than me. You could easily reach the gate ahead of them and open it,' Morr pointed out.

'That wouldn't h– oh I see what you mean,' Motley said with a grin. 'I'll see you again shortly.'

The two runners separated, their courses diverging as Motley put on an impressive spurt of speed. The slight harlequin bounded across the tops of broken pillars, flipped over gaping craters and danced through the ruins with a speed and grace that few living creatures could equal. In a few seconds he was entirely lost amid the rushing darkness. Morr kept doggedly running at his best pace and curved his course off into densest ruins he could see, his klaive held balanced low at his side.

CARAEIS RAN LIGHTLY through the forest of broken stone and twisted metal. He was as deft and agile as any of his race, battle-trained for many differing environments yet he was still struggling to keep Aiosa and the Aspect Warriors in sight. When they had agreed to pursue the incubus he had assumed Aiosa would need him to use his rune sight to follow the Commorrite's black aura. Instead the Dire Avengers had sprung away without a moment's hesitation, almost vanishing before he even began to move. They intended to make the capture alone, Caraeis was sure of it, no doubt as another way to embarrass him before the council when Aiosa made her report.

It had taken him a little while to work out how

the Aspect Warriors were tracking the incubus before he realised they were literally, physically, tracking him. Once he recognised the mundane source of their information he began to notice the tracks himself, unmistakeable large, armoured boot prints filling slowly with blown dust. The fugitive was obviously running with no attempt at concealment at all, the prints were widely spaced, digging deep at the toe as they pushed off. Even so the incubus's lead could only be measured in minutes and judging by the speed the Dire Avengers were moving it must be shrinking rapidly. The incubus's trail pointed unerringly towards the nearest gate, a reality-distorting knot that Caraeis could sense at the edge of his consciousness. There were other gates in the vicinity but this was the strongest focus by far, the obvious escape route.

Caraeis cursed mentally at the perfidy of Commorrites, harlequins and Aspect Warriors equally. He, Caraeis, had seen the crisis-pattern first, and he, Caraeis, had been the one who had calculated precisely how to manipulate it to the best advantage of Biel-Tan. Yet when he put his finely-considered plan into action all the mechanisms he had so carefully wrought span out of control at the first instance, evincing an animus and taste for self-direction he had never anticipated. No calculation he had made indicated that the hidebound pride of the Dire Avengers exarch would be a factor, or that the wandering followers of Cegorach would become involved.

He had tried to dismiss the incident of the warlock

and harlequin runes colliding in his earlier casting. Such unfavourable portents often happened due to malign influences – it was precisely the kind of thing the runes were meant to defuse and could usually be safely ignored. Now he was beginning to wonder whether it had been a more literal omen of their course towards mutual destruction.

Caraeis became aware that the Dire Avengers' course was changing, curving away from a straight path towards the gate. He looked down and saw that the trail they followed was curving too. The incubus must have given up on trying to escape that way. Between the flying wracks of dark vapour blown on the winds it was apparent that the land ahead rose precipitously. Terraces of broken marble and jade frowned down like broken cliffs. They would soon be climbing rather than running if this course held true.

Caraeis thought selfishly that the incubus's tracks would become invisible over such ground, and Aiosa would need him after all. Then he suddenly felt the gate, now off to one side, begin opening and panic thrilled through him to his very core.

'Aiosa! It's a trick!' he mind-shouted desperately to the distant sapphire figure of the exarch. 'The gate is opening! This must be a false trail!'

Aiosa's head snapped towards him and the Dire Avengers paused, as still as statues. 'Can you stop it?' her clipped mindspeech responded immediately.

Caraeis was already bending his will in that direction, trying to prevent reality and webway aligning within the psychically charged arch of the gate. It was like wrestling with a huge door, struggling to keep it shut as unimaginable forces pushed at it from the other side.

'Yes! N-not for long,' Caraeis gasped with the effort. 'Get to the gate! Quickly!'

The Dire Avengers sped away, their armoured forms slipping easily through the ruins. Caraeis clenched his jaw and sank his whole concentration into keeping the gate shut. The pressure was relentless, if he had been in proximity he could have closed the gate with a word but at this distance he could only use his will to hold the winding threads of etheric energy apart. The effort involved made seconds feel like hours, beads of sweat stood out on the warlock's face inside his mask and he ground his teeth together until they felt as if they must break.

Despite his best efforts the portal was still grinding open little by little with unstoppable, machine-like certainty. A few more moments and Caraeis would not be able to stop the gate fully forming. He prayed that Aiosa and her Aspect Warriors were almost there, that they could prevent the fugitive escaping into the trackless infinitude of webway...

'There's no one here,' Aiosa's mindspeech announced abruptly.

Caraeis had a brief impression of a towering arch, multi-coloured energy swirling between its uprights, the gate itself still unstable and unusable. But the dust around the gate was empty, no incubus warrior stood at bay, no simpering harlequin companion was on hand trying to interfere again. Caraeis's concentration collapsed, the gate instantly forming as the impediment to its opening was removed.

In that same instant he became aware of another portal nearby, a temporary manifestation so weak that he had failed to notice it while he was battling to keep the other gate closed. Almost as soon as he became aware of it the new portal vanished again, and with it went any psychic sense of the incubus's presence on Caudoeltih.

Caraeis's mind-scream of frustration was not good to hear.

THE RIBBED ARCHES of the travel tube flashed past scant metres away. Kharbyr had pushed the booster-engines to their maximum and trimmed the triangular sail of the captured raider to catch the best of the powerful, erratic etheric winds swirling down from above. Now he stood braced at the tiller simultaneously trying to control the racing craft and not reveal how close he was to soiling himself.

Fortunately the tube was wide at this point, easily wide enough to accommodate a Raider careening prow first towards city bottom. The soiling parts came from spars, bridges and other obstructions that projected at random from the sides of the tube. Yes, people needed places to dock and perhaps cross over the vertical tube but Kharbyr was finding it hard to believe they needed quite so cursed many of them.

It took every ounce of Kharbyr's skill to sweep

the Raider over, under and around these random obstructions at breakneck speed. He dared not back his speed down even for instant because he was all too keenly aware of the whip-thin shapes of ur-ghuls that could be glimpsed clinging everywhere. Bezieth stood just before the mast, legs braced wide as she toted a splinter rifle she had found in one of the Raiders' weapon racks. She was taking potshots at the crawling ur-ghuls but Kharbyr was far too busy controlling the plummeting craft to see whether she actually hit anything. Xagor was crouched beside Kharbyr's feet in the stern of the Raider watching the metal walls whip past as if he were hypnotised by them.

'Kharbyr! Up ahead!' Bezieth shouted, her voice ringing with alarm.

The vertical tube forked ahead, one branch turning abruptly through ninety degrees to become a horizontal tunnel while the other branch continued down into inky darkness. Kharbyr cursed himself for getting drawn into watching for obstacles instead of the course of tube ahead. He was hard over against the wall of the tube, with the horizontal branch coming up fast on its far side. Something about the black pit they were heading into filled Kharbyr with unreasoning fear, the darkness had an unnatural, surging quality about it that every instinct told him to avoid.

Kharbyr cursed again and hauled desperately for the horizontal tunnel, dragging the prow of the Raider up towards the rapidly approaching opening. Even the craft's gravitic compensators could

not eliminate all of the crushing g-forces generated by the manoeuvre and his vision darkened
as the sleek craft reluctantly obeyed. The branch
was sweeping towards them far too quickly, the
Raider's hull creaking and groaning as it struggled
to level out. Kharbyr cut the engines and furled the
aethersail, but the craft's hurtling momentum was
threatened to pull it apart if he slowed down too
quickly. They weren't going to make it.

To Kharbyr's terrified perception events were
unfurling with glacial slowness. The tunnel branch
was rushing up inexorably towards them, the black
pit was now directly below the Raider's keel and the
horizontal tunnel visible ahead. They were going
to clear the lip of the branch but not by enough to
make the turn into the horizontal tunnel immediately afterwards. He shed speed as hard as he dared,
and then harder still. He felt something give and
the Raider bucked viciously before it began trying
to twist out of his hands into a corkscrew dive. The
tunnel floor rose to meet and it was all Kharbyr
could do prevent them from hitting it inverted and
being crushed like insects under the Raider's sliding hull.

'Hang on!' he shouted uselessly and then all
sound was lost in a grinding, hideous cacophony
of agonised metal.

CHO HAD BRIEFLY experienced a sensation akin to
panic when the lifeforms she was tracking suddenly
became embroiled with a number of others. The
psychic trace was still present – admittedly diffuse

but undeniably present – yet now its potential source, her target, was more obscured than ever in what amounted to a crowd of false suspects. An initial instinct to classify each of the new contacts individually and examine their life-sparks carefully to differentiate them from the initial four contacts resulted in a logjam that virtually paralysed Cho for a split second. Then, from the depths of her memory engrams, emerged a broadly matching universal fit for the majority of the new contacts – ur-ghuls. The target was categorically not an ur-ghul and so all lifeforms fitting that designation were henceforth ignored.

Cho had watched carefully from the flat roof of a structure while a grav-craft bearing eight more anomalous contacts closed in on the first four. Cho's fluted, crystalline spirit syphon had dipped in and out of its housing like an insect's sting as she calculated the potential for her target being revealed by the imminent meeting. Disappointingly the eight new contacts had only hunted the lifeforms designated as ur-ghuls and then been ambushed by the initial four contacts Cho was designating A through D.

The temptation to enter the engagement had been almost overwhelming. Life energies were being spilled before her sensors rods, utterly wasted when she could have drawn them into herself and fed on them to grow so much stronger. However caution was still too deeply rooted in her protocols to simply plunge into the fray and risk everything in an orgy of violence. She continued to watch and wait as the fighting lapped aboard the grav-craft (confirmed designation: Raider). Contacts A through D were soon alone aboard the Raider with contacts E through L extinguished or struggling on the ground below.

The target was not revealed. No changes occurred in lifeforms A through D other than elevated heart rates. The whole engagement was highly puzzling and unsatisfactory in its outcome. It was only when the Raider came sharply about and raced for the distant travel tubes that Cho realised she had made an error by hanging back. The psychic spoor now trailed behind the moving grav-craft like a fuel cell pollutant, the source accelerating at a rate greater than she could equal. Cho poured enough energy into her impellers to push them to integrity-endangering levels of thrust as she swept out of hiding in pursuit of the Raider.

The lifeforms designated as ur-ghuls attempted to impede Cho's progress, leaping at her wasp-like hull as she raced overhead. The impacts of the bodies could do no damage to her armoured, curving carapace, but they clawed and bit at exposed vanes and probes with a strength which indicated they had the potential to inflict harm on her. Quite apart from that factor their attacks were slowing her pursuit of the target by a perceptible margin. Cho quickly reclassified the ur-ghuls as hostile and thrilled as she unsheathed her sting-like spirit syphon.

Baleful energies suddenly played ahead of her hull, a teardrop-shaped negative feedback loop that sucked the very life out of the ur-ghuls caught in its grasp. The wiry troglodytes simply withered in that awful glare. At its touch they shrivelled up into doll-like cadavers of stretched-taut skin holding together mouldering bone as centuries of ageing took place in moments. The survivors broke and fled croaking in terror from the death machine in their midst and she pursued them a short distance seeking satiation. It was weak, vermin-like fare for Cho to feast upon, so unlike the rich-bodied full-ness of a living eldar. Yet quantity had a quality of its own and Cho's capacitors drank in the stolen vitality readily, setting her whole resonation array alive with coursing energy.

Emboldened, she sped away, curving her course to plunge into the open mouth of the travel tubes in the wake of the rapidly vanishing Raider. The craft was plunging vertically down the shaft with reck-less haste, still outpacing Cho's maximum speed. Reluctantly Cho reduced power to her impellers back within safe parameters. There was always the psychic trail to follow. Even if the lifeforms moved fast enough to escape her immediate sensor sweeps the trail would inevitably bring her to the target.

IMAGINE A LANTERN. It's an old kind of lantern con-taining a flame for light, with glass walls and a wire cage to hold them in place. Now imagine that the flame is a dying sun, fat and sullen, caught between walls not of glass but of extra-dimensional force that have pulled it outside the material universe and into the shadow-realm of Commorragh. The lantern's cage is now of steely webs endlessly spun by countless spider-constructs. These webs hold in place distant, horn-like towers that regulate the unthinkable cosmic flux to keep the whole ensemble under control. This is an *Ilmaea*, a black sun, and such is what the dark kin use to light their eternal city.

Several such captured suns orbited Commorragh, artefacts of past ages when eldar power waxed so strong that such prodigious feats were no great undertaking. In realspace a single *Ilmaea* could swallow all the vastness of the eternal city at a single gulp, but each is constrained like a prisoner bound in a cell with only a single chink opening into the world. Their baleful glare lights the frosty spires of High Commorragh and lends a sullen, animal heat to Low Commorragh even as their dying agonies are tapped to supply limitless energy to their captors. Thus even the stars themselves are slaves to the eternal city, bound and exploited like every other resource.

In the context of a Dysjunction the Ilmaea formed vast, open portals that had the potential to turn into giant fusion bombs without warning – a very bad combination indeed. The ordinarily feeble solar flares of the captive suns sped into torrents of blazing plasma that curled across the heavens and fell upon the city leaving only devastation in their wake. Yllithian had seen the other danger with his own eyes (technically they were his eyes now, possession being nine-tenths of the lore). Countless entities from beyond the veil were leaking into the city from the Ilmaea's unstable portals and darkening the skies around them with their obscene swarms. Regaining control of the black suns was vital to the survival of the city during a Dysjunction, vital and incredibly dangerous. That Yllithian had been selected for such an honour made him strongly suspect that the Supreme Overlord desired his death.

He had been assigned the Ilmaea *Gora'thynia'dhoad*, commonly known as Gorath, currently in the seventy-seventh gradient over the city. His orders had been as brief as that with no indication of reinforcements that might be available or what actions it might be wise to take in order to regain 'control' of a rogue star. Yllithian had decided to focus his efforts on the towers surrounding Gorath, seeing no gains to be made in even approaching the extra-dimensional walls of the prison itself. His force flew through flickering, vivid skies of a thousand unearthly hues with gigantic thunderbolts flashing down all about them. His followers had learned their earlier lesson well and spread out to take their chances, racing along at top speed towards their destination.

'We're being followed, my archon,' called Yllithian's steersman shortly after Corespur fell away behind their stern. Yllithian twisted around on his throne to view the crazed skies in their wake. After a moment he saw them, a host of black dots cutting steadily through the air on the White Flames' trail. That was no pack of winged daemons, Yllithian reckoned, it looked like another kabal was trailing him – but there was no guessing to what purpose. Yllithian could only hope they were reinforcements as turning around to confront them in the teeth of the storm was simply not an option.

Constrained though it might be, Gorath still swelled enormously as the White Flames force approached the captive star, becoming a huge black orb set among a billowing backdrop of multi-hued clouds. Tendrils of ebon fire twisted back and forth around the Ilmaea like a nest of snakes. Between them ominous-looking clouds of dark fragments swirled between the flames, winged shapes dancing restlessly through the infernal maelstrom that lashed about them.

'There's another group coming up behind us, my archon,' the steersman warned. 'They're fast – already overhauling the first group now.'

Yllithian looked back, startled by the development and nursing just the tiniest thimbleful of hope. The newcomers were larger and few in number, their distant profile jagged and blade-like as they pushed past the swarm of smaller craft that were trailing the White Flames. They were closing with Yllithian's craft so quickly that they made him feel as if he were standing still. The dagger-shapes rapidly filled out to reveal scimitar-sharp wings hung with missiles, pulsing engines and crystal canopies. It was a flight of Razorwing jetfighters that swept arrogantly past on trails of blue fire to leave Yllithian's craft bouncing through the turbulence in their wake.

Timing, Yllithian thought to himself. For all the

difficulties involved it represented a nice piece of timing on Vect's part to have the Razorwings arrive just before Yllithian's group. That or it was merely a happy coincidence that the Razorwings happened by at the right moment but that seemed too unlikely to credit.

The Razorwings quickly shrank into the distance and became visible only by their engine-fires as they closed in on the black sun. The flight broke up abruptly, needle-thin traceries showing a starburst of divergent courses as they went in to the attack. Each fiery pinpoint seemed to give birth to a litter of tiny offspring as they launched their missiles. Bright, brief stars of light flickered through the flapping hordes before winking out with deadly finality.

Gorath was becoming massive now, its bloated form filling half the sky. Details of the surrounding structures were visible: a faint, gauzy glitter of spun steel and bone-white spines that appeared little bigger than Yllithian's finger joint at this distance. These latter were in fact the kilometres-tall towers that controlled the cosmic forces holding the black sun in check. There were over a hundred such structures around Gorath – far too many for Yllithian to even dream of taking them all. No, the only logical choice was to board the primary tower and see if it could be used to bring the others back under control.

Without warning a river of black fire swept down from above. The rogue solar flare crackled and roared in rageing torrent as it curled past within a few hundred metres of the White Flames' craft. The raw heat of it beat on the decks in searing waves that raised blisters and spontaneously ignited anything flammable. Yllithian's force scattered away from the titanic conduit of flame as it twisted and bucked indecisively for few heartstopping seconds before rushing onward to claw out a new path of destruction elsewhere.

'How much longer to the nearest tower?' Yllithian shouted to the steersman.

'Two minutes, less!' yelled the steersman over the howling slipstream.

'Make it less,' Yllithian snarled.

The double-bladed silhouette of a Razorwing flashed past with a twisting funnel of flapping shapes in pursuit. As Yllithian watched a second Razorwing swept down on the horde and tore ragged holes in it with a burst of fire. A few stray daemons darted towards the White Flames and were met with a withering hail of splinters and darklight beams. The wind roared and crackled like a living flame as Gorath filled more and more of the sky.

'One minute!' the steersman called desperately.

The tower was visible up ahead. It was oriented with its crown towards him and its base pointed towards the black sun. The web around the tower gleamed like delicate brushstrokes of silver against the boiling dark mass of Gorath in the background. He spared a glance behind him to see if they were still being followed and saw that they were, although the pursuing swarm definitely seemed to have thinned. The tower grew from palm-sized disk into a huge, intricate structure that was more like a cluster of barbed towers interconnected by slender arches and flying buttresses than a single edifice.

Yllithian's force dived down towards a wide terrace that clung between the cliff-like flanks of the tower, re-orienting themselves at the last second to place the terrace under their keels. Yllithian experienced a brief moment of vertigo as the barque flipped through ninety degrees and the wall that had been rushing towards them became ground beneath them. Then he was leaping from his barque in the midst of his incubi bodyguards and surveying the chaos around him. Black armoured warriors were jumping down from their Raiders on all sides, hellions and reavers wheeling overhead giving them cover.

Splinter fire crackled out suddenly and Yllithian snapped his attention to the source in time to see distant white figures pouring from doorways in the tower onto the terrace. There was a new sound mixed in with the familiar snap and hiss of eldar weaponry, a deeper, throatier roar of projectile weapons that Yllithian had not heard in a long, long time. It was the sound of bolter fire.

# CHAPTER 21
## BAD LANDINGS

'WHAT IS THIS place?' Morr grated in a tone of bemused contempt.

'You have your memories, I have mine,' Motley said defensively. 'I just needed somewhere safe to get my bearings and rest for a moment. This was the best place to come at short notice.'

They stood on a narrow terrace overlooking an azure lagoon with slender towers of orange-glazed ceramic flanking them to either side. Gaudy streamers floated from a balustrade at the edge of the terrace and banners fluttered from the tower walls in the salt-scented breeze coming off the water. A yellow sun high overhead warmed the air and scattered scintillating diamonds of light across the deep blue water. On the beach below them Morr could see brightly garbed people strolling casually past, chattering and laughing together apparently in complete ignorance of the grim incubus glowering down on them from above.

'I hope you don't want to go back to Caudoelith instead,' Motley remarked pointedly.

'No. I was satisfied to leave that place and our pursuers behind.'

'Hmm, I should think so too, you know you could always try being just a little bit grateful for me getting you out of these frequent jams.'

Morr tore his gaze from the people below and gave Motley a withering look. Motley spread his hands deferentially. 'Mind you it's just a suggestion.'

Morr turned back to the sunlit lagoon. 'You have never fully explained your stake in helping me,' the incubus rumbled. 'To save the city, you say, but you are no citizen of Commorragh. Your kind only wander into the eternal city to perform your morality plays or mythic cycles and then leave, you have no commitment to it or its survival. So why do you so smilingly offer to help me at every turn? Where lies your advantage in all this?'

Motley gazed up at Morr's face helplessly. The incubus looked shockingly aged in the warm sunlight: his cheeks were sunken and cadaverous, the creases around his mouth and brow were more deeply defined, his skin dry and lifeless, the dark wells of his eyes were lit by disturbing gleams of hunger and madness. It was as if Morr had aged fifty years within the last few hours in the webway. The incubus caught Motley's expression and smiled mirthlessly.

'The hunger is upon me. She Who Thirsts

demands her due. Soon I must slay to renew myself or I will become one of the Parched, a mewling half-minded thing existing only on what scraps She might choose to let fall from her table.' Morr eyed the peaceful strollers with intent and then grimaced. 'You said this place is from your memories, so the people are ghosts. None of this is real.'

Motley sighed. 'It was real, and the people were real and so it is still real to those who remember it – which in this case is mostly each other. To put it another way these people are real and we're the ghosts here. You cannot harm them and even if you could I would not permit it.'

'Bold words. Do not imagine I have been weakened by my trials, little clown,' Morr sneered. 'if anything, my inner fires blaze all the stronger.'

'Well… that's good. You'll need everything you can muster for Lileathanir, although there won't be any slaying to be had there either. Sorry.'

'We shall see. You still have not answered my question – why should you care what happens on Lileathanir or Commorragh for that matter? What is it to you?'

Motley pondered on how to explain the concept of altruism to someone who has done nothing but claw and fight for every possible advantage throughout their life. Morr's loyalties extended only as far as himself. He had abandoned his clan on Ushant for the Shrine of Arhra. Duty had bonded him to Kraillach and by extension Commorragh at large but he had turned on Kraillach when the archon fell to corruption. All that held meaning for Morr was the savage code of Arhra, to slay or be slain without morality or compunction, even unto a student slaying their teacher if he saw them weaken. The silence between Morr and Motley drew out painfully until it was clear that Morr was not going to go one step further without an answer that fit into his own peculiar code of ethics.

'Isn't it enough that we both want to save Commorragh that we should act in concert?' the harlequin demanded.

'I accept my duty to Commorragh because my actions on Lileathanir led to the Dysjunction,' Morr replied. 'I will rectify them because should Commorragh fall to entropy the incubi will be destroyed and Arhra's teachings will be lost. You have no such motivation and even less to help me. So explain to me what you gain from all of this or we go no further.'

'Because...' Motley began helplessly before inspiration struck him. 'Because the eldar race is more than just the sum of its parts. After the Fall three completely different societies emerged from the wreckage of what came before: Commorragh, the craftworlds and the maiden worlds. Each of them has preserved some part of what was lost – yes, even Commorragh as much as many would wish to deny it. Each branch has prospered in its own way, or at least not collapsed totally, over all the centuries since the Fall and that tells you something in its own right – these are stable societies. Each has learned to adapt to a terrible new universe that has no rightful place for them in it.'

'So you believe that each should be preserved,' Morr grunted. 'How very noble of you.'

'Oh it extends beyond mere preservation, my dear, cynical friend. There is a fatal flaw present in all three of our societies – all of them look only inward and believe themselves to possess the one, true path forward. If they plan for the future at all it's only with their own people in mind and most can't even think that far. Survival has become the absolute watchword of the eldar race, a sort of siege mentality that has ruled over us for the last hundred centuries. It's leading to stagnation, a polar opposite from the excess that brought forth She Who Thirsts, and so now instead of entropy we fall prey to stasis; a slow, cold death.

'Not everyone thinks that way, of course, there are some in each generation that look up from the mire created by their forefathers and glimpse the stars again. We can still learn from one another, support one another. A shred of hope still exists,' Motley looked out over the lagoon wistfully for a moment.

'So now you declare that you are making a better future,' Morr said flatly. 'I have heard such protestations many times. As chief executioner to Archon Kraillach I sent thousands of similar claimants to their final reward.'

'No doubt, but I'm not talking about overthrowing an archon here,' Motley replied wearily. 'I am talking about reunification of the eldar race.'

Morr snorted with derision at the idea of any true eldar of Commorragh mingling with the pale aesthetes of the craftworlds or the half-bestial Exodites of the maiden worlds. Motley looked up at the incubus curiously, head cocked to one side as he waited to see if Morr could recognise the hypocrisy of his attitude. The incubus gave no indication that it was going to happen anytime soon. Motley rallied himself for one more effort.

'Simply look at our own experiences,' Motley said. 'Archon Kraillach, along with Yllithian and Xelian, wanted to bring someone back who was long-dead – impossibly long-dead. Yes it went horribly wrong but how did they do it? By going to someone who had the power to achieve the impossible–'

'The haemonculus?' Morr rumbled uncertainly.

'No, no, no! The worldsinger – you know, the muddy-footed primitive with supposedly nothing to offer to the magnificent grandeur that is Commorragh. They needed her to make their scheme work and they went to considerable efforts to get her because she could do something that no one in Commorragh could do. Doesn't tell you that the Exodites are far from being beneath your contempt? That they have achieved something in their own right worthy of praise and emulation?'

'No, it denotes that they can be uniquely useful slaves at times.'

'Morr, I do believe that you are being deliberately obtuse for your own amusement – which is something that in an odd sort of way I find to be very encouraging. Let's take a different example instead – you and me. At the point where you discovered that Kraillach had been corrupted you called for my help. You knew that no Commorrite could be trusted to see the job done without exploiting the situation and most likely being corrupted in turn. Have I or have I not been a trustworthy and valuable ally ever since?'

'You have,' Morr admitted grudgingly.

'And yet I am not from Commorragh, and I have no vested interest at stake in it or you.'

'That… is not true,' Morr said with a grim smile. The incubus looked as if he had just solved a complex puzzle that had been nagging at him for a long time. Motley frowned, seemingly discomfitted by the change in the incubus's demeanour.

'You're implying that I have a vested interest? Do tell, please.'

'Of course you have. It's me.'

Motley only smiled in response, motioning politely for Morr to continue.

'You need me because you need a dragon slayer.'

BELLATHONIS RUBBED HIS hands together – both of them, new and old. One was delicate and long-fingered, the other stubby and dark. Well you couldn't have everything, he consoled himself, the acuity of his new digits seemed fine and that was the important thing. Dust flaked down from the ceiling and over his bloody instruments in a most unsatisfactory way that ruined Bellathonis's marginally improved mood. Tremors again, closer this time than the last series. The lab was becoming decidedly unsafe and he couldn't return to the White Flames fortress without running the risk that something worse than Venomyst infiltrators would be there waiting for him.

The haemonculus looked around the chamber, his gaze taking in the three wracks hurrying to pile boxes of equipment onto a crude sled, the sarcophagus they were sadly going to have to abandon, the examination tables with their aggregation of dirt and debris. It was a melancholy sight. He reached down and pulled the fourth of his wracks upright from where he had been lying on one of the tables. Bellathonis fondly dusted the leather-clad, bloodied minion down and set him onto his feet.

'Now go and help the others and take care not to pull those sutures out,' Bellathonis admonished.

'Yes, master, thank you, master,' the one-armed wrack replied unsteadily before staggering away to the sled.

'*Death is coming*,' Angevere whispered at Bellathonis's elbow. He frowned at her tone, there was something off about it: not jubilant or mocking or sneering this time, just fearful.

'That's enough from you, old crone,' Bellathonis said decisively and snapped the cylinder containing the witch's head shut. He hauled the container over to the sled and stowed it carefully among the piles of boxes, cases and jars already there. The wracks milled uncertainly around their master awaiting orders, sensing his distress at having to abandon the lab but unable to offer any help. Bellathonis turned to them and spread his hands philosophically.

'My faithful acolytes,' Bellathonis said. 'It falls to

us that we must move on once again. Though we were here only a brief time it's my belief that great things were achieved in this place, and I shall al–'

The slope of rubble that had buried the cells was shifting, individual chunks of it slipping and rolling down to the floor. A dull spot of cherry red appeared in the midst of the fallen masonry, brightening through orange to yellow to white within a few heartbeats. Waves of palpable heat flowed from the glowing spot and an awful grinding noise could be heard behind it. Bellathonis and the four wracks instinctively began to back away.

'I think we'd best–' was all that Bellathonis could say before the rubble slope exploded in a shower of molten rock and something sleek came surging through the white-hot debris. Bellathonis had only the briefest impression of a silvery carapace and scorpion-like tail before he darted out of sight behind the sled. The wracks cried out in alarm and threw themselves at the intruder without hesitation, which Bellathonis considered a creditable show of fervour if not wisdom.

The one-armed wrack barely even got to swing his cleaver before a nest of barbed chains flailed around his neck and bloodily pulled his head straight off his shoulders. The second wrack managed to snap his dagger's blade against the foe's adamantium hull with an enthusiastic but ill-considered lunge. Two sets of shears caught the wrack at shoulder and crotch before hurling him bodily across the chamber in a hideous show of strength. The unfortunate wrack struck the far wall in three separate pieces.

Bellathonis recognised the assailant as a Talos pain engine. It was smallish, perhaps half the size of full-sized engine, but it had a definitively assassin-like cast to its design. The finest Talos engines were mobile monuments to pain and slaughter, more living works of art than mechanisms with purpose. Bellathonis found the concept of this Talos rather contemptible, akin to hobbling one's offspring so that the resulting pygmies would make better servants.

The two remaining wracks hesitated for a split second and then ran in opposite directions around the Talos. The barbed sting atop the invader's tail flashed and one wrack's torso simply vanished in a mass of flames. The other wrack took advantage of the momentary distraction to charge in behind their metallic assailant and jam a gnarled-looking agoniser rod under its carapace. Lightning flared at the juncture and the machine jerked violently before whipping around with eye-blurring speed to confront the source of its pain. Even machine-life could be hurt with an agoniser, circuits as well as nerves could be induced to a pitch of screaming pain by its touch. The Talos did not allow the wrack to strike again, using its whirling chain-flails to flay the flesh from the wrack's bones with machine-precision.

With all four of its attackers neutralised in a matter of seconds, Vhi turned and came for Bellathonis.

KHARBYR AWOKE TO the popping and creaking sounds of cooling metal. The air was filled with a hot, ozone-tainted smell. He tried to move but that set off fireworks of pain throughout his body and he groaned involuntarily. There were broken parts inside that refused to do anything he told them, most especially down around his legs. He tried to remember how he got there – the last thing he remembered was a speeding Raider with him braced at the tiller... the floor of the tunnel coming up fast towards them. Them? Yes, he remembered now, there had been others aboard the Raider: Bezieth and Xagor, where were they? Why weren't they helping him? He tried to call out their names and that hurt too.

He looked around, moving his head cautiously to keep a foaming black sea of nausea at bay. He was trapped in the wreckage of the Raider. The mast had fallen across his legs, pinning them against the deck. Only the wrist-thick tiller bar had saved his torso from being completely pulped, and now that bar was now bent across him forming part of the wreckage that held him in place. Tatters of the orange and yellow aethersail hung everywhere like bunting, a bizarrely cheery-looking sight against the dark, mangled hull of the Raider.

He called out again. He was helpless to do anything else. Even the act of breathing made the nausea rise and fall in waves. At least he was still breathing, it was starting to seem like Xagor and Bezieth hadn't survived. Kharbyr struggled to remember the crash in more detail. He'd been hauling the Raider across to a branching tunnel, desperately trying to check their headlong descent down a horizontal shaft and turn, turn, turn. A chill came over Kharbyr as he remembered the roiling darkness below, a darkness that every instinct told him to avoid. He'd hauled for the side tunnel thinking they weren't going to make it in time. The prow came up and then he'd seen... he'd seen what?

Kharbyr stiffened, involuntarily hissing with pain. There had been a whisper of sound out in the darkness, the gentle hiss of something gliding stealthily through the air. He didn't call out again. There was something sinister and insidious about the sound that did not presage the arrival of help. A sudden clangour nearby made Kharbyr recoil and set off explosions of pain in his legs that brought him close to retching. Through the haze of agony he saw the familiar, barred mask of Xagor thrust over the edge of the Raider.

Kharbyr croaked wordlessly in relief as the wrack hauled himself over the Raider's twisted gunwales and squatted down beside him. There were fresh wounds on the wrack that oozed sluggishly, deep abrasions that had scoured through his ribbed, hide-like robes and into his equally gnarled, hide-like skin.

'Bad landing,' the wrack said, making no move to help.

'Not... my... fault,' Kharbyr grated through clenched teeth. 'Something... hit us!'

Xagor sniffed and cocked his head to one side as if listening. 'Not by our stalker. It still follows,' the wrack said cryptically after a moment.

'Just... help... me!' Kharbyr snarled.

Xagor shrugged, fishing a small device out of his belt pouches that he pressed against the side of Kharbyr's neck. The pain and nausea vanished as instantly as if a door had been slammed. A vague sense of discomfort was all Kharbyr could feel from his trapped body and legs.

'Now, that's better,' Kharbyr blurted in heartfelt relief. He tried to move again but the discomfort flared alarmingly and he quickly abandoned the effort.

'Nerves blocked, not better,' Xagor said as he started levering the fallen mast out of the way in a surprising show of strength.

'Where's Bezieth?' Kharbyr asked.

'This one does not know,' Xagor grunted shortly. 'Gone.'

The mast shifted with a complaining screech and Kharbyr was free. Xagor reached down and dragged him clear with scant regard for his battered limbs. The wrack set him down and set to work on his injuries, meticulously straightening bones and stitching ripped flesh as he went.

'You – ah – seem to have a lot of experience at that,' Kharbyr gasped.

'A wrack has no worth if he cannot mend broken clients for his master,' Xagor muttered. To Kharbyr it sounded as if the wrack was quoting someone else, Bellathonis probably.

Kharbyr could see over Xagor's shoulder to where the ribbed wall of the tunnel rose a dozen metres away. A few scattered lamps hung from the wall and shed a dim light over the scene. As Kharbyr watched he saw one the lights momentarily eclipsed by something moving across it, a silver crescent that gleamed briefly and was gone again before Kharbyr could be sure he hadn't just imagined it. Kharbyr decided that he didn't need to be sure

'There's something out there, Xagor,' Kharbyr hissed. 'I heard it just before you came. I think I just saw it.'

'Yes. Stalker. Is hunting us,' the wrack said nervously as he looked around. He gave a slight shiver before returning to his work.

'What is it? You said it didn't hit us, what did?'

'This one is not sure…' Xagor said quietly as if the same answer applied to both questions. Kharbyr glared at him silently waiting for a proper answer.

'The… the darkness,' Xagor said after a moment. 'The darkness reached for us, Kharbyr could not see because he was looking ahead, but Xagor saw. It came for us from below.'

Kharbyr's mouth went dry at the wrack's words. 'That was back in the vertical shaft, so what's hunting us now?'

'This one does not know,' Xagor repeated.

Kharbyr thought he glimpsed the silver crescent again, high on the wall. This time he heard the swish of air displaced by a flying body as it vanished from view.

'Why doesn't it attack? We're in no position to stop it dancing on our skulls if it wanted.'

'This one–'

'–does not know, yes I get it, thanks for nothing.'

A fierce tingling started without warning on Kharbyr's chest. At first he though it must be something Xagor was doing but the wrack was busy working on his legs. The tingling grew into a sensation of heat as if someone was holding a flame close to Kharbyr's flesh.

'Xagor! I can feel something! The nerve block isn't – ahhh!'

Kharbyr's body contorted, back arching and limbs flailing as the pain blazed up into an inferno. The injuries from the crash had been sickening but this was far, far worse, something beyond physical hurt that clawed at Kharbyr's soul. Xagor leapt back in alarm as a bright glow began to crawl across Kharbyr's flesh, radiating outward from a pentagonal spot on his chest to encompass his writhing form. Kharbyr unleashed a long, ululating scream that tailed off into grim silence as his thrashing body finally became still. Xagor edged closer uncertainly.

'Kharbyr is–?' Xagor said plaintively just as another spasm gripped the prone form, arching it almost double and sending the wrack scurrying back again. Kharbyr's ragged breaths were just audible, but after a second they changed, becoming a coughing, sobbing sound. Little by little that changed into a burbling chuckle and then what could only be wheezing laughter. Kharbyr sat up suddenly despite his injuries and looked Xagor straight in the eye.

'Excellent. Excellent and distinctly well-timed too,' Kharbyr said with a distinctly un-Kharbyr-like inflection in his voice. 'Oh Xagor, do stop acting so shocked.' Xagor recognised the admonishing tones instantly.

'M-master?' the wrack asked cautiously.

'WELCOME-OFFERINGS!' THE machine-enhanced voice cracked across the terrace like synthesised thunder, cutting across the barrage of weapons fire with a wall of noise. A corpulent champion of Chaos heavily armoured in bile-green plating that leaked pus from prominent boils brandished a rusting sword at the approaching dark eldar. 'YOUR SAC-RIFICE IS EAGERLY AWAITED,' the voice boomed. 'THE LORD OF DECAY EMBRACES YOUR FURY AND RETURNS IT A THOUSANDFOLD! THIS IS A GLORIOUS DAY!'

There was more of the same, much more and Yllithian instructed his armour to block it out. Their enemies comprised two distinct forces – three if you counted the flying daemons, which Yllithian decided could be safely ignored for now. Compared to what they had found at the tower orbiting Gorath the flying daemons were an irrelevance.

Their ground-bound enemies were split into a shambolic horde of possessed and a lesser number of thick-bodied figures in filth-encrusted heavy armour. The latter moved with a singular lack of grace and a kind of crude stolidity no eldar could ever emulate. Mere dogs of the Ruinous Powers, Yllithian told himself, the sort of crudely augmented warriors that the lesser slave races pro-duced and expended by the million. The lie tasted bitter on his tongue. His studies of the daemonic powers had warned of the Traitor Legions and their corruption by the Dark Gods. The legionaries had become champions of Chaos that enjoyed the fickle favour of their deity, and to find them abroad within Commorragh was a dire portent indeed.

Unfortunately they were also very heavily armed. Explosive bolts roared across the open terrace and tore bloody holes in the ranks of Yllithian's disembarking forces. A missile flew up and gutted an incoming Raider in a dirty yellow explosion. Yllithian called in his reavers and hellions to distract the opposing firepower while he led his warriors directly against the onrushing possessed.

Splinter fire scythed down the shambling, putrescent figures like ripe wheat. The hell-born vitality of the fiends availed them little protection against the kind of poisons the White Flames warriors were using: fleshrot, inkblind, scald-lotus, wryther and a dozen other deadly toxins burned, blinded and twisted the stolen bodies of the possessed into useless, fleshy prisons. Warriors armed with Shredders were moving up to liquidate the surviving possessed even as Yllithian's incubi bodyguard cut a path through the flopping, flailing mass.

As they broke through Yllithian saw instantly that his reavers and hellions had failed to break the phalanx of Chaos warriors clustered at the base of the tower. Crumpled bodies, burning jetbikes and broken skyboards scattered across the terrace gave mute testimony to their efforts. The survivors were scattering, jinking and dodging desperately to evade the withering fire coming at them from below.

Yllithian cursed, realising there was still over a hundred metres to go into the teeth of ruinous firepower before his forces could close. The Chaos warriors had already realised the possessed were falling faster than they had thought possible. The wide maws of their big, ugly guns were swinging around, levelling for a salvo that would tear Yllithian's lightly armoured foot troops to pieces.

The howl of engines from above presaged a sudden deluge of sickle-winged shapes diving straight into the Chaos ranks. Hellions, reavers and Venoms swept past at breakneck speed, impaling and decapitating with their bladevanes and hellglaives. For an instant Yllithian thought his own auxiliaries had rallied and returned to the fray before realising his error. The newcomers were from another kabal entirely, their colours familiar to him even in the heat of battle. The Blades of Desire had arrived.

Frenzied wyches leapt down directly into hand-to-hand combat from the decks of speeding Venoms. Yllithian, never one to miss an opportunity, led his incubi into the heart of the struggling mass while the Chaos warriors were distracted. He ducked a snarling chainsword and cut the arm from its wielder with a quick riposte. Rotting face-plates whirled before him as the Chaos warriors fought back with stubborn tenacity.

The hulking warriors were horribly strong and seemed virtually immune to pain. Yllithian saw slender eldar snapped like twigs in their gauntleted grasp, whirling chainblades driven with unstoppable force through the writhing bodies of wyches and bloodied, roaring giants that fought on when they had been virtually cut to pieces.

Yllithian found himself beginning to see why such warriors made such popular arena slaves. They could absorb punishment like Donorian fiends, and took full advantage of the fact. Time and again the hulking warriors shrugged off fatal wounds and unleashed a deadly counterattack. But the Chaos warriors were also fatally slow and clumsy in comparison to the eldar. When a bare-headed warrior grasped at him with lightning-sheathed claws Yllithian simply sidestepped and decapitated his attacker with a backhand flick of his sword. Another attacker came surging forward only to find Yllithian's blade sheathed in his eye socket before he could swing his own rust-covered sword. At Yllithian's signal his incubi bodyguards closed protectively around him, carving him a space in the melee with sweeps of their mighty klaives.

Yllithian glanced around to assess the battle beyond his immediate vicinity. The enemy seemed heavily outnumbered, islands of resistance in a mounting sea. With their formation broken the invaders stood no chance against the ravening dark eldar attacking from all sides. The hulking, armoured figures were dragged down one by one in a frenzy of bloodlust; dismembered and decapitated by the bright, deadly blades of the wyches and Yllithian's incubi.

Across the carnage he saw Aez'ashya weaving a

sinuous dance of death through the last handful of foes. She was wielding twin daggers that shone like crimson ribbons as she carved a bloody swathe through their thickly armoured hides. She laughed lasciviously as she caught his glance, revelling in her moment as a terrible, magnificent goddess of murder unleashed.

Yllithian had a chill premonition as he looked upon her. There was death for him, too, laughing in that unguarded glance – a delectable thirst for his own murder that had yet to be quenched. Vect had sent the new mistress of the Blades of Desire to fight at his side, but under what orders?

# CHAPTER 22
## RETURN TO LILEATHANIR

THE TRAVELLERS STEPPED away from the portal, the silver light of its activation draining away to be replaced by the flickering glow of ice-trapped fires. The travellers' breath steamed in the sub-zero air and the frozen mud beneath their feet was as hard as iron. Around them the living rock walls of the World Shrine had been transformed into a fractured landscape of ice. A pitiful figure was huddled on the slope above, crouching in an attitude that indicated it had waited long at that spot watching the portals for any sign of life.

'It's… it's you? I-I'd never thought to see you again,' the wretch said in a tone of wonder that cracked into hysteria at the sight of the second traveller. 'You and… him!'

'Hush now, Sardon Tir Laniel,' Motley said gently. 'He's come here to help and so have I. I'm sorry it's taken so long.'

The current worldsinger of Lileathanir raked back her greying locks to stare at the shrine's violator unmasked. Here was the one that had defiled the World Shrine and stolen her predecessor, the one who had unleashed such a cataclysm on her world that barely one in ten lived through it. She could feel a gathering rush of emotions in her belly: rage, fear, hate all boiling together into something foul and potent. The shrine shook in empathy, the rock trembling in subliminal response to her anger as hissing flames leapt up behind the ice. Morr returned her gaze steadily, his pitiless black eyes showing no glimmer of sympathy or remorse.

'Sardon!' Motley said less gently. 'It's not your place to judge him for his actions. He's come here to set things right willingly, we can't expect contrition as well.'

Sardon blinked, looked at the warrior again and saw him more clearly: battered, bloodied, a face etched with an awful hunger that could not hide the weariness and desperation in is soul. It was a figure to be pitied rather than hated, a hollowed out, broken puppet propped up only by its vainglorious pride. She had boasted to Caraeis that she would feed the defilers of the shrine to the dragon in vengeance for what they'd done. Confronted with the reality of it she realised there was an all-consuming sickness in the cycle of vengeance. Vengeance begets hatred, hatred begets vengeance. The warrior at Motley's side was as much a victim of it as any. After a moment the trembling of the shrine subsided and the flames sank lower as the dragon spirit returned to a fitful slumber.

'Well then, dark one,' Sardon said eventually as she painfully pushed herself upright on half-frozen limbs. 'You should come and see what you've made.'

Great ice sheets sheathed the World Shrine of Lileathanir. Thick, glassy bulwarks hid the scorched rock and steaming crevasses, fringes of icicles hung from fuming chimneys and frost-rimed boulders. Impossibly, fires still burned just behind the ice. The frozen flames that gleamed through it with undimmed fury, held in check for the present but trembling at the point of bursting into new life.

'You're too late,' the worldsinger said hopelessly. 'I had to do something... I couldn't just sit and wait. I tried to heal it myself, soothe the Dragon, but it only grew fiercer. In the end I was just trying to contain it and I couldn't even do that. Look.'

They looked to where Sardon was pointing. In the depths of the shrine a rough arch pierced the ice sheets, a blackened scar running from floor to roof that oozed smoke and noxious fumes. Red, poisonous light leaked through the crack as if coming from otherworldly depths. In it something was stirring, something vast and unthinkably primordial.

'Ah well, that's... to be expected I suppose,' Motley muttered uneasily before rallying to say, 'but it's never too late! You did a good thing and bought us some time and that's a precious commodity right now!'

Morr ignored both of them, his eyes fixed rigidly on the ominous-looking arch at the far end of the ice-gripped cavern. Without a word he gripped his klaive in both hands and started marching resolutely towards the entrance.

'What is he–?' Sardon gasped before Motley shushed her and whispered in her ear:

'He knows he helped to turn your world spirit to its dragon aspect by stoking all that unreasoning fury and vengeance into what it is now – a rageing beast with quite staggering potential to do harm or, worse still, metamorphose into a form that the Ruinous Powers would welcome as their new plaything. You've been able to quiet the worst of the dragon's effect here temporarily, but ripples of that fury are still causing immense harm elsewhere. Morr has, very bravely in my opinion, volunteered to help quell the dragon in the only way he knows how.'

Morr was wading through a stream of bubbling meltwater up to the crack in the ice. Its vast size was more and more apparent the closer he got to it. His tiny, doll-like figure was visible for just an instant between the roiling fumes before he vanished inside. Sardon drew back and stared at Motley in mixed wonder and disbelief.

'He's going to try and kill it?' she said incredulously.

Motley sighed and shrugged his narrow shoulders pensively. 'He's going to try, yes.'

'But that's impossible!' Sardon cried. 'And what happens if this death dealer does find a way to kill the dragon? What will happen to Lileathanir then? Without the world spirit to protect us we will be left naked to the universe. The daemons will come for us and nothing will be there to stop them.'

Motley spread his hands helplessly. 'I can only believe it's highly unlikely that he'll succeed. All I can tell you is that he'll try. If he fails and the dragon destroys him then it's going to be satiated, its lust for vengeance at least partially fulfilled. That will buy us more time to take further measures.'

'A living sacrifice? That's repugnant. Barbaric.'

Motley looked at the dirty, dishevelled worldsinger in her rough homespun robes and bare feet and he smiled warmly.

'I can't tell you how happy it makes me to hear you say that, Sardon,' the harlequin said without irony. 'However, it might shock you to know that such practices are more widespread and well-established than you might think... in fact I do believe some of its practitioners are just about to arrive, shall we?'

Motley nodded back towards the chamber of portals. When Sardon looked around she could just see the silver glimmer of their activation.


THE RAIDER WRECKAGE was still cooling and creaking around Xagor and Kharbyr. A few dim red telltales on the craft's controls picked out highlights on Xagor's barred mask as he leaned in close over Kharbyr's limp form.

'Kharbyr is true-dead gone?' the wrack asked.

What-had-been-Kharbyr flapped its limbs distractedly like a puppet master testing them for function. It flailed at the nerve block on its neck and eventually pried it loose. It grimaced and then thrust Kharbyr's chin forward aggressively and grinned.

'Ah, that's better. Xagor, when are you going to understand that it's all just meat?' it said in a voice that sounded more and more like Bellathonis with every word. 'Just meat that we push around with our willpower until it doesn't work any more. I've heard that once upon a time and long ago when the meat stopped working that was just The End. One day it was farewell, so long, so-sorry-but-you're-dead-now. Your will to survive counted for absolutely nothing once your personally apportioned slice of meat was dead, rotting – can you imagine it? Well those days are gone and now everyone can live for-ever if they simply plan ahead properly.'

Xagor shook his head. 'This one still does not understand, very sorry, master.'

'All right, very simply and in short words then: You gave Kharbyr a sort of psychic homing device. I used it to transfer my soul into his body. His soul has gone into my body which is very unfortunate for him because mine is dead meat right about now.'

'Is possible?' the wrack seemed stunned by the concept and sat back on his haunches, masked face cocked to one side. 'The master is beyond mighty, beyond death!' Xagor crowed, exulting for a moment before growing very still again. 'Wait… what thing dared kill the master's old body?'

'It was a Talos engine, a very mean little one I was in no position to deal with at the time. It'll be from the Black Descent. Unlike you, Xagor, they refuse to acknowledge my majestic superiority…'

'Master! There is still danger! Xagor has heard Talos hunting close.'

'That couldn't possibly be true... unless there were two machines...'

Bellathonis heard the now-familiar whine of gravitic impellers and caught sight of a flicker of movement above them.

'Oh.'

CHO DRIFTED DOWN towards the target fully confident of her acquisition. A rush of pride and accomplishment ran through her, extending every vane and sensor probe involuntarily to drink in the revised image of the target. Designated target C now fulfilled the precise metaphysical identification parameters stored in her emgrams. Cho had watched the change take place and listened to the target boast of its accomplishment afterwards. Better yet there was a high probability that the target had been fleeing from Vhi at the moment of attack, unaware that he fled directly into the claws of Cho.

The target was aware of Cho's presence now, as was designated target D crouching at his side. This was irrelevant as Cho had already scanned them both for weaponry and found none capable of breaching her spun-metal hide. Designated targets A and B were inactive flatlines, lying together in a crumpled heap beside the wreck of the Raider. At this close range Cho could determine that target B was in fact a contained essence, a life-without-body in a metal prison. No other threats or potential escape routes could be detected within Cho's considerable sensor range, the target was completely trapped with barely enough control of its body to stand up, let alone flee.

Cho slowly extended her spirit syphon. She took pleasure in considering whether to destroy the primary target first and then hunt designated target D afterwards for sport, or whether to simply drain them both with a single wide-setting, maximum-strength feedback loop. Caution came to the fore once again. Designated target D could not be allowed to become a distraction. She should attempt to rejoin the doubtless frustrated Vhi-engine as soon as possible and share knowledge of the kill. Their creator would be proud and recognise Cho's accomplishment. The bothersome fact that Vhi's attack had precipitated Cho's opportunity meant he could still claim a victory of sorts. It mattered not at all. Vhi could maintain his rude pride and sense of superiority while Cho would know that whatever Vhi's claims she was the one that had made the kill.

The calculation had taken only a fraction of a second. Satisfied with her conclusions Cho struck. Baleful energies played over the targets, relentlessly sucking away their life essence. Their bodies began shrivelling as if the march of decades was passing within seconds. Vitality surged into Cho's capacitor-valves in a flood of dark energy – a fine, fortified wine in comparison to the small beer of the ur-ghuls' crude, short lives. Cho crooned with pleasure as she drank it in.

\* \* \*

THE FOOT OF the tower above Gorath was a charnel house. Eldar, possessed and Chaos warriors littered the flagged terrace two and three deep in many places. Even with the timely arrival of the Blades of Desire the toll of the fighting had been heavy and barely half of Yllithian's White Flames kabalites were still on their feet. Overhead a swirl of hellions, reavers and Venoms snarled around the tower answering any shots from the defenders on the upper levels with a storm of fire. Aez'ashya – Archon Aez'ashya as Yllithian reminded himself – sauntered over to him with a hip-swinging gait that was filled with ribald mockery.

'Nice work, Yllithian, you distracted them long enough for my blades to do all the work,' she smiled.

'This kind of butcher's work you are very welcome to,' Yllithian said coldly, 'but sadly I expect our opponents haven't been helpful enough to commit their entire force to be cut up out here in the open.' He gazed up at the enormity of the tower and the ongoing skirmish significantly. Aez'ashya merely shrugged.

'I'm happy to defer to your superior knowledge of our opponent's dispositions,' she said, 'even if I find it a more than a little curious you're so well-informed – these aren't more friends of yours, are they Yllithian?'

'Simple logic, no more,' Yllithian snapped. He kicked at one the bulky corpses littering the terrace. It split open, leaking foul ichor and a sickening stench. 'See? These are mortal servants of the

Ruinous Powers – devotees of the entity we know as Nurgle. An incursion by the followers the plague lord is not just another random manifestation from beyond the veil. If they came here with a purpose I'll wager that it had nothing to do with standing around waiting to get attacked by us. We need to organise our forces and start clearing the rest of the tower from top to bottom. We have to find out what they're doing and put a stop to it.'

'Oh we do, do we?' Aez'ashya purred coolly, deliberately goading him. 'I don't believe that I'm under your command, Yllithian, my orders from the Supreme Overlord said nothing at all about that.'

'Just what did your orders say, Aez'ashya?' Yllithian replied acidly. 'Something along the lines of "follow Yllithian and support him until"… oh I don't know, let's just say…" until further notice?" How close does that sound?' He noticed Aez'ashya's eyebrows twitch upward slightly in surprise and knew that his barb was close to the mark. The pertinent question was really whether Aez'ashya's other orders were to wait for an opportune moment to kill him, but even Aez'ashya wasn't going to be naïve enough to give away that little nugget of information.

Yllithian hesitated momentarily as he tried to decide what to do. He desperately wanted to be away from here as quickly as possible, but leaving before the Ilmaea was stabilised would be a virtual death sentence that Aez'ashya would no doubt be happy to execute. If the forces of Chaos could take over the stolen suns during the Dysjunction then all of Commorragh would be finished anyway, doomed to drown beneath a tide of daemonic filth from above. There was really no option except to go onward.

Just as Yllithian reached his conclusion the tower trembled slightly, a momentary, vertiginous ripple across the entire structure that hinted at the massive forces being focused upon it from elsewhere in the universe. The terrace suddenly lurched beneath their feet and cracked, fissures opening in its surface as whole chunks of it fell away into the blazing inferno of Gorath below. There was a general rush for the towers with White Flames warriors and Blades of Desire wyches elbowing each other aside to get up the shallow steps at their base. As befitted the true state of Commorrite politics Yllithian and Aez'ashya led the charge, their differences and suspicions temporarily forgotten in the face of a common threat.

A set of recessed archways in the flanks of the tower opened into a lofty chamber similarly pierced on all sides. The space was dominated by a wide, spiralling ramp that disappeared up into the ceiling and down through the floor. Muzzle flashes stabbed at the top of the ramp and a spray of explosives bolts bit chunks out of the floor at their feet.

'Up!' both archons cried in unison and led their combined forces storming up the ramp. Through the arches Yllithian glimpsed the last vestiges of the terrace outside collapsing, the air above it filled with a chaotic, spiralling swarm of reavers, Raiders and hellions as the stonework fell away. He was stranded in the tower, at least temporarily, until another platform could be found for disembarkation. He glanced up to see the top of the ramp crowded with hulking green-armoured shapes, muzzle flashes stabbed down at the running eldar like the opening of a set of fanged-filled jaws.

A chain of explosions whipped across Yllithian's shadow field. Dark ink-blots enveloped each impact as the entropic forces of the field dissipated the energy into shadows and dust. Other eldar around him were not so well protected and detonated in bright crimson novas as the mass-reactive rounds penetrated their bodies. The rush of eldar hesitated for an instant as those coming the head of the ramp flinched in the onslaught.

Aez'ashya broke from the wavering ranks as a fast-moving blur that seemed to step under, over and around the hosing streams of explosive bolts as if they were stationary. She sprang up the ramp and vanished into the knot of bestial Chaos warriors at the top, their muzzle flares crisscrossing as they disastrously tried to follow her progress. A rush of fleet-footed wyches overtook Yllithian and plunged in after their mistress, their blades slashing in an intricate ballet of pain.

By the time Yllithian and his warriors arrived at the top of the ramp only twitching corpses lay strewn around in the chamber above with no sign of Aez'ashya and the wyches. The ramp debouched into the centre of a windowless, triangular chamber with more spiralling ramps going upward in each of its corners. Yllithian redirected a few cliques of his followers to go back down and start sweeping the lower floors but his instincts told him the main fighting still lay above. Taking the bulk of his warriors with him he selected the ramp with the most bodies heaped on it and headed up. From above he could soon hear the sounds of combat.

# CHAPTER 23
## INTO THE DRAGON'S LAIR

MORR WADED THROUGH rushing melt water that had a rank, sulphurous smell to it as he followed the arched crack into the ice. The walls soon turned to black rock slick with moisture and gravel crunched beneath his armoured boots. As he moved forward the red glow ahead of him grew ever more intense and sullen. The slick, black walls opened out until he was descending a rough slope into a vast cavern where the far walls were shrouded in darkness and the floor seemed a shifting, bloody sea. A rumbling, subsonic hiss overlaid all other sounds in the cavern, the noise of an unthinkably gigantic serpent or a great host of people muttering and whispering. Morr knew it to be one in the same.

As he descended further into the cavern huge pillars of twisted basalt rose up on all sides to lose their lofty crowns in the gloom overhead. The bases of the pillars were clearly visible. Serpentine coils of crimson energy twisted across the floor of the cavern and around the pillars to form a multi-dimensional cat's cradle of living light. The crimson coils pulsed with vitality: roiling, knotting and shifting as they wound restlessly back and forth.

Morr halted, gripping his klaive in both hands as he readied himself and drew on his last reserves of energy for the battle ahead. He knew that he was confronted not by a physical opponent this time but a metaphysical one. The manifestation of the enraged, dead spirits of Lileathanir lay before him in the cavern, visible now as it coalesced in the broken vessel of the World Shrine. His own perceptions fluttered between interpreting it as the coils of a vast wyrm, a foaming cataract of blood and a blazing river of fire. He was less than a speck beside the all-encompassing power of the world spirit. He was no more capable of harming it than a mosquito is capable of harming an elephant.

The one advantage he held was the composite nature of his foe. The world spirit combined the psychic energy of every living thing that had crossed over into the Lileathanir matrix at the point of its death: Exodites, birds, beasts. The resultant gestalt entity was primal and atavistic, driven by instincts that were by turns nurturing and destructive. Those instincts had pushed it into the dragon aspect of its nature, but there would always be countless spirits pulling it in a myriad of different directions. That was a weakness to be exploited.

He reached up to his trophy rack and lifted from

it the incubus helm he had taken at the shrine of Arhra. That fight seemed so long ago, so important at the time but so trivial now. He gazed into its blank-faced mask for a moment, remembering, before turning it around and slowly lowering the bloodied casque over his own skull. The fit was poor, the internal sensors did not mate properly with his fighting suit, the copper tang of clotted blood assailed his nostrils, but Morr cared not at all. A sense of wholeness and wellbeing flowed into him as he locked the helm in place. He grinned fiercely beneath the mask and raised his voice in challenge, mounting a rocky promontory to whirl his klaive so that it flashed brilliantly in the crimson light.

'I have returned and I challenge you again! Come! Come and match your fury against mine! Never forgive! Never forget! Arhra remembers and now so will you!'

The reaction was immediate, the gestalt consciousness of the dragon suddenly becoming aware of the miniscule speck in its midst that squeaked with outrageous defiance. A vast, triangular shape reared up from the crimson murk. There was the vaguest suggestion of a head with burning spheres like green lamps where eyes could be. Great exhalations of raw emotion gusted from the impossible maw of the being. Morr felt an expanding bubble of conscious recognition sweep over him, the sharp prickle of poisonous hate, the familiar hot wash of rage.

'Yes! Me, here I am! I'm the one! I defied you

then and I defy you now!' Morr shouted into the earth-shaking hiss. 'Now come! Fight me! Learn what Arhra knows!'

Hellfire came raining down and Morr ran for his life, racing downward for the heart of the crimson coils. Beneath the psychic lash of the dragon's fury the rocky slope around him exploded into an avalanche of molten debris. It was impossible to stay ahead of that tidal wave of destruction, the blast wave of it swept him up in giant hands and threatened to smash him down into oblivion. Morr was hurled headlong into the ghostly coils, his klaive carving a ruddy arc as he unleashed his own fury upon the souls of the restless dead.

CARAEIS HAD STEPPED from the portal into the frozen World Shrine of Lileathanir with Aiosa at his heels. The four Dire Avengers that made up the rest of the squad followed and immediately fanned out flawlessly into overwatch positions around the rough little cave. Their long-necked star throwers covered individual fire arcs that all intersected on the two figures that stood waiting for them at the entrance.

'You!' Caraeis snarled, little troubling to conceal his anger.

'Yes, me again I'm afraid,' Motley replied nonchalantly, 'I thought you'd be here sooner than this, trouble with the runes again?'

Caraeis did not respond to the taunt, though the lenses of the warlock's helm that glared at the harlequin were lit with baleful amber fire. Aiosa cut in to ask bluntly:

'What are you doing here and why did you assist the fugitive in his escape?'

'Because this is the place that he was meant to come to,' Motley replied airily, 'and that is my answer to both of those questions.'

'Then where is the incubus now?' Caraeis snapped, rounding on Sardon. 'And why do you, world-singer, now stand beside this... this meddler!'

Sardon blinked in surprise at the warlock's venom. 'The wanderer and his kind have come to Lileathanir since its first settlement,' she said mildly. 'The people of the craftworlds are thought of as our guardians, but children of the Laughing God are known as our friends. In our time of need he has come to us and offered help, a potential solution. What do you bring to the World Shrine? Anger? Recrimination? We have more than enough of that already, we need no more brought to us by outsiders.'

'Solution? What solution?' Caraeis spluttered, fixing his amber-eyed gaze on Motley again. 'My runecastings indicated none of this.'

'The worst kind of solution as far as you're concerned,' Motley taunted with a wide smile. 'One that doesn't involve you: No rung up the ladder to the seer council. No expanded recruitment from the grateful survivors of Lileathanir. No fame. No glory. No praises sung in the Infinity circuit of Biel-Tan for all eternity. Nothing.'

Motley felt he had judged the warlock's true motivations nicely, probably better than Caraeis had ever admitted them to himself. Caraeis's shoulders shook with suppressed emotion as he took a step towards Motley. Aiosa put up a hand to stop him and regarded the harlequin coolly from beneath her impassive mask.

'You charge that Caraeis has been led by ambition? That… desire… has overcome his wisdom?' the exarch asked deliberately.

'It's not my place to charge anyone with anything,' Motley smiled. 'I'm merely putting together everything I've seen and making an observation. I have to ask as a point of interest – what was the plan when and if you finally got around to bringing Morr back to Lileathanir? You were intending to solve the situation how exactly? Tossing him down a crevasse bound hand and foot perhaps? A living sacrifice to appease the dragon?'

'This is ridiculous!' Caraeis shouted. 'You have no right to interfere! You've blackened your hands with the dark kin and now you seek to drag me down into the mire with you. *We* did not do this!' Caraeis swept out his arms dramatically to encompass the shrine, and by extension the whole world.

'No, but you sought to capitalise on it. The dark kin, as you like to call them, were ignorant of the consequences of their actions. If they knew the damage they could cause themselves in the long run they would never have acted in the way they did. Not that ignorance excuses it, of course… it's just that you have no such excuse.'

Sardon looked at the harlequin in shock. 'What do you mean?' she gasped.

'That our friend Caraeis and all of his seer kind

could have foreseen the violation of the shrine and the outcome. They could have acted to prevent it and yet they did not.'

'Every strand of fate cannot be followed,' Caraeis replied with a quiver in his voice. 'Only certain junctions, extraordinary nexii can be affected with the correct application of–'

'Oh please! Stop!' Motley laughed mockingly. 'The strands of fate bend towards a great cataclysm that affects the webway itself and you claim that it was too obscure to foresee, too complex to affect? If that's true you have little value in your current calling and should give serious consideration to finding another path – perhaps pottery, or food preparation.'

'Enough!' Caraeis snarled. 'Where is the incubus? Speak now or–'

Caraeis's impending threat was cut short by a thunderous roar from the depths of the shrine. The rock walls shook and ice fell in splintering sheets as the roaring went on and on; an inchoate, hissing bellow of rage that crashed thought the shrine and made the stones quiver like a living thing. Motley grinned maniacally and shouted above the tumult.

'There! That'll be him, in the very heart of the shrine!' the harlequin yelled wildly. 'And I do believe he's ready to receive you now!'

Without a word Caraeis plunged into the World Shrine with his witchblade in hand. After a split second of hesitation the Aspect Warriors followed, Aiosa giving Motley a long, hard look as she ran past him. Sardon wrung her hands in dismay.

'You're letting them go? They'll be killed!'

'No. Stop. Don't go in there. You'll all be killed,' Motley murmured sardonically as the last of the Aspect Warriors vanished into the quaking shrine. The harlequin's lips were drawn into an unhappy frown, the very picture of sadness and dejection, but behind the mask his eyes glittered with dark, unfathomable amusement.

XAGOR AND BELLATHONIS saw the murder engine approaching, its wasp-like form gleaming in the semi-darkness of the travel tube as it swept down on them from above. The engine was unhurried, confident that it had its prey cornered, and descended slowly enough to allow them plenty of time to realise the hopelessness of their situation. Being devotees of the arts of flesh Xagor and Bellathonis recognised its type immediately: a Cronos parasite engine, a time-thief. Bellathonis recognised more than that, a signature workmanship that he had also seen back at his hidden lab on the miniature Talos engine that attacked him there. He found himself having to grant that a twinned pair of such dwarfs had a certain artistic integrity that he had felt lacking in the singular entity. It still smacked a little of toy-making as far as Bellathonis was concerned.

Xagor was caught still in the act of diving across Bellathonis in a vain attempt to shield his master when the negative feedback loop was established. Dark energies bathed them both, utterly indifferent to the wrack's desperate act of self-sacrifice. Kharbyr – now Bellathonis's – flesh was sinking onto his bones, his face becoming a skull wrapped in papyrus with his dark, shrunken eyes blazing as his vitality was drained away. The haemonculus had never imagined that it would end like this. The very least of his kind were unnaturally long-lived – nigh immortal – and his newly stolen body had been young and fit. Even so the relentless vortex produced by the spirit syphon was stripping away centuries of Bellathonis's lifespan in seconds. Seconds more and he would be nothing but dust and mouldering bones.

The feedback loop ceased abruptly, leaving Bellathonis and Xagor feebly groaning in an advanced state of decrepitude. Bellathonis blinked rheumy eyes and tried to focus on the hovering Cronos engine to see why it had stopped. Perhaps it was going to take its time after all, he thought, indulge in a little torture before it got on with the murder part. Part of him approved.

Curiously the wasp-like engine seemed to have sprouted a distinctly humanoid-looking pair of legs beneath it. Bellathonis realised belatedly that there was a torso too, connected to a pair of arms that had impaled the underside of the Cronos engine with a large, baroque-looking sword. He vaguely recognised the distinctively scarred arms somehow, a petty archon he'd dealt with in Metzuh? Bellathonis couldn't remember anymore, everything seemed dim and half-forgotten. He looked again, unable to shake the feeling that something important was happening.

The murder machine was hanging at an angle with its claws waving frantically, its array of sensor probes and vanes fluttering wildly like a trapped bird. Sparks were pouring out of it where the sword had plunged into its vitals. It seemed unable to move, only bobbing in the air as the sword was ripped free in a disembowelling deluge of components. The gleaming machine sank slowly as if the sword had been its only means of support, guttering and sparking as it rolled over onto its side, lifeless. It was then that a dark miracle occurred, or so it seemed to Bellathonis.

Without Cho's consciousness to control them her capacitor-valves tripped open and all the vitality she had stolen poured out through her resonator vanes at once. The rich, dark prize of spirit-essence she had taken, all the nourishment that should have been presented triumphantly to her creator was instead released back to her prey and her killer. It was macabre feast for Bellathonis, Xagor and Bezieth, a bathing of stolen life-energy that made them young and vital again in accordance with the dark and terrible rites of the eternal city.

In moments flesh filled out and became firm once more, wrinkled skin smoothed and showed the first blush of youth, limbs regained their strength and vigour with the unwitting gift the pain-engine had supplied. It was a long time before any of them spoke.

'Bezieth!' Bellathonis exclaimed finally, still basking royally in the dying radiance. 'I remember now,

I helped you against the Scarlet Edge not so very long ago!'

Bezieth squinted at him uncertainly. 'It is master Bellathonis! Is mi–' Xagor announced proudly before Bezieth raised a hand to cut him off.

'What do you mean? This is Kharbyr, I remember Bellathonis and this isn't him.'

'All possible through the magic of the art, my dear archon,' Bellathonis said with insufferable smugness. 'Forgive me if I don't explain the whole thing over again. We must all keep our little trade secrets, after all. Most fundamentally I must thank you for your timely intervention against the Cronos parasite, I am in your debt and I do not take that lightly. I must ask – how did you manage to surprise it?'

'You certainly sound like Bellathonis, you use too many words like he does.' Bezieth said and shrugged indifferently. Stranger things had happened in Commorragh and especially ones involving haemonculi. 'Your wrack there came up with the idea. We knew that we were being followed by something too wary to attack all three of us together. After the crash we decided to try and use the opportunity to trap it. Xagor gave me something to put me in a kind of trance so that I'd appear dead while he was tending Kharbyr. It took some trust on my part, but Xagor was right – the thing was so busy going after him and you that it missed me altogether. I walked right up behind it and gutted it.'

'Bravo Xagor, very well done,' Bellathonis smiled

indulgently. 'And bravo Bezieth, that was no mean feat to pull off.'

'Yes, yes,' Bezieth said impatiently, 'but it doesn't get us anywhere. I'm expecting the motherlode of ur-ghuls to come sniffing around this crash at any moment, and we're still barely halfway to Sec Magera – unfortunately your predecessor in that body destroyed our only transport and I'm still wondering whether I should take that out on your hide.'

'Hmm, three things occur to me,' Bellathonis said, apparently disconcerted not at all by Bezieth's threat. 'First: ur-ghuls? That doesn't bode well for the state of the portal to Shaa-dom. Second: That going to Sec Magera is a terrible idea, I can take you somewhere much safer and much closer. Third: That Kharbyr probably didn't crash without some help – he is, or rather was, too good a pilot for that.'

Bezieth frowned. 'In that case what happened?'

'Kharbyr-before-Bellathonis said the craft was struck,' Xagor offered. 'This one saw something come up from below. Darkness reaching.'

'Ah. Well then it's probably easier to show you than explain,' Bellathonis said, 'if we can go to the place where it happened.'

Bezieth jammed a thumb towards where the tunnel had branched. 'Back that way, where the ur-ghuls are at.'

'Splendid,' Bellathonis said imperturbably. He attempted to stand but found his damaged limbs still too unserviceable to support him. At his call

Xagor obediently scurried forward to lift his master onto his back, useless legs dangling and arms clutched around the wrack's neck.

'Onward!' Bellathonis called cheerily, and with Bezieth leading they began to pick their way along the travel tube back to the fork.

ARCHON YLLITHIAN AND his White Flames warriors stalked warily up the ramps to the higher levels of the tower. The wraithbone walls showed spider web traceries of cracks that wept pus and foul-smelling ooze. The tower itself shook in the grip of the *Ilmaea* Gorath, the captive sun now so close to freedom. They eventually emerged into another vaulted chamber where open arches on all sides led out onto slender bridges. A profusion of inscribed plinths and jewel-encrusted pillars within the chamber indicated that it had been some form of control room, with the emphasis on had been before Aez'ashya and her wyches had burst onto the scene. Now bolter rounds criss-crossed the space like tiny meteors blasting craters in flesh, metal and stone with equal abandon. Half-seen figures dashed through the smoke and flames, struggling and hewing at each other maniacally.

There were many of the green-armoured Chaos warriors in the chamber, and perhaps an equal number of wyches playing a deadly game of hide and seek among the plinths and pillars. It was easy to see what they were fighting for control over. In the centre of the space a huge crystal floated above the chaos with multi-coloured light leaking from its every facet. Smoky, pulsating tendrils extended from the crystal to penetrate pillars and plinths all around the room. There was a distinct sense of wrongness about the crystal, a poisonous alien taint that flowed off it in palpable waves. It didn't belong in the chamber any more than the hulking invaders did. The White Flames hesitated for a moment on the threshold, an instinctive fear of the warp-spawned gripping even the most hardened reavers among them.

'Shoot it, you fools!' Yllithian snarled. 'Your tormentor stands before you! Shoot!'

In an instant splinter weapons, disintegrator pulses, monomolecular nets and darklight beams slashed upwards. In truth Yllithian had little hope that the floating crystal would prove vulnerable to mundane weapons, but the crystal surprised him by instantly exploding under the barrage, the glittering shards of it scything through the chamber like shrapnel. For the briefest instant Yllithian caught sight of the abomination that had been metamorphosing inside the crystal, a being that seemed too monstrously huge to have possibly fitted within its confines. Yllithian was inured to the worst of horrors but even his black soul was scarred by the sight of the thing, at the terrible sense of closeness of an entity so utterly alien. Waves of sickness radiated from the entity as it writhed. It was attempting to complete its transition into the shadow-realm of Commorragh, to birth itself fully through the rapidly shrinking rents in the Wardings. Yllithian's followers needed no prompting to open fire again.

The tower made a sickening lurch as a torrent of writhing foulness splattered onto the ground beneath where the crystal had floated a moment before. Leech-like, putrid vestiges of the crystal-encased entity went wriggling in all directions like animated offal, hungrily flowing over fallen bodies and struggling fighters alike. Above them blackened remnants of the entity folded back into unseen dimensions like a burned limb being withdrawn.

Bloated, shambolic monstrosities of dead flesh lurched forward to drag the living eldar into their foetid embrace. Once cut off from their progenitor the vestiges of the entity instinctively sought to grow and multiply like microbes. Fire, as ever, proved to be an invaluable ally against the more obscene manifestations from beyond the veil. The bright flare of plasma grenades cut through the murk as Yllithian's warriors fought back against the new menace. The remnants were blasted, burned and hacked into oblivion in a matter of moments, a following rush of clumsily reanimated Chaos warriors meeting with a similar fate. As the last corpse stopped twitching silence descended across the room.

Just a summoning then, Yllithian thought to himself as he led his incubi into the chamber. The pawns of the Ruinous Powers had tried to bring something more powerful through from beyond the veil, a prince or patron from their insane daemonic court. Yllithian's studies of forbidden lore told him that if one Chaos power was intent on Commorragh as a prize then there would be others too. The Ruinous Powers regarded the mortal realms as little more than game boards upon which to play out their endless rivalries. If Nurgle, a force of morbidity and stasis, sought a foothold in the dark city it would automatically be opposed by Tzeentch, the lord of change and vice versa. The Ruinous Powers had been stopped in time though at least here. Yllithian allowed himself to relax fractionally and looked around for Aez'ashya.

It was then that Aez'ashya's wyches attacked Yllithian's warriors. A sudden shout went up and the two forces were instantly at one another's throats. The White Flames found themselves at a disadvantage in the confines of the chamber where the close and bloody fighting favoured the lightning-fast wyches. Yllithian glimpsed Aez'ashya racing towards him through the warring throng with a clutch of her hekatrix bloodbrides close at her back. He quickly backed up a pace to let his incubi form a solid wall in front of him and found himself on one of the bridges leading out of the chamber. The dark, hellish surface of Gorath raged far below and Yllithian could see that the intervening space was filled with darting, swirling Raiders and reavers battling beyond the tower's walls.

Hekatrix and incubi clashed in a deadly fury of swinging klaives and darting blades. One of the hekatrix gave up her life to force an opening for her archon to exploit, dragging aside a klaive for a critical instant even as it slashed open her midriff. Aez'ashya shot through the gap and sprang towards Yllithian with a wild shout of laughter, her knives twin bright blurs as they sought his life.

# CHAPTER 24
## SACRIFICE

THE FLOOR OF the World Shrine on Lileathanir tilted and shook like a ship caught in the teeth of a storm. Rocks and ice rained from above and dashed themselves to pieces all around the group as they ran. Molten rock jetted up in glowing geysers, bulwarks of ice flashed into clouds of steam that hissed and screamed in counterpoint to the thunderous roars coming from ahead.

'By all the gods what has he done?' Caraeis raged as he plunged beneath the arch at the heart of World Shrine. Close behind him the sapphire figures of the Dire Avengers kept pace warily, their exarch silent as they followed the warlock into the dragon's lair.

Caraeis stumbled through the quivering tunnel with witchblade in hand, the chained lightning of his own power coiled and ready to strike. A psychic storm of crimson fury raged ahead of him, and it was soul-shaking in its intensity. His own senses, physical and metaphysical, were deafened and blinded by the dragon's anger but he pushed forward guided by instinct alone.

The warlock emerged from the tunnel onto a slope still smoking and scarred by the sullen glow of cooling rock. Below him was a great cavern in tumult where coils of crimson light twisted and thrashed like a gargantuan nest of snakes. Caraeis could perceive a moving speck of darkness within the energised mass, something constantly tossed back and forth but always at the epicentre of maelstrom. Here was the incubus! Here was the violator that had been sought for so long! The dark one was goading the world spirit into unthinking fury, recreating his crime and magnifying it a thousand times over!

Caraeis plunged a hand into his satchel of runes, grasping one and bringing it forth to hold aloft like an icon. He would destroy the incubus, annihilate the violator utterly and save the world spirit of Lileathanir. It was hard to grasp his own powers and marshal them in the face of the turmoil all around him but grasp them he did. He poured every ounce of his ability into summoning the deadliest manifestation of psychic power that he knew of – the eldritch storm.

A lenticular blaze of blue-white lightning ravened across the cavern, bright bolts crashing into the looping coils as they sought out the dark speck within them with unstoppable force. The rune between Caraeis's fingers blazed with light, growing hotter and brighter by the second as he channelled unimaginable energy through it. The lightning of the eldritch storm clashed with the unleashed fury of the dragon, provoking an earth-shattering howl that bludgeoned the mind and blasted the senses. The rune was shining like a star, its retina-burning image piercing the amber lenses of Caraeis's mask.

It was only then that he realised he had made a mistake.

He had sought the rune of vengeance, he felt sure that was what he had drawn forth from the satchel, but the image burned into his sight was that of the rune of weaving. His concentration was shattered by the shock of recognition, the eldritch storm dissipating in an instant. He flung the treacherous rune away, his mind filling with horror at the implications.

The rune of weaving had many meanings but behind them all lay the weaver of Fate, also known as the Chaos Power Tzeentch, the Lord of Change...

Into his mind there came unbidden the hundreds of times that the rune of weaving had led him upon this path. A push here, a shove there. The guiding rune always twisting at the center of it all, seeming to feed on his ambitions after he first perceived the coming crisis. He felt all the passionate emotion that had raced through his mind in times when he had thought himself calm, the sick realisation that he had been closer to the edge of his sanity than he believed and that he had now passed beyond it.

It was already too late, something was rising from the coils of crimson light, a dark, broken body splayed out as if on a rack. It rose at the head of a serpentine coil of crimson energy, questing, turning back and forth before it fixed upon Caraeis. Momentary silence fell across the cavern, an indrawn breath in the midst of a primal scream. The incubus laughed mercilessly down at him from the head of the crimson serpent before he spoke in a voice like the dry whisper of billon dead souls.

'Fool. Fool to come here. Fool to use your powers against the dragon. Your hubris has become your undoing.'

Somehow Caraeis found a voice in his terror. 'This... this is impossible, how– '

Morr's laughter was a roll of distant thunder. Crimson energies writhed around his limbs, poured from his fingertips in rippling falls of flames. He brought his palms together and a whirling ball of fire sprang into being between them.

'I long since learned to master my rage, to make a weapon of it,' the incubus whispered. He opened his arms wider, the ball of fire growing into a miniature star. 'At Arhra's knee I learned its direction and purpose. I cannot master the dragon, but I can help channel its fury. You angered it and so now I can direct its rage into you... and through your sacrifice this world shall be made whole again.'

Morr opened his arms and the fiery nova swept down on Caraeis with elemental quickness. The warlock marshalled his defences into a sparkling hemisphere of counter-force that sprang into being around him. The barrier shivered with the impact yet it held. An inferno of flames washed over it and it crackled like frosted glass as it resisted the crude, powerful attack. Caraeis enjoyed a brief moment of hope. The incubus was no battle-seer. Even with the limitless potential of the world spirit fuelling the dark one Caraeis still might gain victory with a well-timed counter blow.

Yet the blast did not end, instead it intensified into a roaring firestorm. Caraeis sweated beneath his mask as he hurled all of his psychic strength into maintaining the barrier. He felt as if he were braced against a fortress door that was shaking beneath the assault of a monster outside. He began to pull runes from his satchel to help weave the protective barriers of force more tightly, fumbling as he built a constellation of tiny floating runes around himself. The runes sparked wildly as they sought to dissipate the dangerous levels of etheric energy leaking past the barrier.

Still the assault continued to rage and roar with undimmed intensity. Gibbering in desperation Caraeis reached deeper within himself, *beyond* himself, for the strength to endure. From somewhere deep and forbidden in his mind he heard an answering whisper from a presence he now realised had always been with him. A rushing enormity swelled in his mind, something unutterable, ancient and eldritch. He felt himself begin to expand in readiness to receive it; an arrival that he realised would obliterate him like a wind-blown candle. The idea filled his breaking mind with idiotic joy.

'Caraeis! No!' Aiosa shouted above the fury.

The mind-shout was close by, it was from a familiar source but such things were irrelevant to Caraeis now. His mind had shrunk to a bisected circle containing only the need to maintain the barrier and an indescribable, almost orgasmic anticipation of the arrival of the Lord of Change. He did not look with his altering eyes to see the sapphire-armoured Dire Avengers level their star throwers at his back, did not feel their monomolecular discs spinning through his mutating flesh as Aiosa ordered her Aspect Warriors to cut down the abomination he was becoming.

Mere physical injury could no longer kill Caraeis. He had become a conduit for something too great to be stopped so easily. But even so he could still be distracted by the external input of severed nerves and gouting blood, the circle of his concentration broken by mortal instincts. The psychic barrier wavered as it stood momentarily unsupported by his will. The mountainous pressures of the world spirit's attack – strengthened now through its fear and anger at the approach of the Lord of Change – needed no more than that sliver of hesitation to begin overwhelming Caraeis's defences.

The psychic barrier collapsed sending soul-born fires sweeping down on Caraeis and his constellation of orbiting runes. Rage and burning hate were channelled against the warlock, an endless outpouring that was quelled and dissipated in part by each of the layers of protection Caraeis's had wrapped around his soul. Each defensive rune absorbed unthinkable amounts of psychic power as it flared and failed, enough to destroy cities and continents, but the rage of Lileathanir was an unstoppable, insatiable thing. Layer by layer, rune by rune the defences were stripped away. At last the quailing, tainted soul of the warlock was laid bare and utterly destroyed with a triumphant, earth-shivering roar.

Aiosa and the stunned Dire Avengers fled from the quaking chamber pursued by a rain of rocks and lava. The walls of the exit tunnel shivered as they ground slowly together, seemingly determined to crush the Aspect Warriors in their implacable embrace. Aiosa urged her squad onward, driving them before her like frightened animals until they tumbled out into the World Shrine.

Behind them, sealed in the deep chamber, the lambent tide of violence began to recede, flowing away down the slope and dimming as it went. The looping crimson coils in the cavern were slowed and dissipated by the touch of the returning tide. A rippling colour change was taking place in the insubstantial tendrils as they retreated, a gradual fading through purples and blues to a clear, wholesome green. Where Caraeis had stood was now only a scar in the rock lit by dancing fires. No trace of either the warlock or the incubus remained to be seen.

For the first time in many moons a hushed silence fell across the World Shrine of Lileathanir. Beyond the holy mountain the clans saw stars again in the night sky and the moving stars that were ships in the firmament coming to their aid.

DESPITE BEZIETH'S WARNINGS they encountered no ur-ghuls in the tunnel. She couldn't shake the impression that they had all been spooked by something and cleared out. Perhaps the little murder engine had frightened them all off, but the troglodytic predators didn't scare easily. Once they got closer to the vertical shaft Kharbyr had been so desperately trying to avoid she could see a more probable cause.

Vast, shadowy pseudopods were thrusting up from below, probing at the mouth of the shaft almost tenderly. Bellathonis directed Xagor to carry him right over to the edge without any regard for the sinister ink-black tentacles sweeping past only metres away. Bezieth joined them reluctantly, experiencing a rare twinge of vertigo as she peered over the edge into the kilometres-deep drop. The tentacles seemed to stretch up to impossible lengths from a roiling pit of darkness at the bottom.

'Look at it,' Bellathonis said. 'Aelindrach, the shadow-realm. It has expanded during the Dysjunction by swallowing up more of the city into itself.'

'Then we should be going the other way!' Bezieth snarled, raising her djin-blade meaningfully.

'No, not at all, my dear archon,' Bellathonis said imperturbably. 'I have friends in Aelindrach, contacts even with the ear of the mandrake kings. What you thought was an attack was them reaching out for me, or what they thought was me at the time. The shadow-realm offers sanctuary for all of us during a Dysjunction, trust me on this.'

'With mandrakes? They'll drink our blood and use our skulls for ornaments–' Bezieth said.

'Well the choice is yours,' Bellathonis replied. 'You must either trust me and follow or make your own way, it is all the same to me – Xagor, go ahead.'

The wrack turned and stepped over the edge without hesitation with Bellathonis still clutching his back. The two vanished from view instantly, swept up effortlessly by one of the questing tentacles. Bezieth hung back uncertainly for moment, watching for any glimpse of their falling bodies and listening for screams. She saw and heard nothing.

'Oh to hell with that,' Bezieth muttered to herself as she stalked away from the pit. 'I'd rather take my chances with the ur-ghuls.' She was reduced to being a kabal of one, two if you counted the spirit of Axhyrian and she didn't. Sec Megara wouldn't be such a bad place to start recruiting, certainly a damn sight better than Aelindrach.

YLLITHIAN TEETERED ON the precipice; thousands of kilometres beneath his heels the stolen sun Gorath blazed hungrily, a medusa's-nest of black, twisting fires waiting for him below. Aez'ashya's relentless attack was forcing him back step by step to the edge of the bridge, his blade weaving desperately as he attempted to keep her at bay. Yllithian was a master swordsman in his own right yet he was badly outmatched by her and he knew it.

Only his shadow field had kept him alive so far, a dozen times the inky swirl of darkness had blocked a speeding knife or turned aside a disembowelling thrust. Aez'ashya would know that it was only a matter of time before the energy field failed completely, all she had to do was just keep battering at it for long enough. Yllithian kept expecting his incubi to come up and save him but he was still utterly alone, trapped within an unbreakable web of steel that was tightening by the moment.

Yllithian glimpsed something behind Aez'ashya that surprised him so much it made him momentarily drop his guard. Aez'ahya instantly sprang back out of reach suspecting some sort of a trick. Then she saw it too and her relentless knives hesitated in their courses.

'Is that–?'

The hideous, vibrant colours that had smeared the wardings since the beginning of the Dysjunction were fading. They were dimming and scattering moment by moment like a storm blown away by a fresh wind. Below their feet Gorath was calming as its fiery corona began shrinking back within its normal parameters.

'Yes, it's ending. The Dysjunction is over,' Yllithian said, sidling carefully away from the edge of the bridge as he spoke. Aez'ashya watched him coolly.

'You think this changes anything?' she said.

'Of course it does! It changes everything!' Yllithian exclaimed passionately. 'Clearly our brave assault on the *Ilmaea* has met with stunning success and put an end to the menace. We should be praised and rewarded to the highest degree for our efforts, don't you think? Although naturally that will only work if we're both around corroborate one another's story to Vect.'

Aez'ashya considered this for a moment and laughed.

'I like your thinking, Yllithian,' she smiled nastily, flourishing her daggers, 'but I think that Vect will reward me quite adequately enough when I bring him your head!'

Yllithian took another step back as Aez'ashya tensed to spring. Over the succubus's bladed shoulder he could see his incubi bodyguards pounding down the bridge toward them.

'Then I'm afraid you'll have to see how he responds when you report your failure instead. Vect's terribly unforgiving of that kind of thing as you'll soon come to learn.'

Aez'ashya caught his glance and heard the approaching clatter of their armoured sabatons at the same moment. Yllithian was thrilled to see the anguish in her eyes as she realised she had failed. A few more heartbeats and the mistress of the Blades of Desire would be the one losing her head. He was surprised by the fierce grin she gave him.

'Until next time, Yllithian,' Aez'ashya said spitefully, 'be a darling and try to become more of a worthy opponent by then, won't you?' So saying she turned and leapt from the bridge to apparently certain death in the embrace of Gorath.

Yllithian knew better and cursed as he bounded

to the edge to see her fate. He was just in time to see the blur of a fast moving Venom transport come curving around the tower and intersect with the falling form before speeding away. He was still nodding in admiration when his incubi arrived. He noted with chagrin that only three of them had survived their battle with hekatrix.

'Better late than never, I suppose,' he commented acidly. 'I believe I've found myself the motivation to ensure Xelian returns to lead the Blades of Desire, I like not their new archon.'

AIOSA, HER ARMOUR riven and scored in a dozen places, found the harlequin waiting for her in the World Shrine with a relieved-looking smile on his face. It took all of her considerable self-control not to lay hands upon him and shake him until his neck snapped.

'What did you do?' the exarch snarled dangerously.

'Do? I did nothing but bring people together so that they could mitigate a threat to all of us. Everyone played their appointed part beautifully and now the threat is over. I'm spectacularly happy that you and your warriors survived, and very sorry if I offended you along the way.'

'You sent Caraeis to his death!'

Motley frowned unhappily at the accusation, stepping back with his hands spread helplessly. 'No. He found a doom that has been waiting for him for quite some time. I merely ensured that his sacrifice aided the eldar race instead of the Chaos Powers. Caraeis's overweening ambition did not come entirely from within, Aiosa, surely you must have sensed that.'

Aiosa shook her helm grimly before stopping herself and reconsidering. The tension she'd felt had been real, a sense that the warlock was overstepping boundaries and flaunting traditions without thought. She had repeatedly put it down to youthfulness and arrogance but it had been very real.

'And the incubus?' she said more slowly. 'He was trying to slay the dragon spirit, an impossible task. Did you tell him that he would succeed?'

'I never lied to him, if that's what you mean, he took on the task willingly enough for the sake of his honour and his adopted city. He knew if he went in there he wasn't coming out and that's what I call bravery no matter where you hail from. He should be mourned rather than vilified.'

'He created the situation,' Aiosa said flatly. 'He led the Commorrites that violated the shrine and they brought their doom upon themselves.'

'Morr was a weapon wielded by others,' Motley said wearily. 'He was no more culpable than a gun can be guilty of murder... May I tell you a fundamental truth, Aiosa?'

The proud mask of the exarch inclined minutely and Motley was struck once again by how much like Morr she looked in that moment.

'When I became old enough – and I am very, very old despite my youthful appearance – there came a point when I began to question how many lives a difference in philosophy is truly worth. Upon reaching that point and asking myself that question

I started to consider just whom all the death and destruction that is visited upon our fractured race really serves.'

The slight harlequin looked up into the hard, crystalline eyes of the exarch for some glimmer of understanding. He found none.

# EPILOGUE

*And so I stand revealed at the end of my tale. I, the one called Motley, player and orchestrator both. It would be false to claim that I foresaw every outcome, but it would be fair to say I predicted more rightly than wrongly.*

*It comes to this – the great cosmic joke. All we do is fight against ourselves. The material existence we defer to and rely upon and believe in is illusory; it gives the impression of solidity when in point of fact there's nothing in the universe more destructible and short-lived. It appears from nothing and it goes to nothing while only the soul endures.*

*And you see that's really the key: Immortal souls adrift in an endless sea of aeons eternally at war with themselves, being driven by passions so strong, so primal they have become entities we have come to call gods. Little do those poor souls know that it's their own belief that gives shape to what oppresses them and that they lend it their* strength with every struggle. Poor, lost, immortal souls; they can be crushed, they can be consumed, they can be enslaved, they can be corrupted, but they can never, ever be completely destroyed.

And souls can always be reborn.

## ABOUT THE AUTHOR

Author of the dark eldar series, along with the novel *Survival Instinct* and a host of short stories, Andy Chambers has more than twenty years' experience creating worlds dominated by war machines, spaceships and dangerous aliens. Andy worked at Games Workshop as lead designer of the Warhammer 40,000 miniatures game for three editions before moving to the PC gaming market. He now lives and works in Nottingham.